Praise for Minerva
The R

★A *PopSugar*]

★A *She Reac*

★A *Bookclubz* Recommended Read

"Brilliantly crafted...an irresistible cocktail of smart characterization, sophisticated sensuality, and sharp wit."
★*Booklist STARRED REVIEW*

"*Sparkling...impossible not to love.*"
—*Popsugar*

"*Both characters are strong, complex, and believable, and the cliffhanger offers a nice setup for the sequel. Readers who like thrills mixed in with their romance should check this out.*"
—**Publishers Weekly**

"*Packed full of fiery exchanges and passionate embraces, this is for those who prefer their Regencies on the scandalous side.*"
—**Library Journal**

Praise for Minerva Spencer & S.M. LaViolette's THE ACADEMY OF LOVE series:

"*[A] pitch perfect Regency .... Readers will be hooked.*" (THE MUSIC OF LOVE)
★*Publishers Weekly STARRED REVIEW*

"*An offbeat story that offers unexpected twists on a familiar setup.*" (A FIGURE OF LOVE)
Kirkus

"*[A] consistently entertaining read.*" (A FIGURE OF LOVE)
Kirkus

Praise for Minerva Spencer's *Outcasts* series:

"Minerva Spencer's writing is sophisticated and wickedly witty. Dangerous is a delight from start to finish with swashbuckling action, scorching love scenes, and a coolly arrogant hero to die for. Spencer is my new auto-buy!"
-NYT Bestselling Author Elizabeth Hoyt

"[SCANDALOUS is] A standout...Spencer's brilliant and original tale of the high seas bursts with wonderfully real protagonists, plenty of action, and passionate romance."
★Publishers Weekly STARRED REVIEW

"Fans of Amanda Quick's early historicals will find much to savor."
★Booklist STARRED REVIEW

"Sexy, witty, and fiercely entertaining."
★Kirkus STARRED REVIEW

Praise for S.M. LaViolette's Books:

"Lovers of historical romance will be hooked on this twisty story of revenge, redemption, and reversal of fortunes."
★Publishers Weekly STARRED REVIEW

"A remarkably resourceful heroine who can more than hold her own against any character invented by best-selling Bertrice Small, a suavely sophisticated hero with sex appeal to spare, and a cascade of lushly detailed love scenes give Spencer's dazzling debut its deliciously fun retro flavor."
★Booklist STARRED REVIEW

"Readers will love this lusty and unusual marriage of convenience story."
-NYT Bestselling Author MADELINE HUNTER

"Smart, witty, graceful, sensual, elegant and gritty all at once. It has all of the meticulous attention to detail I love in Georgette Heyer, BUT WITH SEX!"
RITA-Award Winning Author JEFFE KENNEDY

More books by S.M. LaViolette & Minerva Spencer

THE ACADEMY OF LOVE SERIES
The Music of Love ✓
A Figure of Love ✓
A Portrait of Love ✓
The Language of Love*
Dancing with Love*
The Story of Love*

THE OUTCASTS SERIES
Dangerous ✓
Barbarous ✓
Scandalous ✓

THE REBELS OF THE *TON*
Notorious ✓
Outrageous* July -ordered
Infamous*

THE MASQUERADERS
The Footman — 14.95 ✗
The Postilion*
The Bastard*

THE SEDUCERS
Melissa and The Vicar — 13.95 ✗
Joss and The Countess — 15.95 ✗
Hugo and The Maiden*

VICTORIAN DECADENCE
His Harlot — 14.95 ✗
His Valet — 13.95 ✗
His Countess — 18.95 ✗
Her Master*
Her Beast*

ANTHOLOGIES:

BACHELORS OF BOND STREET — 8.95 ✗
THE ARRANGEMENT ✓
*upcoming books

A Portrait of Love

Minerva Spencer
writing as S.M. LAVIOLETTE

Crooked Sixpence CS P Press

CROOKED SIXPENCE BOOKS are published by
CROOKED SIXPENCE PRESS

2 State Road 230
El Prado, NM 87529

Copyright © 2020 Shantal M. LaViolette

All rights reserved. No part of this publication may be reproduced, distributed, or transmitted in any form or by any means, including photocopying, recording, or other electronic or mechanical methods, without the prior written permission of the publisher, except in the case of brief quotations embodied in critical reviews and certain other noncommercial uses permitted by copyright law. For permission requests, write to the publisher, addressed "Attention: Permissions Coordinator," at the address above.

To the extent that the image or images on the cover of this book depict a person or persons, such person or persons are merely models, and are not intended to portray any character or characters featured in the book.

If you purchased this book without a cover you should be aware that this book is stolen property. It was reported as "unsold and destroyed" to the Publisher and neither the Author nor the Publisher has received any payment for this "stripped book."

First printing December 2020

ISBN: 978-1-951662-43-1

10 9 8 7 6 5 4 3 2 1

Any references to historical events, real people, or real places are used fictitiously. Names, characters, and places are products of the author's imagination.

Photo stock by Period Images
Printed in the United States of America

Chapter One

London
1803

Honoria ran down the stairs as if winged death were snapping at her heels.

It was ten minutes past noon; he would be here, already. She would have missed *ten entire minutes* of his company.

Of staring at him.

Of *worshipping* him.

She skidded to a halt outside her father's studio and checked her reflection in the shiny brass urn that sat on a plinth across from the door. The belly of the vase stretched her eyes and made them look long and narrow while shrinking her overlarge mouth into a prim, bow-shaped moue. Honey wished she looked like this imaginary girl instead of the pale, gangly, and big-mouthed reality that stared back at her every day in her dressing room mirror.

She wrinkled her stubby nose at her distorted brass reflection and hissed, sticking out her tongue and giggling at the evil image she'd just created. All she lacked to be truly horrifying were fangs.

He's in there, an unamused part of her mind pointed out.

Honey pinched her cheeks to give them a bit of color and pushed her waist-length far-too-curly hair back over her shoulders. Her father would not let her wear it up until her next birthday, when she would be sixteen. For an artist Daniel Keyes could sometimes be a stickler for propriety and—

"Hello."

Honey jumped and yelped, no doubt resembling a huge, startled mouse in her hideous brown painting smock.

Correction, a huge mouse with a red face.

She didn't want to turn around but she could hardly stand there all day staring at the door. She swallowed noisily, as if her throat had rusted shut and then slowly, ever so slowly, turned on one heel.

Eyes the color of hydrangeas stared down at her, their corners crinkling.

Lord Simon Fairchild.

Even his name was beautiful.

But nothing compared to his face and person. Not only was he beautiful, but he was also taller than her. At over six feet Simon Fairchild didn't exactly tower over her five feet eleven inch frame, but it was near enough. And it made Honey feel—for the first time in her fifteen and three-quarter years—almost petite.

He was golden and broad-shouldered and graceful and he looked like a hero out of a Norse epic, all chiseled angles and fair perfection. His sculpted lips curved into a smile that released butterflies into her body.

"My lord," she croaked, dropping the world's clumsiest curtsey.

He grinned and took her hand, bowing low over it. "Good afternoon, Miss Honoria." His voice was warm honey and it pooled low in her belly, the sensation … disturbing.

She blurted out the first words that leapt to mind, "You remembered my name."

And then she wanted to hide.

His lips twitched and Honey only just stopped herself from smacking her palm to her forehead or crawling behind the big moth-eaten tapestry which covered much of the opposite wall.

Of course, he remembered her name, she'd only met him yesterday.

He clasped his hands behind his back, his broad shoulders almost blocking the light from the cathedral window at the end of the hall. He was dressed for riding, which meant he would change into his portrait clothing once he entered her father's studio.

Thinking of Simon Fairchild changing his clothing gave her a swirly, hot feeling in her belly and made her palms sweat. And she seemed to be salivating more than necessary, as if her mouth were anticipating a delicacy.

Say something, you fool! Ask him something. Keep him here. Don't let him get—

"Are my sittings keeping you and your father in the city this summer, Miss Honoria?"

"No, we stay here most of the time."

He raised his eyebrows and nodded encouragingly.

"We rarely go into the country," she added lamely, unable to come up with anything better.

But then inspiration struck. "Will *you* be going to the country, Lord Saybrook?"

"I no longer hold that honor, Miss Keyes," he reminded her gently.

Her face heated yet again. "Oh, yes of course. The duke now has a son. You must be very—"

She bit her lip; he must be very what? Would a man be happy that he was no longer a duke's heir?

Lord Simon flashed his lovely white teeth. "I'm very happy *and* relieved."

"You do not wish to be a duke?"

"No, I do not. Not only would it mean my brother's death, but the position entails altogether too much responsibility in my view. Besides, I have other plans."

"Other plans?"

"Yes, I wish to live at my country estate and breed horses."

Honey could not imagine the elegant man-god across from her rusticating and living the life of a mere country squire. She leaned against the doorframe to her father's studio, aware it was rude to keep a guest in the hall, but not wishing to share his attention with her father just yet.

"And you cannot do that *and* be duke?"

"Oh, I suppose the right kind of man could, but I wish for a quiet life, not responsibilities in Lords and the management of hundreds of lives. No, the country life is the life for me. I'll be happy on my much smaller estate." He paused, his look speculative, as if he suddenly realized that he—a man of twenty—was confessing his aspirations to a mere fifteen-year-old.

Honey had seen the look before; every person she associated with was older than her. She'd never gone away to school, had no close relatives her age, and only socialized with her governess or her father's friends. Being young had never bothered her before, but suddenly, it felt . . . limiting.

He bent low to catch her gaze, which had dropped miserably to his feet. "But you can't possibly find my boring plans of interest. While I'm off mucking about in my stables you'll no doubt be whirling around ballrooms and breaking young men's hearts."

Honoria could not think of a single thing to say that would not be humiliating.

So—" he said when she remained stupidly mute, his mouth ticking up on one side, his gaze merry yet gentle.

It was impossible not to smile when he was smiling.

"So?" she echoed as the two of them stood staring at one another.

He chuckled and shook his head, as if she'd said something amusing. He gestured behind her to the studio door, which she was blocking with her body. "I'd better get inside. I believe I'm late and your papa is probably going to give me the raking I deserve."

Honey stepped aside, gawking like the smitten fool she was. He opened the door and again gestured. "After you, Miss Honoria. That is if you are going to join us again today?"

"Of course, she is," Honey's father boomed from inside the bright, sunny room, where he was preparing his work area. His voice acted like a catalyst and Honey tore her eyes from Simon's perfect features and bolted inside.

"Good afternoon, Papa."

Daniel Keyes gave her an approving smile as she went to her easel and then turned to Simon Fairchild. "My daughter will one day be England's premier portrait painter," he said, speaking with such certainty, pride, and love that Honey's heart threatened to expand right out of her chest.

Lord Simon cut her one of his devastating smiles. "So, you will be painting a portrait of me while your father paints his?"

"Yes," Honey said, pulling the cover off her much smaller canvas. She was glad to look away from Lord Simon's distracting person; her wits were already scrambled from their brief conversation in the hall.

Her painting was coming along quite nicely, not that she would show it to anyone until it was completed. And even then ....

"Right now my daughter spends half her day studying and the other half honing her art. Once she is eighteen, and her schooling is over, she will be free to decide how to spend *all* her time," Daniel Keyes said as the younger man stepped behind the large screen in the corner of the room.

To change his clothing.

Honey reminded herself to breathe and forced her gaze away from his head, which was visible above the screen. Her own face heated and she tried to control her breathing, which was soughing in and out just like their ancient butler Dowdle after he had climbed two sets of stairs.

"And will I get to see the portrait *you* are painting, Miss Keyes?"

Her head jerked up just in time to see him toss his waistcoat over the top of the screen. Which meant he was only wearing his shirt. His thin, fine, soft, muslin shirt. His eyes met hers as he did something behind the screen. Put on a coat? His other waistcoat?

Honey swallowed; her father and Lord Simon were waiting with raised brows.

"I don't know yet," she mumbled.

"An artist's prerogative," Daniel Keyes said with a laugh. "She might not even let *me* see it, my lord."

Her father was right. There were plenty of sketches and paintings that were only for her eyes and she rather suspected this painting might be another.

***

On Lord Simon's fifth visit he asked her father if he could take Honey for a ride in his high-perch phaeton.

Hyde Park was thin with people, but Honey still felt as if she were on the top of the world in his tall carriage with *him* beside her. It was the most magical afternoon of her life.

Until his next visit, when he took her to Gunters.

Miss Keebler, her governess, came along for that treat, but even the presence of her dour chaperone couldn't dampen the day.

All that month Lord Simon took her places or dined at her father's house and spent evenings mixing with the many artists and actors who comprised Daniel Keyes's social circle, which included Honoria, who'd been allowed to eat dinner with her father's guests since turning fifteen.

Part of her knew Lord Simon was only spending so much time with her because London in the summer was devoid of most of his usual friends and entertainments. But she didn't care.

He took her on strolls after his sittings and they sat in the park together. Always with Miss Keebler nearby, of course.

He told her about Everley, his home in the country. His face glowed when he talked about building new stables and the improvements he would make to the house, which was Tudor and always in need of repair.

He spoke of growing up with his brother on the great estate of Whitcomb and told her tales of ghosts in the castle and how he'd once dressed up in a sheet and terrified his nurse, earning the worst paddling of his youth.

Honey told him about growing up surrounded by artists and how she'd begged her father not to send her away to school. How she planned on taking over the management of the household when she was sixteen and taking care of him. She shared her dreams that she might go to the Continent someday—when it was once again safe to travel—and see all the great art she'd only been able to read about.

Honey knew it was unheard of for her father to require so many sittings—in fact, he usually finished his portraits after no more than ten meetings. But, for whatever reason—maybe because he knew how greatly she enjoyed it—he had the young nobleman visit the house over a period of thirty blissful days and *sixteen* sittings.

Honey wished it would never end.

***

"Will you accompany me for an ice, Miss Honoria?"

Honey looked at her father as she laid aside her brush and he nodded, the somewhat distracted look in his eyes telling her that he was still deep inside his work.

Daniel Keyes turned to Lord Simon, who'd emerged from behind the screen, once again dressed in his street clothing. "Did you bring that yellow bounder today?"

Simon—Honoria thought of him by his Christian name, now, although only in the privacy of her own mind—smiled. "No, sir, I'm afraid it will have to be my brother's clunky old boat."

Her father chuckled at this characterization of the ducal barouche, which Honey had ridden in once before. "Why don't we have a glass of something reviving while my daughter does whatever it is that women need to do before going out to eat ices?"

Honoria loved her Papa for many reasons, but especially for giving her this chance to change into the new dress she'd just purchased—hoping for a day like today to wear it.

She rang for the parlor maid to help her change—she didn't have her own lady's maid—and was down in her father's study just as the men finished the amber liquid in their glasses.

They stood when she entered, and she wanted to weep with joy when Simon's eyes widened appreciatively.

Her dress was a crème silk with a dozen rows of tiny primrose ruffles around the bottom, a spencer in the same yellow. Matching silk lined her bonnet, the wide ribbon tied in a floppy bow beneath her right ear.

"You look lovely, Honoria," her father said, his eyes uncharacteristically serious, as if he knew how important this last outing was to her.

"Thank you, Papa."

Not until they were seated in the big carriage, Miss Keeble beside her, did Simon speak.

"That is a smashing outfit, Miss Keyes. I'm glad it's such a clear, sunny day so we can show off both you and that very pretty bonnet."

Honoria tried not to preen at his words, but it was difficult to keep her smile from growing into a grin.

They spoke about her father's portrait, which he would deliver sometime next month.

"I daresay my brother will plan some party for the unveiling. You will come with him to Whitcomb, of course?"

Had she heard him correctly? Was he inviting her to his family's home? "I—I shall have to ask my father," she said in a breathy voice that was likely inaudible above the street sounds.

"When you visit, we can ride out to Everley, which is not far from the duke's home."

"That would be lovely." It was all she could force out, her mind too busy imagining herself mounted on a magnificent horse beside him, galloping across a stark, lonely moor.

He spoke of his home and family on the brief ride and his words were like a siren's song that held her entranced.

Carriages lined both sides of the street outside Gunter's; clearly they weren't the only ones to have such an idea on a beautiful day.

"It will be stuffy inside and the tables outside are taken," Simon said. "Shall we enjoy our treat in velvet-lined comfort?"

Honey and Miss Keeble agreed and Simon gestured to one of the waiters. Once they'd placed their orders they sat back and watched the fluctuating crowd, many of whom seemed to know Simon.

Honoria was deep inside a fantasy where she and Simon were married and leaving for their country home tomorrow, only stopping to take leave of their many, many friends when Simon uttered a word—just one single word, but one that pulsed with more emotion than she'd heard from him in an entire month.

"Bella!"

Simon's enraptured expression sent her plummeting back down to earth. He was gazing at three women who'd stopped beside the carriage. To be precise, he was only looking at *one* of the women, and with his heart in his eyes.

Honey stared, too. She—Bella—was the most beautiful woman that she had ever seen.

"Hello, Simon." Bella smiled up at him as he scrambled down from the carriage. Her cherry red lips parted slightly to reveal dazzling, white teeth. She had skin like proverbial porcelain and navy-blue eyes. Her hair was brown, dark enough to look black, the ringlets glossy and luxurious beneath her straw bonnet.

Simon wore an expression she'd never seen before: abject worship.

Honey felt something crack inside her chest: Simon loved this beautiful creature.

"Mrs. Frampton, Bella, Agnes—what are you doing in London at this time of year?"

His words seemed to come from the bottom of a very deep well, and it was all she could do to remain upright in her seat.

The older woman—Mrs. Frampton—Honey supposed, answered him, "Agnes is getting married next month and we needed a few last-minute pieces of this and that." She was speaking of one daughter, but her eyes were on the other—the one who looked like an angel come to earth—right before her faded blue gaze flickered to Honoria.

The gesture was minute, but Lord Simon had impeccable manners. Usually.

A flush covered his beautiful, high cheekbones when he realized that he'd neglected his hosting duties. "Mrs. Frampton, Miss Agnes Frampton, and Miss Arabella Frampton, I have the honor of introducing you to Miss Honoria Keyes and her companion, Miss Keeble. Miss Keyes is Daniel Keyes's daughter."

Nods and smiles all around, but Honoria could hardly take her eyes off Arabella Frampton long enough to even remember what the other two women looked like. Either could Simon.

A waiter appeared with their ices.

"Would you care to join us?" Simon offered, blissfully unaware that his six words were like an ax to her heart.

"Yes, please do," Honey said mechanically when four pairs of blue eyes turned her way.

The women did a very unconvincing job of demurring and Simon opened the barouche door and gestured inside. "Please. We shall be a bit cozy but I'm sure Miss Keyes will not mind?"

Nobody noticed that her smile was more suited to a death mask and Honey soon found herself staring across at the three newcomers, Miss Keeble now beside her.

The strawberry ice she'd ordered tasted like ashes and she wanted to be back at home, in her bed with the blankets pulled over her head. And never come out.

Later, she couldn't recall a single word that was spoken, her only memory Simon's expression and the way his eyes had lingered on the dark-haired beauty every chance he got.

She slept very little that night, her once vibrant world suddenly gray and colorless.

The next day was his final sitting and Honey had planned to remain in her room and avoid seeing him—hopefully ever again. But her father put an end to that hope at breakfast.

"You look as though you didn't sleep well, Honey. What is the matter?" he asked when she joined him in the sunny breakfast room that overlooked the back garden.

Honey usually had a healthy appetite and her father would have been suspicious if she'd refrained altogether so she served herself the smallest possible portion of everything from the sideboard.

"Just a bit of a headache, Papa."

"Hmm." He laid aside the newspaper he had been reading and gave her a piercing look, his eyes so similar to hers it was like looking in a mirror. "I know you've grown to like young Fairchild, my dear, but—although you do not act it—you are a girl of fifteen and he is a man of almost one-and-twenty. He is a good and kind gentleman so I've given you more latitude than a wise father probably would have." He frowned. "I often regret not sending you to school and giving you an opportunity to mix with young girls your age. Perhaps—"

"Please, don't Papa." She laid down her fork and knife and met his worried gaze. "Don't. I would be miserable if you sent me away. I would miss you and you know that painting is everything—"

"No, my dear, not everything. Don't forget about life. About love. About experiencing joy—which is what you have been doing recently. Without experience in love, loss, pain, joy, and *life* one cannot make great art."

Honey didn't tell her father that after yesterday she now had far more familiarity with pain than she would have wished for.

***

Honey jerked her gaze from The Most Perfect Man in Britain and glanced at the clock: it was almost two-thirty. Soon it would all be over. Soon her father would lay down his brush for the last time and say—

"Well, my lord, it appears I have captured enough of you to satisfy even *my* exacting mistress." Daniel Keyes laid down his brush.

Simon, who'd been telling them about his plans for the remainder of the summer, smiled at Honoria. "You mean your daughter, sir?"

Daniel laughed. "I meant my muse, Lord Simon, but you might have something there." He looked over at Honey and raised his eyebrows. "Well, are you going to put poor Lord Simon out of his misery and show him his portrait?"

Before Honey could answer there was a sharp knock and the door opened to reveal their ancient butler, his face red with exertion.

"Good Lord," her father paused in the act of wiping his hands on a turpsy rag to frown at his servant. "Have you been *running*, Dowdle?"

The old man was too busy gasping for breath to answer. Instead, he held up a rectangle of cream-colored paper.

"For me?" Daniel Keyes took a step toward him.

Dowdle shook his head. "A post chaise is waiting outside." He handed Simon the letter. "For Lord Saybrook,"

Honey was surprised at their butler's slip with Simon's title; Dowdle was usually such a stickler for propriety.

Simon tore open the letter and Honey watched as every bit of color drained from his face. He swallowed hard enough to be heard all the way across the room and then looked up.

"You'll have to excuse me, sir. It's … well, It seems my … my nephew developed a chill and a cough and—" He waved his hand in a churning motion, as if he were stirring the very air around him in the hope it would stimulate the correct words.

His face was stiff and his eyes wide with horror. "My nephew, the young Marquess of Saybrook, has died. I must leave immediately for Whitcomb."

Chapter Two

Village of Whitcomb
Fourteen Years Later

Simon, Marquess of Saybrook, had been to the St. George Inn several times in the weeks since he'd finally been able to leave his bed. It had been his cousin, Raymond, who'd first persuaded Simon to go out for a pint—or six.

"It'll make you feel more yourself to visit some of your old haunts," Raymond had cajoled when Simon had initially demurred.

It had taken only one night out with Raymond to convince Simon that his cousin was correct.

After that first evening, he'd gone to the cozy pub again and again, both with and without his cousin. It seemed the better he felt physically, the more he needed to drink.

He'd soon discovered that he liked the St. George far better than the chambers he kept at his brother's sprawling monstrosity, Whitcomb.

He and Raymond had taken rooms that first night—when neither of them had been in any condition to make the half-hour ride back home—and Simon had stayed at the inn several more times since.

Tonight was one of those nights.

A hot, rough hand slid over his chest and a silky-smooth leg wrapped around one of his thighs, pulling him from his thoughts. "That was lovely, my lord."

Simon snorted at the serving wench's lie; he'd mounted her roughly and ridden her with all the finesse of a soldier on leave.

This was their first time together, but he'd seen her before—each time he drank at the George—and he'd ignored her overtures for weeks.

The reason he'd made no move to bed her until then was the sliver of decorum that had somehow lodged itself in his conscience. Whoring so close to home—so close to where his mother and niece lived—had seemed very wrong. What if word of his activities were to make its way to his brother's house?

But tonight—after the set-to he'd had with Wyndham earlier—Simon had decided he'd be bloody pleased if word of his debauchery reached his sanctimonious brother's ears. Perhaps Wyndham might even release him from the shackles he'd bound him with if Simon behaved revoltingly enough.

And so, when the barmaid had delivered his fifth—or was it sixth—drink, lowered her pert bottom onto his lap, and then slid her questing hand between his thighs, he'd spread them wider for her.

Soon afterward, he'd taken her up to his room, where he'd mounted her like a man who'd not had a woman in a long, long time. Because he hadn't—not in almost two years.

Simon felt her stroke the scarred side of his torso and turned to face her.

She snatched away her hand, her eyes round. "I'm sorry, my lord, does that hurt?"

He took her hand and placed it between his thighs. "No, but these do."

Her expression shifted from worried to wicked and she giggled, her skilled hand massaging his sensitive jewels.

Simon groaned and closed his eyes. "That feels bloody wonderful."

She moved closer, positioning herself to have better access to his body. Her other hand stroked him from groin to chest, teasing his remaining nipple until it was hard and tight, and then moving to the other side, to the mass of scar tissue.

"What happened, my lord?" Her fingers were gentle and so tentative he could barely feel any pressure. The scars were thickest on his torso and very little sensation remained, although he ached like the devil after a day's exertion.

Simon opened his eyes and blinked up at her through the gloom. She was younger than he'd thought, her harsh features softened by the bounteous brown hair that now framed her round face and hung down her back. He didn't know her name but now seemed like the wrong time to ask. Instead he took a handful of hair and began to wind it around his fist, gradually pulling her lower.

"Exploding shrapnel," he said, the two words a bit like shrapnel themselves. Her forehead wrinkled and Simon explained. "A cannon ball that breaks into many pieces in order to spray death and destruction more broadly."

Her fingers traced the shot pattern down his side to his hip and he tightened his grip on her hair and tugged. She sucked in air through clenched teeth, her eyelids becoming heavy at his rough handling, the look of wanton lust on her face making his prick throb.

He took her hand from his chest and kissed her palm.

"The Frenchies are evil buggers," she said, her voice husky.

Simon laughed—in between kissing the rough calluses on her hand and tonguing the sensitive skin between her fingers—but there was no humor in it.

"It was one of ours, love. It had some flaw and exploded; the entire side of the cannon came apart. A big section of the barrel hit my mount." Poor Hector. He'd been a fine horse and had made it through seven years without a scratch. But the chunk of iron had taken his head off as cleanly as a cleaver. Simon knew it could have been his own head just as easily. People told him he was lucky.

"I was lucky," he said out loud, just to see what the words tasted like—how they felt.

They tasted like ashes and felt like nothing.

Her hand moved from his balls up his hard shaft and it was Simon's turn to suck in a harsh breath.

"Yes, you were very lucky," she murmured, her eyes roaming his body, the look in them an odd mix of morbid fascination and lust. Well, it was better than horror, which is what he'd expected to see. All his life he'd enjoyed the admiration of women and had come to expect it. Simon had to admit he'd wondered—even worried a little—if those days were over. He felt a hot rush of gratitude, heavily mixed with lust, for the woman above him: the first woman to see his scarred body naked.

He released her hair and hand and grabbed her hips, lifting her off the bed. She squealed and wiggled and the skin up and down his left side burned like fire as he held her aloft. He wanted her again; he'd redeem himself and do better by her this time.

"Now it's your turn to get lucky," he said, as she spread her legs and reached between them to take his length in her hand. Simon lowered her body slowly onto his stand and thrust into her at the same time, the savage, deep penetration causing both of them to gasp with pleasure.

"Oh, *my lord.*"

He groaned at the need in her voice and closed his eyes and began to move, pleased to discover that alcohol wasn't the only way of escaping his thoughts.

***

Meanwhile, in London . . .

"Hello? Are you there, Honey?"

Honey startled at the sound of her name and turned.

Her friend and housemate Serena Lombard stood in the open doorway, a puzzled expression on her face. "Is anything amiss, my dear?"

Honey realized she was standing in the middle of the room staring at the letter. She held up the ivory paper with the black wax seal.

"What is it?"

"A letter from the Duke of Plimpton."

Serena's eyebrows rose. "Hmm, Plimpton—didn't your father once paint him? Wait, that was his brother, the Marquess of Saybrook, wasn't it?"

Honey's pulse pounded in her ears at the sound of his name: the first time she'd heard it spoken aloud in years.

Serena's forehead creased with concern. "You *are* feeling ill, aren't you? You are as pale as a ghost. What is it?"

Honey turned away and folded the letter with jerky, clumsy hands.

"Honey?" Serena's fingers landed on her shoulder.

"I'm fine. Just a bit light-headed. I-I'm afraid I missed breakfast this morning," she lied. It took three swallows to get rid of the lump in her throat and she forced her face into some semblance of self-possession before turning to her friend.

"Shall I ring for tea?" Serena asked in her slightly accented voice.

"Tea sounds perfect. And perhaps some of Una's butter biscuits. After all, one does not receive a piece of mail from a duke every day. I shall meet you in the parlor in ten minutes and tell you all about it," Honey promised, giving her friend what she hoped was a reassuring smile.

"I'll round up everyone and send for tea."

The door shut behind her and Honoria's brain spun like the colorful wooden whirligig Serena's young son had made for their back garden. The Duke of Plimpton—after all these years? She had not thought about the duke for a long time. But his brother Simon was a different matter. *He* still managed to escape from the Newgate-like prison she'd constructed in her mind just for him. It didn't matter how thick she made the walls or how small the gap between the bars, Simon's shade always found a way to escape and come find her.

Honey's feet took her in the direction of her private storage cupboard, which she kept locked at all times. She stood on her tiptoes and felt for the key on top of the smallish wardrobe. It had been some time since she'd unlocked the door.

There wasn't much inside, in fact the cupboard wasn't anywhere close to full. Four canvases leaned against each other, protected by old sheets.

The first was a painting of her mother.

Although Honey had no memory of the woman on the canvas it was her father's work and his love for the subject was evident in every stroke. It was his finest work, in her opinion. She knew it was wrong to keep it hidden in the dark but it was her *only* reminder of both her parents and that somehow made it intensely private.

The second portrait made her smile. It was the first painting she'd ever done. She could not have been older than five. It was, of course, a portrait of the person she loved most in the world: her father. It bore a striking resemblance to Daniel Keyes and it brought to mind his reaction the day she'd painted it. Joy and love and pride had shone brightly from his handsome face, so strongly that even now the memory warmed her like a comforting blanket.

The third was a portrait of her. Her father had done many of her over the years—over a dozen, several of which still hung on the walls of their house. But this one? Well, this was special. He'd painted it not long after finishing Lord Simon's portrait that summer.

Daniel Keyes had been a self-absorbed man in many ways, but not when it came to his daughter. He'd known it would have been unbearable to expose her unrequited love to questions, but this painting was proof that he'd felt every ounce of her suffering in his heart. Just looking at the pain in her eyes was enough to make Honey's throat tighten

She was beautiful in the portrait—far prettier than she was in life—her eyes like shards of broken ice, haunted, turned in on an internal landscape that was pure pain.

The portrait reminded her how her fifteen-year-old self hadn't believed that her bleeding heart would keep beating. Yet here she was: hearty and hale all these years later.

Her hand shook as she pulled the sheet from the fourth painting and looked into the smiling hyacinth-blue eyes of Simon Fairchild, the Marquess of Saybrook.

As it always did, the breath froze in her lungs. Honoria had painted many portraits in the past fourteen years but in none of the others had she captured the pure light and human essence of a subject as she had in this one.

Her technique was far superior now to what it had been over a decade ago, but she'd never painted anything better. The laughter in his eyes was so vivid she could hear its echo.

Honey dropped the cover back over the image that had haunted her far too often over the years. Simon wasn't the only man she'd been fond of, of course, but no other man had inspired such depth of feeling.

She knew he'd gone to war because she'd read his name in the paper—first among the missing, and later when he'd returned. Both times she'd wept: first with sorrow and then with relief.

Why had he gone to war? What had happened to the young woman—Bella—and his plans for a life in the country?

Honey sighed and locked the door on those questions and dozens of others.

She went to the small mirror beside the door and inspected her uninspiring reflection. Her heavy hair had come loose from its severe moorings and long tendrils floated around her narrow face like a dun-colored gloriole.

To be honest, her narrow face with its pale gray eyes were significantly more appealing with disheveled locks as a frame, but it did not suit a woman of her age and position, so she did her best to tidy the loose strands without actually unpinning and re-braiding it all. The result was good enough for an afternoon tea with her housemates, who were spinsters like Honey.

A diminutive garden packed with blooms separated her painting studio from the small house where she'd spent her entire life. After her father died, she'd chosen to set up her painting studio in the carriage house, rather than his studio. It was foolish, but she'd left the studio untouched, not a shrine to him, but a place so full of his essence that she could not bear the thought of dismantling it.

As Honoria traversed the narrow walk that led to the back door of the house she noticed that Freddie's peonies—the size of cabbages—had bloomed and died. It was another summer of her life, her twenty-ninth summer.

That notion was vaguely depressing but she was in no mood to ask herself why that was, not today.

Freddie—Lady Winifred Sedgwick—glanced up from the small writing desk in the corner when Honey entered the parlor.

"Serena will be here in a moment. She has become embroiled in a battle of wills."

"Ah, a skirmish between Mrs. Brinkley and Una?"

"Who else." It was not a question. Their housekeeper and cook were both the best of friends and the worst of enemies, depending on the day.

Honey dropped into her favorite seat, a battered green leather wingchair that had been her father's favorite. She swore she could still smell the unmistakable combination of turpentine and bay rum she associated with him even though he had been gone eight years. He'd died not long after her twenty-first birthday, passing away in his sleep—a quiet death utterly unlike his passionate, flamboyant life.

The door to the parlor swung open and Honey smiled. "Hello, Oliver. Have you escaped your lessons?"

Serena's ten-year-old son dropped a creditable bow. "Mama said that I might come down for tea."

"And Una's biscuits?" she teased. He grinned and came to sit beside her. Honoria ruffled his messy brown curls. "What have you been working on? I haven't heard any explosions lately."

"Mama said no more experiments with the electricity maker." He sounded mournful about that.

"How do you manage to entertain yourself in the face of such deprivation?"

"She gave me an automaton." His smile was blinding.

"Ah. And have you taken it apart yet?"

He gave her a scoffing look that told her what he thought of such a foolish question.

Freddie came to join them after depositing a small pile of correspondence on the salver by the door. "He is making his own automaton, aren't you, Oliver?"

"*Oui, Tante.*"

Oliver called them all *aunt* and spoke a fluent mix of French and English that was beyond charming.

The door opened and his mother, accompanied by Mrs. Brinkley, with the tea tray, entered.

"Thank you, Mrs. Brinkley," Honey said to the tiny housekeeper, who was looking a bit fierce.

"My pleasure, ma'am." She plunked down the tray and then bustled from the room, no doubt headed back to the kitchen and a resumption of hostilities.

Beside her, Oliver's stomach grumbled and Honey gave him a look of mock, open-mouthed shock.

He flushed. "*J'ai faim.*"

"English today, Oliver," Serena reminded her son. "Did you get a letter from Miles?" she asked Freddie.

"Yes," Freddie said, gesturing to the single page on her desk. "You may read it. He says he won't be back from the country for at least another week."

Miles Ingram was a friend of theirs who'd been the dancing master at the Stefani Academy for Young Ladies, where they'd all taught before the school closed last year.

There'd been seven teachers and they'd grown as close as siblings over the years they worked together. And now they were scattered to the four winds: Portia had gone to the wilds of Cornwall; Annis lived with her Grandmother in the tiny town of Cocklesham; and Lorelei with her brother and his family at his vicarage just outside York. Only Honoria, Serena, Freddie, and Miles remained in London.

Freddie busied herself with distributing tea, small sandwiches, and biscuits.

"Well?" Serena demanded. "Will you put us out of our misery, Honey? What does the duke have to say?"

"Perhaps she would like to wait until we've finished eating?" Freddie murmured.

"Oh, bother waiting," Serena said.

Honey laughed at her friend's impatience. "Very well, I shall read it to you." She opened the letter and spread the single sheet out on her lap.

"*Miss Keyes,*

I am writing to you at the recommendation of Viscount Heath, whose wife's portrait you painted this spring. I have seen the painting and found your rendering of the viscountess to be accurate without excessive flattery or over-indulgence."

Honey couldn't help chuckling at that. "Perhaps I should print that on my calling card—*Accurate portraitist not given to flattery or over-indulgence?*"

"Keep reading, my dear," Serena urged.

"*I would like to engage you to paint my wife and my daughter, who is sixteen and—*"

Serena clapped her hands and bounced up and down on the settee, jostling Freddie beside her. "Oh, Honey, that is marvelous."

"Does he mention his terms?" Freddie asked, ever the practical one.

"He asks that I respond with *my* terms and the earliest date I will be available." She placed the letter in Serena's outstretched hand.

"When will you go?" Serena demanded, looking up from the letter, which she was cradling as if it were spun glass.

"Goodness, I've only just learned of it. I've not even decided if—"

"*Pffft!* Don't be coy. You know you will do it. How could you not? A duchess and her daughter. His Grace is quite well off, isn't he?"

Honey's friends did not know of her girlhood infatuation with the duke's younger brother. Why should they? Who told their friends such embarrassing private details? She shuddered at the thought of disgorging such a pitiful confession.

"Honey?"

Serena and Freddie were watching her with expectant expressions.

A slight knock on the door made her jump.

It was Nounou, Oliver's nurse.

Serena smiled at her son. "You may take some of Una's biscuits up to the schoolroom."

Oliver—who'd been behaving with remarkable composure for a little boy in the middle of a tedious adult conversation—placed another three biscuits on his plate and dropped a careful bow before following the French woman from the room.

Honey waited until the door closed before clearing her throat and asking Freddie the dreaded question. "What do you know of the Duke of Plimpton and his current household?"

Winifred Sedgewick made her living as a matchmaker, even though she despised the term, and there was very little about society that she did not know

"I know His Grace has been married for almost eighteen or so years and that his wife was the Duke of Stanford's youngest. She is delicate and cannot have more children. I believe the daughter is their only surviving child."

So, the duchess had never had any more children after their only son died.

"The duke's younger brother, the Marquess of Saybrook, is heir presumptive," Freddie continued, unaware of the chaos the name caused in Honoria's breast.

"Ah, yes," Serena said in between bites of biscuit. "He was at Waterloo." She paused and frowned. "Was there not something odd about his return?"

"Yes," Freddie said, "he was not found until three days after the battle. I have not seen his name this past Season, so I daresay he is still mending."

Honoria knew all of this. She'd followed the story of his return like a woman obsessed. She took a sip of tea; her hand was white from squeezing the cup's handle and she forced herself to relax.

"I cannot imagine what he must have endured," Freddie said, shaking her head.

"Do you think he lives with his brother?" Honey asked.

"That I do not know. Why do you ask? Oh, that's right—" Freddie said before Honey could answer, "I recall now, your father painted his portrait."

"What was he like?" Serena demanded, dipping a biscuit into her tea and then popping the soggy mess into her mouth, licking her fingers.

Honey bit back a smile at her friend's free and easy ways. She could hardly imagine the scandal the voluptuous Frenchwoman must have caused during her brief sojourn among the *ton*.

"It's been a long time since I last saw him, Serena." Fourteen years, three weeks, and five days. Not that she was counting.

Serena gave one of her very gallic shrugs. "You must remember something about him?"

Honey sighed—why bother lying? "He was the most gorgeous man I've ever seen."

Serena's biscuit froze an inch from her open mouth and she frowned, her expression one of disbelief. "Surely he is not more handsome than Miles?"

Honey's face heated, but she jerked a nod.

The Frenchwoman chuckled. "Hmmm, that must be a rare sight to see."

Honey turned away from her knowing look and fussed with the handle of her teacup.

"I believe he stayed with his brother when he first returned," Freddie said, mercifully changing the subject. "But he does have an estate of his own."

"Yes, Everley." Honoria's voice was barely a whisper. She set down her cup and saucer with steady hands and then looked at her friends. Freddie's beautiful, inscrutable face remained expressionless but Serena met her gaze with a bold, challenging stare.

"Well?" The irrepressible Frenchwoman broke the uncomfortable silence, her hazel eyes sparkling. "When will you leave?"

Chapter Three

Simon was flying.

Or the very next thing to it.

The sorrel stallion with its flaxen mane was not only beautiful, but he was also as enamored of speed as his master. Bacchus was his name but Simon would have done better to name him Mercury he was so fleet.

Simon gave Bacchus his head when they approached the end of the path that opened onto the long and somewhat hilly drive leading down to Whitcomb. Bacchus knew the road well and his powerful muscles exploded. The wind was so fierce Simon swore he could hear it whistling past the scarred remnants of his deaf ear.

His muscles bunched and stretched like that of his mount, the damaged skin of his face, throat, and torso burning. The pain was almost cathartic and it reminded him that he was alive, something he needed to tell himself at least a dozen times a day.

"I'm alive," he whispered.

The wind ripped away his words but they pounded through his mind and body. He *was* alive.

Thundering hooves and blurring trees cocooned him.

Alive.

He crested the ridge—and almost collided with a post chaise that was ambling down the center of the road.

"Holy hell!" His voice was so loud it caused the big stallion between his thighs to startle.

Life shrank to a fraction of a second as Simon shifted his weight and flexed his legs, sending Bacchus charging toward the slight gap to the right of the carriage.

He was vaguely aware of the postilion using his entire body to wrench his team to the left. The carriage skittered sideways and the wheels rolled into the soft, damp soil beside the drive.

Simon thundered past without slowing, his heart pounding louder than the wind. He laughed, the sound mad to his own ears.

He was alive.

***

Honey looked out the window just in time to catch a glimpse of the most beautiful man she'd ever seen.

And then the chaise lurched to the side, throwing her, her book, and her cloak to the floor. Luckily, the cloak went before Honey did and softened her fall so she was more startled than hurt when she landed on her knees.

She held onto the seat as the carriage bounced over rough ground, waiting until the vehicle began to slow before pushing herself up until she could grasp the leather strap beside the door.

The pounding of her heart thundered in her ears, and not just because of the scare.

He was here.

Honey closed her eyes and relived the lighting-fast image of a Norse god on a magnificent mount. The image—no matter how fleeting—had shown him to be just as beautiful as before.

Simon was here.

The chaise shuddered to a halt and shook her out of her stunned reverie.

So what if he was here? What difference did that make? She'd known it might be the case. She'd prepared herself for seeing him again. Or at least she'd thought she had.

Honey grimaced at her pitiful dithering and released the strap, collapsing back against the squabs as the chaise shifted on its springs.

The door opened and the burly groom appeared in the opening. "You all right, Miss?" His homely face was creased with concern.

"Just a little shaken up. What happened?"

His expression shifted from concern to disgust. "Naught but a lunatic, riding hell-bent for leather. Beggin' your pardon, Miss." He pushed back his hat and scratched his head. "He came out of nowhere and went past in a blur—riding the damned finest piece of horseflesh I've ever seen," he said with grudging admiration, and then grimaced, "Beggin' your pardon, Miss," he added, again.

Honey wanted to roll her eyes; men and their horses. "Are we close to Whitcomb House?"

"Aye, naught but ten minutes away."

She smoothed her navy blue traveling dress over her lap with shaking hands.

Good God. I will see him again in only minutes.

"All right then?" the groom asked.

She mustered a smile and nodded. "Yes—yes of course. I am fine and ready to resume the journey."

He closed the door and soon they were rolling.

Honey stared out the window and tried to sooth her jangled nerves, but the beautiful profile and flash of golden hair were stuck in her mind's eye—a problem with artists. She would have known that classical profile—distinct enough to grace a coin—anywhere. Hatless with buckskin breeches, black clawhammer, and tall leather boots completed the brief picture. He'd looked vital, not damaged at all. He looked like a Corinthian—or at least that is what she imaged they looked like, those men who relished their own physicality: bruising riders, crack marksmen, determined pugilists, and other such overtly masculine foolishness.

Her stomach quivered at the image her mind would not relinquish. How could she endure the proximity of such a beautiful, vital, distracting man? It was simply too—

Calm yourself.

The cool voice was like a blast of frigid air waking her from a fevered dream.

Suddenly her anxiety was annoying rather than crippling; she was nine-and-twenty, not fifteen. So what if he was here? She wasn't painting *him*, she was painting the duke's wife and child. She was here to work, to build her reputation as a portraitist and a commission for a duke was a powerful thing—could be a powerful thing—if she concentrated and did her best.

You are a woman grown—no longer a tall, skinny, gangly fifteen-year-old, the logical, soothing voice in her head reminded her.

She snorted. No, she was now a tall, skinny, gangly twenty-nine-year-old. Good Lord. Hadn't she learned anything in fourteen years?

The racing of her heart told her she'd not learned much—at least not when it came to Simon Fairchild.

The chaise crested the ridge and Honey gasped. "Oh my goodness." Her eyes darted wildly as she tried to take it all in. Massive oaks flanked both sides of the drive at regular intervals, allowing glimpses of rolling parkland beyond. This was no house, not even a mansion—it seemed to stretch for miles and resemble a mediaeval township.

Honey had heard Whitcomb compared in size and character to Knole House and now understood why it was considered a national treasure. Her fingers itched to sketch it and she knew she would need to come back to this vantage point.

The sun was already low in the sky when the carriage rolled onto the cobble drive that curved in front of the massive entrance.

A blond man dressed in a dark coat and buff pantaloons waited at the foot of the shallow stone steps that led to arched doors at least fifteen feet at their peak, the heavy, weathered wood bound with intricate iron strapping.

Over the entrance the dragon and greyhound of Henry VIII supported the Royal Arms of England.

Even before the carriage had come to a full stop the man strode toward her, two liveried servants following in his wake. For a moment, Honey's heart thundered in her ears: *Simon?*

Impossible, Simon had just passed her carriage.

The man's resemblance to Simon became superficial the closer he came. While he was blond, his hair was not Simon's striking gold. He was shorter—perhaps even shorter than Honey—his build stout rather than lithe and well formed. His eyes were blue, but sky-blue rather than hydrangea.

"Welcome to Whitcomb House, Miss Keyes. I am the duke's cousin, Raymond Fairchild." He helped Honey descended from the carriage. "The duke had wanted to greet you but, unfortunately, he's indisposed. How was your journey?"

"It was lovely, thank you."

"Excellent, I'm glad to hear it." He looked so overjoyed that Honey actually believed him. "I daresay you would like a cup of tea and an hour to rest." He gestured toward the house, not waiting for an answer. "His Grace will see you in the library before dinner. But come, I will show you to your rooms."

Honoria followed the shorter, bustling man into a hall that was straight out of Shakespearean. Her jaw sagged as she gazed up at the four-centered-arch ceiling.

"This is the Great Hall and was built in the 1490s," He said, not slowing. "The older parts of the house are not used as much as the South Wing, which was added in the 1740s and affords far more convenience and comfort. The family dines in the smaller dining room when not entertaining. His Grace has requested that you dine with the family." His tone said the request was not really a request.

They ascended ancient flagstone steps that turned twice at ninety-degree angles and opened onto yet another long hall, this one heading back in the direction they just came.

"This may seem a rather odd way of reaching the South Wing," he said in a confiding tone, as if reading her thoughts, "But it will make more sense shortly."

They passed through a lengthy wood-paneled hall; the dark wood floor covered with an ancient carpet runner that muffled their steps. Heavy iron sconces lighted their way at intervals and a massive rose window at the far end added an almost religious air.

He turned down a hallway on the right before they came to the spectacular window, leading them down an almost identical corridor.

"Is it only the duke and duchess and their daughter who live here?" Honey asked as they ascended what felt like half a story, entering a much wider and airier hall illuminated by cathedral windows with intricate tracery.

"His Grace's mother, the Dowager Duchess of Plimpton and his brother, the Marquess of Saybrook, also live at Whitcomb." He cut her a quick smile. "As do I." He took yet another right, this hallway narrow and windowless.

Lord, she was so lost she could wander for weeks.

"The only one of the family to keep chambers in the East Wing is my cousin, Lord Saybrook."

Honey blinked at the disapproval she heard in the jovial man's voice. So, the marquess was … difficult? Or was that merely the opinion of an envious poor relation?

They turned yet another corner but this time she staggered to a halt.

"Goodness," she murmured.

"This is the older of the two portrait galleries," Mr. Fairchild said, his increasingly distant voice causing Honey to resume walking, her head swiveling wildly to take in the staggering number of portraits that covered the high, paneled walls, jammed together so tightly that the frames touched in places.

Good God—she recognized the unmistakable style of Holbein. *Holbein*! She made an undignified squeaking sound. Her portrait would hang in a collection which contained one by Hans Holbein?

"Miss Keyes?"

Pulling her eyes away from the portrait—the subject a middle-aged man with no great physical beauty, but with a countenance so *knowing* that Honey felt as if he were looking right at her—was like pulling a heavy wagon from deep, sucking mud.

"Yes?" she said dazedly, turning her head and blinking, as if she'd just been blinded by a lighthouse lantern.

"This way, please. It is just a little farther."

Honey hurried after him, pointedly keeping her eyes from the flow of portraits that assaulted her peripheral vision.

Later. She would come back later. This gallery would be reason enough to learn the layout of the maze-like house.

Something Mr. Fairchild had just said sank in.

"Did you say this was the *old* gallery?"

"Yes, the new gallery is on the first floor. That is where the newer portraits hang."

Like her father's portrait of Simon Fairchild.

Honey's heart pounded like a young girl's facing her first assembly: Simon *and* more paintings.

They ascended yet another set of stairs, these wooden and carpeted with a rich maroon and gold pattern that seemed to levitate above the floor. Honey felt almost guilty stepping on such lovely, intricate work. She had never seen its like.

"And here we are," he said, flinging open the first door on the right.

Honey gaped. She was vaguely aware that she was spending far too much time with her mouth hanging open and shut it.

The sitting room was a cream and lemon-yellow shade that felt crisp and cool. Delicate, spindle-legged chairs and a low-slung settee were arranged in front of a massive fireplace with an off-white marble mantle and surround.

"Through this door," he opened a door to the right, "Is your dressing room." The room was monstrous and Honey's paltry collection of dresses would scarcely fill a corner of one of the huge armoires. A washstand, dressing table, clothing chest, several chairs, damask covered chaise longue, and large bathing tub near a fireplace weren't enough to make the huge room feel crowded.

"And here is your bed chamber." This last door opened to the most opulent room of the three. A monstrous four-poster bed held pride of place, curtained and canopied in the same lemon yellow and cream, but with hints of gold. Rich velvet drapes covered the floor to ceiling windows that made up part of one wall.

Honey realized that he was waiting for some reaction.

"These rooms are lovely and quite … spacious."

"This is the family's section of the house. This room used to belong to his grace's grandmother."

"How kind of the duke to treat me with such generosity and condescension."

Mr. Fairchild's expression said that he agreed. "He is quite excited that you are here to paint our dear Becca and the duchess. Do you ride?" he asked.

"Adequately."

"Well, I'm sure you won't be working all the time, so I hope you'll allow me to show you some of the beauties of Whitcomb."

Before she could answer the door opened and a footman entered with her portmanteau.

"Ah, here is your baggage," Mr. Fairchild said. "I've taken the liberty of ordering a light tea and I will send up a maid to assist you."

"You're most kind," Honey murmured.

"Is there anything else I can arrange for you, Miss Keyes?"

"No, thank you. This is all very lovely."

"The duke's study is at the other end of the Old Gallery. Ring the bell and a servant will escort you. His grace will expect you at seven."

"Thank you." Honey didn't bother telling Mr. Fairchild that she'd be able to find her way back to those portraits asleep and in the dark.

Chapter Four

Honey was ready a full fifteen minutes before her meeting. Rather than sit in her room staring out at the view—admittedly quite a remarkable one that provided a sweeping panorama of the topiary and past that, the deer park—she made her way back to the old gallery.

The wide, black and white tiled corridor was partly illuminated with windows set high above, perhaps thirty feet. The angle of the light was such that it would never touch directly on a painting.

She noticed that she was actually walking on tiptoes as she made her way down the length of the hall, as if approaching a holy relic. Well, for her this *was* the equivalent of a holy relic.

Her gaze flickered greedily across the collected booty of centuries: a Van Dyke, a Devit, a Seymore—complete with trusty steed, a Dance-Holland, a—she gasped and lurched toward a portrait slightly smaller than those beside it—a *Hogarth*! The subject, a beautiful woman whose eyes and expression invited the viewer into her boudoir, indeed, who promised and *enticed*—

A door down the hall swung open so violently it crashed against the wall hard enough that she could feel the vibration in her feet.

"You can go sod yourself, Wyndham!" The roar filled the hallway, although its owner was still inside the room.

Honey had never heard the voice pulse with so much rage when she'd known him, but she recognized it all the same.

Instead of simply scurrying away—as she should have done—she stood motionless, her eyes riveted on the gaping doorway. A soft murmur broke the silence—the person who was currently being yelled at, she supposed.

"Ha!" The word dripped with loathing and fury. "I don't bloody *care*; haven't you been listening? The whole place can go to the devil and you along with it. I'm telling you for the last time, Wyndham—do *not* meddle in my affairs ever again or I swear you shall live to regret it." The enraged speaker catapulted out of the open doorway.

Even though Honey was frozen, he must have noticed something out of the corner of his eye because he stopped and whipped around to face her.

She gave a small, nearly inaudible, gasp of surprise. *Good Lord.* What had *happened* to him?

He surged toward her with an odd, lurching gait that drove her back a step, raw rage rolling from him like waves of heat.

"Who the *devil* are you? And what are you doing lurking about and listening at keyholes?" He kept walking, driving her back and back, until she hit the wall and felt something sharp jab her hip. The thought that she might have damaged a priceless painting was even more horrifying than the furious man stalking her. She turned to look over her shoulder and nearly fainted with relief when she saw it was only the corner of a plinth bearing a marble bust.

A hand grabbed her arm ungently and swung her around. The face that scowled down on her was not far different from the beautiful portrait she'd painted all those years ago—at least on the right side.

But the left side had been vandalized with angry red scars that had destroyed the smooth, high-boned beauty. The slashes and gashes and pits bore the slick sheen of recently healed wounds. His magnificent golden-blond hair had been cropped brutally close, doing nothing to hide what remained of his left ear or the deep horizontal groves that began at his jaw and deeply scored his cheek. He glared down at her with the same beautiful blue eyes, but the left eyelid was pulled down at the outside corner, the stretched skin giving the eye a perpetually sinister cast. He'd been tall and lithe when she'd known him but now his broad shoulders were heavily muscled and massive rather than slender.

It was Simon, but it was not Simon.

The man in front of her was a byproduct of war: a more intense, distilled version of his prior self. He was sinew, muscle, and bone—all softness and excess flesh had been burnt away. What remained was pure warrior, a man branded, bent, and distorted by violence.

This was not the Simon she knew, nor did he appear to know her.

The crushing realization left her sick inside; he looked at her with no recognition at all in his glorious eyes. He did not know her.

Honey wanted to weep.

"Simon." The word was quietly spoken but it cracked like a bullwhip in the cavernous hallway.

Both Honey and Simon Fairchild startled, as if they'd been caught in the act of something indecent, yet still they could not look away from each other.

Rather than release her, his hand squeezed tighter while his jaw worked, as if he were chewing his options and found them indigestible. His eyes narrowed and the nostrils of his fine, aquiline nose flared as he struggled to impose some modicum of control—as he appeared to remember that it was not *her* he was angry at.

He dropped her arm as if she'd scalded him and spun away, his expression—on both the angel and monster sides—disdainful. He pushed past the other man without speaking and lurched down the hall, his steps awkward but swift.

The air in his wake crackled and Honey felt as though she'd been picked up by a powerful cyclone and tossed aside, her ears ringing, her soul battered.

"Miss Keyes?"

Honey had never met the Duke of Plimpton in person. By the time her father finished Simon's portrait the duke had merely sent a lackey to collect it, the grand ceremony planned for its unveiling never spoken of again.

His Grace the Duke of Plimpton looked nothing like Simon. He was a paler, slighter, and far less noticeable man than his younger brother in just about every way except for his cool dignity and quiet power.

Unlike Simon, the duke's hair was a nondescript brown. His features were regular and not unattractive, but, on the whole, unexceptional. He lacked Simon's size and was not much above medium height, lean and compact rather than broad and towering like his younger brother.

Only in the shape of their tilted eyes did she see any resemblance. But where Simon's were the Egyptian blue of a Raphael painting, the duke's were a dull gray that was every bit as nondescript as the rest of him.

Simon Fairchild was a blazing star while the duke was the distant and unknowable dark side of the moon.

He also looked quite ill. There were dark smudges beneath his eyes and his skin had an unhealthy sheen. Honey supposed this was the *indisposition* that Mr. Fairchild had mentioned.

The duke gestured to the open doorway. "Please, come inside my study."

Honey's legs wobbled a little as she crossed the carpeted hall between them.

He shut the door and gestured to the two chairs arrayed before a desk. "Have a seat."

His desk was a slab of almost black wood supported by scaly gilt legs that looked as if they had once belonged to some monstrous mythical creature. It was the most magnificent piece of furniture that she had ever seen and it should have made the man standing behind fade into insignificance. But the duke's understated authority bent the grandeur of the room to his will and she realized he might not *look* as physically imposing or handsome as Simon, but he possessed enormous presence.

Honey lowered her still-trembling form into one of the brown leather chairs across from him. She'd been around artists all her life so she was accustomed to high-strung emoting, but even her father had not been as mercurial or violent as the man out in the hall.

"Welcome to Whitcomb, Miss Keyes. I hope you are not too fatigued from your journey?"

Ah, so they were going to pretend like the human hurricane in the portrait gallery didn't exist. That was fine with Honey.

"Not at all, your grace." She was pleased by her cool, level tone and could see by the slight lessening of tension in the duke's face that he was relieved that she'd decided to play along.

"Thank you for arranging such a luxurious carriage." The duke had, in fact, seen to all the facets of her journey and had not stinted.

"I am pleased you have accepted this commission, Miss Keyes. Your father's portrait of my brother captured his spirit and is one of my favorites." He paused and she smiled at his kind words. "He was a great artist and I am sorry for his passing."

"Thank you, your grace."

"Would you care for something to drink before dinner?" He gestured to a selection of decanters on a table not far from his desk.

"No thank you, your housekeeper was kind enough to provide a cup of tea in my room."

Pleasantries out of the way, his attitude became brisk. "It will only be the family at dinner tonight. My wife does not dine with us as she is unwell. My daughter, Lady Rebecca, my mother, my cousin—whom you've met—and my brother—" a minute flicker of irritation disturbed his calm façade but quickly passed. "will dine with us this evening. We entertain from time to time, and you will, of course, join us."

"Thank you," she murmured.

"Perhaps you might explain your preferred method of work so I can inform her grace as to what is expected?"

"I will need a few sessions to become acquainted with Lady Rebecca and the duchess. During these sessions I will make sketches. I will also look at the gowns and accessories they have chosen as well as discuss the preferred setting or background. I like to give the subjects the final approval in all such matters but sometimes my guidance can be helpful for aesthetic reasons."

He rested his elbows on his desk and glanced down at his interlaced hands for a long moment before looking up. "My wife will not be able to sit for protracted periods of time."

Honey didn't think the duke looked as if *he* could sit for protracted periods of time, either. She hoped that whatever ailed him was not an influenza or something contagious.

"I understand and I will take as many sketches as I can during the time I'm allotted. I will endeavor not to overtire her grace."

"Thank you, Miss Keyes, I can see you are thoughtful as well as accommodating and I appreciate both characteristics." He stood, indicating their brief meeting was over. "I shall see you at dinner—please ring for a servant to show you the way."

Honoria waited until the door closed behind her to smile at what his words had implied: that she was kind, accommodating, and *bland*—for an artist.

The other artists, friends, and hangers-on who'd surrounded Daniel Keyes had often commented on Honoria's calm, even-tempered nature. People had never stopped marveling that she was nothing like her larger-than-life father, with his unconventional clothing, wild hair, and flamboyant personality.

"How can you paint without passion?" more than one of her father's friends had asked her.

Only Daniel Keyes had never made Honey feel deficient about her temperate disposition.

"All of this," he'd said to her once, waving one ring-encrusted hand to encompass his unconventionally garbed person. "Is showmanship, Honey. A person does not need to be ostentatious to be a real artist. And you, my love, are not only a real artist, but you also possess a very rare quality in that your company is soothing and rejuvenating."

Honey supposed she could have chosen to be insulted by his words. After all, it was a commonly held belief that a woman had to be passionate in order to inspire passion. But, instead, she'd found his assessment of her to be comforting.

One of her father's lovers had once had the poor judgement to chide Honoria during a dinner at their house. "You are far too mild to ever be a truly successful artist, my dear. You must not appear so sedate. Try to cultivate an air of mystery, even if you do not *feel* mysterious." Honey recalled how the woman's cool eyes had flickered over her person, unaware of Daniel Keyes's gathering wrath at the end of the table.

The woman's full lips had folded with distaste at the conclusion of her inspection. "Lord knows your person is too ... *unusual* to hide, so you might as well make the best of what you have and dress with more flair."

She'd found the woman's advice amusing rather than insulting but her father had responded with all the anger and emotion that Honey could have desired in a champion, banishing his erstwhile lover from their lives before dinner had even ended.

Honey had not, even for an instant, considered taking the woman's ridiculous counseling. It wasn't that she didn't enjoy brighter colors and more interesting styles—like the *avant-guarde* clothing her friend Serena wore—but such garments never looked quite right on her.

She had long ago accommodated herself to the fact that she looked like a governess rather than a famous artist. The same went for her behavior and bearing; she was calm to the point of phlegmatic, but that was the way she was made and no amount of artificial emoting would change that.

Thinking about emoting turned her thoughts to Simon Fairchild. And thinking about Simon Fairchild stripped away everything she'd believed herself to be—cool and collected—and left her raw, furious, and hurt.

*So, it seems there is something—or some*one—*that can change your torpid bearing, Honey.*

She snorted at the taunting thought but she couldn't deny the truth of it.

What stung even more was that Honey had kept Simon Fairchild on a pedestal for fourteen years and he'd not even remembered who she was.

***

Simon slammed the door to his chambers with unnecessary force and stalked into his dressing room.

His valet was fussing with clothing but put his work aside and turned to help Simon, who waved him away.

"I'll undress myself, Peel." Simon yanked off his cravat and tossed it to the older man, who'd been with him before he'd joined the calvary and then served as his batman through the grueling years on the Continent. Peel knew him better than any other person on earth, the poor bastard.

To Peel's enduring displeasure, Simon often joked their relationship was very much like a marriage, but without the bedding. Peel was a bloody prude when it came to such humor.

"Ring for a bath," he ordered.

"Right away, my lord."

He left Simon alone without anyone to growl at. That was just as well; Simon was in such a vile mood he wouldn't bear his own company if he could find some way around it.

He was behaving badly and shaming himself and yet he could not seem to stop arguing and fighting and yelling with Wyndham at every opportunity. He needed to get away, but his brother kept him on such a tight leash it chaffed.

He snatched a decanter off the highboy dresser and poured a stiff shot of brandy. Drink was the only way he'd found to escape himself—at least with his clothing on—even if it was only for a little while and even if the price of escape was high.

And even if his brother would always be waiting for him at the end of what little bit of escape he could snatch for himself.

Bloody, damned Wyndham. Why could he not leave Simon be? Why must they have the same argument time and again? Why was the man so relentless? Where did he get such strength? Why couldn't he just accept that Simon was not cut from the same cloth as he was and would be a disaster as duke?

Besides, what did Wyndham care who took the title after he died? He would be *dead* for God's sake. Who cared about what happened after they died?

Simon had his hands full worrying about what happened while he was alive. In fact, he would rather *not* worry about it. Or anything else, for that matter.

That was a childish attitude and utterly unreasonable, but he didn't care; arguing with Wyndham always brought the worst out in him and it always had. The man was colder than an iceberg in December. The angrier and irater Simon became, the calmer and more distant Wyndham became.

It was a challenge to see if Simon could draw a rise out of him. Not that he'd ever managed such a feat. No, all he managed to do was fly into a pelter and make a bigger ass of himself.

His brother's image rose up before him and Simon frowned; Wyndham had looked quite ill earlier. In fact, Simon thought he'd looked rather the worse for wear for a while now.

Can you blame him? You are probably driving him into an early grave with your idiocy.

Simon clenched his jaws against the unwanted—but likely true—chastisement.

"Blast and damn and bloody hell," he muttered, putting his brother from his mind with a forceful shove.

He shrugged out of his coat, grimacing at the pain the small motion caused in his neck and shoulders. Would it always be that way? Would his skin burn and ache for the rest of his days? Another thing alcohol was good for—the pain. Not that there weren't better things for pain, things he'd enjoyed far too much during the war.

Simon jerked his thoughts away from that dangerous subject.

He tossed his coat over a chair and unbuttoned his waistcoat, forcing himself to use his left hand. It was not nearly as damaged as the rest of his left side since his hand had been in front of his body when the cannon exploded. But it still burned like hell whenever he used it for fussy tasks like unhooking buttons.

The doctor had cautioned him against mollycoddling his left side, telling him the more active he was, the quicker the pain would go away. Not that it would ever go away completely. Some activities, he'd told Simon, would exacerbate the injuries. Activities like riding, the only thing that made life worthwhile.

He grimaced at the self-pitying thought and slipped into his favorite robe, a battered green and gold silk banyan that had been with him throughout the War and which he associated with better times. It had been a garment he'd worn after surviving each uncertain day; something he'd only donned once he was clean of blood and grime and death. It was a symbol of cheating death yet again and a reminder of those nights when he'd been hot and hard and lucky enough to find a willing, eager woman to celebrate with.

Simon shook his head at the foolish thoughts. Memories of days that had been both better and worse; memories so old and faded they might as well have belonged to some other man. *This* was his life now: a sort of half-life that Wyndham insisted on foisting on him.

You could have a different life—a better life.

Oh yes, that he could. Just as soon as he danced to Wyndham's bloody tune and married a woman of his brother's choosing.

Only if he capitulated to Wyndham's demands could he have the life he'd always wanted. Well, part of it, at least—the part that didn't include Bella.

Ahhhh, Bella, his snide mental companion taunted. *But she is long gone. You can't even remember her face and yet you cling to her memory—and your anger—like a child.*

So what if he couldn't always recall Bella's face? He couldn't recall lots of things, but that didn't mean they hadn't happened.

His head had been batted about more violently than a cricket ball over the past decade and a half, but he could recall Bella—and what his brother had done to her—clearly enough.

He would *never* buckle to his brother's demands and take a wife. Indeed, he would never marry.

You need a woman, not a wife.

"Shut the hell up," Simon snapped, and then realized he was bickering with his own mind as if he were some sort of lunatic.

He threw back the remains of his glass, bared his teeth at the pleasant burn, and poured himself another. He paused, the glass halfway to his mouth.

Perhaps the annoying voice in his head was right: he needed a woman. Lord. When was the last time he'd had sex with someone other than his own hand?

It was exactly two weeks ago, the voice provided helpfully.

That was true. Not since the night he'd bedded Lily Bancroft, the serving wench at the St. George.

His intention of fucking his way out from under his brother's thumb had dissipated the following day when he'd realized he'd be using an innocent bystander in his war against Wyndham. Not that Lily was either innocent or reluctant to be used—those being her own words.

"When will I see you again, my lord," she'd asked as she'd gathered up her scattered clothing.

Simon's head had been pounding, his conscience no longer numbed by ale. "I'm not sure that is wise."

"Why? Do you fear for my reputation? It's too late for that."

Simon had winced at her justly mocking tone.

"I'm a grown woman, my lord," she'd said standing before him naked to prove her point. "My Tommy died in Spain so I'm my own mistress now."

He'd felt doubly appalled by the knowledge that he'd just bedded a serving wench who was also a war widow.

Like a coward, Simon had slunk away and not gone back, since— even though his cousin nagged him nightly to join him on his carouses.

Simon flexed his left arm; the taut, scarred skin tingled, but was not painful. At least not much. He was better every day and even the worst of his wounds was well on the road to healing.

Peel appeared in the open doorway. "Will you have a shave before dinner, my lord?"

Simon looked up from his red, rough forearm. Dinner?

He stared at the fragrant, golden liquid in his other hand, suddenly recalling the tall, skinny wench he'd found lurking outside Wyndham's study. Who the bloody hell was she? She'd looked familiar but he couldn't recall ever meeting a woman so tall. Her wide, gray eyes hovered in his mind—surprised and outraged. He smirked at the memory. *Well, that's what you get for listening at keyholes, missy.*

He took another drink and realized Peel was still waiting. "Dinner, eh?" He'd been eating in his room more often than not these days, but he couldn't help but admit to some curiosity about the woman he'd just met. Perhaps she would be dining with the family?

Well, what the hell else did he have to do? He snorted and then quaffed the contents of the glass. "Yes, a shave before dinner, Peel."

Chapter Five

Simon Fairchild didn't appear in the dining room until the middle of the second course.

He was far more formally dressed than he'd been earlier, but also far less sober. Even before he opened his mouth, she knew he'd been drinking. She could *smell* him when he dropped into the seat beside her, his damaged side facing her.

"Sorry I'm late," he said to nobody in particular and not with any conviction. His glazed eyes flickered over Honoria, the duke, his cousin, and the dowager duchess before landing on his niece. His sarcastic smirk shifted into a smile that looked genuine.

"Well, look at you, Becks—you're prettier than a princess. What's the occasion?"

Lady Rebecca was undoubtedly the duke's daughter. She'd inherited his somewhat nondescript hair color and her neat, even features were in no way extraordinary. She was far from robust looking for her age and appeared younger than her sixteen years.

"I'm going to an assembly." Lady Rebecca smiled and flushed a rosy shade that made her average features pretty; Honey knew *that* was the expression she wanted to capture in her portrait.

Lord Saybrook paused in the act of lifting the glass of wine the footman had just filled

"Ahh, an assembly. A bit of practice before you tackle the Season proper?"

"Lady Partridge says there is no harm in such an entertainment even though we are not yet out. Sarah and Lilian will be with me."

The marquess took a gulp of wine that drained half the glass. "Well, I daresay you'll have all the young cockerels squaring up to dance with you. I suppose we should expect lovelorn swains playing flutes and violins and reciting bad poetry below your window from now until whenever?"

Only his cousin Raymond laughed.

"*Simon*," the duchess scolded, but her expression was indulgent as she chastised her younger son.

Lord Simon gave his mother a tolerant smile and the tension that had accompanied him into the room dissipated a little.

The dowager duchess shared her pale gray eye color and mousy brown hair with her eldest son and granddaughter. Honey wondered if Simon's father was the source of the unusual hydrangea eyes and antique gold hair. Simon looked more like his cousin Raymond than he did the rest of his family.

"Simon," the duke said, taking advantage of the break in conversation and fixing Honey with his cool gaze. "This is Miss Honoria Keyes, who has come to paint Cecily and Rebecca. Miss Keyes, this is my brother, the Marquess of Saybrook."

Simon paused in the act of loading his plate with food and turned his body toward her, as if his neck were unable to do the work. His golden eyebrow arched, the one on the scarred half of his face lifting only halfway.

In the well-lighted dining room, she could see the gouges and wounds were bad enough on their own, but their puckered edges tugged on the healthy skin, distorting his image like an old, pitted looking glass. One long red scar ran perilously close to the bottom lashes of his left eye. He'd been fortunate that his eye had been spared, although she doubted that he would feel that way.

They held each other's gaze and Honey saw recognition gradually shift his features.

"So *that's* who you are?" His teeth flashed white in his tanned, scarred face. "Honey." He gave a delighted laugh.

The duke cleared his throat and Simon glared at his brother's disapproving expression, what little humor he'd felt quickly draining from his face. "What the devil are you frowning at, Wyndham, that's her name."

All eyes turned to Honey.

She could control her expression, but not, unfortunately, her skin. Her face heated and Simon Fairchild's smirk grew along with her flaring color. She cut him a look of cool dismissal, but that just made him grin more.

"Little Honey Keyes, all grown up," he said, chuckling.

"Simon," the dowager murmured.

"You know each other?" Raymond asked, looking intrigued.

Simon just laughed and threw back the rest of his wine. Honoria had never seen a man drink so much, so fast. Even her father's wild friends had behaved with more decorum. At least around her.

When it appeared that Simon would not answer Mr. Fairchild's question, Honey said, "Yes, we met when he was sitting for a portrait with my father."

"Ah, interesting," Mr. Fairchild said, although nobody else looked particularly interested.

"Miss Keyes has just finished painting Viscountess Heath." The duke sounded as calm as ever, but Honoria thought there was a tightness around his mouth that hadn't been there before his brother's arrival.

"Is that so?" Simon asked, pausing with his loaded fork half-way to his mouth. He gave an evil-sounding bark of laughter. "Heath, eh? I remember *her.*" He shot the duke a look of pure mischief. "Why the devil would Heath want *her* image memorialized? Isn't she the one who—"

The dowager's fork clattered against her plate and the duke spoke over the din. "You are thinking of his *prior* wife, Simon." His tone was as sharp and brittle as a shard of obsidian. "Lord Heath recently remarried."

The marquess grunted. "Ah, he turfed out the old wife and got himself a young, pretty, fecund one, did he? Giving you ideas, Wyndham?" The look he gave his brother was unpleasantly suggestive.

The duchess gasped and frost swirled around the duke; he appeared to grow larger. "You will recall where you are, Simon."

Lady Rebecca looked confused and Raymond's avid gaze flickered between the brothers as if he were watching a badminton match.

Simon gave an ugly chuckle. "As if I could ever forget. You know how to get rid of me, Wyndham; I'll leave anytime you like, Brother." He forked the food into his mouth, looking gratified by the duke's silent glower.

The rest of the table was poised and waiting for whatever gem Simon might deliver next, but he took his time before appeasing anyone's curiosity, chewing and swallowing several mouthfuls before taking another barbaric gulp of wine, waving for the footman to refill his glass and turning his flaming blue gaze on Honoria.

"Your father did a fine job on my portrait." He raised his scarred hand in a vague gesture that encompassed his face and person. "But things have changed, as you can see. Perhaps you could make some changes to your father's work? Or maybe you'd like to take a run at me yourself? Yes, that's a better idea; we could hang them together, sort of a before and after thing?" His tone was taunting and his eyes glinted with either anger or intoxication or both. He turned away so that she could see only the damaged left side. "I daresay I'd make a captivating subject."

Before Honoria could open her mouth, or even think of anything to say, the duke spoke.

"That is an excellent idea, Simon. Why didn't I think of it myself? A wedding gift." His tone was benign but a taunt lurked beneath it.

Simon was getting married?

The thought was like a kick to the chest. Fortunately the moment was too fraught with tension for her to sink into despair. No, she could do that, later.

Honey wasn't the only one who thought the duke's words were mocking. The marquess' mouth screwed into an ugly scowl and his fine nostrils flared, like a warhorse scenting battle and blood.

"I daresay Miss Keyes has a full schedule," the dowager interjected before her grown sons could commence fisticuffs at the dinner table. The older woman gave Honoria a beseeching look.

Honey wanted to remind the surly, sarcastic, *hateful* man that she *had* painted a portrait of him already—not that he'd ever seen it—but she was still stung, humiliated, and reeling that he'd not remembered her.

She was having a difficult time getting her mind around that—in addition to the news of his impending marriage.

All those hours they'd spent together had meant nothing to him. She was a fool of mythic proportions; all these years she had carried a torch for this—this drunken, oafish, savage.

Ugh. It was too humiliating to be borne.

Honey banished her rage—for now—turning her attention to the duchess, who looked more than a little miserable. What must it be like to watch her two grown sons rip up at one another like ill-behaved children?

Honey took the pity she felt for the dowager and forged it into cold disdain before turning to the man beside her with a smile of insincere regret. "I appreciate your gracious offer, Lord Saybrook—I daresay you'd make a fascinating subject—but I have a busy calendar."

Rather than be insulted, he gave an abrupt bark of laughter. "Oh? And just what is so important that you can't push it off?"

Honoria actually had no other commissions, but she was hardly willing to tell *him* that. She grabbed the first name she could think of. "I'm engaged to paint a portrait of Lord Alvanley's favorite spaniel."

All eating ceased and the room was as silent as a tomb.

And then the marquess threw his head back and roared.

"Well," he said once he'd stopped laughing. "I guess you've put me in my place, haven't you?" And then he turned his attention to his plate, as if finished with both her and polite discourse.

"How did you decide to become a painter, Miss Keyes." Lady Rebecca's voice was soft and tentative, her eyes flickering to her father as she spoke, as if looking for approval. The duke's eyes softened and Honey was stunned by the flash of love she saw on his face. He was not an emotionless aristocrat after all—he loved something, some*one*, a great deal. Did he love the girl's mother as much?

She dismissed the thought as none of her concern and smiled at Lady Rebecca. "When I was a little girl my father would give me paints to keep me busy while he worked. After a few years he noticed I not only had an aptitude, but an interest in painting, so he began to train me in earnest."

Simon's head swiveled around and he fixed her with his burning gaze. "How lucky for you that he cared what interested you, Miss Keyes."

Honey blinked at the barely leashed rage beneath his words. She looked at the duke; he was watching his brother with a stillness that reminded her of a predator stalking its prey. Just what was going on between these two men?

Again, the dowager came to the rescue. "Your grandfather was Baron Yancey, was he not?"

It took no small amount of effort to pull her gaze from Simon, who was still staring at her.

"Yes," Honey said. "My mother was the baron's youngest daughter. I'm afraid he died before I was born, so I never met him."

"Your grandfather was a close acquaintance of my late husband."

"Now there's an endorsement," the marquess muttered, but so low Honey thought she was the only one who heard it.

The duchess waved away her almost untouched plate and a footman took it. "Lord Yancy's family was quite a large one, if I recall correctly."

"There were ten children, ma'am."

"Ah, I did not know it had been quite that large."

"It would have been even larger but seven did not survive." Honoria had never met her grandmother but could only imagine the woman must have been worn out by so much pain—both the physical strain of childbirth and the emotional pain of losing so many children.

The dowager's eyes flickered to her elder son, as if she'd suddenly realized the subject she'd inadvertently introduced.

But the duke didn't appear to have heard, his gaze still fixed on his younger brother.

Simon was methodically consuming the contents of his plate and appeared uninterested in either the subject of infant mortality or large families.

In fact, he did not speak another word for the duration of the meal.

Not until the women rose to leave did the marquess open his mouth again.

He stood and went to his niece, dropping a kiss on her cheek. "Have a jolly evening, Becks." He walked past Raymond, ignoring his cousin entirely, and then paused beside his brother, his smile sliding off his face like ice shearing from an iceberg. "I'll leave you to your port, Wyndham. I'm for town." He kissed his mother's hand and gave Honey a mocking bow before leaving.

The duchess turned to Honey once the door had slammed shut behind her son. "You must be tired from your journey, Miss Keyes. Perhaps you care to retire?"

"Thank you, your grace. I am somewhat fatigued." Honey didn't tell the older woman that the tense dinner had been far more tiring than the long journey.

Chapter Six

The following morning a maid delivered a terse message to Honey along with her hot water.

It was from the duchess: her grace would see Miss Keyes at three o'clock.

But what about Lady Rebecca?

Honey commenced to wash and dress; she would seek out Lady Rebecca after breakfast and ask her when they might have a sitting.

Once she was ready to face the day, she rang for a servant to take her down to the breakfast room, where she found the duke just finishing his meal.

He rose when she entered the airy room, which had French doors open to allow in fresh air from the warm, sunny morning.

"How was your first night at Whitcombe?" the duke asked after she'd served herself from the array of chaffing dishes.

"I fell asleep before my head even hit the pillow." She nodded at the footman who offered her coffee.

"I am pleased to hear it." The duke took more coffee, himself, even though his plate was nearly empty. "Do you ride, Miss Keyes?"

"I do, although it has been quite some time."

"I'm sure you will find something in the stables to suit your level of comfort. You are welcome to take the gig, of course, but the loveliest parts of the area are not accessible by cart or carriage." He closed the newspaper that had been open beside his plate. "I know you will do the painting in London, but I have instructed Philips, my house steward, to show you several rooms which I believe have suitable exposure, if you would like to use them for anything."

"Thank you, your grace, I look forward to seeing them." Honey couldn't help being amazed by how different he was from his brother. Not just different looking, but different acting. She could only suppose his position mediated a certain amount of dignity and steadiness not necessary in a younger sibling. In truth, he quite reminded her of herself—at least when it came to presenting an unflappable appearance to the world.

In the daylight she realized he looked older and far more drawn than he'd appeared yesterday evening. Whatever was ailing him, seemed to be taking its toll. His brown hair was liberally dusted with gray at the temples and there were deep grooves bracketing his mouth. The lines radiating out from his eyes did not look like smile lines. In fact, she could hardly imagine such a cool, remote man smiling.

But then she remembered the loving look he'd given his daughter at dinner last night and decided he must have hidden depths.

He looked up, meeting her scrutiny. "I understand you will be seeing my wife this afternoon."

"Yes, I will meet her at three o'clock. I was wondering where I might find Lady Rebecca—perhaps we might have a sitting this morning?"

"My daughter has gone to a function with her grandmother today, but she will be ready for you after breakfast tomorrow morning."

So, that meant Honey would have the first part of today to herself.

The duke stood. "I must meet with my bailiff for most of the day but if you have need of me you can always ring for a servant."

"Thank you, your grace."

The duke rose to leave just as the door opened.

Mr. Fairchild stepped into the room, a smile on his face, his gaze on Honey. He opened his mouth, as if to say something, but then jumped a little when he noticed the duke standing to the side of the door. "Oh, your grace." He looked nonplussed. "How are you this morning?"

Plimpton's mouth compressed into a line, as if the question displeased him. "I am well, thank you, Raymond." He paused, giving his cousin a piercing look that made the other man's face reddened. "Are you still going to Lindthorpe today?"

"Er, yes, sir. I'm afraid I'm getting a rather late start."

The duke merely stared.

"But I shall be on my way within the hour," Mr. Fairchild added when it was clear the other man was waiting.

The duke nodded. "Very well."

Once the duke had gone Raymond Fairchild turned to Honey, his expression a mix of mortification and something else? Irritation? Anger?

"Did you sleep well on your first night at Whitcomb?" he asked, walking to the sideboard.

"Yes, thank you, Mr. Fairchild."

He chuckled. "Now, now—none of that. Please call me Raymond." He turned and gave her a smile that deepened his resemblance to Simon.

Well, what else could Honey say but, "Please call me Honoria."

"A lovely name. What was it that Simon called you last night?" he asked, taking the seat across from her.

"Honey is the name my father called me. That is likely where Lord Saybrook heard it," she said.

"Ah, so it is a family name for your intimates." He made a clucking sound with his tongue. "You'll have to forgive Simon," he said, and then began to methodically demolish the contents of his plate.

"What do you mean?" Honey asked.

Raymond took his time chewing before taking a sip of coffee. "Oh, just that he tends to be a bit, er, uncouth at times. I'm afraid his animosity toward the duke seems to be getting worse. Sometimes I fear that Simon might—" He paused and pulled a face. "I'm sorry, I shouldn't be speaking so frankly."

Honey didn't think so, either. But that didn't mean she didn't want to know what he'd left unsaid. Did he think Simon might do his brother harm? He'd certainly behaved hatefully enough toward him yesterday.

They ate in silence for a moment, her conscience telling her to leave the matter be, her curiosity spurring her to speak.

Curiosity won. "I actually heard the tail end of a, er, disagreement yesterday," she said.

Raymond's eyebrows shot up and he nodded; his cheeks stuffed full, giving him more than a passing resemblance to a chipmunk. He gulped down his food and dabbed his mouth with a napkin. "I'm afraid it is a daily occurrence," he admitted. "As the duchess cannot have any more children the duke is understandably eager for Simon to marry and have a child. Simon, on the other hand, has no intention of marrying to please his brother."

Honey was ashamed by the surge of joy she experienced at that information.

The door opened and a footman entered, his presence putting a halt to any more enlightening comments. Honey couldn't help thinking that Raymond looked a bit relieved—as if he'd already said more than he should.

He finished his meal quickly—obviously eager to get about his errand. "I shall see you tonight at dinner," he said.

Once she was alone, Honey allowed her thoughts to wander back to Simon Fairchild, a subject which had been uppermost in her mind first thing this morning.

His behavior—both times yesterday—had been appalling. He was nothing like the man she'd once known. He was like a keg of powder that was rolling too close to flames. She wondered if the duke, a man who appeared to be carved from ice, understood just how raw and on edge his brother was.

She also wondered what time the marquess came down to breakfast.

Put Simon Fairchild out of your mind and enjoy this unexpected afternoon of freedom, the cool voice of reason in her head ordered.

Honey sighed and spread marmalade on a slice of toast, took a sip of delicious, dark coffee, and then munched while gazing out at the lovely scene beyond the French doors, her mind still on the man who'd taken up far too much space in her head these past fourteen years.

Well, the habit of a lifetime was hardly likely to be broken in just one day, was it? But Simon had certainly done an excellent job of demolishing the shrine she'd worshipped at all these years. It would be up to Honey herself to complete its destruction.

***

After breakfast Honey changed into her serviceable navy habit, caught up her satchel, and headed in the direction of the stables.

There was nobody visible as she passed under the grand archway into the courtyard. Male voices and the sound of horse hooves came from a gap in the three buildings and she followed the sounds to a large, enclosed arena, coming up behind a half-dozen men who were either leaning or sitting on the fence that surrounded the arena.

They were watching as a man dressed in top boots, shirtsleeves, and buckskins guided a magnificent horse through its paces.

The man's back was to her but she would have recognized Simon Fairchild's broad shoulders and guinea gold hair—no matter that it was closely cropped—anywhere.

The horse he was training was stunning—an inky black stallion whose body was so powerful he would have resembled a draught horse if not for the proud, arched neck and finely boned head. Honey had never seen an animal with such muscular hindquarters and forequarters that moved so fluidly. She could see by the horse's flared, quivering nostrils and the iron tension in its enormous frame that it was not yet fully broken.

Simon's fine muslin shirt adhered to his muscular body as he worked both himself and the animal. Honoria had never watched the training of a horse before and found his patience with the stallion both impressive and at odds with his behavior toward humans.

She recalled his dreams from all those years ago: to live in the country and breed horses. What had happened to that dream? Why had he gone to war and then stayed in the military for all that time? As the heir to a dukedom it was unusual that he'd fought, at all.

Honoria felt movement beside her and had to look down a good six inches to find a wiry, grizzled man touching his cap and smiling up at her.

"Beggin' yer pardon, miss. I'm Wilkins, the duke's stable master. I'll wager yer looking for a horse and are wondering if ye came to the wrong place." His voice rose as he got to the end of his sentence and it worked like the crack of a whip on the loitering men.

It also drew the attention of Simon, who brought the lathered horse to a graceful halt.

"That's a good fellow," he said, reaching out a gloved hand to stroke the glossy black neck. The horse stiffened at his touch but did not pull away. Simon scratched the stallion's mane until the beast was pushing against him like a dog, asking for more. He chuckled and spoke softly into the horse's twitching ears.

Honey could not pull her eyes away from the sight of the two big, magnificent animals. "The horse is beautiful but appears rather wild," she said to Wilkins, who was still beside her.

"Aye, Master Simon be breakin' him slow-like. Horses love 'im. He's gentle and sparin' with the whip and gets quick results."

The marquess summoned one of the stable lads who vaulted over the fence and cautiously approached the stallion. Simon spoke a few words to the boy, who led the horse toward the stables.

Once horse and boy were gone, he looked over at Honey, the expression on his ravaged face unreadable. "Good afternoon, Miss Keyes," he said, striding toward her with his odd, slightly uneven gait, "Have you come to inspect the stables?"

She frowned at his taunting tone, as if she'd stepped over some line by coming there. "Inspection is not one of my duties, my lord. Your brother gave me permission to borrow a horse whenever I pleased."

He smiled at her acerbic response, the smooth, undamaged side of his face pulling up while the other half only twitched.

Even scarred and limping he oozed a potent masculinity that made her feel restless and it was a struggle to remain cool beneath his hard, blue gaze. "That is a lovely horse, my lord. I do not recognize the breed."

He began to pull off his battered black gloves, finger by finger, never taking his eyes from her. "Loki is a cross between a Friesian and Andalusian."

"The trickster," she said stupidly, struggling for something else to say—some way to hold his attention, just as she had all those years ago.

His smile grew, as if he could read her as easily as one of his horses. "Saddle up Bacchus and Saturn for us, Wilkins," he said without looking at the stable master.

Wilkins dipped his head. "Aye, my lord," he said, and turned away, leaving her alone with Simon.

Honey did not dare glance directly at the open neck of his shirt even though every particle of her being urged her to take another— more leisurely—look at the V of hard chest and the sweat-sheened cords of his tanned neck and the—

Take hold of yourself! The voice was like a lash and startled her from her mesmerized state. She swallowed, forcing herself to meet his eyes, which glinted with uncomfortable emotions.

"Are you going for a ride, my lord?" She hated how wobbly her voice sounded, but she hated the pregnant silence more.

"I am." He smacked his palm with his gloves, the ropey, powerful muscles of his exposed forearms flexing. "With you."

Honey blinked and shook her head before she could stop herself.

"Why not?" he asked, sounding amused rather than annoyed at her immediate rejection. He tucked his gloves into the waist of his buckskins, rolled down his sleeves, and then plucked his waistcoat off a nearby post and shrugged into it, not bothering to button it.

"I shan't be going to ride," she lied, lifting her satchel as proof. "I'm going to sketch."

He deftly swung his tall body over the arena fence, landing with a soft thump in front of her, so close she could smell horse, leather, and his sweaty, sun-warmed skin. She took a step back.

He took a step toward her. "I'll come along to help you carry your things."

She lifted her satchel again, like a talisman to ward him off. "But this is all I have; I don't need any help."

"I'll help you find the best spot." He took another step.

Honey frowned and took another step back—the *last* one she was taking, she told herself. She tilted her chin and stared up at him. What a novelty; there were not many men taller than her five feet eleven inches. Simon's eyes were a good three inches above hers.

"The best spot for what?" she asked in a breathy, annoying voice.

"For whatever you want." He took a step, and—curse her!—so did she. Her shoulder hit something hard and unyielding, the doorframe—reminding her of how he had stalked her this same way yesterday.

Impotent anger flamed in her breast as he closed the small bit of space between them and she did nothing to stop him.

His eyelids lowered and his smile disappeared. "Nowhere left to run, *Honey*." His breath was hot on her temple.

She shook her head and the navy-blue feather in her hat brushed at his forehead.

"I wasn't running," she said, her voice cracking. She tried not to let her eyes wander from his burning blue gaze, tried not to stare at the ruin that was his face, but her eyes kept sliding to the left.

He laughed softly and turned his scared, pitted side toward her. "Difficult to look away, isn't it?"

She could only stare.

He turned to give her his undamaged side. "Such beauty and horror, all in the same package." His white teeth flashed in his face and his hand shot up. For a moment she though he was going to touch her but he reached higher and pulled down a strip of white— his cravat—from the post above her head. He dropped it around his neck and turned away, disappearing into the stables.

***

Simon had no idea why he was taunting her. Boredom? Perhaps.

Raymond had joined him at the St. George last night, the first time in two weeks. His cousin had spent about forty-five minutes chiding   him—loudly—for   arguing   with   Wyndham—making something of a scene himself in the tiny public room—until Simon had finally told him to bugger off if he didn't have anything else to talk about.

Once Raymond left—in a huff—Lily sat her delightfully plumb bottom on his lap and kept him company through several pints. She'd wanted him to come upstairs, but he'd begged off and ridden home more than a little worse for wear.

Miss Honey Keyes had been on his mind for a good part of the night and again when he had woken at dawn, hard and wanting, and tossed one off.

After that he'd taken out Loki. He had hoped his vigorous ride would have work the restlessness from his system, but here he was, still as twitchy as a cat with two tails.

Simon stared at Miss Keyes's shoulders as she rode up the narrow path ahead of him. She was stiff in the saddle, her body telling him she didn't like riding, or at least she didn't like riding in front of him. Or maybe she just didn't like *him*.

The right side of his mouth kicked up at that thought. Well, she didn't need to like him; she was nothing more than a distraction and it was just her bad luck that she'd wandered into the stables when she had. He was irritable. And angry. He wanted to do something rash, but he was—quite frankly—too damned bored with himself and his tedious situation to bother coming up with anything inventive to infuriate his brother.

And then *she'd* come along, looking at him with those cool gray eyes that could be leaden one moment and melting ice the next. They were extraordinary eyes in an unremarkable face. Well, except for her mouth—he liked that, too. It was too big for her small face and put the wrong ideas into a man's head. At least a man who wasn't very nice.

She had a long upper lip that was thin but shapely and a lower one that was plush and full and inviting for all that she tried to keep it prim.

And her height? He estimated she was close to six feet and improbably fine-boned and delicate, like bone china.

He remembered her—now. Pieces had come back to him slowly throughout the night—not entire memories, but wispy cobwebs— some of which stuck, some drifted out of reach. But he'd begun to flesh out the picture—or portrait, rather—until he had a clear enough recollection. The sittings during that odd, hot summer in London, his conversations with the serious, mature, and lonely young girl—those memories had all paled after his nephew died.

The duke, who had been cold before his son's death, lost all remaining traces of the brother Simon had known and worshipped as a boy. On the outside he appeared the same calm, unshakeable Wyndham, devoted to his duty. But the loss of his son—four-month-old Edward— had been the death blow for Wyndham's humanity.

Simon had watched it happening for years, with each death of his three children a little more life had leaked out of his eyes. At first Wyndham had looked haunted, and then harried, and—finally—just lifeless. Four children and only Rebecca had survived—and she was less than robust.

It had been unbearable to witness; Simon could only imagine what it must be like to experience.

He'd been overjoyed when he heard the doctor advised the duke and duchess against another pregnancy. Even though the decision had doomed Simon as heir, he could not stand to watch what another death might do to his brother.

As for the duchess? Well, it was difficult to say what his sister-in-law felt or who she loved, if anyone. Simon had never seen Cecily Fairchild show one particle of affection for her only daughter or her husband.

Wyndham had wanted Cecily—Simon could still recall just how mad his normally calm brother had been for the icy beauty—and now he was stuck with her.

Simon snorted. *Be careful what you ask for ...*

For all Cecily's die-away airs, Simon suspected his sister-in-law would outlive everyone else in the family.

The woman was cold through and through, which Wyndham had not discovered until too late.

Or maybe his brother had accepted her aloofness but believed that his love would change her?

If that had been his hope then Wyndham had spectacularly miscalculated.

Simon felt sorry for Rebecca with a mother like that. Their own father had been a cold, inhuman bastard but at least their mother loved him and Wyndham to distraction. She still loved them, for all that Simon had behaved like an ass for the past decade and a half.

He realized he was gritting his jaws so hard that his teeth hurt and forced himself to relax. Why was he thinking about any of this—about the past? It was ancient history and felt like something from five lifetimes ago. It must be the woman in front of him who was bringing it all back.

Simon studied Honoria Keyes's rigid posture and was suddenly glad he did not have to look into her clear gray gaze. Something about the way she looked at him made him ... anxious.

Well, at least that was part of the reason for his anxiety.

The other part was his brother's unswerving demand that Simon marry, which was beginning to drive him mad.

Simon glared through a red mist of frustration and noticed how far they'd come. "You're going to take a right at the fork, Miss Keyes."

"Where are you taking me?" she asked without turning.

"It's a surprise."

She stiffened even more, which he hadn't thought possible, but remained quiet.

Simon grinned; she was a self-possessed little thing—always had been, now that he was starting to remember.

His memory, like the rest of him, had not finished out the War unscathed and it took a great deal of mental energy to unearth the past. Sometimes he felt like he was digging for buried treasure, although that was gifting what he usually discovered with too much value. For the most part, the memories he found were fragmented and pale, and often not worth the effort.

He didn't know why his memories hid themselves—and for the most part he didn't care—but he would have liked to remember that particular summer—the summer of 1803—in better detail.

He had been a golden child, his life spread out before him like a sumptuous buffet prepared solely for him.

Simon scowled. What did it matter what he remembered? The past was long dead and gone.

The road forked and the trail became steeper.

Honoria Keyes twisted slightly in her saddle to look at him. "My lord, where are we going?"

"I told you, it is a surprise."

"Is it much further? I have an appointment with her grace at three o'clock and I do not wish to miss it."

That made Simon laugh.

"You may think that is amusing, my lord, but it just so happens to be the reason I am here." She twisted a little more when he didn't answer.

"Turn around and watch the trail, Miss Keyes," he advised.

She made a huffing noise but did as he bade.

"I'm not laughing at you; I'm laughing because you don't have to worry about missing an appointment with my sister-in-law. Cecily is there, in her quarters, all day, every day—like a spider in her web. I doubt she remembers either what day or time your appointment is; if you show up at midnight it wouldn't matter to her. It is likely she will not receive you if it does not suit her. The duke is the one who wishes for this portrait, not Cecily."

"That may be so, my lord, but it matters to me."

"I'll have you back well before three o'clock."

She had nothing to say to that.

They rode in silence for five more minutes, until the narrow path opened into a small grassy glade.

"Pull up right here, Miss Keyes."

Simon swung down off Bacchus and approached Saturn and his rider. Miss Keyes was staring in open-mouthed shock at the vista before her.

"It's magnificent," she said, her tone one of awe.

"I told you it was the best spot."

She looked down at him, her eyes still wide with wonder.

Simon reached up and took her by the waist. She was slender, but he felt curves in the right places. He lowered her to the ground without touching any other part of her and she looked away, her face flushed and the vein in her temple pulsing. Was that from excitement or disgust? He knew he wasn't pretty to look at anymore and could no longer assume women would appreciate his attention or touch.

He watched her walk away, the breeze causing the feather in her hat to dance. He turned to unstrap her satchel from the saddle and bring it to her.

"Thank you," she said absently taking the bag without looking at him, her attention on the view before them.

Simon knew he should have felt insulted at her sudden dismissal of him, but he was amused. After all, how could a scarred, bitter stranger compete with the spectacular view from the hill known as The Wrekin?

He followed her gaze and looked out over the plain below; it felt like looking out from the top of the world, even though they were only half-way up the hill.

You couldn't see Whitcomb or Everley from here, but there was Charles Frampton's estate. Only Frampton and his wife lived there now. Bella was married and gone, with a family of her own. Bella, a woman he'd loved so much he'd wanted to die when he learned she had married another—at least what he could remember of that time— and all thanks to the bloody Wyndham. He remembered his brother's interference in that part of his life well enough.

Simon turned his back on the view and his bitter memories.

"I'm going for a walk," he said, throwing the words over his shoulder and not bothering to look back.

Chapter Seven

Honoria let out a sigh of relief as she watched Simon's broad back and golden head disappear into the scrubby trees that surrounded the small clearing. The tension slowly drained from her shoulders and back.

Being in his vicinity was like standing too close to a raging inferno. Worse, actually. A fire wouldn't mock you, argue with you and follow you.

And mesmerize you.

Why was she standing there right now? She should have asserted herself. Instead she had let herself be borne along like a leaf on a strong wind.

Honey shook her head and lowered herself shakily onto one of the big boulders that were tumbled about as if a giant angry child had flung down a handful of pebbles.

That was what Simon Fairchild was like—an angry child. But in a man's body.

Honey pulled out her sketchpad with a trembling hand. What was wrong with her? Was this all it took to discompose her famous cool and calm? One scarred angry man? She should be thrilled he'd turned out to be such a hateful beast. At least she no longer cherished the golden memory of him, which was fading more with each moment she spent in his presence.

She opened the book, flipping past drawings of Serena, Oliver, Freddie, and Miles in their garden. The first blank page she could find she began to fill with sketches. Not sketches of the magnificent scenery, but sketches of him.

Over and over and over she drew him. Scarred on one side, scarred on both sides, unscarred, Simon young, fresh, and unscathed by life; Simon as a scaly beast with claws, a long tail, a spiny frill of bone encircling his head like a mythical beast. And on and on.

Gradually her hands stopped shaking.

For over a decade she had idolized and worshipped a dream. Not a man, but a dream—a golden, childish fantasy. Honey shook her head in disbelief. Was everyone this stupid? Or only her? Did every woman develop enduring infatuations, even in the face of no encouragement?

Was she this way because she'd been raised by her father, no female influence in her life other than the relative strangers who had only tolerated her to get close to Daniel Keyes?

Honey had a sudden, burning desire to talk to Freddie. They'd known one another for years yet neither of them had ever spoken about their pasts and their experiences with men.

Not until that moment did Honey realize how strange such an omission was. Freddie was her closest friend—oh, she loved Serena, Miles, Portia, and the others, but Freddie was special to her—yet she'd never told her about the chamber of her heart where Simon Fairchild still resided.

"What have you got there?" A deep voice demanded right beside her ear.

Honey shrieked and flung up the sketchpad.

A hand shot out and grabbed it before it hit the ground.

She jumped up and spun around. "Give that back," she demanded, trembling with fury.

But he wasn't paying her any attention. Instead, he was staring down at the drawings, flicking through the half dozen pages she'd filled with his image.

"That is my property. Give. It. Back." Never in her life had she felt such rage.

A tiny voice tried to be heard through the fury that enveloped her like a whirlwind: *Why are you so angry? Let him look, you've always shared your sketches with your subjects.*

That was true, she had. But none of that mattered right now.

"*Lord Saybrook.*"

He glanced up, but only briefly. "These are amazing." He flipped a page, shaking his head. "You *are* a bloody genius."

She flinched at his vulgar language and reached out, not caring what became of her sketches any longer, just not wanting him to take yet another piece of her without her permission. The ripping of paper filled the air, silencing the nearby birds.

"Bloody hell," he yelled, suddenly giving her all the attention she wanted and more. "What the devil are you doing?" He held up his hands in a placating gesture. "I've let go. Stop it—you're destroying it."

She was too furious to care and savagely crushed the sketchbook, her awkward, rough actions causing pieces of ripped paper to detach from the binding and swirl away on the breeze.

Simon grasped at two pieces that flickered quickly beyond his reach.

"Stop," he repeated, his voice almost anguished. "You're *ruining* them."

Honoria marched back to her bag, not caring if he followed. But if he dared to touch her or her possessions she would—she would … kick him.

She yanked open her satchel and rammed the crumpled sketchbook inside, her hands shaking so badly she couldn't fasten the buckles.

A big hand landed gently on her shoulder and inexorably turned her around.

"Look at me," he ordered. He took her chin between his calloused fingers and tilted her face until she couldn't avoid his piercing blue gaze.

She jerked her head from his distracting grasp, blinking through tears, which only made her angrier. Why did he make her so *emotional?*

"Why are you so angry?" he asked.

"Because it is *mine* and you have no right to take my possessions," she forced the words through gritted teeth.

"You're right, I didn't. I'm sorry. I promise I won't try and look again. But you didn't need to ruin them."

"They are mine to ruin."

Her words surprised a laugh out of him. "Yes, that is true. But still—"

Honey twisted away from his hand, which still rested on her shoulder, and went to stand by the boulder that was nearest the cliff's edge, her breathing ragged, her vision strangely blurry. What was wrong with her? Why had she reacted—overreacted—in such a way? She was *never* so wild.

A loose strand of her hair curled and eddied in the slight breeze. She sighed and adjusted her hat, her hands smoothing and tucking as if they had eyes and minds of their own. When her hair felt restrained, she jabbed in a hatpin.

Her rough handling knocked the feather loose and it fluttered toward the cliff's edge. She lunged to grab it, but it danced and swirled out of reach.

"I'll get it." Simon leapt over the rock she was leaning against.

"No, no, you mustn't, it's—"

He paid her no mind, instead stepping out onto the small rock ledge that hung over nothing but air.

Honey's throat constricted as he stood on the very edge, where the feather whirled round and round, its beckoning motion luring him further and further. The toes of his boots scraped as they slid over stone. His body was angled forward, his arm outstretched—

Honey froze, unable to move, speak, breathe, or scream.

For one sickening eternal moment he hung balanced on the edge, his body hanging out in thin air. And then he lunged and she squeezed her eyes shut.

"Got it!"

Her eyes flew open to see him spinning on his heel away from the precipice, a triumphant smile on his ravaged face, his blue eyes sparkling the way they had so long ago. He grinned down at her, his smile slowly draining from his face. "What's wrong? You look as if you've seen a ghost."

"You—You—"

He nodded encouragingly. "Yes, me. Me what?"

"You almost *died.*"

His eyebrows shot up, one sleek and blond, one crisscrossed with red scars. "Hardly—I just leaned over to fetch a feather."

"You leaned over a *cliff*." She didn't even recognize her own voice, which was high and shrill.

He gave a dismissive shrug that made her hands *ache* to hit him. "You're a bit too dramatic, Miss Keyes. But I suppose that is all part of the artistic temperament—drama and such."

"No," she snapped, the staccato sharpness making him jolt. "I am not at *all* dramatic. You could ask anyone who knows me. I am the calmest person I know. I am staid, collected, some have even called me *phlegmatic.*"

"You?" His disbelieving gaze flickered back to where he'd taken her sketchbook and she'd behaved like a lunatic.

Her cheeks blazed at the memory and Honey snatched the feather from his outstretched hand and spun around. "I'm leaving." She grabbed her satchel without stopping and marched toward where the horses stood grazing.

She was fumbling with the straps that held her bag to her saddle when he stopped beside her and lifted it from her hands.

"Here, let me. You are not doing it properly. And you're squashing your fetching feather. Would you like me to—"

"No." She flinched away and jammed the feather into her satchel before thrusting the bag into his hands, tapping her toe while he secured it.

When he'd finished, he turned to her, his face so expressionless it *was* an expression: that of a man forced to deal with an irrational female. She felt a growl building deep in her chest.

"Ready?"

She lifted a foot, preparing to put it in his cupped hands. Instead, his hands slid around her waist and he picked her up. Yes, he lifted eleven stone as though it were nothing.

He didn't toss her or drop her like a sack of oats, he placed her gently on the saddle like one set a delicate object on a high shelf; it was a demonstration of physical power that left her breathless.

He also held her waist a bit too long before releasing her, the heat and strength of his fingers burning through the layers of cloth and sending more distracting messages to her already raddled brain.

The Simon of fourteen years ago would never have touched her so casually or intimately. This Simon was not the kind, sweet gentleman from her past. Honey questioned whether he was a gentleman, at all.

Rather than leading the horse toward one of the rocks to mount he held the reins lightly in one hand along with the pommel and then flung himself into his saddle in a graceful motion.

She was still staring when he looked over at her, his eyebrows arched. "What is it?"

"I've never seen anyone mount that way."

He gave a careless shrug. "It's amazing how dodging bullets can motivate one to acquire such skills." He gestured for her to precede him and they rode the entire journey back to Whitcomb without exchanging a single word.

Chapter Eight

Her grace was not available when Honey presented herself at her chambers at precisely three o'clock.

"She is not feeling well today," a diminutive, openly hostile servant told her, keeping Honey standing in the hallway while she did so.

"I see." She hesitated, wondering whether to ask when the duchess *would* be ready.

"The duchess will send word when she is ready for you."

The woman did not wait for a response before closing the door in her face.

"Miss Keyes?"

Honey turned to find Lady Rebecca hovering in front of another door down the long corridor, dressed as if she had just come in.

"Good afternoon, Lady Rebecca."

"Did you just finish your sitting with Mama?" the girl asked, pulling off a pair of canary-yellow kid gloves.

"Her grace was not feeling well today."

Lady Rebecca gave her a knowing look that made her appear older than her years. No doubt the girl was accustomed to her mother's ways.

"Is there a time when we could sit down for a chat?" Honey asked.

Lady Rebecca visibly perked up. "I have time now, if you like?"

"That would be perfect."

"Come into my sitting room."

The room Lady Rebecca led her into was surprisingly sedate and mature for a school-aged girl.

"I'll ring for tea and change my dress," she said to Honey, untying her bonnet. "I shan't be more than a few minutes."

"I'm in no hurry," Honey assured her.

The layout of the apartment was like hers, with the addition of another room that appeared to be a private schoolroom of sorts. She supposed the rather fragile girl was schooled at home. That must be a lonely experience in this rambling house.

When Lady Rebecca returned, she showed Honey into a second, much smaller, sitting room that was off the schoolroom.

"This is one of my favorite places," the girl told her, looking quite pretty against the dark rose silk that covered the walls.

"It is a charming room." Indeed, with its cloth-hung walls and thickly carpeted floor it felt like a cocoon.

"Do you mind if I take some sketches while we talk?"

"Oh. Not at all." Rebecca's eyes dropped to the sketchpad Honey took from her satchel. "Will you allow me to see the sketches after you've finished?"

"I will. And will you allow me to look at your wardrobe? And perhaps see what you wish to be painted in?"

The girl's thin cheeks flushed with pleasure, and Honey thought her response was sweetly naïve, but also a little sad as it demonstrated her loneliness. Lady Rebecca put Honey in mind of an orphan, even though both her parents were alive and living with her. So far nobody had mentioned the duchess—except the duke, at their brief meeting. It was as if the woman didn't occupy the same world as the rest of her family.

That is not your concern; you are here to paint Lady Rebecca, not pry into her life.

Honey silently acknowledged the truth of that statement and brought her attention back to the task at hand.

"Do you have any idea what kind of background you might like?"

Lady Rebecca's eyes widened. "You mean I may choose?"

"Of course. It is a picture of you, after all."

"Hmm, let me see—" A secretive smile tugged at her lips as she pondered.

Honey began drawing and had almost a minute to study the girl before Rebecca came back to herself.

"Oh," she said, her eyes dropping to the sketchpad and immediately assuming the stiff, watchful pose of a person being observed.

"I could see you were thinking of something," Honey prodded, her pencil still moving. "Something that made you smile—what was it?"

Lady Rebecca's eyes flicked up and met hers. "I was thinking, if it would be proper, that you might paint me with my horse?" The girl's pink blush deepened. "I know that I do not look strong enough to enjoy riding," she said, echoing Honey's thoughts. "But appearances can be deceptive."

"You are right—it is never wise to judge by appearances. And I think a portrait with your horse would be charming. Perhaps on our next meeting we might go for a ride?"

The remainder of the sitting went quickly, and Honey accumulated dozens of quick sketches as the girl relaxed.

The portrait of Lady Rebecca, at least, would be easy and pleasurable.

***

Simon did not show up for dinner that evening.

Honey told herself she was glad he'd stayed away but that was a lie. His absence made for a far quieter meal, but it also meant the conversation was rather tepid. At least in her opinion.

The duke appeared slightly less ill but was preoccupied and the dowager kept casting nervous glances at the empty chair, which left only Mr. Fairchild—or Raymond, as he'd again insisted she call him, Lady Rebecca—and Honoria to carry the conversation.

Raymond shouldered the bulk of the conversation, talking about a large gaggle of geese that had wandered onto the grounds at one of the duke's nearby properties—a place called Lindthorpe, which he'd visited today.

While he made them all laugh describing his rather frantic efforts to dodge the aggressive birds, there was a tinge of hostility beneath his words that said the task hadn't been nearly so amusing at the time.

"Did the masons arrive?" the duke asked, his soft voice causing Raymond's shoulders to stiffen.

Honey observed the two men as they discussed some repair or other. She couldn't help noticing a certain tension between them. The more she watched them interact, the more she thought the awkwardness originated with Raymond.

The duke was civil and polite with him and behaved no differently than he did with any other adult, except perhaps Simon, with whom he allowed some irritation to show.

Raymond, on the other hand, acted as if he were walking the plank. His answers to simple questions were jerky and defensive.

Honey wondered if the duke was really such an exacting employer.

Or perhaps this was just a natural awkwardness that came with working for one's relative? Would the duke ever discharge his own cousin?

Rebecca asked her about riding tomorrow and they discussed which habit she should wear and where they should go.

"Don't you require good light for such a thing?" The dowager asked when there was a lull in the conversation

"Not for making sketches, those I can do anywhere."

"Miss Keyes showed me some of her sketches today," Rebecca said, visibly excited. "They are very clever. In one of them she had me riding a horse even though we were sitting in the Rose Salon."

"How marvelous," the dowager agreed. "I understand some painters like to keep their process a secret. I know the gentleman who painted me would not let me see it until it was unveiled. Is that how it is with you, Miss Keyes?"

"I am always happy to share sketches. In fact, I will do a number of different poses and Lady Rebecca shall choose whichever she likes best." Honey knew the girl had her heart set on an equestrienne image, but might change her mind when she saw the sketch she'd made of her in her cozy sitting room, smiling with a look of mischief as she contemplated some question Honey had asked.

"How many drawings do you typically make?" the duke asked.

"I might make dozens of them; I will only do oil sketches for the best."

"An oil sketch?" he asked, sounding genuinely interested.

"They are quick paintings—like sketches in color." Lady Rebecca glanced at Honey for confirmation.

"That is an excellent description. I will do several of these over the next few sittings."

"But she will paint my actual portrait in London, Papa."

The duke nodded. "So, I understand."

"Some painters do the portrait during sittings," Lady Rebecca informed him, clearly pleased that he'd joined in the conversation and wishing to hold his interest. Her neediness made Honey's heart ache.

"That is how mine was done," he said.

The Thomas Lawrence portrait of the duke was a masterful piece. It hung in the gallery beside her father's painting of Simon.

Honey had seen Lawrence many times while growing up and admired the kind, if morose, genius.

"I daresay you had six or seven sittings for your portrait, your grace?" she asked.

"It was around that number. He began my portrait in May of '98 but urgent business pulled him away. I did not sit again until later that year."

Lawrence had visited her father often during that period. Honey had been very young so she hadn't known the rather scandalous cause of his grieving—the death of Maria Siddons, and his love affairs with both daughters of famous actress Sarah Siddons—until years later.

That was hardly a subject for the dinner table so Honey steered the conversation in another direction.

"My father was the same—he required sittings to work or he would not accept a commission." That had meant many clients went elsewhere, where they could have a portrait painted at their convenience. Even so, her father had never lacked for subjects.

"I think it is interesting that you do not employ the same method, even though your father taught you how to paint. You must have a very good memory to paint the way you do?" Raymond asked.

"I do have a good memory for faces, but I require sketches to remind me of the smaller details."

"How long will it take after you begin?" Lady Rebecca asked.

"I can never say for certain, as every subject is different. Unlike my sketches, however, I like to keep the final process to myself until I am finished."

Rebecca paused in the act of spooning a mouthful of floating island to her mouth. "Why is that?"

"I've found that—"

The door to the dining room opened and the marquess stood in the opening. Even from across the room Honey could see he was not swaying this evening as he had yesterday.

"Sorry I'm late," he said as he entered, his eyes on Honey.

She narrowed her eyes at him and willed herself—without success—not to blush. He was late? *Late?* There should be a new word to describe showing up for dinner during the dessert course.

He took his seat beside her. "Good evening, Miss Keyes," he murmured.

She ignored him.

"Please have Cook send something for Lord Saybrook," the duchess told the footman who appeared behind Simon's chair.

"I stopped in the kitchens and spoke to Cookie on my way back from the stables," Simon said to his mother. "She's already sending something up." He lifted the glass the servant had speedily filled for him, took a deep swallow, and then turned to the duke. "I was out on Bacchus and heard the most piteous racket in that copse near Craig's property. It was one of his hounds, caught in a snare. The poor old gaffer was in quite a state." He glanced at his niece's interested face, frowned and then added, "Suffice it to say that some assistance was needed."

"I see," the duke said, his expression losing its sternness upon hearing Simon's reason for his tardiness. "It was good of you to take the time and help him," the duke added softly.

Simon shrugged and turned to his niece, clearly disinterested in speaking with his brother. "And what have you been up to today, Becks?

"I had my first sitting with Miss Keyes, Uncle. She was just telling us about her process and how she doesn't show the finished portrait to anyone until it is completed."

Simon gave Honey a sardonic look, his jaw working slightly, as if he were biting back several choice retorts before saying, "I'm sorry I interrupted such an interesting conversation. Tell us, Miss Keyes, why is it that you don't wish to share sketches or—"

"Not her sketches, Uncle. She showed me the ones she did of me today."

"Oh, did she?" He smirked at Honey and she knew they were both recalling her hysterical behavior earlier in the day. "How interesting. But you don't do the same with your portraits. And why is that?"

Honey would have liked to ignore him, but the rest of his family were all waiting with interested expressions.

"There exists something of a ... well, discourse, for lack of a better word, between myself and my work in progress." She could see the girl did not understand. "For example, sometimes I will paint something and decide later it simply does not fit. If I've not shown anyone else, I don't feel as though I have committed to my work." Judging by the looks on their faces, she'd lost them all.

The door opened and three footmen entered, each bearing a large silver domed cover. The marquess turned toward his food, clearly more interested in it than Honey's answer. She couldn't blame him; she'd made a hash of it.

Surprisingly, it was Lady Rebecca who came to her rescue. "I think I understand. If it is just you, then you don't have to be concerned with other people's expectations. I feel the same when I am practicing a piece of music. I would rather work on it by myself before I share it with others." Her cheeks flushed, as if she realized that she'd volunteered too much. "I just like things to be perfect before I let others hear it," she mumbled.

"That is very much how I feel," Honey said. "There have been times when I might even paint over a canvas completely if I were dissatisfied."

Lady Rebecca goggled. "*Everything?*"

"I have done that in the past. I don't like to do it, but if something seems off to me I don't want to keep it. I've had sitters become upset by such drastic measures so it is better to wait until the end."

"Does such a thing happen often?" the duke asked.

"Thankfully, no. But sometimes ..." she chewed her lip.

"Yes?" he prodded.

"Oh, sometimes there can be—for lack of a better word—a streak of such things. My father had a dreadful streak one year. He had three commissions and ended up repainting every one of them from scratch." She chuckled. "It was *not* a happy year in our house."

Amusement gleamed in the duke's eyes, the unexpected emotion making his plain features austerely handsome. "Ah, the temperamental nature of artists." He cocked his head. "Yet you seem decidedly *un*temperamental."

Simon glanced up from his food at his brother's words, his smile apparent even while he chewed.

Odious man.

"I'm sorry to say it is true, I am—generally—possessed of a calm, measured demeanor."

The duke's eyebrows arched. "Sorry? But why?"

"Oh, it seems very *un*artistic to be so *un*temperamental."

He chuckled at that. "Surely all that matters about an artist is the quality of their art?"

"In the end, that is true. Still, it does help to have a bit of atmosphere. Take Lord Byron, for example."

"Lord Byron," Lady Rebecca repeated somewhat breathlessly.

The duke pressed his lips together. "I believe I would rather *not* take Lord Byron." He glanced at his daughter. "Trust me, my dear, such behavior may make for amusing reading but his behavior cannot be pleasant for those in his life." His eyes flickered over his younger brother before settling on Honey, who couldn't help nodding her agreement. She found Byron's behavior repellent enough that she could not enjoy his admittedly compelling poetry.

"Temperamental people can make for a decidedly unpleasant existence." His grace didn't look at Simon, but his meaning was clear.

His brother paid him no mind.

Instead, Simon was staring at Honey, his gaze intense and … speculative. It was a gaze that left her feeling unsettled and slightly anxious.

Just why was he looking at her that way?

Chapter Nine

Simon was as sweaty as his mount when he and Loki trotted into the stable courtyard.

Just as he was about to dismount his cousin emerged from the stables, along with his lurching groom, Taft.

The two men appeared startled to see him.

"Be more careful next time," Raymond snapped at his servant. "That's all then. Be about your business, man."

Taft scuttled back into the stables just as Wilkins came out, no doubt having heard hooves on cobbles.

"Raymond," Simon said, nodding at his cousin and handing the reins to Wilkins. "Have trouble with your man, are you?"

Raymond scowled. "Oh, he's as thick as a bloody plank and needs a cuffing to keep him in line."

Simon cocked an eyebrow at his cousin's harsh words.

Raymond had always been far too abrupt and high-handed with servants. Simon could only assume that was because his cousin had spent his first years without them and had never really learned that a gentle word worked far better than rude or demanding ones.

Raymond dropped his gaze, as though he knew what Simon was thinking, and turned to Loki.

"A lovely animal," he said, taking a step toward Loki as if to pet him, and then wincing back when the temperamental stallion jerked away.

"You'd better keep your distance," Simon said, trying to keep the irritation from his voice and failing. His cousin was a timid horseman and that made him a danger around a high-strung animal like Loki. "I'm afraid he's still a bit of a savage," he added, when he saw that his sharp words had made Raymond's rather jowly face darken.

Wilkins took the reins from Simon, cutting Raymond a dismissive look. The stable master had no patience with a man who didn't know his way around a horse and didn't hesitate to show it.

Simon felt a pang of sympathy for his cousin, but Raymond really did bring it on himself. And he treated Wilkins the same way that he treated his idiot groom, Taft.

"Did he behave hiself, my lord?" Wilkins asked, rubbing the big stallions chin as if he were a kitten.

Simon scratched Loki's slick powerful neck, pleased when the animal pushed into his touch, rather than shying away. "Not too much."

Wilkins chuckled. "Aye, that's right enough, Master Simon. He be broke, but not broken. Ye've done a bang-up job."

"Yes, well, we've got more work ahead of us. But give him some extra oats," Simon said gruffly as he turned away, his face heating from the other man's praise. He couldn't think of a man he respected more than Wilkins. Well, except for his brother. No matter how much he hated Wyndham at times, he respected him.

Wilkins was one of the best horse trainers in Britain. He'd been a groom back when Simon's father had still been alive and was only a few years older than Simon. The two of them had been as thick as thieves once, drawn to each other through their mutual love of horses. It had always been Simon's plan to poach Wilkins from the duke's household when he took up residence at Everley.

He snorted, brushing his forearm over his sweating brow. *That* dream was still as far out of grasp as it ever was, thanks to Wyndham.

"I'll release your inheritance when you marry or turn five-and-thirty." His brother had said in his cold, implacable way the last time they'd fought. Well, the last time *Simon* had fought. Wyndham never fought. Never raised his voice. Never got angry. Never let even one emotion slip from his viselike grasp—not even when Edward died.

"Er, Simon?"

Simon turned at the sound of Raymond's voice and found the man only a few steps behind him. He hadn't even realized that Raymond had followed him.

"Yes?" he asked, once again needing to rein in his impatience. Simon tried not to be cruel to his cousin, but Raymond, with his cringing, fawning ways made it difficult.

He'd lived with Simon's family since he was five—ever since Simon's father had brought him to Whitcomb. Although Raymond had never mentioned his past, Simon knew his cousin had been living in squalor when the old duke had learned of the existence of his youngest brother's only child.

"Er, I was wondering if you wanted to accompany me to Lindthorpe. His grace wants an assessment of the stables there and I thought you might be able to give me your opinion?" Raymond asked.

"Lord, Raymond—why don't you just call him Wyndham? I've heard him tell you to do so a thousand times."

Raymond shrugged, his expression the strangely dogged one that always made Simon feel bad for snapping at him.

He heaved a sigh and stared at his cousin, absently smoothing his worn leather gloves as he considered the invitation.

Lindthorpe was a good-sized property that Wyndham had recently purchased. It was only about an hour or so away from Whitcomb and Simon was a bit of curious about the place. It was old—built during the early Tudor period—and had belonged to the Earl of Templeton's family for generations. Simon knew the earl had gotten into hot water with poor investments and had needed to sell the ancient estate.

"Did my brother put you up to inviting me, Raymond?" he asked, smiling sardonically at the shorter man.

"No. The duke was to accompany me, but he's not—" Raymond grimaced. "He's not feeling well."

Simon frowned. "Lord—again? Is it the same thing? His stomach?"

"I believe so. You'd have to talk to the doctor, who just arrived a while ago."

The small hairs on Simon's neck lifted at this news. "Good God—as bad as that? I should probably go to him and—"

"Now is not a good time," Raymond said. "In fact, his grace told me to ask you to stop by at half past three."

Simon nodded. "Very well."

"It was not the duke who suggested you accompany me; it was my idea. I'd like you to look at the stables and advise me as to what should be done."

When Simon didn't immediately answer, Raymond added. "I'd like your company, Simon. It has been a long time since we've spent much time together. Well, other than drinking down at The George."

Simon opened his mouth to make an excuse but then saw the same yearning and admiration on Raymond's face that he had seen ever since his cousin had come to live with them, a lonely orphan a year Simon's senior. Even though Raymond had been older, he'd always behaved like a younger relative, following Simon around like a besotted puppy.

"All right. Thank you," he added, feeling like an arse at how thrilled Raymond looked at his grudging courtesy.

"I'm leaving first thing tomorrow."

"I'll be ready."

Simon left Raymond to his business and headed toward the house. He came out from under the big stone arch just in time to see the flash of a familiar navy-blue cloak disappear behind the rose hedge.

Simon strode off in her direction. Why not? He had two hours to wait before he could go see Wyndham.

Worry stabbed at him as he pondered his brother's unexplained illness. While it was true that Simon was angry at the duke's behavior toward him—namely holding Simon's inheritance hostage to force him to marry—he loved his brother a great deal.

Simon was tired of fighting with Wyndham and scheming—rather fruitlessly, truth be told—ways to get out from under his brother's thumb.

Later today, when he went to him, he'd talk to Wyndham rather than yell. They used to be the best of friends when they were younger. It was time to stop his childish behavior.

Buoyed by that thought, he hastened his pursuit of Miss Keyes; he might as well amuse himself while he waited.

Simon passed through the meticulously maintained knot garden and into the manicured park. Miss Keyes wasn't far ahead of him, heading in the direction of the maze. Simon slowed his pace; it wouldn't do at all if she saw him.

The maze at Whitcomb was a superlative example of its kind. Hundreds of years old and towering a good ten feet tall, it was a tricky puzzle—at least for those unfamiliar with it. The pathways had narrowed over the centuries as the carefully pruned plants grew and expanded. Curves, sharp angles, dead ends, repeating patterns, one-of-a-kind diversions—all of these and more contributed to a massive rolling green of confusion or delight, depending on one's perspective.

There were two entrances to the maze and Simon took the same one Miss Keyes used. At the first fork he noticed a small piece of paper impaled on a twig on his right. His smile turned to a grin and he plucked it off and put it in his pocket.

He followed the paper trail, removing each piece. Two times, when she encountered dead ends and tried the alternate paths he had to force his way into the dense hedge to hide as she passed him, close enough that he could have reached out and touched her. But that would have spoiled all the fun.

He followed her for perhaps a quarter of an hour. And when he was sure she'd gone the wrong way, yet again, he made his way to the heart of the maze—which wasn't in the center at all, but off to the northwest corner, yet another trick played by the ancient designer.

A massive fountain surrounded by a half-dozen stone benches sat in the middle of the eerily quiet space. Simon took a seat and faced the only entrance, preparing himself for a long wait.

***

Honoria began to wonder if the maze was haunted.

Even as the ridiculous thought entered her mind, she felt embarrassed. She was the least fanciful person she knew.

But her pragmatic, practical mind couldn't explain the mysterious disappearance of a dozen pieces of paper. She must be far more lost than she'd believed—so lost that she'd gone down a different path entirely. She stopped at yet another intersection, this one heading in two directions.

Although the day was mild her head grew hot and her dress started to stick to her.

She untied her cloak and threw it over the arm that held her increasingly heavy satchel. She'd stopped wanting to reach the center of the maze fifteen minutes ago. Now she just wanted out. She looked up at the sky but the sun was dead above her, giving her no clue as to where she'd entered.

How long would she be out here before somebody came looking for her? *Would* anyone come looking for her? In this household people seemed to come and go without comment or notice. She could be in here for hours—days. She could *die* in here.

A shiver rippled up her spine before she could stop it.

"You are acting like a fool, Honoria Keyes." Her voice sounded muffled and far away, the encompassing walls of greenery swallowing up the sound. She inhaled until it felt like her lungs would explode, held it, and then exhaled.

After repeating the calming exercise twice more, she took a left. That's what she would do: take only lefts until she could not.

She shoved the remaining pieces of paper into the pocket of her cloak and began walking.

She'd taken six lefts and was beginning to feel a lightness in her chest when she came up against a dead end.

She groaned, turned, and took a right.

Now she would only take right turns.

Part of her brain—a part she was desperately trying to ignore—told her there was no rhyme or reason in this approach.

Honey took three right turns and then stopped. Directly in the middle of the narrow path was a piece of paper. One of *her* pieces of paper.

She picked it up and turned it over, and then over again, as if it might tell her something. In its way, it did: somebody was playing tricks on her.

She crumpled it up and added it to the others in the pocket of her skirt. When she got to the next turn there was a piece of paper in the middle of the left path. She snorted and went in that direction.

At each intersection there was a piece of paper. She followed the trail until it opened out into a surprisingly big clearing with a giant fountain in the middle.

And Simon Fairchild lounging on a bench, squinting against the sun, a blade of grass between his smiling lips.

"You." It was all she could manage but it was probably more dignified than hurling her bag at his head.

His smile grew into a boyish grin and he held out his arms, as if to present her with a prize. "Me."

Honoria stood frozen in place. It was the first time he had looked anything close to human since her arrival.

The fatuous thought infuriated her. So what if he was smiling?

She reminded herself of what she must look like—damp hair loose, messy, and spiraling, her face red and sweaty. All thanks to him.

Simon patted the bench beside him. "Come and have a well-deserved rest."

"Ha!" As if sitting that close to him would do anything other than maker her redder—sweatier.

Honey ignored him and walked—no, *flounced*—to the bench on the opposite side of the magnificent fountain. She dropped her bag on the ground and gazed up at the water-spouting centerpiece in wonder.

"Perseus and Andromeda."

She glared across the distance at him. "Is that right, Lord Saybrook? And here I thought it might be some other man on a winged horse rescuing a woman chained to a rock."

He laughed as he came to stand beside the huge fountain, leaning a hip against the marble trough where Andromeda was lashed to a chunk of marble.

"How do you like our maze?" he asked, tossing the blade of grass he'd been chewing onto the perfectly manicured lawn.

Honey spread her cloak on the stone bench and sat, taking her time before answering. She made her mouth into a prim, disapproving line and then looked up. "I *would* have enjoyed it a lot more if somebody hadn't stolen my markers."

"But that's cheating—leaving a trail of breadcrumbs."

"Cheating?" She had to raise a hand to shield her eyes from the sun before cutting him a look of scorn. "I'm sorry, I didn't realize there were rules about navigating a maze." Her voice faltered as he came toward her, stopping directly in front of her, his broad back and shoulders blocking the glare from blazing into her eyes, the placket of his worn leather breeches mere inches from her face.

"There," he said, looking down at her from his six plus feet. "Better?"

She dropped her hand. "How long have you been waiting here?"

The undamaged side of his mouth curled into a smile. "Not long before you—I followed you here."

"Don't you have better things to occupy your time than stalk me?"

"No."

It was not what she had been expecting him to say and her body exhibited a mixed bag of reactions: joy, terror, curiosity, anxiety, yearning. She picked curiosity. "Why?"

"Because I wanted to."

Well. One could not really argue with that, could one?

They stared at one another in silence for what felt like a very long time. The maze held them in its quiet embrace, nothing but the gentle hum of insects and the very distant chirp of a bird or two.

"You painted a picture of me," he said.

Truly, the man was an expert at throwing her off balance. Not that she'd been feeling particularly balanced since finding him waiting for her.

"I beg your pardon?"

"While your father painted his portrait of me, *you* painted yours. I've only just recalled that."

"What of it?" She threw the words out with as much carelessness as she could muster. As if she hadn't been hoarding the image of him like other people hoarded gold or jewels.

"I'd like to see it."

Honoria was glad she was seated. "Well, you can't."

His brows snapped into a line. "Why not?"

"Because I no longer have it."

That surprised the odious, conceited wretch.

"What did you do with it?"

She shrugged. "Painted over it, I daresay. Not that I can recall."

"You painted over it?" His voice was higher than normal and she had to bite her lower lip to keep from smiling.

"Yes, it was just like I said at dinner last night."

"What did you say at dinner?"

She gave him a look of mock surprise. "Weren't *you* at dinner last night?"

He ignored her sarcasm. "Clearly I missed something important."

"And why would that be I wonder?" She tapped her chin with her forefinger and rolled her eyes skyward, as if searching her memory.

He sighed heavily. "Likely because I wasn't paying attention. Now, tell me what you said."

"That artists frequently paint over pictures that do not please them or are not right somehow. After all, why discard a perfectly fine canvas?"

"Ah, that's right. I recall now." He chewed the inside of his mouth for a moment before saying, "So, which was it?"

"Which was what?"

He cast his eyes skyward in a mocking echo of her recent look. "Did it not *please* you or was something not *right?*"

Honoria gave a careless wave of one hand. "That was a long time ago, my lord. I hardly remember."

He gave a low, dangerous chuckle while slowly shaking his head from side to side. "Oh Miss Keyes, what a fibber you are."

Her heart bolted like a horse that had been roughly spurred. "What do you mean?"

"I want you to paint me."

"So you already said. However, as *I* said, I am engaged after I complete these two portraits."

"What? Alvanley's dog?" He gave a bark of laughter. "That's very droll."

She couldn't help the smile that tugged at her lips.

"If you do sittings of me while you are here you can paint me after you've finished with Cecily and Rebecca. It would be very economical for you."

She snorted. "You can't be serious."

"Why can't I?"

"You already *have* a portrait." And it was glorious. Honey had seen it hanging in the newer of the two galleries after she'd left the breakfast room. Her father had done an inspired job of capturing Simon's younger self. Physical beauty and a zest for life had blazed out of eyes that were surely the color of heaven. It wasn't her father's masterpiece—that was the portrait of Honey's mother—but it was close.

"That is who I *used* to be." He smiled grimly. "Back when I was young and innocent and foolishly optimistic. I wish for a portrait of who I am now."

"You mean now that you are old, debauched, and bitterly pessimistic?"

He laughed. "*Exactly.*"

She opened her mouth, and then closed it. And then opened it again. "I understand your appearance is different," she said hesitantly, flushing under his sardonic gaze. "But surely you are the same person?"

"Are you the same person as you were back then at what— fourteen? Fifteen?"

"I was fifteen," she said, spurned that he did not remember.

"Are you the same as your fifteen-year-old self?"

Against her will, she gave the question some consideration. Was she? She almost laughed out loud. In one way she was: she was still infatuated with the man across from her. She flushed with shame and anger.

When she looked up it was to find him watching her, his expression intent. How long had she waited for him to look at her like that—as if he wanted to consume her? Or at least to consume what she was thinking, if not her person.

Honey shrugged. "In essentials I am the same. In experience, well, of course that is different. I am older, I have more experience in the world, I—"

"Have you been painting all this time? Did you ever go away to school?"

She should have been annoyed by his interruption, but she was too flattered by his interest. "I did not go to school."

"Ah, yes, I recall you had a governess—a dragon of a woman who breathed fire at me."

"That was Miss Keeble."

"She accompanied us on our little jaunts."

So, he *did* remember.

"So, the redoubtable Miss Keeble was your teacher, then?"

"For a while." Honey hesitated, wondering how *much* of herself to share. "But she left—and so did the one after her. Our household was rather unconventional and most of them did not care for the schedule my father kept. By the time the third one left I was seventeen and spending more time on my painting."

"So you never left home?"

Something about his question made her bristle. "For several years I worked at an Academy for Young Ladies."

"You were a schoolteacher?" He eyebrows shot up, the left one almost as high as the right.

"What, don't you believe I'm qualified to teach art?"

He gave a derisive snort. "Don't be foolish—what a bloody waste of talent."

She flushed at both his language, his dismissal of her life as a waste, and his backhanded compliment. "For your information, my lord, I *enjoyed* teaching. It gave me a chance to hone my methods but left me with ample time to take commissions."

The sun disappeared behind a white fluffy cloud and he dropped down beside her, moving with the fluid grace she remembered from all those years ago.

Her body tingled on her right side and she inched to the left.

He picked up her bag and set it on the bench between them. "There, a barrier for your safety, darling."

Honoria flushed at the endearment and his mocking tone. Of course she didn't feel safe—nor was she his darling. She wouldn't have felt safe with a two-foot-thick wall between them. Simon Fairchild was the most dangerous man she'd ever met. Not that she thought he would hurt her—at least not physically. But in every other way? Yes, absolutely.

He was like a narrow trail over a treacherous mountain pass or a night with no moon: dangerous.

Honey swallowed for the umpteenth time, the noise an audible gurgle deep in her throat. She could not help it; his proximity made her frightened, giddy, and anxious.

She lowered her eyelids in what she hoped exhibited ennui or sang-froid or one of those emotions only the French seemed to have names for. "And what of *you*, my lord? You're so eager to point the finger at me and my shortcomings, I recall you said you were going to retire to your house in the country and breed horses." Honey paused, willing herself not to say what she was about to say. "And weren't you betrothed? Bella something-or-other? Did you get lost on your way to the altar and end up on the Continent?"

A cloud moved across his eyes, much as one had just dimmed the sun, and a muscle ticked beneath the scarring of his damaged jaw. Honey felt like she was at Astley's and had just tied a pork chop around her neck and then flung open the door to the lion's cage.

She opened her mouth to take back her taunting words, but he was faster.

"What a good little listener you were, Miss Keyes, and what an excellent memory for details you have," he purred, his gaze burning through her and into his past.

The seconds ticked away and Honey thought that perhaps she had been lucky and that was the end of the conversation. But then his eyes sharpened and fixed on her again and his mouth curved unpleasantly.

"And what of you, *Honey?*" His face pressed close to hers, as quickly as an asp. "Why are you not married with a few brats in the nursery? Or are you a martyr to your art—no room for anything but your *passion* for painting?"

His eyes were hard and his mouth unsmiling. Why was he so hateful? What had happened to that beautiful, kind, thoughtful young god she had worshipped?

Foolishly, she leaned closer, until their noses almost touched. "I have not given you permission to use my name, *my lord.*"

Honey must have wanted what happened next. Why else would she have gotten so close to a man who bore more than a little resemblance to a smoking volcano?

He slid a warm hand around her neck, his broad palm and long fingers wrapping around her throat in a way that made her feel fragile and small.

"I wonder what you taste like, Honey." And then he lowered his mouth over hers.

A soft grunt broke from her chest and she sagged against him, her body as insubstantial as a cobweb in a breeze.

His lips were … well, there wasn't a word for the heat and texture of his mouth. Who could have imagined such tantalizing softness could coexist with such brutal, hard words?

His other hand joined the first, two fingers on each hand sliding up beneath her jaw while his thumbs tilted her chin, positioning her for his pleasure as his lips pressed against hers and opened.

His tongue, warm and slick, flickered along her lower lip and darted inside, making her gasp with surprise.

"Shhhh," he murmured, stroking into her again, deeper this time, and then again and again.

Her body was shaking with suppressed, confused emotions and her hands clenched at her sides, clutching at air.

"Put your hands on me, Honoria," he whispered into her ear, before trailing hot kisses and licks down her throat, nuzzling beneath her chin to get to the hollow at the base of her neck.

Honey closed her eyes and reached for him.

Chapter Ten

The tiny, shrill voice of reason that Simon had last heard sometime early in the War shrieked at him to stop. The woman was obviously a virgin—perhaps even when it came to kisses, which she accepted with adorable awkwardness, but hadn't yet returned.

Simon had not meant to touch her, but when she'd leaned toward him, bad thoughts—or good ideas, depending on which way one looked at it—had ricocheted around inside his head.

His recent amorous activities over at The George had opened a door that had been closed since that fateful day in June. Hell, for a good long while before Waterloo.

Kissing her was the least of what he'd been thinking about. He told himself that he was behaving quite well in comparison to what he really wanted to do to her.

But that other voice in his head—his conscience? —was not convinced by the argument and harangued him.

Somehow that chiding voice found the strength and volume to be heard: *She's an innocent, not a lusty bar wench intent on adding another notch to her belt by sleeping with the local lord's feckless brother.*

Simon was temporarily distracted by the observation, but he couldn't stop himself and he didn't want to, so he shrugged the voice away, easily dislodging his weaker, better angel from its perch.

Good God, she was sweeter than anything he'd tasted in a long, long time.

He plunged into her mouth while holding her steady, her willowy body pliable, soft, and hot in his hands, her tongue clumsy but enthusiastic to return his attentions. She was a tall woman but her bones felt as fine as those of a bird.

Her hands were awkward on his torso but her touches were eager enough to make him hot and hard with desire.

She had elegant but strong fingers and Simon wanted to feel them on his bare skin.

He yanked the long tail of his shirt from his buckskins, took her by the wrist, and shoved her hand beneath the fine muslin. For a moment he thought she might bolt, but then her fingers slid up over his belly, toward his chest. He released an explosive sigh at the feel of her long, cool fingers on his hot skin.

His cock was full and cramped in his snug leathers and he shoved it to one side—as if that would somehow ease the discomfort of his condition—before resuming his own explorations.

Her gown was made of some light, summer-weight fabric and designed to be loose-fitting. He could feel the boning of her stays beneath it as he lightly caressed up her side. She shivered but did not pull away. In fact, her second hand joined the first beneath his shirt and she shifted her body to better access him.

He shivered when a touch softer than a fluff of down trailed over his hardened nipple before drifting to the wreckage that was his left side. The disfigured skin had suffered extensive nerve damage but the tissue-thin skin remained oddly sensitive.

She made a noise somewhere between a choke and a gasp; Simon pulled away just enough to see her face.

Her dazed gray eyes were coal black, the pupils enormous. While she stared up at him her hands widened their range of motion, stroking from his nipples to the waist of his buckskins, the tips of her fingers slipping beneath the leather and brushing low on his sensitive belly, coming tantalizingly close to the swollen head of his prick.

"Mmmm, that feels so good," he praised, leaning close to kiss her parted lips, penetrating her with a teasing flick of his tongue.

He stared, transfixed, as innocent lust transformed her features, her raw desire making his erection ache so hard it hurt.

Simon knew that he could mount her right where they sat; he could lift her onto his lap and sheath himself balls-deep in her tight, virginal heat.

Yes, he could take her, but he wouldn't.

Not even he was such a dog as to deflower a woman on a cold, stone bench.

Simon had just sucked in a ragged breath to do his gentlemanly duty—even though he'd stopped being a gentleman years ago—when she once again found his right nipple and commenced to circle the sensitive nub with erotic insistence.

A low, animal groan escaped him and his hand moved up her side and over her stays until he cupped the gentle swell of her breast. He despised himself and what he was doing, but then despising himself was nothing new.

He flicked his thumb over the thin bodice that could not conceal her taut bud and her hands froze on his body as every particle of her being focused on where his thumb was touching. He could feel the rapid palpitations of her heart beneath his palm and it reminded him of a hummingbird. A trapped, powerless hummingbird.

Christ.

She was breathing so hard and fast Simon thought she might lose consciousness.

He drew in every ounce of will he possessed and was just about to pull back, to release her, when her hands tightened on his torso, her fingernails grazing his nipple.

He almost screamed at the jolt of pleasure that ripped through him. The leash he'd kept on his desire snapped and he claimed her mouth again, harder and deeper this time, both his thumbs teasing and circling her small, thrusting nipples.

"Open my breeches," he murmured in a voice that was thick and hoarse, licking and sucking the hot, damp skin of her throat hard enough to mark her.

She stiffened as if somebody had inserted a rod up her spine and snatched her hands from his body.

Simon closed his eyes and exhaled noisily. Part of him—the hard part—wanted to howl in sexual frustration. But the rest of him congratulated himself on avoiding the despicable, and ultimately unwise, action of deflowering a virgin.

Simon brushed her delicate jaw with the back of his fingers. "It was the right decision, Miss Keyes. I have nothing to give you that is worth having," he whispered, leaning in to deposit a light peck on the cheek.

He stood and began tucking his shirt into his buckskins. Her eyes dropped to his distended breeches and the thick, hard ridge that was the only thing he had to give her.

Her lips were swollen and slick from what was—he wagered—if not her first kiss, then certainly not far behind. Her sharp, jerky motions as she put herself back together told him that she was not just embarrassed, she was angry—at both Simon and herself.

Later, when she was alone with her thoughts, he knew that she would start hating him for exposing her to such mortification.

Simon felt a pang that she would hate him, but that was just as well; he had nothing to give her and everything to take.

He held out a hand. "Come," he said, more brusquely than he felt, "I will assist you out of the maze."

Simon wasn't surprised when she ignored his hand and stood without his assistance, her eyes like daggers made of gray ice.

"I can find my own way." She snatched up her satchel, her delicate nostrils flaring with suppressed fury, pink slashes of color high on her cheeks.

Lord, she was lovely when she was angry.

Simon doubted that she'd appreciate that observation just now so he dropped his hand. "As you wish, Miss Keyes. If you aren't out in an hour, I shall send help."

His words didn't elicit so much as a twitch of a smile.

"The only help I want from you, *my lord,* is to stay away from me for the duration of my time at Whitcomb." She turned, took several steps, stopped, and spun around. "In fact, don't come near me ever again." And with several long strides, she disappeared into the maze.

Simon couldn't argue with her; the best thing she could do with a man like him was turn her back and walk away.

Chapter Eleven

After the debacle in the maze, Simon headed directly to Wyndham's chambers.

His brother was just dismissing his valet when Simon entered his room.

Simon frowned as he took in Wyndham's haggard appearance. "Wasn't the doctor just here? Why aren't you in bed? You look like hell."

"Yes, he was. Because I am feeling better. And thank you for your kind words," Wyndham said, a gleam of humor in his slate-gray eyes.

Simon huffed out a breath as he followed his brother into the adjacent study. "I'm not speaking in jest, Wynd. What the devil is wrong with you?"

Wyndham sat at the small secretary desk and took a sheet of paper out of the drawer. "The doctor said I have a chronic stomach ailment," he said, taking a quill from the standish and beginning to write.

"What does that mean? Will it just go away? Or is there something you can eat or drink to make it better?" Simon shoved his hands through his hair, annoyed by his brother's calm, aloof attitude. "Is this serious, Wynd?" he finally asked, his face heating at the fear and tinge of hysteria he heard in his own voice.

Wyndham glanced up at him and gave him a slight, weary smile. "Doctor Morton assures me that it will go away on its own, given time," he said, turning back to his letter. "It is not life-threatening," he added softly.

Relief rolled over him at his brother's words. "Well, thank God for that. I have no interest in stepping into your boots at any point—and *certainly* not now." He strode over to the cluster of decanters on the glass table beside the fireplace. "These are empty," he said, lifting one decanter and then another.

"Daley must have been interrupted before he could refill them. Take a fresh bottle from the cabinet," Wyndham said, sanding his letter.

Simon took out a bottle of brandy. "Do you want one?" he asked, pouring three fingers into one of the cut crystal glasses.

Wyndham hesitated, and then pulled a face. "No, I'd better not. The doctor recommends a bland diet that does not include alcohol. Besides, he just cupped me so enthusiastically I'd probably swoon from even one sip." He sanded his letter and then took off his signet ring.

"Ah, probably wise," Simon agreed, lifting his glass and drinking enough for both of them. "So," he said, watching as his brother melted wax and sealed the letter he'd just written, "what did you want to talk to me about?"

Wyndham removed his spectacles and set them aside before tossing the letter onto the salver, along with several others. "I'm going to have a house party in two weeks."

All the good will Simon had been feeling toward his brother began to dissipate.

"Tell me this isn't going to be the sort of house party that is peopled with eighteen-year-old chits, Wyndham."

"I am inviting several eligible females, along with their parents," Wyndham continued, as if Simon had never spoken.

"Unless you're inviting them for you, Wynd, you might as well not bother." Simon slammed his unfinished drink down on the end table, stood, and strode toward the door, yanking it open.

"I understand you went riding with Miss Keyes."

Simon spun around on his heel. "What of it?"

"She is not to be toyed with, Simon."

"I'm not *toying* with her, Wyndham."

Oh, you lying villain, Simon's conscience chided.

Simon grimaced, infuriated that the bloody voice was right this time.

"Don't worry," he snapped, before his brother could call him out on his shameless lie. "I'm going to Lindthorpe with Raymond in the morning. That should stop me from ravishing your portrait painter if that's what is concerning you."

"She is an employee in my house, Simon, it is up to me to protect her. If you are looking for a suitable woman to shower with your attention you shall shortly have several appropriate candidates to choose from."

Simon felt as if a rope were tightening around his neck; would the man never stop?

"Sod off, Wyndham. Just bloody sod off. After I'm finished at Lindthorpe I shan't be returning to Whitcomb. It's past time I got the hell away from this place. I can't bear one more day of your pompous meddling without resorting to violence." Simon flung open the door hard enough that it cracked against the wall, and then strode out into the corridor, only to slam into Raymond.

"Good God, Raymond. What the devil are you doing lurking about?" he snapped, his cousin's wide-eyed gawking only infuriating him more. "I'll be ready to leave at seven o'clock in the morning. You can pick me up at The George, where I shall be staying the night," he added, loud enough for his brother to hear.

***

After Honey had changed her clothing, cooled off—both mentally and physically—and eaten a light lunch, she went to meet her second subject.

She'd just reached the landing that led to the family wing when she heard a familiar voice shouting somewhere to the left of the staircase.

"—after I'm finished at Lindthorpe I shan't be returning to Whitcomb. It's past time I got the hell away from this place and you. I can't bear one more day of your pompous meddling without resorting to violence." The sound of a door slamming followed, and then some garbled voices.

Honey turned right and scurried down the hallway that led to the duchess's chambers—which were thankfully in the opposite direction.

She hesitated in front of the duchess's door, giving her heart a moment to stop pounding.

Simon's furious words and not-so-thinly veiled threat replayed inside her head.

Just what had that argument been about?

What happened to your resolution of a mere half-hour ago—in which you swore to avoid both thinking of or talking to Simon Fairchild ever again?

Honey gritted her teeth; yes, that was true. She *had* planned to avoid him. But that didn't mean she couldn't be curious. Did it?

Oh, Honey.

Honey thrust everything but her work from her mind and knocked on the door.

She was just about to knock again when the same sour crone as before opened the door.

"Oh," the servant said, eyeballing Honey as if she'd come to beg the duchess for alms rather than paint the woman. "No more than a half-hour," she cautioned before opening the door enough to allow her to slip sideways into the room.

Honey smiled down into her hostile face. "Of course," her easy acceptance caused the other woman a look of surprise.

The maid led Honey through the apartments, a rather vast collection of rooms that must be some distance from the duke's if that is where Simon's voice had been coming from.

The duchess received Honey in her boudoir.

Cecily Fairchild was every bit as gorgeous as her name.

She looked nothing like her daughter. Indeed, it was hard to believe the tiny, delicate woman was even old enough to have an adolescent daughter. She was the opposite of Rebecca in not only coloring and beauty, but she had an aloof, almost chilly, demeanor. She also appeared every bit as fragile as the duke had intimated.

"I hope you will excuse meeting in such an intimate setting," she said from her perch on a sumptuous chaise longue, which was upholstered in ice blue velvet that flattered her delicate, porcelain looks. She wore a frothy crème-colored peignoir and matching slippers, her cornsilk-colored hair artfully arranged as if she'd just risen from bed. Which she very well might have.

Her chambers were done in shades of crème, blue, and silver and made Honey feel as if she had stumbled onto a heavenly cloud; all the scene lacked were cherubs plucking harps.

Honey felt even taller, gawkier, and ganglier than usual, aware of every inch of her almost six feet of body.

Her grace was a tiny woman whose limpid blue eyes and smooth skin were as youthful looking as her daughter's. The only sign that she was ill, aside from her retiring airs, were the two rather feverish spots of color on her cheeks.

"I'm sorry I could not see you when you came before. I'm afraid it was not a good time for me."

"It wasn't a problem, your grace. When I left, I encountered your daughter and we had our first session."

The duchess blinked, looking surprised to hear she had a daughter. "Oh."

There was a moment of awkward silence as Honey struggled to come up with something to say.

Thankfully, the maid appeared with a tea tray, setting it on the table in front of Honey.

"Will you pour, Miss Keyes?" the duchess asked. "I'm afraid I only have so much energy each day."

"It would be my pleasure."

"Plimpton tells me you wish to have several sessions where—" she frowned. "Well, I don't know what you wish to do."

"I just wish to get to know you a little and also make sketches. Milk? Sugar?"

"Neither, thank you."

Honey gestured to the plate of delicate pastries, which the duchess waved away.

"I trust there will be no problem having the sessions here?" Her grace glanced vaguely around her, as if seeing her own room for the first time.

Honey was in the process of putting a few pastries on her plate and looked up.

"Not at all. I would like to make several sketches the way you will eventually be posed, which is something else we should discuss. This room would make a very lovely setting—do you envision this as the background for your portrait?"

"Plimpton wishes for a full-length portrait but I do not wish to be standing."

Honey nibbled her pastry as she examined the sumptuous room, beautiful woman, and expensive, graceful furnishings. The duchess did look lovely draped across the blue velvet chaise longue with its gilt legs. And the room was undoubtedly her natural—and perhaps her only—milieu. It did not sound as if she left her chambers, even to dine.

A full-length horizontal portrait would be quite stunning and unusual.

"I believe we can contrive something that will satisfy you both," Honey said, her mind already racing with possibilities.

"Plimpton says you shall be painting Lady Rebecca. Will you want the both of us here during these, er, sessions?" A plaintive note had entered the duchess' soft voice.

Honey used the delicate, lace edged napkin to remove any crumbs from her fingers. "I have already arranged for sittings with your daughter—separately."

The duchess sighed. "Yes, that would be best. Rebecca is rather restive and does not care to sit for long periods." She gave Honey a fragile smile. "It might be better if you conducted some of your sessions with her in an outdoor environment. My daughter loves riding and so forth."

Honey couldn't help being grateful that Rebecca wasn't there to hear the dismissive way her mother spoke about her.

As a girl, she'd always wished for a mother and now she realized they weren't always the loving parents of her fantasies.

"Your grace?" It was the sour-looking servant. She gave Honey a narrow-eyed look before turning back to her mistress. "You know it's time for your midday rest."

"Ah, yes. Thank you, Stapleton. I *am* feeling a bit weary." The duchess sighed, as if a strenuous activity awaited her. Why would she need a nap when all she did was lie around all day?

Wisely, she kept her wondering to herself.

Instead, she stood. "I shall leave you now. Shall we say tomorrow, the same time?"

The duchess looked at Stapleton, who pursed her lips and gave a grudging nod. "No longer than a half hour."

Honey forced a smile. "Of course."

The maid frog-marched her to the door and then shut it in her face.

Honey stood in the same position as less than thirty minutes earlier: staring at the duchess's door.

She turned and began the long process of returning to her room.

At the current pace—less than thirty minutes a day, and with half the meetings cancelled—she'd end up staying at Whitcomb for half a year just to get the sketches she needed.

Oh, and you'd just hate that, wouldn't you? Trapped in a house with Simon Fairchild for six months.

With a pang, Honey thought back to the yelling she'd overheard earlier. If what she'd heard was true—about him leaving—it didn't sound like she'd have to worry about Simon bothering her again.

Chapter Twelve

Two Weeks Later ...

Simon woke up confused, the bed linens twisted around his naked torso like a thick, damp vine.

Dim gray light seeped through the combined shutters and drapes that he'd kept closed for the past week and, for a moment, he thought that was what had woken him: sunlight.

But then something rumbled—a door being repeatedly struck by something hard, like a fist—and his brother's muffled voice came from the other side of the heavy oak.

"Simon, open the door." The duke paused, as if he could hear Simon's sluggish brain struggling to come awake. "Don't make me fetch the innkeeper."

Simon groaned and let his head fall back on the pillow before croaking. "What the devil do you want?"

"Open. The. Door."

He stared at the whorls on the ceiling, the once-white plaster-stained tea-brown from centuries of candle and fire smoke. The boards squeaked outside the door, as if his brother were preparing to go downstairs and drag the innkeeper up here. To be a witness to the duke scolding Simon as if he were a ten-year-old boy.

Simon sighed as he swung his feet over the side of the bed, levering himself up. He winced when not-yet-healed bullet wound snagged on the rough woolen blanket. It had been almost twelve days since he'd been injured, but the damned thing still hurt like the dickens.

When he was standing, he realized that he was naked and briefly considered slipping on his robe, which was draped over the back of the chair; he decided against it. Maybe if he made Wyndham uncomfortable enough, he would leave sooner.

He wrenched open the door and smirked at his brother. "Good morning, your grace." He gave him a shallow, mocking bow.

Wyndham frowned slightly but otherwise did not acknowledge Simon's nudity. He brushed past him into the room. Simon was more than a little disappointed. Was there *nothing* he could do to get a reaction out of his brother?

"Shut the door, Simon." The duke tossed his hat onto a table cluttered with books, empty wine bottles, and dirty crockery. Lily—who also acted as The George's maid—had been less than friendly to Simon after he'd politely refused her services in his bed.

He hadn't refused because he'd not wanted a wench—because he bloody well had. Rather, he'd refused because every time he closed his eyes, he saw that damned Honey Keyes in his mind's eye.

As much of a bounder as he could be, he drew the line at bedding one woman while thinking about another.

"Here," Wyndham said, snatching up Simon's robe and throwing it onto the bed before lowering himself into the room's only chair.

Simon was tempted to simply walk out of the room and down the stairs, out of the inn, and all the way to Everley. The only thing that stopped him was the fact that he had exceptionally soft, sensitive feet.

He slammed the door and then flung himself onto the bed and bunched the pillows behind him before lounging back and clasping his hands behind his head. He stared across his naked body at his brother.

Wyndham sighed—the equivalent of another man yelling. "I have seen you naked, Simon, more than I care to recall. Believe me, you are not shocking me or making me uncomfortable."

His cool, weary words caused a flush to surge up Simon's chest and neck.

Yes, his brother had seen him naked. And helped him piss and shit when he'd been too sick to do either of those activities unaided. He'd done things for Simon that no human being should ever have to do for another—no matter their age, gender, or relationship.

Wyndham had come to Belgium to find him upon reading Simon's name among a list of the missing.

And, because the Duke of Plimpton never failed at anything he set out to do, he'd found Simon in a filthy, cramped hospital in the chaotic aftermath of the battle. He'd been naked under a pile of other naked men for three days after the cannon exploded and knocked him unconscious. Scavengers had taken every stitch of his clothing and belongings, which he couldn't imagine were in such good condition given *his* condition.

The only difference between Simon and the other naked men had been that he was still alive. Barely. Somebody—he never discovered who—had found him and brought him back to the hospital. None of his wounds had been life-threatening, which had been the only reason he'd survived for three whole days and nights.

However, by the time he received medical care, his injuries were badly infected.

Wyndham must have thrown enough money around to buy a small village because the next time Simon woke up, he was in a humble room, but one that was clean, quiet, and private.

Wyndham had hired a woman to help him care for Simon, but even wealth and power only went so far in the days after the Battle of Waterloo and the duke and Simon's man, Peel, had done the lion's share of the nursing.

His brother had cared for him for six weeks, until Simon's infection was brought under control and he was well enough to travel.

So, that was yet another thing Wyndham held that over his head, along with Simon's inheritance: saving his bloody life.

"What do you want, Wyndham?" he asked, not having to feign the exhaustion in his voice.

"How is your arm?" his brother countered, looking at the ugly, raw mark on his right shoulder.

"It's fine." He paused and studied his brother; the duke looked in the pink of health. "You are looking far better, yourself."

"I feel much better," Wyndham admitted.

"Tell me, did Raymond ever find the fool who shot me?" he demanded, not with much hope.

"Whoever it is has also poached hundreds, if not thousands, of pounds' worth of game. Raymond only returned from Lindthorpe this morning, but whoever the man is, he's elusive." His brother sounded peeved, which mean he was actually infuriated.

Simon pitied the poacher when Wyndham finally got hold of him.

He'd been shot just as he and Raymond were leaving Lindthorpe after their brief sojourn. The trip would have been a relaxing one if not for the bloody poacher, who'd not only hit Simon, but nicked Raymond's mare, who'd then thrown his cousin.

Poor Raymond had been injured worse than Simon; so bruised and battered from his fall that he looked as if he'd gone ten rounds with Gentleman Jackson himself.

Simon had been surprised by how much he'd enjoyed that time with his cousin. They had done some hunting, a bit of fishing, explored the big estate, and had stayed up each night reminiscing.

He'd been reminded, for the first time in years, how pleasant Raymond could be when he wasn't trying to curry favor with Wyndham.

His cousin could not seem to understand that Wyndham would never give him the sack—no matter how ineptly he might sometimes manage his brother's many properties.

While it was true that Raymond served as a sort of steward, he was family first and always. Wyndham was loyal to a fault when it came to supporting his relatives. Of course, he also expected their loyalty and obedience, in return.

"When are you coming home." The duke crossed an impeccably booted foot over one knee and eyed him like a surgeon wondering how much rot he would need to cut away and whether the patient would survive the procedure.

"Home? You mean to Whitcomb?"

Irritation flickered across his brother's impassive features. "Yes, Simon. When are you returning to Whitcomb?"

"Maybe never. I like it here."

"And how are you paying for this little sojourn?"

That made him smile. "It seems I have excellent credit in these parts."

"Not after today," the duke replied coolly.

Simon's smile slid from his face. "You bastard."

"How long are you going to do this, Simon? How long will you insist on thwarting me?" For once, Wyndham did not sound as cool as a January wind. Instead, he sounded like a man who was nearing forty and rapidly losing what little patience he had with an heir who refused to marry and propagate.

"I guess I'll do it until I'm thirty-five."

"Not without money."

Simon felt his features twist into a sneer that he knew to be twice as unbecoming thanks to his injuries. "I might not have money, but I have plenty of possessions I can sell. I can live long enough on the proceeds of those sales. My existence for the next ten months won't be luxurious, but I will survive. Trust me, *your grace*, living above an inn is paradise compared to being on campaign. I can wait you out." By the end of his soliloquy Simon was beginning to enjoy himself. But then his brother reached inside his immaculately cut coat and drew out a battered and filthy piece of paper.

"What the devil is that?" Simon asked.

"Everything you have is in my name—or have you forgotten?"

"What?"

Wyndham's eyebrows arched. "Don't you recall? When you were ill—delirious with fever—you signed this." He tossed it to Simon.

Simon opened the folded piece of paper and read the brief contents. It was like a punch in the face. He had no memory of writing the words on the page, but it was undeniably his handwriting.

He crumpled up the paper and threw it at his brother, who easily caught the projectile. "You bastard," he said through gritted teeth. "You know I only wrote that because I thought I was going to die."

Wyndham gave an elegant, ducal shrug. "It is too bad your letter does not say that. It only says all of your worldly possessions are mine."

"No magistrate would believe that."

"That might or might not be true. However, the word of a duke will suffice until I have liquidated all your possessions—all your horses, including that lovely new mare you just purchased. By the time you get the issue before a magistrate—provided you can find the money for such a legal action—everything will be gone."

It took Simon three gulps before he found adequate air. "You fucking bastard."

Wyndham nodded, untouched by Simon's venom. "Perhaps, but it still doesn't alter the fact that you don't have a penny to your name." The duke sighed, looking unspeakably weary. "Come home, Simon. Marry a respectable woman of breeding, produce two sons, and then you may do whatever you wish." He waved a hand, his heavy gold signet glittering on his smallest finger. "You may live above a taproom, cavort with serving wenches, breed horses, set up an entire houseful of mistresses—anything you desire once you have done the one thing I ask. I will not only release your inheritance early; I will put all the wealth of the dukedom at your disposal."

Simon shook his head. "That really is all that matters to you, isn't it—the dukedom? An heir. You don't give a damn about anyone else."

"I give a damn about hundreds of people, Simon. It is my duty to give many damns—and it will one day be yours, and then your son's." His eyes glinted. "I am the Eighth Duke of Plimpton. Our line has been unbroken for hundreds of years." He leaned slightly forward, his taut posture more telling than his cool expression or tone. "Do you even know how singular that is?" An almost fevered look spread across his cold, emotionless features. "Do you?" He did not wait for an answer. "Because of *me* and my inability to get an heir this may be the first break in hundreds of years. If the title goes to Raymond—"

He didn't need to finish his thought; Simon knew what he meant. Raymond had always had a problem when it came to cards. Simon had given him hundreds of pounds over the years and he knew Wyndham would have done the same. Putting the dukedom in the hands of an inveterate gambler was, indeed, a concern.

But it was not *Simon's* concern. Besides, he would do his duty during his lifetime and be a responsible steward. But did he have to dance to Wyndham's tune for the cause?

He knew that Wyndham's answer would be *yes*.

His brother's features shifted subtly, until he looked out at Simon through eyes that would have done some long ago religious zealot or too-enthusiastic member of The Inquisition proud.

For the first time in Simon's memory, his brother *burned* with emotion and it scared the hell out of him.

He lost all desire to taunt or mock. "But you are not the break, Wyndham. I will inherit. There is *no* break. Everything will go on as usual. You know I will not be profligate or reckless or—"

"But that will never happen, Simon."

Simon squinted. "What do you mean?"

"I mean that you are intent on killing yourself. I can read it in your face. Every day that passes and your head hits the pillow is a miracle." Simon opened his mouth to deny it, but Wyndham wasn't done. "I *see* it. I *feel* it, Simon. You are not interested in living. I don't think you are interested in anything—not even the horses you claim to love."

An image of himself reaching over the cliff to retrieve Honoria Keyes's feather flickered into Simon's brain.

Wyndham nodded as though Simon had admitted to something. "Yes, you don't want to live. You haven't wanted to live since before your injuries."

This time Simon was too shocked to argue—too shocked by his brother's perception. He was also bitterly envious of other man's memory. He could no longer recall so much of his past. It was like looking at something through a cracked and filthy window, he could see images, but they were smoky and unrecognizable.

"I don't know what happened to you during the war to make you the way you are, Simon, but I do understand the result—your lack of desire to go on living." It was as close as Wyndham had ever come to admitting the unimaginable pain of losing one child after another.

A lump of remorse blocked Simon's throat and he had to swallow several times to overcome it. He was so bloody tired of fighting with the brother he loved that he opened his mouth to capitulate—to give him what he wanted and marry one of the young women who were probably even now infesting Whitcomb.

But then, out of nowhere, Bella's tear-stained face rose up like some specter from a Shakespearean play.

I love you, Simon. I will always love you.

He had no recollection of the circumstances surrounding that memory—he didn't know the day, or even the year—but it left a bone-shaking rage in its wake.

This was the man who had made Simon this way: Wyndham.

His brother had destroyed his chance of marrying the woman he loved and living the life he'd always hoped for.

Wyndham's machinations were the reason that Simon had gone to war in the first place.

It was because of Wyndham that he was a broken, damaged wreck of a man.

Simon let fourteen years' worth of fury ooze into his sneer. "You haven't a clue what is in my mind, and I have no intention of *ever* sharing my private thoughts or plans with you."

Wyndham's eyes shuttered at Simon's animosity, the little glimpse of himself that he'd so briefly displayed was gone without a trace.

A chill settled deep in Simon's bones. Wyndham was not a man to cross, and yet Simon had done so again and again and again. And now—

The duke stood and pulled on his gloves, the snug brown leather tightening over his knuckles as he flexed them, as if for a fight. "I have paid your shot here through tonight but the innkeeper knows it is the last money he will see from me. I daresay you could remain here indefinitely and he will not dun you. You can soak up his food and drink, occupy his best room without pay," he hesitated, "or *fuck* his employees, and he will allow it—even if it ruins him."

Simon felt dizzy and breathless as he realized how inexorably his brother's web had closed around him.

"You're inhuman." The words were barely a whisper.

Wyndham nodded. "I am. Don't fight me, Simon, you cannot win. Come home by tomorrow. I will expect you at dinner, which will be a bit of a send-off for Miss Keyes. As you've not been home for some weeks you might not be aware that she has completed her work here and will be going home to commence the portraits."

Oh, Simon had been aware. Very aware. Staying away from Miss Keyes—and thereby avoiding ruining her life—had been his chief reason for relocating to the St. George.

He'd removed himself from temptation the morning after that disastrous day in the maze—the day he'd discovered that he wouldn't be able to keep his hands off her if he remained.

Wyndham cleared his throat. "I have also invited guests to stay at Whitcomb for the next fortnight and I will expect you to do your duty and help entertain them." He plucked his hat from the table where he'd tossed it and turned on his heel, leaving without another word.

The door shut with all the finality of a judge's gavel sentencing a doomed man to hang.

Chapter Thirteen

Honey dressed with extra care for her last dinner. She was flattered the duke had organized something of a party for her final meal, although she knew the house guests had come to stay a full two weeks, not only for this dinner.

"I will of course compensate you for the time it takes to accompany the portraits back to Whitcomb when they are completed," he'd said when he called her to his study to tell her his plans.

Honey would take the duke's portraits wherever he wanted, no matter how horrible his brother was.

You mean no matter how <u>absent</u> Simon is ...

When Honey didn't immediately respond the duke had looked up from a ledger on his desk, his eyes hidden behind glinting, gold-rimmed spectacles.

Honey smiled through gritted teeth. "Yes, of course, your grace."

"I would like to organize a larger celebration around their unveiling, perhaps a ball. I would be honored if you would attend."

Honey had never attended a ball in her life so the invitation sounded magical. And if part of her regretted the duke's obnoxious brother would probably not attend, well, that was all for the best.

Besides, she'd become accustomed to his absence in her life over the last few weeks; accustomed to the fact Simon Fairchild didn't care if she lived or died—if he even recalled her existence.

Which is a good thing, she reminded her frowning reflection, a very good thing.

Honey reached into the small jewel case she'd brought with her and took out the exquisite strand of pearls that her father had bought for her eighteenth birthday. She clasped them around her neck and it was as if someone had lighted a dozen candles in the room. The pearls managed to endow both her dress and her person with a lustrous sheen.

Her gown, the nicest thing she owned—purchased for one of her father's exhibits just before he died—was out of date but suited her to perfection. It was an unusual antique gold that made her hair glow and her skin appeared burnished rather than freckled. She screwed in the small pearl studs that matched and then stood, smoothing the rich silk over her hips to examine her reflection.

She was still close to six feet tall—no gown or jewelry would ever diminish that—but she looked her best. She was girded—just on the off-chance Simon Fairchild made an appearance. If he did, she would show him that neither his absence, nor what they'd done in the maze, mattered even a ha'penny.

Of course the fact that *he* was the only thing on her mind right now told her that was patently untrue.

She picked up her gold beaded reticule and scowled at her face in the mirror. "Well, the habits of a lifetime are unlikely to be erased in a month," she told herself.

The words should have eased her mind and made her feel stronger. Instead, they just made her feel sad. After all, what kind of person would be happy about the death of a dream?

***

Simon had been drinking since the evening before, which had been his last night at the inn.

"My Da says this is your last night, my lord," Lily had said when she'd thumped down his pint, spilling a good third of it onto the table.

Simon couldn't help noticing that her expression had not been one of regret.

He frowned at the memory of the hostile barmaid and raised the glass of port to his mouth, tipping it back all the way. Thanks to his brother and Miss Keyes, The George was no longer a hospitable place for him to spend either his days, or his nights.

Oh, Simon. Blaming your infatuation on a poor woman who did nothing to deserve your oafish attentions?

He grimaced at the too-accurate observation.

His fixation on Honey Keyes was more than a little unfortunate, not to mention unfair to the woman. He would have liked to blame his behavior on Wyndham, but his brother was in the right when it came to ordering Simon to leave the artist alone.

Still, he could blame his brother for taking advantage of that bloody letter Simon had written when he'd thought he was dying.

The superior voice in his head had no response for that.

Simon finished the few drops left in his glass and glanced around at the table of men. Nobody was speaking to him or paying him any mind, which was just the way he liked it. When he set down his glass it made an overloud *clunk* on the polished wood, drawing glances from several guests.

Simon didn't care. Instead, he looked around for the port decanter.

It was at the end of the table, next to his brother.

The duke was staring at him in a way that should have left nothing but a smoking black hole in his chair. Simon grinned at him and gave a mock salute.

Although it had only been a scant twenty or so minutes after the women had left the dinner table, the duke stood. "Shall we join the ladies?"

Most of the port glasses at the table still had liquid in them, but nobody demurred. Wyndham was the Duke of Plimpton, after all. Except for five exceptions, most of the guests were nothing more than country gentry, thrilled to have caught the attention of such an august personage.

Simon rose to follow the other men.

"Simon. A moment, if you please." Wyndham's quiet words should have frozen the port in its heavy crystal decanter and filled the room with an icy fog.

Simon heaved a sigh and plopped back down into his chair.

"Close the doors," the duke ordered the two footmen who were always present outside any room Wyndham occupied.

The duke turned his attention to Simon once they were alone. "You are drunk."

Simon looked up at his brother's uncharacteristically blunt words and grinned. "As sharp as ever, old man."

"You are not just shaming me, Simon. You are shaming our mother."

Simon recalled a glance the duchess had given him just before dinner, when he'd arrived in the drawing room where all the guests had assembled. The duchess had, for once, looked older than her years.

He ignored the embarrassment that roiled in his belly. Instead, he sneered at his brother. "Well, she has you to thank for that, doesn't she, your grace?"

"This behavior is beneath you."

Simon lurched to his feet and jabbed a finger in his brother's direction. "And it is beneath *you* to have invited Lady Rosamond and Lady Margaret and the other two whose names I can't recall, dangling them in front of me like so many worms on hooks." He shoved a hand through his hair, barely resisting ripping it out by the roots. "Christ, Wyndham—those are *girls*. Is Margaret even eighteen?"

"All four young ladies are of impeccable birth and the perfect age," Wyndham said through clenched jaws. "And her name is Rosalind, not Rosamond. Because you have refused to consider a Season in London, I must now bring candidates *here*."

"Listen to yourself: *Suitable candidates!* Do you think you're delivering some speech in bloody Lords?" he snarled. "I don't care if you line the table with naked virgins, Wyndham, I'll not marry any woman of your choosing. I'm not your damned blood stock, to be bred when and to whom you please." He reached down and grabbed the half-empty drink of the man who'd been sitting beside him, threw the contents down his throat, and then hurled the glass at the massive mirror that hung over the equally massive fireplace.

The detonation was surprisingly loud and the sound of shattering glass must have been heard even rooms away.

Rather than upsetting his brother—as it would a *normal* man—the duke merely straightened his already impeccable cuffs and strode toward the door. "Your presence will not be required in the drawing room." He opened the door and left, the enormous slab of wood shutting soundlessly behind him.

***

Honey could not recall ever being more embarrassed on another person's behalf in her entire life. The poor duchess was whiter than parchment, her gray eyes wide.

The sound of Simon's yelling—if not the actual words—was audible in the big drawing room.

So was the sound of breaking glass.

Honey made her way through the clutch of speechless guests toward the older woman, afraid the dowager might lose consciousness she was so pale.

"I was wondering about the provenance of this painting, your grace."

The duchess's vague gaze slowly focused on Honey's face. "Painting?" she repeated, the soft word loud in the stone silence of the room.

Honey took her arm, which trembled beneath her hand. "May I show it to you?" She didn't wait for the stunned woman to comply before leading her toward the far wall—away from staring eyes, to where a settee had been placed across from the painting in question. "Why don't you have a seat, ma'am?"

The old lady's body trembled as she lowered herself onto the divan.

Just then the door swung open and Honey glanced up to see the duke entering. He smiled coolly at his guests, who were milling in a tight group.

As far as she could see, his ducal dignity was unimpaired by the scene they had all just overheard.

"Lady Rosalind," he said, turning the not insubstantial force of his personality on the pretty young girl. "Will you entertain us with some music?" He gestured toward the doors that had been opened between the big drawing room and adjacent music room.

Before the petite, delicate blonde could open her pretty, bow-shaped lips her mama stepped forward. "She would be delighted, your grace."

The guests moved toward the music area and the Duke of Plimpton looked toward where Honey waited beside his mother.

The dowager immediately stood and gave Honey a brave smile. "Will you accompany me to the music room, Miss Keyes? Lady Rosalind's performance on the piano is not to be missed."

The duke had been wise to insist on music. By the time Lady Rosalind had played three songs, followed by two other young ladies, the atmosphere had relaxed, if not returned to normal.

Card tables had been set up in the drawing room and tea arrived while they split into groups.

Honey found herself paired with a local squire, playing whist against the dowager and the squire's wife.

When the clock struck midnight, the party broke up.

It was a sign of the dowager's distraction that she did not demur when Honey offered to escort her back to her chambers.

The duke gave Honey the closest thing she'd seen to a smile when he saw her lead his mother out of the drawing room.

Not until they reached the stairs did the older woman speak. "I am sorry, my dear. What a dreadful hostess I am, requiring an escort from one of my guests." The duchess's voice was breathy after their climb.

"Not at all, ma'am. I have been meaning to visit this wing for some time." She glanced at a painting that hung between two sconces and then stopped, turning around. "Good Lord," she gasped. "Tiziano Vecellio."

"What's that my dear?" the dowager asked before turning to peer at the painting, as if only now seeing it. "Oh, yes, a Titian. My husband believed we should not keep all the best pieces in the galleries. He liked to look at them as he came and went from his chambers." She blinked owlishly at the painting, which was a rather wicked depiction of Bacchus and Ariadne. "This was one of his favorites and I have left it here."

Honey heard the exhaustion in her voice and wrenched her eyes from the glorious canvas.

"I must apologize; you are tired and yet I stand here gawking."

The dowager chuckled and they resumed their journey. "I can see how it is for you with art, my dear. My husband was the same way, if you can believe it. His old nurse once told me that it had been his dream to be a painter in his youth." She frowned. "His father could not permit such a thing." She cut a glance up at Honey. "My husband was the only child to survive out of seven, you see. The burdens of the dukedom descended on him early, just as it did my own son."

"His grace was young when your husband died?"

"Yes, not yet ten-and-seven." She shook her head. "You would not have recognized the boy he was—so happy and boisterous." She saw Honey's look of amazement. "Oh, yes. He was a sweet child. Not that he is not a good man now, of course. But so much death and disappointment has taken the light from him. From both my children." Her voice wobbled and she shook her head. "Forgive me, my dear. You should not have been here these past weeks. The family is not fit for company and it must have been uncomfortable."

It *had* been uncomfortable, but Honey could hardly say that. "I have greatly enjoyed my time here."

The duchess patted her hand. "And I know that Rebecca has enjoyed having another young person around."

Honey was amused at being called *young*. "I have enjoyed her, too." And she had. Her sittings with the younger woman had been more like sessions between friends. It pained her to leave the obviously lonely girl in this house of swirling emotions.

A portrait hung not far from the next door and Honey paused.

"It is my husband," the duchess said, stopping beside her. "This was the earliest of his portraits," she explained. "The others hang in the gallery."

Honey had seen them; they were both magnificent. But they were of an older man, his expression stern and uncompromising. This picture, on the other hand—

"Dominic was only twenty in this picture," the duchess said, her voice wistful.

"He was very handsome." The former duke might have been mistaken for Simon in the right light. The clothing and hairstyle were of another age, but the mesmerizing hydrangea eyes and sharp, achingly handsome features were almost identical.

"I was so flattered when he noticed me," the dowager said. "He was eight years older and that was my first Season." She cut Honey a shy, twinkling look, "I was not homely, but neither was I a diamond of the first water." She sighed. "But Dominic—" she broke off and shook her head, as if at a loss for words. "Every woman adored him and yearned for him. But he chose me."

Honey could not read her expression. There was pride, and maybe some love, but also regret.

"I recall your grandfather, Miss Keyes," she said, her pale cheeks reddening. "He was so—"

"Wild?" Honey suggested. At least those were the few stories she'd heard about her mother's father, the infamous Baron Yancy.

"Oh, indeed. He was very wicked. Of course, we all adored him."

Honey saw the truth beneath her tremulous smile. So, the duchess had loved Honey's grandfather, but had married a duke?

Her heart ached for the sweet older woman, who'd probably been made to give up the feckless, impoverished baron in favor of a powerful, wealthy duke.

But if she hadn't, Honey wouldn't be standing there right now.

The duchess resumed walking and a few feet away she stopped in front of a massive crème and gilt door. "Here we are, at last." She smiled up at Honey. "Thank you for your kindness, my dear. You are a good girl."

Honey dipped a courtesy. "Sleep well, your grace." She waited until the door closed before turning back, stopping to examine the various pieces on the walls more closely.

The previous duke had exquisite taste and it was difficult to pull herself away. Still, she hardly wanted to be caught here when the duke eventually returned to his chambers, which were in this wing.

Honey decided she would take the long route back to her rooms and pay one last visit to the new gallery.

She was passing the duke's study when the sound of glass breaking stopped her. Something else shattered, followed by a loud, pained grunt. Honoria stood frozen outside the massive oak door and listened.

There was nothing … and then a groan.

She bit her lip and raised her hand to knock, and then froze again. What was she doing? What if the duke was in there? Or what if—

The door swung inward and she jumped back, an undignified squeak escaping before she could stop it.

"Well, if it isn't Miss Honey Keyes." Simon leaned his forearm against the doorframe and smirked down at her. "Eavesdropping again, are you?"

Chapter Fourteen

Honey was speechless, not from being mocked, but by Simon's haggard appearance: he seemed to have aged ten years since dinner—at which he had not looked particularly healthy, either.

Blood was dripping from his hand and dropping in soft pats on the carpet.

"You've hurt yourself."

He swayed slightly and she realized he was very, very drunk.

"Do you have a handkerchief?" she asked.

When he didn't answer, she looked up from his bleeding hand. His full lips were pulled down at the corners and his nostrils were pinched and white, as if he were angry at something—or someone.

Her?

Honey shook her head at the foolish thought. He was drunk; it didn't matter what irrational thoughts were running around his drink-sodden brain.

She pushed him in the chest, harder than she'd intended, and he staggered back inside the room.

Honey shut the door behind her and held out her hand. "Give me your handkerchief."

His expression was now dazed rather than hostile, but he complied without arguing. Honey took the opportunity to study him while he clumsily fished a crisp white square from the pocket of his coat.

His cravat was half-untied and wrinkled and there was wine or port stains on it. Both his coat and waistcoat were unbuttoned and the black superfine coat looked creased, as if he'd been sleeping in it. Her eyes went to the big leather sofa across from the fire and she saw the glitter of broken glass beside the end table and a throw rug in a pile on the floor.

Honey couldn't have painted a more illuminating scene: he'd been drinking and had lost consciousness.

She snatched the proffered handkerchief from him. "Sit."

She didn't wait to see if he obeyed but went to the collection of decanters that sat on a long rectangular table against the wall. There was a metal bucket with half-melted ice and an empty bottle; she removed the bottle and took the bucket.

Simon was sitting on the couch beside the wreckage when she returned, seemingly unaware of the glass at his feet.

Honey set the bucket on the floor and sat down on the settee as far from him as possible yet still close enough to reach his hand.

She opened the reticule that dangled at her wrist and took out her own, smaller, square of cotton. It bore her initials, neatly embroidered in one corner, courtesy of Freddie, who did the most exquisite needlework Honey had ever seen.

She grimaced, it was a shame to use such a beautiful item, but it was all she had, and calling servants to witness the drunk, scarred man's humiliation did not seem wise. Even though he deserved every bit of pain and humiliation he received. But his mother did not, and servants loved to talk—and Simon Fairchild had already provided them with plenty.

"Give me your hand."

She didn't look at his face, instead concentrating on the cut, which was across his palm, just above the fleshy heel. It was a good-sized slash but it was not terribly deep and the bleeding had already begun to slow. She dipped his cloth in the icy water and began to clean away the blood.

"How did this happen?" she asked without looking up.

She felt him give one of his characteristic shrugs. "I don't know."

She glanced up.

His beautiful, empty eyes were steady on hers, his voice unslurred. For all that he'd been swaying, he certainly sounded frighteningly sober.

Once she'd cleaned the cut, she took her own handkerchief and folded it diagonally, which made it barely big enough to tie around his palm. He had large hands with long fingers, the nails well-kept but the skin hatched with scars and the pads of his fingers rough.

She recalled that his hands had once been elegant and soft; now work-swollen knuckles disturbed their clean, long lines. He was not idle, for all that he seemed to spend a great deal of time drinking or drunk.

"There," she said, releasing him once she'd snugged the knot. She looked up.

He was staring at his hand, which he raised and then gingerly flexed, grimacing slightly.

"Yes, I'm sure it smarts," she said, although he'd not spoken.

He raised his hand to his face and examined her work, turning his fist to and fro. "You've ruined a very nice handkerchief on me."

"Yes, I have."

He looked up and then grinned, his boyish amusement making her heart lurch. "Not much of a bedside manner, Miss Keyes."

Honey gave him a frosty scowl and then began to stand.

His hand—the one without the bandage, landed on her forearm. "Stay a moment."

She hesitated, half-standing, half-sitting.

"Please."

She heaved an exaggerated sigh to hide the leaping sensation taking place in her chest. "Fine. But only a moment." She pulled her arm out from under his hand and sat, scooting as unobtrusively as possible in the opposite direction.

"You are leaving tomorrow?"

"Yes."

"So soon?"

She couldn't help it, she snorted. "Soon? I've been here for weeks—almost a month."

"It doesn't seem that long."

Anger flared in her chest. "How would you know? You haven't been here."

That made him smile. "Oh, did you notice my absence? Did you miss me?"

"No," she snapped.

He laughed softly, the sound dangerous. "Don't lie to me, Honey."

She shot to her feet. "Good night, *my lord.*"

"I'm sorry," he said, instantly contrite. "Please, don't leave angry. I won't misbehave. I promise, Miss Keyes." He put his hands behind his back, as if to demonstrate his harmlessness.

She stared down into eyes that brought back memories that had been cherished and wrapped in gold tissue for fourteen years. *This* was the Simon she knew: gentle and sweet and honest. He was still in there, somewhere. Perhaps if she stayed with him, she might—

Leave. Leave now.

The voice was so sharp and loud she would have sworn it came from somewhere inside the library.

But apparently not, because Simon did not seem to hear it.

Instead, he waited—his stunning blue eyes curious as he stared at her.

Now, Honey! Leave now—

She sat down again.

His lips curved. "Thank you."

Honey studied her clenched hands and unclenched them, forcing them to lie flat and supine in her lap.

"I've been thinking about when I sat for my portrait."

Her head jerked up. "I thought you didn't remember me."

"I didn't, at first."

She flushed, the shame of being forgotten fresh all over again.

Simon shook his head. "I can see you don't understand. I have … problems remembering things."

"Problems?"

"Yes."

"What kind of problems?"

"It's difficult to explain."

"Well, try."

Rather than be offended by her tart tone, he gave her a slight smile. "It started during the war, after I'd been injured the first time."

Honey hadn't known he'd been injured more than once. But why should she? It wasn't as if the papers published news of each and every injury an officer suffered.

She settled back a bit more. "What happened?"

***

Simon wished he'd never started down this road and looked for the quickest way off of it. But he had her attention and he realized that he'd do anything to keep it.

"That's the thing—I can't recall any of it. One moment I was on my horse, heading down a rocky incline, the next—" He shrugged. "I woke up in a bed three days later. Nothing more than a few scratches on my body," he lied, not wanting to tell her about the fragments of human bone and iron they dug out of his back. "But there was blood running from my ears and I had no memory of anything."

"You mean, no memory of your injury?"

"No, I mean anything. I didn't even know my own name."

"Oh my God," she whispered. "How dreadful."

"Yes, it was the most terrifying thing I've ever experienced. Even worse than Waterloo. It lasted for three months. People told me who I was, of course, but my life seemed like somebody else's—like someone in a book."

"What finally made you remember?"

Simon opened his mouth to tell her about the night it all came back and then recalled to whom he was speaking: little Honey Keyes. He looked into her worried gray eyes and shuddered. Thank God he'd caught himself in time. He could just imagine telling her how his men had smuggled a Spanish whore into his makeshift hospital room.

Given his reputation for philandering, they had—rather bizarrely—hoped that vigorous bed sport would jog his memory and remind him of who he used to be and what he used to do. Perhaps it hadn't been bizarre at all, because he'd woken the next morning knowing who he was.

Simon saw that she was staring at him intently, waiting for him to finish the story.

He said, "A friend of mine from Eton came to see me and suddenly it all came crashing back—everything other than the injury itself."

"How fortunate you were," she said in a wonderous voice.

"Yes," he agreed. "I was fortunate."

"And yet you never remembered what happened?"

"No, I never remembered." That much was true, at least.

"And nobody who'd been there that day saw anything?"

Simon hesitated. Why tell her nobody else survived that charge? Why tell her that two hundred and fourteen men had died—all except him: Lucky Fairchild. That was what some people took to calling him—although only behind his back.

Lucky Fairchild lying in a pile of dead bodies, most of whom bore bayonet wounds through their necks and torsos—the signs of thorough enemies. All except for Simon, who'd only had a stab in the arse.

Ha. *Lucky.*

He met her anxious gaze and lied, yet again. "Nobody was close enough at the time. There were no witnesses to what happened." He didn't tell her that he'd been able to figure it out well enough even without a witness. A piece of artillery or bullet must have hit the man riding beside him, and a piece of that man—or his horse—must have hit Simon. Or maybe just the sheer percussive force knocked Simon off the horse. Or maybe his head got kicked on his way toward the ground. Or after he hit the ground. It didn't matter; it was not a tale for a lady's ears.

"I'm afraid my memory has never been the same since. I've … well, lost a great deal of the past."

Her eyes were suddenly shining with unshed tears.

"Here then," he said. "What's this?" His heart skipped uncomfortably in his chest. "Don't worry, love. I was fine. Hector was fine."

Her lush lower lip quivered. "Hector?"

He gave what he hoped was a reassuring smile. "Yes, my horse, Hector. He came out of it without a scratch. No problems with his memory, either."

She gave a choked, watery laugh, but her eyes glistened even more.

Hell.

"You mustn't look that way—it was a long time ago. I am all healed, none the worse." He held his hands out, palms up. "See?" But his words seemed to have the opposite effect and one fat tear slid down her down her cheek.

"Oh bugger, don't do that," he begged, as a second and then a third followed, until there were two solid trails.

On impulse he reached out and brushed at one tear-stained cheek with the back of his fingers. Instead of pulling away, she pressed her soft cheek against his palm.

It was all the encouragement he needed and his arms slid around her.

"Here now, shhh," he murmured into her thick wheat-blond hair, which smelled of lemons.

"I'm sorry," she said against his shoulder, her voice muffled. "I don't know what is wrong with me. I always seem to be either yelling or crying around you. What is it about you that makes me so emotional?" She gave a watery gurgle of a laugh. "It's just—"

"Yes? What is it?" he asked, not wanting to move, not wanting *her* to remember where she was—who she was with—and pull away.

He could feel the tension in her body as she struggled to find the words to answer.

Finally, she just shrugged. "It's just such a horrid, horrid waste."

Simon knew exactly what she meant. Yes, war was a waste—a tragedy for everyone involved. It stunned him that she—who had never seen it first-hand—could know that so viscerally. He pulled back and looked down at her, needing to see her face.

She blinked up at him, her lashes glittering with tears, the tip of her small nose red, her lower lip full and tremulous.

So, of course he kissed her.

Chapter Fifteen

The prudent part of Honey's brain was hoarse from screaming *Run!*

Honey didn't care if the voice was right—in fact, she was certain it was. But she simply did not care about anything other than having his lips on hers, his body against hers. He was Simon—not sneering and cruel—but the Simon she remembered.

Unlike in the maze, this time when his mouth opened over hers, she knew what to expect; she even knew what to do.

She touched his tongue with the tip of her own and his arm tightened, pulling her so tight to his body that she could hardly breathe.

Their tongues tangled as Honey invaded him as ruthlessly—and probably with as much finesse—as a marauding Viking.

Her hands were trapped between them and it was a struggle, but well-worth it, to push away just enough to slide her fingers beneath his coat. His torso was hard and hot and her body flamed at the memory of his skin beneath her fingers.

While she was frantically tugging at his shirt he massaged her back in long, hard strokes, his touch firm and strong as he traced the outline of her body, his clever fingers quickly finding the top edge of her stays beneath the thin silk of her gown.

He made a noise of frustration and, without warning, picked her up by her waist and set her across his lap, the action pulling her hands from his body.

"But—" she mumbled, her mission to expose his skin to her hands thwarted before its successful completion.

"Shhh," he whispered, kissing her with renewed vigor. This time, when his tongue swept between her parted lips, she sucked him into her mouth.

He groaned, accepting her invitation and exploring her deeply, his thorough, demanding kisses leaving her breathless and dizzy.

Honey's eyelids fluttered shut as he began to nibble and kiss his way down her chin to her throat, his free hand lightly stroking her midriff in ever increasing circles.

His mouth arrived at her chest and she felt the hot, slick tip of his tongue trace the top edge of her snug bodice. She shuddered as his finger inadvertently brushed over a taut, pebble-hard nipple pressed against the silk.

And then he did it again.

The third time he did it, she realized it was no accident.

Honey arched into his hand as he palmed her breast.

"So sweet," he murmured. "But I need to taste you."

Warm, strong fingers slid beneath the already low neckline of her bodice, pulling the thin fabric beneath her breasts, the taut material forming a shelf that pushed them higher.

A vague image of how wanton she must appear—sprawled and half-naked—coalesced in her mind but Honey ignored it, instead arching her back and presenting herself to him like a pagan offering.

Warm breath bathed her exposed breasts and she whimpered when his hot, wet mouth closed over her nipple, the erotic shock sending a bolt of lightning to her sex.

What the devil do you think you are doing? the voice in her head demanded, louder this time.

Louder and oddly … *male* sounding.

Honey's eyes flew open.

The Duke of Plimpton was standing behind the couch, hovering over them, his angry gray eyes burning into her.

Chapter Sixteen

Honey gawked up at the duke and screamed.

Simon pulled her protectively toward his chest while simultaneously twisting around to see what had made her yell. She felt his body jolt when he saw his brother.

"Goddammit, Wyndham, what the hell do you think you are doing?" he roared, holding Honey's unresisting body against him while his hand fumbled between them to pull up the crushed, damp silk of her bodice.

"Gentleman, will you please excuse us." The duke's voice was as chilly as a hailstorm.

Honey could not see his face and did not want to. She burrowed into Simon's shoulder like the coward she was.

The door closed with a snap and Simon spoke low into her ear. "I am going to release you, but only if I have done an adequate job of fixing your gown," he hesitated. "Have I?"

Honey dragged a hand up over her bosom; she was covered. "Yes."

He shifted her off his lap far more carefully than he'd put her there.

Honey stared up at him, her face scalding; he looked murderous.

"Are you all right?" he asked softly, his gentle tone showing the murder in his eyes was not for her.

Again, she nodded.

He flashed her a quick, hard smile and then turned to where his brother waited.

The duke was leaning against the front of his desk, his arms crossed over his chest, his gaze on Honey rather than Simon. "I apologize for what my brother—"

"You *never* apologize for my actions!" Simon surged to his feet with balletic grace—no sign of his earlier intoxication evident in his motions. He was in front of the duke in half a heartbeat and his fist connected with the side of his brother's face with a sharp crack even as the other man ducked.

Honey's hands flew to her mouth. "Simon!" The word came out a strangled sob.

He lifted his hand to deliver a second blow.

Honey could see that the duke had recovered from the first, but instead of defending himself or attacking, he simply waited.

Simon's fit froze in midair, inches from his brother's face. "Fight me, you bastard."

The duke didn't so much as twitch.

Simon dropped his arm and made a sound thick with disgust. He spun around, fixing Honey with an incendiary glare. "You should go, Miss Keyes."

The words were the verbal equivalent of a slap and Honey flinched. Before she could respond, the duke spoke.

"No, Miss Keyes. Please stay. This involves you as much as my brother." He extracted a snowy white square from his impeccably cut coat and dabbed at the blood at the corner of his mouth.

Simon clenched his jaw and shook his head. "There is no *this* Wyndham."

"Unfortunately, there is, Simon. Although you may have not noticed, Lord Renshaw, Albert Grayson, and four other gentlemen were with me a few moments ago. I foolishly thought to bring them back to *my* library," he gestured to the shattered decanter, "and I stupidly thought I might enjoy a glass of *my* brandy with them." Although he'd never raised his voice, he was more menacing than a cobra. "But what do I find? I find you. Dishonoring one of our guests."

Honey swallowed and stood. "Your grace—"

He turned to look at her and the rest of her words died in her throat.

"You, Miss Keyes, are ruined." His soft words hung in the air like a thick, unpleasant London fog.

"No," she said, shaking her head vigorously. "I am not a girl in her first Season. I do not need to protect my reputation to attract an offer of marriage."

A look of pity flitted across his granite features and it made her blood run cold. "No, Miss Keyes, you need to do something even more delicate and difficult—you need to convince the aristocracy that you are the type of woman they can permit into their homes. The type of female they can trust their wild, young heirs with for private sittings. The type—"

"That is *enough*, Wyndham," Simon said.

The duke merely looked at his younger brother.

Honey could not see Simon's face, but she knew there was a battle going on between the men. Only the soft ticking of a clock disturbed the brittle silence.

And then Simon's shoulders slumped. "Christ."

The duke nodded and straightened, his arms falling to his sides. "I will give you a few moments together."

And then he strode from the room.

***

Damn, damn, damn, damn. The words were like the insistent cawing of crows in Simon's head.

He turned to the woman. To *Honoria*.

She was staring across the room at him with the terrified eyes of a prisoner at the dock.

Christ. Fortunately, he did not speak the profanity out loud, this time.

He ran a finger around the disaster that was his cravat, wondering why he was so bloody hot when the room felt as frigid as a tomb.

Simon forced a neutral expression onto his face. Or at least as neutral as a man with half of his face in ruins could appear.

"Will you sit?" he asked. She looked as skittish as an unbroken filly, and rightfully so. She'd found herself trapped between two men who'd been fighting each other for almost fifteen years.

Tonight Honoria Keyes had become a casualty of their war.

She sat and Simon lowered himself into the chair across from her. Best not to sit beside her as it seemed like that led to trouble. Still, hard to imagine what worse trouble there could be other than this.

His gaze flickered over her wrinkled gown and loose hair and he cleared his throat. "Miss Keyes—"

She held up one hand, palm out. "Stop," she said, just in case he did not understand her gesture. "I know what you are about to do, and there is no need. I won't say *yes* in any case."

Simon felt oddly affronted. "What?"

"I would not marry you no matter what the incentive or motivation."

Well, hard to misinterpret *those* words.

Simon couldn't help smiling at her fiery spirit. "You know my brother is correct. Word will leak out, somehow. It always does. Even if he threatens those men with dire consequences."

"I understand. But his grace does not understand *me*. He does not understand that I can weather this storm. My father left me enough money to never need to paint another portrait." Her angry gray eyes flickered over his person. "I will not be pressured into a hasty marriage with a man who does not want me."

Simon tried to hide the almost crippling relief her words brought, but some of that must have shown through because her expression turned even grimmer, which he'd not believed possible.

"Don't worry, my lord. I wish to be shackled to you even less than you wish to be chained to me."

Simon flinched at the raw loathing in her eyes.

She stood, and his body automatically followed. She held out a staying hand, her gaze bleaker than the Outer Hebrides in winter. "I showed myself in; I will show myself out."

And in a rustle of golden silk, she was gone.

Simon slumped back into his chair, his mind a whirl of shame, regret, and relief. He dropped his head into both hands and shook it slowly back and forth. He couldn't have said which emotion was strongest.

***

Honey's eyes blurred with tears and she all but ran from the room.

"*Ooooff!*"

Strong hands gripped her shoulders and kept her from toppling backward.

Honoria recognized the duke's face through her tears of rage.

"Steady on, Miss Keyes," he murmured, not unkindly, releasing her once she was steady.

"I'm sorry, your grace, I should have looked where I was going."

He ignored her apology. "I am sorry about the way this has come about, ma'am, but I am pleased that you will soon become a part of this family."

She gave a better, slightly hysterical laugh. "Thank you, sir, but I will not marry your brother." She turned on her heel and began the journey to her room.

"Miss Keyes."

She stopped because he was the sort of man a person naturally obeyed.

But she refused to turn around.

The hallway was carpeted so she could not hear his footsteps. But she was not surprised when his voice came from right behind her.

"I'm afraid you must marry my brother, Miss Keyes."

What little remained of her control shattered and molten anger oozed through the cracks. Honey spun around. "I beg your pardon, your grace, but I must do no such thing. You may control this household and those who live in it, but you do not control me."

His eyes narrowed in a way that made her throat so tight it was hard to breathe. How had she ever believed this man was bland or nondescript? He was like the razor-sharp edge of a blade, like the venom-slicked fang of a snake.

Honey swallowed but held her ground.

"I ask you not to go against my will on this matter, Miss Keyes."

"Or what? You will cancel my commissions and refuse to pay me for my time?" She raised her chin. "Go right ahead. I will be glad to leave this place behind and never return."

"I will pay you for your time and I still expect the portraits to be delivered."

His emotionless tone drove her beyond common sense, beyond self-preservation.

"Or what?"

His thin lips flexed, but it was not a smile. "I do not engage in the exchange of baseless threats, Miss Keyes." He paused to let *that* sink in and do its work.

Goose pimples rose on her naked arms, but she refused to look away.

"None of us have any choice in the matter of your marriage to my brother. I cannot have my family's name dragged through the filth in this way. My brother has dishonored you in my home, in front of my guests. He knows there is only one thing to do now, and so do you."

She shook her head. "Trust me when I say I am deeply grieved by any harm I have inflicted on your family name. But you are the Duke of Plimpton. Surely your credit in the world is high enough to suffer such a setback." She rushed on, not waiting for an answer. "In any case, I will not sacrifice my future for your reputation. I will get commissions, even with this black mark against my name." She gave a shrug that was far more insouciant than she felt. "And if I do not, I will simply pack up my things and go to the Continent. My father left me in a position that does not require me to either marry or work."

She might as well never have spoken.

"I will give you two weeks to consider my brother's offer and return the appropriate response, Miss Keyes."

A disbelieving laugh broke from her. "I don't *need* two weeks, your grace. The answer is emphatically *no*." Honey shook her head and tried to calm down. "This will pass, sir—for both of us. We are strong enough to weather such a small tempest."

The duke nodded slowly. "That might be true—*you* might weather this scandal."

Honey cocked her head, as if she were straining to recognize a tune, but could not quite hear the notes. "I beg your pardon?"

"I understand Lady Winifred Sedgewick lives with you—the Earl of Sedgewick's widow," he added, just in case Honey didn't know who her dearest friend was.

The tiny hairs on the back of her neck rose. "What of it?"

"She is a woman of limited means who makes her way as something of a matchmaker."

"Why are you asking about her?"

"Two weeks, Miss Keyes." He turned and opened the door to the room she'd just left.

"Your grace," she said, but he did not stop. "Why are you asking about Lady Winifred?"

He disappeared inside the library and the door clicked quietly shut behind him.

Chapter Seventeen

Honey could not believe how thrilled she was to be back in smoky, smelly, crowded London; back in her relatively small, snug house; back in her less than luxurious bedchamber—at least when compared to her accommodation of the past weeks.

Freddie, of course, knew something had happened to Honey during her trip their very first night.

They had eaten dinner together, just the two of them, since their other housemate, Serena, was now working at the country home of the wealthy young industrialist Gareth Lockheart.

"You look different, Honoria," Freddie said as they sat down to tea in Honey's favorite room, the tiny sitting room she thought of as the parlor.

"I've got oodles of freckles on my nose, haven't I?" Honey said, purposely misunderstanding her friend's gentle probing. "I'm afraid I was outside in the sun and forgot my hat several times."

Freddie was the last person to ever push or pry. As close as they'd been for the last six years, they had never spoken of their pasts.

Oh, Honey had talked about her father, of course, but never about her girlhood infatuation with Simon Fairchild.

An infatuation which had officially ended just after midnight on her last day at Whitcomb.

"Have you seen Miles?" she asked her friend, hoping to lead the topic away from herself.

"Yes, he has returned. He will come to dine tomorrow if you are free."

Honey reached across to take the teacup and saucer. "I have no plans." She shook her head at the offer of biscuits and sat back in her favorite chair, kicking off her slippers and tucking her feet beneath her.

Ah. Home.

"When will you start the portraits?" Freddie asked, stirring milk into her tea.

"After I have a few days to rest." The last thing Honey wanted to think about her first day home was the past few weeks.

"And what about you? Anyone new in my absence?"

"I have just met with the Duchess of Shearing about her twin daughters."

"Ah," Honey nodded. "I understand she can no longer walk."

Freddie's dove-gray eyes, so different than Honey's muddy gray, clouded over. "Yes, she has become worse, until she cannot even walk with her cane." She shook her head. "And not yet forty."

"What is wrong with her, do you know?"

"I don't believe even the doctors know. In any case, I am very grateful to Lady Cleaves for recommending me to her. Shearing is a stickler and I'm not sure he will approve of his wife's idea to engage me."

Honey knew many people did not view Freddie's *business* with approval. A widow with no means was expected to either remarry, drudge for her family, or starve. Not stand up on her own two feet and take charge of her future.

Honey set her cup in her saucer. "When will you know?"

"The duchess did not say, but the girls have run wild, according to her. They will need the rest of the year if they are to be ready for next Season, which she has indicated is the duke's expectation."

Honey had never met His Grace of Shearing, but she had once seen him when she'd accompanied her father to the Royal Portrait Gallery. He'd been older than her father and had emanated the same cold power she'd felt around Plimpton. They were the men who shaped Britain, and, by extension, the world. Honey shivered.

"Are you cold?"

She looked up to find Freddie watching her with quiet concern. "No, just tired. I think I shall have an early night."

That night had been over two weeks ago, and only recently had Honey begun to feel normal.

Part of her had been privately counting the days until she would openly defy the duke.

Well, it was now seventeen days after returning to London, and the sun was still shining—albeit behind grit, smoke and haze—and Honey had survived Plimpton's displeasure.

She'd heard not a whisper about the scandal of that night, proving that the duke's power to quash rumors was greater than he'd expected.

Honey spent the best five hours of the day—the early morning—in her studio. She'd started Rebecca's portrait first, since she found that she missed the young girl.

Not until there was a tap on the door did she come up for air.

"Lady Sedgewick is in the parlor, Miss. Did you want to join her for tea? Or should I bring you a tray?"

Honey put down her brush and reached back to untie her smock. "I need to take a break for an hour. Tell her I'll be right up, Mrs. Brinkley."

Honey rarely worked past one or two o'clock and decided that she would spend the rest of the afternoon going over the account books, which had sat untouched since before her journey to Whitcomb.

Freddie was already preparing the tea by the time Honey came into the parlor. Her friend's pale porcelain complexion was even paler than usual.

"Are you unwell?" Honey asked.

Freddie fixed her with her silvery stare, the delicate skin beneath her eyes bruised.

The smile she gave Honey was, on the surface, the same as usual. But something was not right. She handed Honey her tea, along with two biscuits.

"Thank you," Honey said, absently. "What is wrong, Freddie? You look exhausted."

"I'm afraid I had some rather disappointing news yesterday and it disturbed my sleep."

The room was cozy and warm, but Honey's hands felt like blocks of ice. "What is it?"

"I received a message from the Duke of Shearing letting me know his daughters would not require my services."

"Why?"

Freddie's eyebrows arched at the abrupt question. "I don't know, my dear. It is hardly the type of thing a duke would be likely to share." She took a sip of tea.

"Well, it's rather rotten of him, but I daresay something will come along," Honey said, far more heartily than she felt.

Freddie nodded absently.

Honey took a sip, lowered her cup, and sighed. "Please, you haven't told me the whole of it, have you?"

"I just received this." She held up a piece of pale green parchment.

"What is it?"

"Lady Mayfield has changed her mind and, it seems, won't need me for her niece after all."

The duke's voice was clear in her mind. *"She is a widow of limited means who makes her way as something of a matchmaker."*

Honey's full teacup hit the threadbare Aubusson carpet, bounced twice, and then clattered to a stop on the exposed wood.

"Goodness!" Freddie set down her own cup and saucer with the flawless grace for which she was so well known. "What is wrong, Honoria?"

Honey just shook her head, struggling to speak. "Nothing," she croaked, unable to stop shaking her head. "Nothing." She stood and went to the bell pull that she almost never used, giving it two sharp yanks.

Freddie came to stand beside her and laid a hand on her shoulder. "You are frightening me."

"I need to send a message. Immediately," she added, staring out the window that looked over the back garden, usually her favorite view. Today she did not even see it. Instead, she saw the duke.

"I ask you not to go against my will on this matter, Miss Keyes."

Honoria closed her eyes. Oh God.

The door opened behind her. "Miss Keyes, you rang?" her housekeeper asked, her voice breathy from running and pulsing with concern.

"I need to hire a messenger."

"A messenger?" Freddie and Mrs. Brinkley said at the same time.

"I'm going to quickly write a letter and I need you to summon a boy to deliver it to The Swan with Two Necks. I will pay for their fastest rider."

Mrs. Brinkley nodded. "Very good, ma'am, I shall go fetch someone."

The door shut and Honey strode to the small writing desk.

"Honey."

She stopped and turned at the unprecedented sound of Freddie raising her voice. "I'm sorry Freddie—I don't mean to act so dramatic. It's just that I suddenly recalled something I forgot at Whitcomb."

Now Freddie's confusion was complete. "Whitcomb? But what could be that important? You will have to pay a great deal to send such a message."

Honey couldn't bear to tell her friend that Freddie would have to pay a great deal more if she didn't send the message.

Chapter Eighteen

Simon was accustomed to the way the old woman's eyes widened and then quickly slid away from his damaged face.

It was the same reaction he got from anyone who wasn't either a cretin or under the age of twelve; those were the ones who openly gawked.

"I'm here to see Miss Keyes." He held out a card and the old woman took it in a hand that looked to be covered in flour and squinted at the card.

Too late, it occurred to him she likely could not read. "I am Lord Saybrook," he said.

She heaved a sigh. "Aye. Well, tha best come in."

Simon almost smiled; what an unusual housekeeper.

"I be Cook here, not a footman or butler," she grumbled, making Simon wonder if he'd spoken out loud.

She started toward the stairs and then seemed to recall his presence. "Come along now, if they want tha I don't wish to make a second trip. If they don't." She shrugged, not bothering to elaborate on that contingency.

Simon followed her hunched form up to the second floor where she stopped in front of the third door. Simon could hear voices on the other side.

She pounded with a fist the size of a ham, leaving white knuckle marks on the mahogany wood before seizing the handle, opening it a miserly crack, and shoving her head in the gap.

Honey's voice came from the other side of the door, "Yes, Una?"

"Ye've a caller. Lord Lanebridge or summat."

Simon snorted, diverted. Too bad Wyndham wasn't here to enjoy such treatment.

The room beyond was utterly silent.

There was the sound of somebody clearing their throat and then, "Please bring him up."

"Well, I already did that, didn't I?" the old crone snapped, pushing past Simon and stomping back toward the stairs.

"Lord Saybrook," Honey said, coming to take the place her cook had just vacated, her body blocking the entrance

He bowed, still holding his hat and cane. "Miss Keyes."

She just stared.

Simon tapped his hat on his thigh, wondering what the convention was in this household. Should he put his hat back on?

She looked down at the tapping and sprang to life.

"Oh, goodness—Una didn't take your hat and cane." She snatched both from his fingers and stepped aside. "Do come in. We were just finishing tea."

Beyond her were two others, a beautiful blond woman and a man who looked vaguely familiar.

"Lord Saybrook, let me present Lady Winifred Sedgwick and Miles Ingram."

The light came on at the sound of the man's name. He bowed low to the icy-looking blonde and then turned to the other occupant. "It's been a long time, Captain Ingram."

Ingram's mouth curved but his smile never reached his eyes. "I've cashed out. Just Ingram will be fine, Saybrook."

"Please, have a seat," Honey said, when the silence began to stretch.

Simon took a seat on the settee, the last unoccupied place to sit in the tiny room other than the writing desk or window seat.

"Would you care for some tea? This is cold but I could ring for more?"

Simon smiled, tempted by the thought of the contumacious cook playing parlor maid. "No thank you." He turned his gaze back to Ingram, whom he suddenly recalled with startling clarity. "How is your hand?"

The other man's eyes flickered. "Better than no hand."

Simon supposed it was the only thanks he'd ever get for saving Ingram's hand, not to mention his life. Not that he was interested in gratitude.

"You two were acquainted in the War?"

Simon let Ingram answer Honoria's question. "Yes, I met Lord Saybrook. Once."

Tension poured off the other man in waves.

Well, well, well. Here was another damaged dandy.

Simon had to smile. Ingram even looked a little like him—or at least what Simon used to look like: tall, blond, blue-eyed, handsome, charming.

Well, Simon was still tall and blue-eyed.

"Are you staying at your brother's house in town, my lord?"

Simon turned at the sound of Honoria's voice. "I don't know yet. I've only just arrived."

Her eyes flickered over his dusty riding clothes, which her friend—Lady Sedgewick—had frowningly noticed when he'd walked into the room.

"Could I have a moment with you, Miss Keyes. Alone." It was rude, but Simon was exhausted after the long ride.

The countess colored and Ingram seemed to double in size like a venomous exotic reptile. Simon ignored them both.

If Ingram had some sort of lingering bone to pick with him then Simon would love nothing more than to thrash it out with the other man at some point. But that wasn't what he was there for today.

"Of course," Miss Keyes said, her face redder than her friend's. "Perhaps a walk in the garden?"

Simon opened the sitting room door and shut it behind her.

"They don't know," he said flatly as he followed her down the stairs.

"No, they don't."

She led him onto a small terrace that led to a pretty garden.

"There is a bench just over there." She pointed but Simon was looking at her face, which had gone beet red as she recalled the last time they'd been in a garden with benches.

He followed her down a path surrounded by neatly pruned rose bushes and toward a tiny sitting area with only one bench. She sat all the way on one side.

Simon remained standing. "The duke tells me you have reconsidered my offer."

Her gray eyes blazed up at him. "Did he tell you what he did?"

"No, but I can imagine. Did he pressure you by threatening your career?"

"Worse. He threatened Lady Sedgewick's livelihood and she is not like me—she does not have a comfortable home and a nest egg. She needs to work for her bread and the duke has already snatched two pieces from her grasp."

If she expected her words to surprise him, she was destined to be disappointed.

"I already told you, Miss Keyes: my brother will do whatever is necessary to get what he wants. You should be glad he has only meddled with a few of your friend's potential clients. It is easily within his power to make her a pariah."

The color drained from her cheeks. "What kind of monster is he?"

Simon felt a protective twinge toward his brother at her words.

"He is a powerful man. That is what they are like, Miss Keyes. That is how they get and keep power." Simon shrugged. "And you and I are just as vulnerable to his will and whim as your friend, Lady Sedgewick You can fight him, but you've already seen some of what he is willing to do." He saw the frustrated fury in her taut face and felt a pang of sympathy. "I am sorry about that night and what it has led to. Truly."

"I am an adult, not a child, my lord. I was there that night, half of what happened is my fault."

Simon did not think it would be wise to argue the matter. He also didn't see any point in telling her that her life would be a disaster when word of what they'd been doing in his brother's study finally came out. Which it would—things like this *always* came out. The duke could only hold them in fear for so long. And when the truth came out? It would not be Simon who would suffer. I would be Honoria Keyes and anyone who associated with her. It was not right, or fair, but it was the way of things.

He realized she was still waiting for an answer from him. "I can tell you from personal experience that I have never won a battle of wills against my brother. Never. But his winning streak may be at an end."

She frowned, rightly suspicious. "What do you mean?"

"I mean I know a way we can thwart him."

Hope flared in her eyes. "You mean I won't have to—"

"No, you will still have to marry me. But afterwards," he felt a grin take control of his mouth and knew it was not a pretty sight. "Afterwards we can beat him."

"How."

"I know you do not wish to marry, but I am willing to make a bargain with you."

"What kind of bargain?"

"My brother wants me to marry because he wants an heir."

"But *you* are his heir."

He didn't want to tell her what Wyndham thought: that Simon would not live that long.

"The duke is worried I'll never marry. His purpose in life since the moment he learned that his wife couldn't have any more children has been to see me married." He gave her a tight smile. "I will let him think he has achieved that purpose. For a time."

She shook her head. "I don't understand any of this. I know why I would marry you—your brother has made it patently obvious that I must do as he says. By why are you buckling to his will? Wouldn't it make him equally angry if you continued to refuse to marry? Why become his pawn in this?"

Again, he knew she would not believe that any part of his decision sprang from gentlemanly or chivalric reasons. Hell, he wasn't sure he believed it himself.

So, he decided to tell part of the truth. "I want my life back—I want to be at Everley, getting on with doing what I planned all those years ago. My brother holds my inheritance and has the power to continue to do so until I marry or turn thirty-five. Even then, he can make matters uncomfortable. Besides, if I'm married to you, he will stop throwing young girls like Lady Rosalind into my path. If I'm married to you, he'll stop hounding me. As for us presenting him with an heir? Well, he can hardly do anything to either of us if one is not forthcoming, can he?"

Simon watched as understanding bloomed in her eyes.

A pink stain spread over her high cheekbones. "Please speak plainly, sir."

"Very well. I mean that we shall marry, but we will have no children. Ever."

She gasped softly. "You would deprive yourself of children to spite your brother? That is how far you will go to thwart him?"

Wyndham's face rose up in Simon's mind—how he'd looked upon learning that Cecily had lost their first child. And then the second, and the third. And then after his fourth child had died.

No. It would not be a deprivation to avoid such pain. Women and children were fragile and the childbirth process was a brutal one. He had seen enough death in the war to last him a thousand lifetimes. The very last thing Simon wanted in his life was to surround himself with more death. Women died in childbirth all the time, infants with them. He'd been too stupid to avoid the war, but he *could* avoid this.

He looked up at her. Honoria Keyes did not need to know all that—nobody did.

So, instead, he just nodded and said, "Yes, that is how far I am willing to go."

***

Honey felt as if he had slapped her. Perhaps she had misheard him? She had to make certain.

"So, you mean—"

"I mean, no children. Ever. That is the only way to win against the duke. Deny him what he wants."

The logic was sound. It was also twisted beyond anything Honey could have come up with. This man was as bad as the Duke of Plimpton, as cold and as devoid of anything that constituted a human heart. And all in the pursuit of his goal, which was to deny his brother *his* goal.

Honey laughed. Simon frowned, but said nothing.

She shook her head, too rattled to play guessing games. "You are not offering me children or a family. Just what are you offering, my lord?"

"Marry me and you will have security, a respectable position in society, and the freedom to paint when and where you want. You will also have your own life: Freedom, Miss Keyes; I will not stand in your way and you will not be tied to either a husband or a home."

So, these were her two options: she could destroy her dearest friend's life or live a childless, loveless existence—not that she had cherished any expectations for either of those things for many years. But not cherishing them and being told you would never have them were two different matters, entirely.

Still, if Simon were actually willing to take such extreme measures to exact revenge on his brother then he was the last man on earth who *should* have children.

They would suffer together.

The anger inside her was so potent and cold it surprised even Honey. There was no point to any of this soul-searching—it didn't matter what she wanted. The duke would crush the people she loved if she did not do what he said. Subject closed.

Honey had too many questions and most of them she didn't want to put into words. She picked the least repulsive one.

"Where would we live?"

He looked surprised, as if he'd expected more resistance.

"Wherever you like. I will have Everley as soon as we marry. I will also have access to my inheritance, so if you want to live in London, we may buy a house, or you may continue on as you are."

Honey could only stare; she could not believe this is what her life had been reduced to. And she truly could not believe that she had ever thought she was in love with this man. How could he marry her for no other reason than to foil his brother?

She wanted to kick him out her front door and down the steps of her house, but she had already seen what the duke could do in only a few weeks.

She thought about Serena, Miles, even Portia, Annis, and Lorelei, although they were far away from London. The duke would be a man with a long reach.

Honey forced herself to look at the man beside her, the man who would probably be her husband for as long as she lived. A man who wanted no children of her body—who wanted that part of their marriage not even to exist.

It was insulting—no, it was *beyond* insulting. But she told herself she no longer cared. Being married to him—as much as she now hated him—would present no problems. At least not like it would have if she had still loved him.

"So, we shall get married and then return to our respective residences and go about our lives?"

He nodded. "Just so."

"And people will not consider this strange—us living in separate houses? Separate cities? This won't make people talk?"

"What do you care?"

"Part of the reason I'm doing this is to preserve some vestige of my reputation so that I might continue my work." She didn't bother keeping the sarcasm out of her voice.

"Fine," he said shortly. "There are over twenty bedrooms at Everley and other rooms that would be suitable for painting. We can cohabitate and yet never actually see each other's faces." He gave vent to an irritable sigh. "Trust me, Miss Keyes, if you wish to project an image of a normal aristocratic marriage, we shall be able to do so with little effort."

Honey knew he was right. She'd lived at Whitcomb long enough to witness an *aristocratic* marriage first-hand. She had never actually seen the duke and duchess in the same room, yet nobody seemed to notice anything untoward.

Regardless of how the duke and duchess chose to live, projecting an image of a normal marriage would be important for Honey.

She never wanted her friends to find out why she'd had to marry. She already knew that Freddie would fight this wedding tooth and claw if she learned that Honey was only agreeing to this sham to protect Freddie.

And if Miles ever learned what the duke had done to Freddie?

Honey recoiled at the thought; she knew Miles would call out the duke for attempting to destroy his friend.

Her friends loved her and would rush to defend her, ruining themselves in the process.

She eyed Simon, who was waiting with a mildly interested expression.

Honey had to force herself to say the next sentence. "And we will have lovers, just as all members of the aristocracy seem to do?"

The undamaged side of his face darkened and Honey was more than a little surprised that such a man could still blush.

After a long, awkward moment, he shrugged. "You may have as many lovers as you wish, so long as there are no children."

It was her turn to blush. She did not tell him there would be no lovers. She had lived for twenty-eight years and had only kissed a man in the past month. The likelihood of her kissing another was less than slim.

Honey looked at the man who had been her dream for fourteen years. Part of her wanted to hit him with a brick and part of her wanted to weep. But the rest of her knew there was no way to avoid this.

She jerked out a nod. "Fine. I will marry you. But I absolutely do not want a grand ceremony."

Chapter Nineteen

This is your last chance, Honey. It's not too late," Miles said.

Honey looked into Miles's anxious blue eyes and smiled calmly. It wasn't an act; she actually *felt* calm this morning. "I am ready, Miles."

She was. She had been up since before dawn and had been wide awake and ready when Freddie knocked on her door to help her with her wedding day preparations.

Now they were sitting in St. Olav's, waiting for the groom to arrive.

The three of them had arrived at the odd church early. It had amused Honey that her friends had eyed the gruesome entrance gate on Seething Street with more than a little trepidation.

"You picked this church?" Miles asked for at least the fifth time.

Honoria smiled. "Yes, Miles. I picked this church. My father used to bring me here. He greatly enjoyed the macabre atmosphere.

"Yes, an excellent spot for a wedding."

Freddie laid a hand on his arm to quiet him, which she'd been doing almost constantly over the last three days, making Honey wonder—not for the first time—if there was more than friendship between her quiet friend and the gorgeous dancing master.

"I still can't believe you didn't tell the others," Miles persisted.

By others he meant their friends from the Stefani school.

"I'll tell them afterward," Honey said, yet again.

She didn't want them all rushing to London to attend the grim little ceremony. She especially didn't want to answer the questions they'd ask—especially her friend Serena, who could have worked for the Inquisition.

"I want to tell you something," Miles blurted, as if the words had used a battering iron to break free of his mouth.

"Miles—" Freddie began.

"No, Freddie. I shan't forgive myself if I keep this from her." He turned back to Honey, his usually lazy blue eyes burning. "Your betrothed was rather well-known on the Continent."

Honey said nothing. Part of her wanted to hear what he had to say; part of her felt like she was engaging in gossip about a man to whom she owed her loyalties. Or at least *some* loyalty.

"Whenever there was a mission or skirmish or anything dangerous—something that no sane man would volunteer for—Major Lord Simon Fairchild would be at the top of the list. That is how I met him." Miles shoved a hand through his soft golden curls, the action uncharacteristically jerky for such a graceful man. "He was part of a small group composed of four men from my unit and one other man who knew the way—Saybrook. Our mission was what is called a lightening attack. The target was a country estate where the frogs were said to be holding three officers captive." Miles's brow was sheened with sweat even though the church was cool.

"Miles, you don't have—"

He continued as if he didn't hear her. "Fairchild was only supposed to show us the way, wait in a separate location for us to complete our mission, and then return without us if we did not come back after twenty-four hours." He let out a shaky sigh. "We walked right into a trap. They weren't keeping any officers at the old house—at least nobody alive. Not only that, but they were not using the location as a prison. Instead, it was a staging area and they were an advance group."

Miles swallowed hard; his gaze distant. "They started torturing us, one after another, working in a quick, brutal fashion that told us they'd soon be on the move again. I thanked God that Saybrook would be able to get back to HQ and tell them the truth—that it was—" he broke off, gulped, and shook his head. "Never mind what it was. Two of the men with me were dead within six hours. They were working on me and another man when the door swung open and Saybrook came striding in." He made a sound of utter amazement at whatever it was he saw in his mind's eye. "He walked in with a grin on his face, his steels—holstered at his waist—trailing blood. He had a pistol in each hand and he shot both men dead center. One of them was so close to me that—" he stopped abruptly, as if suddenly recalling to whom he was speaking.

He cleared his throat and then continued, "The other man they'd been torturing was already dead and I was not far behind him. Saybrook paused long enough to throw my coat over me and reload his pistols. He then slung me over his shoulder and carried me out of there."

Miles gave a snort of disbelief. "There was a trail of dead bodies leading from the room where we'd been held captive all the way out of the house. There were Frenchies *everywhere*. I am not exaggerating; Saybrook can walk between bullets. We should have both died a dozen times getting out of there." He stared at Honoria with anguished eyes. "Three of my best friends died that day but Saybrook waltzed into that house as if he didn't have a care in the world, plucked me up like a baby from a pram, and hauled me away without even a scratch."

Honey did not know what to say—did not know why he told her this, although she was grateful that he had.

"I'm telling you this," he said, as if reading her mind, "Because I want you to know two things. First, Saybrook only does what he wants to do. Always. He should have gone back to HQ with the information. Instead, he jeopardized thousands of lives disobeying orders and coming for me. Second, and far more important for you, Honey, that man does not care if he lives or dies. Because that was not the first time that he pulled such a stunt and it wouldn't be the last. He was not famed for his behavior—he was *notorious* for it."

The ancient wooden door behind them opened with a screech and they all three turned.

There stood Simon, his tall body limned by the light.

"Good Lord," he said, "don't tell me I'm late?"

***

"I Simon Bevil Charles Fairchild do take Honoria Agnes Keyes …."

It was really happening; Simon was getting married.

He had been in an odd fugue state ever since arriving in London.

After leaving Honey's house that first day he'd gone directly to Doctors Commons and laid out the twenty guineas for a special license.

With that in his pocket he had gone to Grenier's Hotel, which was conveniently located and suited his plans: Tedious plans that involved purchasing clothes, ordering new boots, dropping in at Whites—not an activity he was looking forward to—and generally making himself presentable.

Simon had not been in big crowds or mingled with people who didn't know him since returning from Belgium.

He had always believed that he had a strong constitution, but after stopping at several busy posting inns, he was fed up with being gawked at.

He was also exhausted.

After procuring the license he'd fallen into his bed and slept until noon the following day. As a result, he'd been late to his meeting with his wife-to-be, who'd appeared to be in the midst of a domestic whirlwind when he was shown into her parlor.

Her glorious hair was hidden under an ugly mobcap and her gown was old and out of style and generally a good match for his own clothing—a reminder that his plans for the rest of the day included shopping.

Once she'd seated him and placed an unwanted cup of tea in his hands she went on the offensive. "Have you made any arrangements for the service?"

Feeling like the greatest dolt in the nation, Simon admitted he had not. What the devil had he been thinking? Or not thinking?

"I wish to marry at Saint Olav's."

He had wracked his brains but had come up with nothing.

She'd noticed his blank look. "Seething Lane."

The name conjured up skulls and a cemetery, but not a church. "I seem to recall a rather unusual—"

"That is the lychgate—it has a skull frieze."

Ah, yes. Rather macabre but fitting for a union that had been forced on her, he supposed. "I have no issue with your choice," he'd said, taking a sip of tea and biting back a grimace. He would have to tell her after they were married that he hated tea.

"As the ceremony is supposed to be two days hence perhaps you might make arrangements. Today."

Simon had smiled at the silky sarcasm in her voice; his wife-to-be was not a shrinking violet. That was good, he did not like spiritless women. "I shall handle it," he promised. It was dreadfully short notice but he suspected a proper donation would help ease matters.

She'd sniffed and they enjoyed their beverages accompanied by the tick of the mantle clock and the muffled sound of street noises.

"I should like Lady Sedgewick and Mr. Ingram as my witnesses."

"I'm glad to hear it—I don't have anyone."

"What are your plans after the ceremony?"

For a moment he'd wondered if she thought he would be heading off back to Whitcomb on Loki.

"Plans?" He'd blinked, feeling sluggish and stupid that he could not seem to keep pace with her. "I haven't any plans—I suppose I thought you would want some sort of feast here afterward." Lord, didn't that sound grim? His justifiably hostile wife, her two hostile friends, and Simon.

But she'd surprised him. "I would like to dispense with a wedding breakfast and leave for Everley immediately."

"Ah." Finally something he had an answer for. "That might be a bit of a problem."

"Why?"

"There are tenants there until the end of the month. Wyndham—in his wisdom—had already terminated their lease after I returned from Belgium. But as they've occupied the place for decades he thought it generous to give them a few extra weeks to pack their possessions."

"So where did you plan to take me?"

"Back to Whitcomb. There's plenty of room."

She'd puffed up like an angry hen, her eyes as hard and gray as balls of lead. "I will not stay under your brother's roof."

Simon had experienced a twinge of pity for his brother; Wyndham had earned himself an enemy for life, it seemed.

"I see. Well, that does present a problem. Especially since all the roofs we currently have access to are his." He'd glanced around at her tiny parlor. "Or here."

Her grimace told him what she thought about him living in her house.

They'd stared at one another.

After an hour of question and answer, ruling out Plimpton House, Wyndham's hunting box in Leicestershire, another in Devon, and several others, they had finally decided to spend the next few weeks in Brighton. She had refused the fashionable house the duke owned there, so Simon had agreed to whatever hotel she wanted.

"Lord Saybrook?"

Simon looked up and realized the vicar, Honoria, and their two witnesses were all staring at him. And he was in church, getting married.

He cleared his throat and looked beseechingly at the vicar. "I beg your pardon?" he asked when it became clear he would receive no help from his wife-to-be.

"The ring, my lord? Do you have one?"

That was one thing he did have. He reached into the pocket of his coat and extracted a diamond of obscene proportions. His new wife sucked in an audible breath at the dazzling, tear-drop-shaped monster and even the vicar appeared momentarily stunned.

Their two witness, he noted smugly, looked awed, for a change.

"Please repeat after me …"

Simon did, and then they were man and wife.

Chapter Twenty

"A re you sure you don't wish to stay one more night?" Freddie
asked, uncharacteristically anxious as she helped Honey finish
the last of her packing.

Honey had packed most of her clothing the day she'd spoken to
Simon, who'd informed her they had no home and had—insanely—
believed that she would stay within a mile of his brother.

She snorted at the memory of his stunned expression and stuffed
a pelisse into the remaining portmanteau. *Men!*

Freddie quickly removed the wadded-up garment and folded it
properly.

"Are you quite sure you will be alright, Honoria? I still don't
understand why you are doing this." The personal comment was
unprecedented and went to show how worried her friend was.

She took Freddie by the shoulders and sat her down on the bed.

They'd had three whirlwind days to sort through household
matters and the logistics of moving her most important possessions to
Everley.

There had been no time to talk about why she was marrying a
man her two friends did not seem to like—or at least trust.

Honey could only be glad her other friends were not here for the
fiasco.

"Take lovers," her friend Portia had once advised her female teachers, scandalizing all of them except Lorelei, who was frequently vocal about the oppression of females in marriage after reading some tract by Blake.

Of course, Portia herself had recently married and seemed to be happily in love, so presumably her advice would now be different.

Not that Honey's marriage was even close to being a love-match. *At least not on his side ...*

Honey hastily pushed that thought from her mind and concentrated on Freddie and her worries. "I am happy with this marriage—thrilled, in fact." She made herself smile.

"You don't look happy. And I do not understand why things have proceeded with such haste? Why have you not allowed us to tell anyone? And why—"

"I'm not pleased about the speed at which things are happening, but that's rather my fault." The only thing she'd shared with her friends about why she was getting married—that was true—was the episode in the duke's study and the half-dozen witnesses. Freddie, far more than Miles, understood why she must marry the man.

Her friend nodded but her cheeks developed two rather alarming red spots.

"What is it Freddie?"

"About tonight."

"Tonight?"

"Yes, your wedding night."

It was Honey's turn to blush. "Oh, that."

"Do you know what will happen?"

Honey did not tell her that nothing would happen—that this was to be a childless marriage. Instead she nodded. "I was raised around artists. They are rather indiscreet," she said, hoping that would be enough to put an end to a topic that was mortifying them both.

Freddie took her hand in a crushing grasp. "If you find it too unbearable, just know that it does not last forever."

Honey blinked at the loathing and passion in Freddie's normally cool eyes. She'd heard women complain, in vague ways, about their husband's carnal desires, but none of them had looked as horrified as her friend. Not for the first time did she wonder about the other woman's brief marriage to the Earl of Sedgewick. Part of her wanted to ask Freddie what had happened, another part feared what she might learn.

But now was hardly the time to ask, even if her friend was willing to share.

Honey told herself that she should feel glad she would never have to worry about *that* part of marriage. But those two kisses—and more—with Simon made that a difficult belief to cling to. It was even more difficult to put those memories out of her mind—to put them in that locked room with all the other thoughts and emotions that were too uncomfortable to consider in the harsh light of day.

Honey looked at the watch Freddie wore pinned to the bodice of her gown and stood. "I must hurry, he will be here soon."

***

The chaise to Brighton was not as luxurious as the one the duke had arranged for her trip to Whitcomb, but Lord Saybrook said it was the best he could find on such short notice—after she told him that she would not ride in the ducal coach he'd planned to use.

Not only was the carriage less spacious and comfortable, but this time she was not alone in it. This time her long-legged, virile, hooded-eyed husband was with her.

He had assisted Honey into the front facing seat, said a mocking goodbye to Freddie and Miles—who'd glowered at him—and hopped inside, dropping into the seat facing her before rapping on the roof.

He looked across at her as the carriage sprang into motion. "Well, Lady Saybrook."

Honey started at the name; she had not even considered the title. She was a marchioness and would one day be a duchess. The knowledge left her cold.

She lifted her eyebrows at her husband.

"Oh come," he said, unrepressed by her quelling look. "We are in this together now. We used to be friends," he saw something on her face and chuckled. "Alright, amiable acquaintances? How is that?" He didn't wait for an answer. "My point is that we once got on well enough. We ought to make the best of it, don't you think?"

He was right, of course. They were now stuck with one another. Perhaps they could find some manner of living together that would be good for both of them.

She looked into his expectant eyes and opened her mouth. And then she remembered what he'd said about no children and taking lovers, and all her good intentions flew out the carriage window like frantic sparrows.

"I would like to get some rest," she lied, secretly pleased when his mouth tightened at her snub.

She closed her eyes and laid her head back.

***

Simon wished he were riding beside the carriage on Loki, as he had first thought to do. But instead he'd decided to make peace and ride with his prickly new wife.

Unfortunately, he had sent Loki back to Whitcomb so now he was stuck with her, unless he wanted to rent a job hack at Grunstead, where they would spend their first evening as a married couple.

He brooded on that thought as he stared at her. He could tell she wasn't sleeping even though he couldn't see her eyes. She'd tilted back her head and exposed the long, elegant expanse of her throat. His groin stirred as he recalled the last time he'd seen her head thrown back like that.

Part of the reason that he'd agreed to his brother's plan to marry Miss Keyes was the memory of that night in the study.

Simon liked his new wife in a variety of ways—her responsive body being only one of them. She was a fascinating blend of the girl she used to be and the woman she had become. She did not trust him, and he could not blame her. Simon did not—could not—trust himself. Not with so much of his mind a mystery to him.

Recently, however, memories of her had begun to pop up in his raddled mind like plants pushing through long-dormant soil.

Simon now recalled that she had worshipped him all those years ago. He had been flattered back then. What man did not like female attention—especially young men and especially such naked adoration?

But he had also been dismissive of her hero worship. After all, a great many young ladies had looked at him with similar admiration in their eyes. It was lucky for Honey that he'd been an honorable sprout and had handled her with kid gloves.

Honey's father had taken additional steps to ensure Simon's good behavior.

"My daughter has no experience with either boys her own age or handsome young men, my lord." Daniel Keyes had been an imposing man, far more masculine than Simon had envisioned a painter would be.

"I understand, sir," young Simon had said with the respect he'd shown his elders back in those days.

"Do you?" Danger had glinted in Keyes's eyes.

"Should I stop taking her for ices and such things? I've made sure she has her governess or a footman or —"

"No, I do not wish you to stop. It would break her heart—which will happen soon enough when you leave. I just wanted to make sure you understood the power you have over her."

Simon pulled his eyes from the vulnerable architecture of his wife's neck and turned his gaze to the carriage window.

But his thoughts were not so easily pulled from the past.

Memories, it seemed, were like weeds. Once he'd begun unearthing them, he could not stop others from thrusting their way into the light of day.

One of the memories he would have preferred to stay buried was the day that he'd learned of his nephew's death.

Simon had gone directly to Whitcomb after leaving Daniel Keyes's studio, riding through the night, reckless and terrified and ill with fear—for his brother. He truly did not think Wyndham could weather such a loss. Not again.

He'd returned home to find the transformation had already taken place: his brother was nothing but an animated shell; hard, impervious, and unyielding.

The days before the funeral had been agonizing and Simon had yearned for even a glimpse of Bella, whom he'd not been alone with for almost two months. But he'd learned that Bella and her mother and sister had decided to extend their stay in London.

He'd swallowed his disappointment; there would be time for Bella after they had put his nephew beside his siblings in the family crypt.

The ceremony had taken place in the small chapel at Whitcomb and the only attendants were Wyndham, Simon, and their mother. Not even Cecily had attended.

The duke had called Simon to his study directly afterward, poured them both drinks, and bade him to sit.

"I have news for you."

Simon could still recall that moment—the last time he'd been truly happy. Oh, it wasn't as if he'd been happy that day, of course.

He'd mourned his nephew's passing and his family's pain. But always with the knowledge that Bella waited for him; at the end of it all, she would be there.

"Arabella Frampton has married."

For one moment, he foolishly marveled that there could be two women in England with the exact same name.

Surely, he must have misheard?

But no, his brother had demolished that hope. "She married a Scottish earl, some acquaintance of her father's—MacLeish."

The glass Simon had been holding, a ruby crystal shot through with clear chevrons—glasses that had allegedly served Henry VIII when he'd stayed at Whitcomb—shattered. Cool liquid had seeped through the black satin funeral clothing he still wore.

Wyndham's gaze had flickered over the shards of glass and rapidly disappearing brandy but he had not moved.

"When?" Simon demanded.

"Yesterday, in Scotland. I believe they made a brief stop at her parents' house after returning from London and heading to MacLeish's estate some hours north of Edinburgh."

He'd barely heard his brother's words through the roaring in his ears.

"Simon? Simon!"

Even now, with so much of his past drifting back into place, Simon had no clear recollection of the days and weeks that followed that discussion.

The next memory he recalled was his brother dragging him from a London brothel and hauling him back to Whitcomb.

He had nightmarish flashes of shaking and shivering, a prisoner in his room, desperate for the oblivion that only the milk of the poppy could bring.

To this day Simon had no memory of who'd introduced him to the magical substance.

"You were poisoning yourself, Simon." His brother had said when Simon woke bound hand and foot to his bed.

A man in an old-fashioned black suit had lurked in the duke's shadow, like a witch's familiar.

"Doctor Hanley operates a special asylum where he has experience with such matters. I have arranged for him to treat you here, in the comfort of our own home." Wyndham had gestured for the spindly, nervous-eyed man to come forward, black leather bag in hand.

"I'll need to bleed you, my lord. And then we can begin—"

Simon had lunged from his bed, stopped only by the thick leather cuffs that held him to the four posts.

"If you touch me, I'll kill you," he'd snarled only inches from the man's sweaty, wide-eyed face.

The doctor had stumbled back, but the duke had merely nodded at someone behind Simon's head.

Two enormous hands landed on his shoulders to stop him from thrashing, while another set of big hands gagged him.

Simon fought like a demon, but the duke had employed men the size of oaks.

He'd been carefully subdued, restrained, and forced to endure the good doctor's nightmarish treatments.

He'd been imprisoned, fed gruel and watered wine, and bled for days.

Finally, one morning he woke up cool and lucid, his hands and feet no longer restrained. His body no longer slick with sweat and stench. It was as if a fever had broken.

He'd felt shame at how he'd behaved. His brother had lost three children and had still gone on living. Simon had lost a woman who had agreed to marry another man—clearly she had never loved him—and he'd behaved like an animal.

He had vowed to start a new life that day. And he had, for all of nine days, until Bella's sister delivered the letter to him.

It was her youngest sister Mary who'd found him when he'd been riding back from some estate errand for the duke.

"I'm not supposed to be here. Father would kill me." Mary h ad thrust a wrinkled rectangle of paper at him. "It's from Bella—I have had it for months, but you were away."

The paper had smelled of roses—Bella's scent.

Simon had torn open the letter with shaking hands.

"*My Beloved,*" both her looping, girlish hand and endearment had made his legs so weak that he'd left his horse grazing and gone to sit under a tree before continuing.

"*By the time you receive this I will be gone—beyond your reach in every sense of the word. My father is forcing me to marry an acquaintance of his from Scotland and—*"

Simon had cursed so loudly that his startled horse had cantered beyond his view.

Forced? But why? Mr. Frampton had always liked Simon.

Why?

Then he'd read the rest.

"*MacLeish is my father's age. A giant, cruel man who smells of port and unclean skin. He looks at me as if I were a chop of lamb and I shiver at what he will do to me when we are wed and I am in his power.*"

Simon had closed his eyes, too disgusted, furious, jealous to even see straight.

He'd forced himself to read on.

"*My father says His Grace of Plimpton came to see him the day after his son's death.*"

Simon could still recall the sickness that had unfurled in his belly at his brother's name.

"*You are his heir and he cannot have you marrying a mere baronet's daughter. He told my father to arrange this marriage and he offered more money than my father could turn away for my bride's dowry.*

I have only ever loved you, my dearest, sweetest, most gentle Simon. I will give my body to another man, but my heart will always belong to you.

Forever,

Your Bella"

"My lord?"

Simon's head jerked up; his wife was staring at him.

"What is it?" she asked, her forehead furrowed with concern. "You look almost murderous." She glanced out the window, as if to see what might have angered him.

Simon had allowed himself to slip into the past and had worked himself into a state; he was not fit company for anyone—especially not his virginal wife.

"Nothing is wrong," he lied, his voice gruff with anger—at himself. "I'm merely sore from jouncing in this bloody carriage."

There was a heavy silence and then, "Do your injuries pain you?"

"No." Yet another lie.

"Are you angry with me for declining your brother's coach?"

He turned on her, cruelly pleased when she flinched away from him.

"You had better understand one thing about me, *my dear*, I don't care enough to be angry with you."

She flushed deeply at his ugly words but sat up straight, no longer cringing away from him. Good, Simon wanted her anger, her hate. At least it made him feel something.

"You behave like an immature child. Only a short while ago you said you wished to make something of this marriage. Now you are speaking to me as if I am lower than dirt. Make up your mind—if you still have one."

Simon laughed, delighted by her fire. "You give as good as you get, don't you, Honey?"

"Don't call me that."

"Why not, it's your name?"

"It is a name for people who love me, and whom I love."

Her words were like nails dragging across his raw scars and he couldn't believe how much pain they left in their wake.

"Am I permitted to call you Honoria." It wasn't a serious question.

She scowled across at him. "If you have to speak to me at all, I'd rather you address me as *my lady.*"

Simon laughed. It seemed he'd chosen a wife worthy of him. At least when it came to hating.

Chapter Twenty-One

The sun had already set when they reached Grunstead.

Simon knew it was unusual to stop on the journey to Brighton but traveling in such confinement for too long was unbearable to him. Besides, there was no rush; they would be staying in a hotel in Brighton, they could just as well stay in one on the way there.

As the chaise rumbled toward the posting inn, something occurred to Simon.

"You don't have a maid."

He could barely see her face in the gloom of the carriage, but he could hear her snort. "You are only noticing that now?"

Simon ignored her question. "How will you see to yourself—change your clothing and whatnot?"

"The same way I have been doing all my life. You have no personal servant, either."

That was true, and Simon would bloody well miss the man, he knew that, already. "My valet has a constitutional dislike of riding across country like a maniac and I needed to be in London quickly—as you well know. Peel will join us in Brighton. You will need to engage a maid in Brighton."

"I will need to do no such thing."

He clamped his teeth down on an annoyed retort.

Already his brother would be angry to learn that they were not using the ducal coach, they had no outriders, and they weren't staying in the family house in Brighton.

The last thing they needed was more reasons for Wyndham to interfere in their business—or their marriage.

He should tell her that the duke would have conniptions if he learned Simon's wife was traveling without a body servant.

Yes, that's what he *should* do

But he was feeling miserable. And misery, it was said, loved some company.

"Time for lesson number two, *my lady*, this is a marriage of convenience. That means you'll behave in a way I find *convenient*. So, you'll engage a maid. Not only will you require such a person to see to your upkeep, but you will need her if you are to observe propriety."

An ugly laugh came out of the darkness. "Since when have you been concerned with propriety?"

Simon wasn't, he just felt like bossing her about for some unpleasant reason. He thought about telling her that, just to see her reaction. But he was too tired right now to enjoy a proper row. Perhaps later.

Quit being an arse, Simon. It's not her fault—none of it.

He stifled an irritated snarl at the voice, which was, once again, correct.

He inhaled deeply and then exhaled slowly. "I should not have spoken to you in such a manner," he said, and then waited. When she said nothing, he continued. "My brother, as you have seen, is a stickler for propriety. It would be better if he didn't learn you were traveling without a servant."

"Better for *whom*?"

He gave a weary laugh. "Us."

Before she could argue further, insult him, or accept his apology, the chaise rumbled to a halt.

Simon opened the door before the servant could get to it, eager as hell to get out of the stuffy carriage. He kicked down the steps and turned to assist his wife. She ignored his outstretched hand and held the side of the carriage instead as she descended.

Simon stared at her until she looked up at him and then he offered his arm. Whatever it was she saw on his face, she put her hand on his forearm and they entered the inn in silence.

The innkeeper was ready and waiting and they found themselves settled in their respective rooms in a flatteringly brief amount of time.

Once he'd washed his face in the basin of hot water provided and changed his cravat, he knocked on the adjoining door and reached for the handle.

It was locked.

"My lady?" he called through the heavy wood when there was no answer. He rattled the handle, his temperature rising. Was he really standing on the other side of a locked door from his wife of less than ten hours?

Her muffled voice came from the other side just as he was considering kicking it down. "What do you want?"

"Unlock. The. Door."

There was a long, annoying moment before the tumbler turned. The door opened a crack, barely enough to expose one eye. "What do you want, my lord?"

"Are you really going to make me converse with you through a door?"

"Yes."

Simon tapped his foot, his gaze locked on her single gray eye. The pupil was a pinprick, telling him more clearly than words what she felt about him.

"I'm going to have dinner sent up—when do you want it?"

"With you?"

"Yes, *with me*, in the private parlor." For one blasted moment he thought she was going to throw the invitation in his face or insist he eat in the public room. Simon honestly had no idea how he would respond.

"I shall be ready in an hour." The door snapped shut and the lock turned. Simon dropped his forehead onto the rough wood and closed his eyes; this was not an auspicious beginning.

***

Honey sagged against the door and worried her lower lip between her teeth. Why was she behaving this way? He had apologized and she was acting like a shrew. She had agreed to this marriage and now she was behaving as if he had forced it upon her.

You're still angry that he does not wish to have carnal relations with you.

Even though she was alone, Honey's face flamed.

"No. I am *not*," she said aloud, through gritted teeth.

And then felt like a fool for arguing with herself.

She crossed to her dressing table and stared at her reflection in the mirror, as if seeing herself would help her to admit what the problem was. She hated him, but she still loved him. She shook her head—how was such a thing even possible?

Because he hurt your feelings.

She ignored the voice, pulled the hatpin from her hat, and unpinned her hair—Honey's crowning glory, her father used to say.

She had to admit that her hair was pretty, even though she wasn't.

Oh, she wasn't ugly—she was worse: nondescript.

How she'd yearned to look like Portia Stefani. The half-Italian, half-English woman had features so bold they should have been unattractive. But there was something compelling in her flashing black eyes that was even more attractive than conventional beauty.

Honey adored the delicate, cool beauty of Freddie, or the fairy-like delicacy of Annis. Even Lorelei Fontenot, who could at best be called *unusual* looking with her small, triangular cat face and bushy black brows, would have been preferable to almost six feet of boredom.

She coiled her heavy braid into a coronet and secured it with a fistful of pins.

That only makes you look taller.

She didn't care.

Or so she told herself.

Honey had believed that she'd gotten over regretting her unfortunate height and bland looks years ago. It could only be her proximity to Simon that had brought such insecurities back.

Even with his hideous scarring he was mesmerizing. He'd been a very pretty young man, but he was now a battle-scarred Odysseus back from over a decade of war.

But was he back? Had any part of the Simon she'd once known—and loved—returned? It seemed to Honey that his body was here, but other than a few lightning-quick flashes, she'd seen nobody recognizable behind his achingly beautiful eyes.

Not that she was finding this new version of Simon any easier to resist than the old. As snappish and cruel as he could be, he still enthralled her.

"Fool," she accused her reflection, running her hands lightly over the smooth cap of hair, turning to the side to inspect her "crown." The simple style suited her and she looked her best. Not that she suspected the man waiting for her would even notice.

***

By the end of the meal Simon's spirits had, if not risen, then at least not fallen any further.

His wife had been a different person since sitting down to supper.

First, she had accepted his apology and then offered one of her own.

"I behaved badly when you offered to engage a maid for me." She admitted while spooning soup into her mouth, her eyes downcast.

Her apology made him feel restless. He'd opened his mouth to say it was no bother, but she wasn't finished.

"And I especially apologize for throwing your offer of friendship in your teeth earlier." She set down her spoon and looked up. "You are correct. We are married. There is no point in making life a misery for each other. I accept your olive branch." She hesitated and then gave him a shy smile, "Besides, I should hate to let your brother think he had forced us into something against our will and made us miserable."

Simon laughed. "That's the spirit, my lady."

"Please, call me Honoria."

Simon tried not to mind that she kept her pet name from him, but small steps were better than none.

They ate their meal and conducted careful conversation. He talked about his horses and she talked about her paintings.

Simon watched her eat the last of her berries and cream, aware the smudges beneath her eyes had not been there only a few days ago. He resolved to ease her tensions tonight. Truth be told, he'd been more than half-hard for three days thinking about their wedding night. He was a bit surprised—but beyond pleased—that she did not seem more anxious about losing her virginity. He could only assume her friend Lady Sedgewick had soothed her nerves on the topic.

Simon could have used somebody to sooth *his* nerves a little. He'd never bedded a virgin and had no interest in making a woman weep—especially not in bed. Still, it would just be the one night that was uncomfortable and then he would have access to her tall, willowy body on a regular basis—or at least whenever she chose to stay at Everley.

He picked up his wine and took a sip, his mouth curving into a smile. Perhaps marriage would not be so bad, after all.

Chapter Twenty-Two

Honey had just tied on her nightcap and crawled into bed when there was a soft tap on the door that led to the corridor, not the connecting door.

She frowned. "Yes?"

"It is Simon."

She swung her feet down to the floor and bit her lip. *What did he want?*

"Honoria?"

She rose, snatched her dressing gown off the back of the chair, and opened the door beyond a crack, but not much.

He held up a bottle with two glasses. "May I come in?"

"I was just getting into bed."

His eyes flickered to her nightcap and a notch formed between his unnaturally blue eyes.

The hand holding the bottle lowered. "Please?"

Honey realized the delicate peace they'd established at dinner was in the balance. Already. She stepped back and gestured to the small sitting area before the fire.

"Have a seat."

He held up the bottle. "Would you like a glass of wine?"

She shook her head. "I've already cleaned my teeth."

He expelled the air in his lungs slowly. "I see. Well, would you mind if *I* had a glass."

It did not sound like a question to her. "Please do."

She took a seat in the chair, leaving him the loveseat. He glanced at her, the loveseat, and then poured himself a glass and sat.

"So," he said.

She swallowed. "So."

"You were getting into bed."

She nodded.

"Weren't you forgetting something?"

Honey frowned. "I don't think so." He took a drink of wine. A *big* drink. "Did I forget something?" she asked when it seemed he was finished speaking.

"This is our wedding night." He looked up from his glass of wine, his pupils expanding, until his blue irises appeared almost violet.

Honey opened her mouth to acknowledge the truth of that statement but froze.

No.

He could not mean that. He couldn't.

Could he?

"I thought we had begun to make up our differences over dinner," he said.

She nodded vigorously.

"I thought perhaps we might continue to make them up in bed."

"What?"

His eyebrows arched. "It is our wedding night. I wish to bed you."

She felt light-headed. "But—"

"But?"

"You said you did not wish for children."

His brows descended. "I don't."

"But … I thought you meant—" She didn't want to say it. She couldn't say it.

Honey knew the exact moment he understood what she meant.

He set down his glass with a clatter. "Good Lord. Don't tell me you thought—" he stopped, interrupting himself with a rough bark of laughter.

"What is so funny?"

"Oh, it's not funny—well, maybe only in the tragic sense."

Honey got to her feet and he rose with her, taking a step toward her in that fast, silent way he had of moving sometimes. He took her shoulders in his big hands; the look on his face made every part of her body clench. *Every* part.

She dropped her gaze to the carpet.

Warm fingers slid beneath her chin and forced her to look up.

Honey recognized that heavy-lidded amused expression from the day in the maze. "It never occurred to me that you would take my words that way. I assumed you would know there are ways of engaging in sexual congress without a child resulting; otherwise, mankind would be cheek-by-jowl by now."

She shuddered at the word *sexual* which she'd never heard spoken out loud before, even her father's friends had not dared use such a word in her presence.

His hard eyes softened. "You look very pretty when you blush like that."

She ignored the bolt of pleasure and desire she felt at his compliment and shook her head. She could not endure this again—not the tender touches, the emotions, and then his cold, empty stare afterward. Or him disappearing for three weeks.

No, she could not.

"This is not what I agreed to, my lord. You made me believe this was to be a marriage in name only."

Any softness in his gaze evaporated like steam from his heated glare. "I did not."

"You did."

His scowl deepened. "No. I did *not*. I said I didn't want children, and I was very specific about that. I never said that I didn't want to bed my own wife."

She jerked away from him. "Don't speak to me so vulgarly."

His mouth twisted into a travesty of a smile—a sneer she had not seen since that first day at Whitcomb: ugly, hard, and mean. "That's not vulgar, darling. Vulgar would be if I said I wanted to fuck you."

Honey took another step back, shaking her head. "I don't know what that word means, but I can guess." Her face burned at having to admit her ignorance in such areas. "I do know I will not be sharing your bed."

His jaw tightened and a dangerous light glittered in his darkened eyes. "You are my wife." The words were as soft as a snake's hiss.

Honey crossed her arms tightly over her chest. "I married you believing we would have a marriage in name only. That is what you promised me." And it had almost killed her believing he didn't want her. And now? Now he thought he could just change his mind, use her like a puppet because there was nobody else at hand? She swallowed the weakness she felt welling inside her at the thought of him touching her like he did that night. She steeled herself against her own treacherous body—that's all it was, her own lust.

"We had a bargain, my lord. Are you now going back on your word because I am in your power? Does your word mean nothing?"

He was on her in a heartbeat. His hands around her upper arms, holding her in two hot vises. "You know nothing of my word and what it means, *my lady*. It would be wise not to impugn it."

"I'm sorry," she said, "I should not have said that."

His eyes flickered from hers to her mouth to the high neck of her gown and back. "I don't know about that. Perhaps plain speaking might have saved us from this misunderstanding. But now that we've spoken plainly—"

"There is no misunderstanding. You said no children. When I asked you about l-lovers you said we were both free to take them."

He snorted. "Did you think I meant to take one on our wedding night? Was that *your* intention."

"No, of course—"

He released her as if she were a hot coal and stepped back. "Don't repeat yourself. I know what you thought." He flicked a contemptuous gaze over her huddled, cringing form. "And don't worry about me forcing my attentions on you—I've never needed to do that, not even now that I'm not so pretty as I once was. This is the last time I will step foot in your bedchamber." He dropped a mocking bow. "Good night, my lady."

And then she was alone.

Chapter Twenty-Three

Simon should have gone through the damned connecting door.

As it was, he took four wrong turns before finding himself in front of his door. And then he fumbled with his key and dropped it twice, knocking his head hard on the rough wood when he bent to pick it up.

"Christ," he muttered, massaging his throbbing forehead as he rammed the key into the lock. The door yanked inward and he staggered along with it.

"My lord?" A sleepy-eyed housemaid peered up at him.

"Oh." Simon had forgotten about her.

She dropped a hasty curtsy.

"Everything all right and tight here?" he asked, annoyed by the slur in his voice.

"Yes, my lord. I told her ladyship I was to stay in case she needed me, but she never did, sir."

Simon fished a coin out of his coat and handed it to her, only realizing when her eyes all but bulged out of her head that it was gold. Oh well, *somebody* should be happy on his wedding night.

"Is that all you need, my lord?"

Simon looked into soft brown eyes that bravely held his gaze and avoided the mess on the left side of his face. She was a girl—not more than fifteen or sixteen, but he could see that she knew what she was offering. His groin showed signs of stirring and he scowled, horrified by his own body's urges. "Get out," he said hoarsely.

She fled.

He made his way unsteadily to a chair and dropped into it. Too hard, it appeared, since it gave way beneath him with a deafening crash.

His tailbone would have screamed if it had a mouth.

Simon *did* have a mouth and the connecting door flew open in response to his yell.

His wife stood in the open doorway, her eyes wide and terrified. "What happened?"

He closed his eyes and groaned, in too much pain to speak.

"Simon?"

He opened his eyes to find her leaning over him.

"I don't like that cap. Take it off." It wasn't what he'd thought would come out of his mouth.

She pursed her lips, but, surprisingly, held out a hand. "Take my hand."

She was stronger than she looked, but it still wasn't enough to deadlift thirteen stone. He shook off her hand and rolled onto his hands and knees, pushing himself slowly and unsteadily to his feet.

Bloody hell! It felt as if he'd snapped his tailbone off.

Her shoulder slipped beneath his arm.

"What happened?" she asked as they hobbled toward his bed.

"The chair broke."

"I *see* that. How?"

"I sat in it."

She made an unfeminine snort and shoved him onto the bed before turning to go.

"Wait, my—Honoria," he corrected when he recalled she'd given dispensation to use that name.

She turned around. "What?"

He waved toward his feet, all four of them. "I need some help."

"Ring for the boots," she snapped.

"They'll be sleeping—it's one o'clock in the morning."

She crossed her arms and stayed where she was. "I know."

Simon couldn't argue; he was too damn tired. He fell back on the bed with a thump. He would sleep with his boots on, he'd done it dozens of times before.

Something—or someone—tugged on his leg. "Sit up, Simon. I cannot lift you; you'll need to help."

Simon opened his eyes and tried to push his torso off the bed. He couldn't.

"Oh, for pity's sake." Slender but strong hands grabbed his arms and yanked him into a sitting position.

He smiled. "You're strong."

She grunted and grabbed one of his top boots, staring down at it, as if wondering what to do.

"Pull," he offered.

She fixed him with an irritated look. "You don't say?"

Simon laughed.

"I'm glad you are enjoying yourself, my lord. I would rather be sleeping." Without waiting for a response, she yanked on his boot.

Simon wasn't expecting it and slid right off the floor, landing again on his enflamed tailbone.

He yelled a few words one didn't say in front of ladies.

The only lady within hearing dropped down beside him. "Oh, I'm so sorry. Are you in pain? I didn't mean to hurt you. Here," she slid an arm under his neck, which was bent at an uncomfortable angle, and leaned closer. "Let me help—"

He pressed his mouth against hers, reveling in her softness for a long moment. When she didn't pull away, he drew back. She was frozen, like a deer surprised in the woods, her big gray eyes dark.

"You taste sweet, like berries and cream."

She squinted, as if he were mumbling and she couldn't understand him.

"Or like peaches." He shook his head, hoping that would stop his mouth. "Or—"

Whatever he'd been about to say was muffled by her soft mouth crushing his lips.

***

He tasted like brandy and smoke, which Honey discovered tasted better than an ice from Gunters. Or anything else she'd ever sampled in her entire life.

His lips parted beneath hers and she sank into him, slanting her mouth to reach deeper, tonguing him with a clumsy, desperate need which shamed and frightened her.

How had she ever thought she could avoid this? Not even one night—not even twenty-four hours—and she'd already given in to him.

Given in? You are plundering the poor man more thoroughly than Rome sacked Carthage.

She pulled away and he moaned.

"No, don't go, Honey."

He might be three-quarters of the way to unconsciousness but his arms were like iron strapping.

Honey squirmed. "Come, Simon, let's get you up on the bed."

He gave a low, wicked chuckle that rumbled through her body. "I thought you'd never ask." He released his death grip and they staggered up together, until he was seated and she was standing before him.

His big hands slid around her waist and he pulled her between his spread thighs, his grip gentle but unbreakable. Not that she was struggling—how much danger could he be in this condition?

"Mmmm." He lowered his forehead onto her belly, his arms wrapping around her. "I know," he slurred into her nightgown, his breath hot even through the heavy flannel of her gown. "You smell just like honey." He gave a deep groan of satisfaction.

"Simon?" she said when he remained motionless. "Is aught amiss?"

When he didn't answer, Honey laid a hand on his shoulder and gave a gentle squeeze. "Are you ill?"

The only answer she got to her question was a soft snore.

Chapter Twenty-Four

Simon woke up coatless, shirtless, but still wearing his breeches and boots.

He also woke up with an armful of warm woman spooned along the front of his body.

The room was still dark, which meant he'd not slept that long. He was pleasantly numb, which meant the copious amounts of wine he'd drunk had yet to entirely wear off.

And he was also amazingly hard.

He nuzzled her hair, which had escaped her ugly cap, and inhaled deeply. She smelled sweet and pure and—

"Simon?"

"Hmm?"

"Are you awake?"

Part of him was. "No."

She shook and he realized he'd made her laugh, which just made him harder—something he'd not believed possible.

She started to move and his arm tightened like a snake around its prey. "Where are you going?"

"Nowhere, I just want to turn around."

Simon thought of his mouth, and how much drink he'd poured into it last night and knew his breath could melt iron. "No, you don't," he assured her. "Just lie here for a while. Please," he added when he felt her stiffen.

She heaved a put-upon sigh. "For a little while."

He nuzzled her neck, kissing the small hairs. She stiffened even more. "What?" he asked, although she hadn't spoken. "I'm just sniffing you."

"With your mouth?"

He grinned. "No, that I was using to taste you."

She shook her head, as if in defeat. A good sign, that.

He nuzzled her again. This time, he felt her body soften against his.

"That's good," he whispered, nipping her ear lobe. "Relax." He loosened his arm and stroked down her side. She was wearing not only a nightgown, but also her dressing gown. Far too many clothes. Still, he could work around that.

He made himself be patient, stroking her body in languid motions, avoiding any of those areas that might cause her to react skittishly. He petted her like a cat; like a long, slender, lovely cat that he resolved to make purr.

"Does your head hurt?" she asked, just when he thought she might have fallen asleep she felt so relaxed against him.

"No, I'm lucky that way. Or maybe unlucky, depending on how you look at it." He let his hand drift off her arm and onto her hip. She stiffened and he moved back up her arm; she relaxed again.

"What do you mean *lucky?*"

"I mean if I had a sore head after drinking a barrel of wine I might not do it the next time. But I've always woken up feeling as fresh as a daisy." And hard, so bloody hard. He pressed his hips against her bottom and she jumped.

"Shhhh," he murmured, petting her, this time lingering on her hip. "Does this feel good?" he asked when her body remained tense.

She nodded.

"There is no harm in making each other feel good, Honoria." He stroked again, inching closer until the front of his distended breeches rested in cleft of her heart-shaped bottom. She shuddered.

And then she pushed back ever so slightly.

Simon felt like throwing his head back and howling in triumph. Instead, he kept stroking.

"Did you sleep?" she asked after a few moments, her quickly heating body telling him that she was not as cool as she sounded.

"A little. Did you?"

She shook her head, and Simon allowed his fingers to graze her pelvis, ghosting close to her sex, but never touching her.

"Why not?" he asked, moving his fingers into safer waters for a moment, just until her heart stopped pounding against her ribs hard enough to break them.

"I couldn't."

"Oh?" he breathed the word behind her ear, and licked her, a nice, long lave up the back of her neck. She tasted salty and sweet and made him almost insane.

Her body thrummed under his mouth and her breathing stopped.

"Honoria, breathe, darling." He ran his hand lightly over her mound, the heat of her scorching even through two layers of clothing.

She shuddered and pushed back against him.

Simon had to catch his lower lip in his teeth to keep back his groan. This time, when he stroked, he also tugged up her nightgown a little.

"You were telling me why you couldn't sleep, sweetheart." He felt her jolt at the endearment and smiled.

Stroke, tug.

"Oh. Well, because."

Stroke, tug.

"Because?"

Stroke, tug.

"I've never slept with anyone before."

Her words reminded him that he would be the first man to enter her body and the thought made him throb so powerfully he became dizzy.

Stroke, tug.

The tips of his fingers grazed naked skin and it was his turn to shudder.

"Are you cold?" she asked.

"A little," he lied. "You're so warm." He should have felt like a scheming worm, but when she snuggled back against him, her soft, rounded cheeks grinding against an erection hard enough to cut diamonds, he felt like a bloody king.

On his next sweep, his hand encountered a warm, smooth thigh.

"You've pulled up my clothes." She sounded surprised and confused—but not angry.

"I have," he admitted. Why hide what he was up to? "I want to touch your skin. Do you like the feel of my hand?"

Again she swallowed noisily, but nodded.

He wasn't sure how much longer he could stop himself from flipping her onto her back and plowing into her. Perhaps, if she let him, he could content himself with giving her pleasure rather than taking her virginity, which didn't seem quite right when he was still jug-bitten.

He nuzzled her, inhaling her scent, kissing her whisper-soft skin. "Will you let me touch you? Will you trust me not to hurt you—only to give you pleasure?"

An eternity passed ... and then she nodded.

***

Never in her life had anything felt so good. Not only did his tall, strong body feel heavenly molded to hers, but his hand—

He stroked her again, his fingers gently combing through the curls covering her mons, skimming lightly over something so sensitive that a low moan escaped her tightly clenched jaws.

Simon pressed tighter, his arm coming beneath her body, crossing her chest diagonally and pulling her tight while he pushed the hard ridge of his desire against her bottom and lower back, grinding against her so hard it hurt. But it was a delicious pain.

"Do you feel that Honoria—my desire?" The words rumbled through her body as he ground against her yet again, harder this time. "I want you so much."

This time when he touched her, he parted her sensitive, swollen folds and she bucked in his arms.

"Sh, sh, sh," he murmured, his finger drifting away from her core toward her entrance. She stiffened when he gently probed. "It won't hurt," he promised, sliding a digit into her wetness.

Honey's shuddered at the sudden breeching.

"Mmmm," he hummed, his chest vibrating against her back, his finger sliding in and out of her suddenly slick body while his thumb rubbed the skin just beneath the nub that occasionally woke her in the middle of the night.

An irresistible pressure built inside her—the indescribable sensation spreading and intensifying.

"Oh God, Honoria—you're so hot and tight. I wish I could see you … taste you"

She jolted at his raw words, every muscle in her body clenching.

"I can't wait to bury myself deep inside you—to stretch you and fill you." And then he bit her shoulder—*hard.*

Honey gasped at his animalistic claiming and intense waves of joy radiated from her sex, flooding her body with exquisite pleasure.

"Oh, darling," he said, his voice wonderous. "Did you come already?"

Honey had never heard the word used that way before, but her thighs were slippery and wet and knew what he meant.

"Such a good girl to come for me," he murmured.

Why the word *come* was so much more vulgar than *orgasm*, she didn't know, but her sex tightened in response, the subtle action sending yet more distracting sensations rippling through her body.

Deep down, beneath the wits-destroying pleasure, some part of her reeling mind rebelled at being called a girl.

But another part—the greater part—thrilled at his effortless mastery of her body.

"Do you want me to stop?" he offered. His fingers—both the one resting on her mound and the one buried inside her passage—stilled and he held her gently, nuzzling her neck with light kisses and nips.

Honey pressed back against that most fascinating—and still hard—part of him and shook her head.

He gave a growl of approval and resumed his erotic caressing, careful to avoid her too-sensitive pearl, his hands far more confident on her body than hers had ever been.

His thick finger stroked in and out of her virgin flesh.

"Can you take a little more—for me?" he whispered, pushing a second finger alongside the first. He groaned, "God, Honey, you feel so beautiful, I can't wait to see you."

She whimpered softly at the feeling of being stretched, preening at both his praise and his touch. Not so deep down she knew that she'd be ashamed by her actions later—by her desperation and her raw need for him.

Later, Honey. You can worry about all of that later. For now, just take what he offers.

She didn't need to be told twice.

He pumped her steadily, his other hand teasing the tight bundle of nerves that he'd called her bud.

Honey didn't realize that her hips had begun to pulse in counterpoint to his thrusting until he murmured against her temple.

"That's right, sweetheart, use my hand for your pleasure." He ground his erection against her bottom, his hips moving rhythmically. "Yes," he urged so quietly she could hardly hear, his deft fingers stroking and penetrating, the sound of her own wetness making her squirm with a blend of mortification and arousal.

"Will you come again for me, darling?" Teeth grazed the back of her neck as the shocking words exploded like tiny bombs inside her body.

He curled a finger inside her, grazing some part of her that made her cry out and buck.

A low chuckle vibrated through her body. "Scream as loud as you want, darling, bring down the house." He stroked her again and again; white lights exploded behind her eyelids and pleasure swamped her, both exquisite and excruciating.

But still he would not stop.

Honey barely had time to recover before he pushed her toward another peak, his mouth rough on her neck, biting, sucking, licking.

"Just one more time for me, Honoria," he begged, his hips grinding rhythmically against the small of her back, his fingers driving her over the edge.

"That's right," he growled against her throat, his body jerking in violent but controlled thrusts. "Come with me." He stiffened, his arm circling her waist and crushing her while everything inside her surged and spun, pulling her into a warm, blissful darkness.

Chapter Twenty-Five

The next time Simon woke up there was pale yellow light coming through the blinds and he was alone.

The cold, sticky feeling against his abdomen told him it had not been a dream; he'd come in his bloody breeches while rutting against his wife.

He smiled as the memory of last night came back to him. Good Lord; touching her had been delicious.

Simon rolled onto his back, his hand going to the placket of his buckskins. He unbuttoned himself, roughly shoving both his leathers and drawers down to his thighs and freeing his aching cock.

He was hard again, just as he always was in the mornings. He wished Honoria were still beside him, but he knew that he'd already received far more than she'd intended to give him. Not that the realization stopped him from wanting more.

Simon brought his hand to his face and inhaled her scent, his smile turning to a grin as he recalled her screams; she had some lungs. They would have heard her in the stables, over and over and over again. He absently stroked a hand over his chest, abdomen, and down to his pulsing erection while he reconstructed the fingering and grinding session he'd shared with his virginal wife.

He hadn't done such a thing since he was a young male; who would have believed that sex without penetration could bring so much enjoyment?

His shaft throbbed and strained in his fist as he imagined burying it inside her tight body.

"Christ," he groaned. When was the last time he'd wanted a woman so much? When was the last time he'd wanted *anything* so much?

He closed his eyes against the unwanted thought and worked himself with ruthless efficiency.

The familiar sensation of his calloused palm dragged him back to the Continent, back to the war. He'd pleasured himself more as an adult on campaign than he had as an adolescent at Eton.

Actually, school and war were not entirely dissimilar, he thought with some amusement, his fist slicking as he stroked.

In between the mad, violent moments of terror, pain, and fear there had been long, tedious expanses of dreadful anticipation. A man could go insane worrying and waiting to die, so keeping oneself amused was paramount. And there were limited distractions when one was alone, in a tent, in the dark.

Yes, one's priorities in life were both clearer and less elevated when one's head might get split open by lead at any moment.

Thoughts of wars and long, cold, lonely nights gave way to the insistent pumping of his fist and Simon was building toward his climax when a tiny sound disturbed him.

He opened one eyelid a crack; there was his wife, fully dressed and ready for travel, standing in the doorway between their rooms, her eyes and mouth as round as wagon wheels.

Even in the midst of his arousal he realized this was probably the first time she'd seen a man's penis in all its glory. Simon waited for her to realize he'd opened his eyes and seen her, but she couldn't tear her gaze from his cock.

Which made him painfully, gloriously hard.

He liked her eyes on his body; he *liked* masturbating in front of her—something he'd never done for a lover before.

Bloody hell! He was ten times more aroused than he'd been mere seconds earlier.

Too damned aroused.

His body began to shake and his fist stroked faster, harder. Rational thought fled and Simon's eyes rolled back in his head. Pleasure seized him in its brutal grasp and squeezed. His back arched off the bed and every part of him froze as heat pulsed out of him, splashing onto his belly and chest.

A short time later, after Simon finally came back from his small, exquisite, slice of death, Honoria was gone.

***

Honey couldn't look him in the eye. Not without jabbering or fainting or otherwise giving away what she had seen.

She could not seem to keep her eyes off his body, however. At least not for long.

She repeatedly pulled her gaze back to the window and away from his muscular thighs—clad in skin-tight buff pantaloons that fueled her already rampant imagination—or his broad shoulders and powerful chest.

But then, like the hands of a clock, her eyes slowly moved back around to the same position.

Simon sat in the seat across from her, his eyes closed and his long, well-thewed legs bent and spread in the confines of the chaise.

He'd come down to the private parlor for breakfast when she was almost finished. Not that she'd eaten anything. No, she'd crumbled toast, pushed eggs around her plate, and stirred four spoons of sugar into her tea. She didn't even *take* sugar in her tea.

Over and over and over again the same scene played in her mind. Simon's scarred, muscular body, naked to mid-thigh, to where he'd shoved down his buckskins, the soles of his black leather boots planted on the bed, knees splayed wide while he did ... *that*.

Honey realized she was staring at his spread crotch again and her eyes flew up. She almost fainted with relief when she saw he was still sleeping.

Thank God.

Because that's all she needed—for him to catch her staring at his groin.

She massaged her pounding temples—hard—and closed her eyes.

Why hadn't she left immediately?

Because you liked it.

Honey gritted her teeth at the sanctimonious, accusatory voice.

But it spoke the truth: she *had* liked it. Or at least her body had.

As she'd stood there and spied on him the same tight, hot feeling as the night before, when he'd made her—she shuddered at the memory—*scream*, had begun to build deep within her womb.

Unfortunately—or perhaps fortunately—the same feeling had not come at the end of all her panting and clenching, which was just as well. He would have noticed her for certain if she'd yelled as she had twice—actually *three* times—the night before.

Honey wouldn't be surprised if her face was permanently stained red. She'd seen the truth in the eyes of every stranger she'd encountered that morning: The entire inn had heard her screaming last night and they all knew why.

It didn't matter that they were newlyweds, which she'd heard Simon tell the innkeeper, and that such behavior was expected. She was mortified to the bone.

Right from that first awkward ride to see the view at Whitcomb Simon Fairchild had caused her to behave in ways that were not normal or regular for her.

Honey didn't know who she was when she was with him.

And God help her: all she wanted was to be that woman again. And again.

"You look as if you are in pain, my lady."

Her eyes flew open and met his.

"You're awake," she said stupidly.

He nodded gravely. "I am awake."

Why did she feel as if there was more to those words than their face value?

He stretched and tried to rearrange himself in the cramped carriage, grimacing as he shifted on the seat.

"I'm sorry."

He glanced up. "For what?"

"For refusing to ride in the duke's traveling coach when you suggested it. I daresay it is far more luxurious than this."

"It is."

They rode in silence—awkward on her side, at least, although he looked contented enough to gaze out the window.

Honey kept seeing him as he'd been on the bed. His body slicked with sweat; his taut belly ridged with muscle. Even the scars he bore—and there were many—seemed to make him more attractive, more … dangerous.

But then she recalled how sweet he'd been last night, how slow and patient with her. It was obvious he had not experienced sexual release last night or he would not have needed to do such a thing this morning. Would he?

Honey had been insensitive to his needs last night, too immersed in her own pleasure to think about him.

"You're doing it again," he said, a trace of a smile on his lips.

"Doing what?" she asked, although she knew exactly what he meant.

His smile grew a few degrees warmer. "When is the last time you went to Brighton?"

Although she resented the way he'd ignored her question, she couldn't help being grateful to talk about something less anxiety-provoking than what she'd been thinking about.

"My father took us there for three summers starting when I was seventeen."

"For any particular purpose?"

"At first it was because of a woman who lived there most of the year."

Perdita Davis had been a beautiful widow who'd hidden her dislike of Honey from her usually astute father for all but the last few weeks of their association.

Honey had disliked the woman every bit as much.

Dislike? Or was it jealousy, you felt?

She scowled at the thought. *I was not jealous.*

Simon interrupted her internal feuding. "Your father did not wish to remarry?"

"I don't know."

"He didn't enjoy female company?"

She frowned; just what was he getting at?

"He did," she admitted, "But he never seemed to come to the sticking point."

"Why do you suppose that was?"

"I don't know."

Simon's smirk grew and he turned to look out the window.

"Why are you smiling like that?"

"Because you are a bad liar Honoria."

Honey stiffened. "I don't know what you mean."

He sighed, as if she were a tiresome child refusing to eat her dinner or finish her sums. "He didn't remarry because of you and you know that. He loved you more than anyone else."

Guilt flooded her at his words. "What of it? I loved him just as much."

"I know you did. What did you think of the lovers he took?"

When she didn't answer, he laughed.

"What?" she demanded rudely.

"You should see your expression."

"What about it?"

"You were jealous; you disliked those women who came between you."

"That's not true," she retorted.

He just smiled.

She opened her mouth to deny it again, but then stopped.

Why bother lying? It had driven her to distraction when her father's lovers had invaded their happy life. Even though she'd been young, she'd known that jealousy was an ugly, damaging emotion; she'd tried to hide her feelings, but of course her father knew her better than anyone.

She had always suspected, at the back of her mind, that he had remained unmarried because of Honey.

While she loved him all the more for it, she couldn't help feeling guilty that she'd deprived him of intimacy. He'd been so young when he died—only forty-five—and her mother had died decades before, leaving him alone to raise their daughter.

Honey had forgotten that unpleasant aspect of her character— her capacity for jealousy. How like her new husband to make her remember it. After all, he was so good at eliciting other unpleasant behaviors.

"I doubt that you kept him from remarrying, Honoria. I imagine his devotion to you irked his lovers and that he saw that," Simon said. "All those women must have known they would never be first with him. And so it should be." He smiled at her—this expression pleasant rather than a smirk. "I thought your relationship was marvelous. I remember burning with envy watching the two of you."

"You did?"

"I did." He shifted on his seat, grimaced, and then propped one booted foot on the bench beside her. "My mother loves me and my brother very much, but she had to keep herself from showing it. My father didn't want us coddled—not an unusual attitude for fathers to take with their sons—and he wouldn't permit my mother to do so."

"I have never understood that belief—that showing love somehow weakens a person, the giver and the recipient. I think my father's love made me a stronger person."

"I agree. But I also think it took its toll." Honey opened her mouth and he raised his hands in mock surrender. "Don't rip up at me, which I can see you're about to do. Do you wish to have an honest discussion or would you like to discuss banalities? Because I'm more than willing to speak about the weather, the state of the roads, the—"

"What did you mean, about his love taking its toll?"

"Well, he raised you without any other children, he didn't send you to school, and he made no effort to find you a mate—did he?"

Honey could not believe his audacity. "For your information he offered to send me to school but I did not wish to go."

"And if a child refused to eat anything but chocolates, should a father agree?"

"That is hardly the same thing."

"I think it is exactly the same. A parent makes decisions that take into consideration the welfare of their child—not just their child's preferences. I think your opportunities were narrowed by his love."

She crossed her arms and looked out the window. But he was having none of it. He dropped his foot and leaned toward her, his forearms resting on the long bones of his thighs. "Have you ever had a beau?"

Honey glared at him. "What does that have to say to anything?"

"Answer the question."

More than anything, she wanted to lie. But she knew he'd spoken the truth earlier—she was a dreadful liar. "That is none of your affair."

He sat back, his look of smug satisfaction beyond galling.

"For your information, I have known several fine young men," she snapped. That much was true, although she'd not felt more than a passing interest in any of them.

He didn't answer, just looked at her through slitted eyes, as if he could hear her every thought.

"What does it matter if I haven't?" she demanded irritably. "I daresay you've had enough lovers to crew a ship. Has that made your life so much better? So much happier?"

Instead of answering, his expression became speculative; his lips moved but no words came out.

"What are you doing?" she asked.

"I'm trying to recall how many it takes to crew a brig—or did you mean something bigger—perhaps a galleon?"

Honey opened her mouth, closed it, and then raised her hand to smother the laugh.

"That's better."

She shook her head, annoyed at how he was able to manipulate her mood. "You always do that."

"What do I always do? Head off an argument?"

"No, say and do things to disconcert me."

"You mean like last night?" His eyelids lowered a fraction and she knew exactly what he was thinking.

Her cheeks burned. "No, I mean like right now."

His mouth twitched and he turned to look out the window.

Honey fiddled with her reticule, which lay in her lap beside a book she'd brought but not yet opened. How could a person read with somebody like Simon Fairchild a foot away?

"Why did you wish to break the journey rather than traveling all the way through?" she asked.

He cut her a glance. "Did you not enjoy your sojourn in Grunstead?"

Her face, which had just begun to cool to a normal temperature, flared. "Tell me, my lord, do you *try* to be provoking, or does it come naturally?"

This time his lips did more than twitch before he turned back to his window view. "I broke the journey because I don't care to be confined for long periods of time." The words were quiet but his tone told her plainly that he did not wish to discuss the matter. Honey could only assume it was yet another of his many scars, this one on the inside.

She picked up her book and pretended to read.

***

They settled into their spacious rooms at the York Hotel and then enjoyed a leisurely tea in their private parlor.

Simon offered to leave Honoria to rest after the journey, but she was eager to explore.

"Anything in particular you wish to see?" he asked, leading her past bowing, liveried servants and out of the hotel lobby.

"May we ramble for a bit?"

And so they were rambling.

The populace in Brighton appeared more genteel than that in London and Simon was amused by the way passing pedestrians studiously avoided staring at his injuries. His wife, however, felt otherwise.

She gave a huff of annoyance as two passing women almost ran into a streetlamp while pretending not to gawk. "Is it always this wretched? People staring and pretending not to stare?"

He drew her closer to his left side as they passed a trio of gaping, giggling girls. "You cannot blame them."

"Yes, actually, I can." She flicked an affronted glance up at him and Simon realized, not for the first time, that she honestly did not seem to be offended by the wreckage of his face.

"Doesn't it bother you to be stared at?" she demanded.

"No." It was true, it didn't. Although it *did* become rather exhausting. "But I must say I'm not accustomed to so many people."

Her hand tightened on his forearm. "I'm sorry—why did you not say crowds bothered you?"

Nothing bored Simon faster than speaking about things like scars and injuries and anything else to do with his past.

He stopped and pointed to a straw hat in the bow window of a shop. "Do you like that?"

She blinked and for a moment he thought she might not let loose of the topic, like a terrier with a bone. But she was too curious.

She stared at the ridiculous female confection. "It is pretty," she rather grudgingly conceded.

"I want to see it on your head." He pulled her toward the shop entrance.

"But I don't need a hat."

"We are not speaking of need. We are speaking of want. Like." He leaned down to whisper in her ear as he opened the door, "*Desire.*" And then gave her a gentle push into the shop.

Chapter Twenty-Six

Honey had never been in a dress shop with a man before. Well, except her father when she'd been younger.

Truthfully, she hadn't been in many dress shops, period. She usually sent her measurements to a woman who'd been making her dresses since she was a girl. She liked pretty clothes, but when you were almost six feet tall it felt foolish to stand in the middle of a shop and pretend that anything could possibly make you look feminine.

The shopkeeper, one of the smallest women she had ever seen, gazed up at them with sparkling green eyes, her own clothing so outrageous it was difficult to look away: a bright pink silk gown with yellow ribbons for trim, and tiny kid boots of apple green; she resembled a spring garden.

She folded her hands together and smiled, as if Honey were the answer to all her prayers. "Oh, I know why you've come in! The hat—the red hat."

Simon chuckled. "I can see we've come to the right place."

The next few hours were a whirlwind of delight. It turned out that her new husband was a more patient shopper than any of her friends except Freddie. Freddie adored shopping and could spend hours debating the merits of a single gown.

After the hat had been tried on and admired—even Honey had to admit the tiny straw brim with the crimson ribbon around the crown and towering, fluffy feather suited her better than any she'd ever worn—the clever shopkeeper somehow eased pattern books and fabric swatches into Simon's hands and parked him in a comfortable wingchair.

"I can see you are a man of fashionable discernment," Mrs. Fenton said, her eyes glinting as she studied Simon's expensive but loose, not particularly well-fitting clothing. "Please peruse the latest plates from Paris while I show her ladyship a few of my premade garments."

She whisked Honey into a back room while her assistant arrived with tea and biscuits.

The dressing room turned out to be almost as large as the shop front and just as luxurious. Yet two more assistants entered from behind a heavy silvery gray velvet curtain, bearing gowns. Honoria had to smile; she'd not even seen the diminutive woman communicate with another person except her and Simon.

"This," Mrs. Fenton said, taking a gown of the most delicious crème lace over dull gold silk, "Is made for one such as you."

It was one of the most beautiful garments she'd ever seen. But it was also far too short.

Before Honey could open her mouth, Mrs. Fenton laid the gown across her lap and flipped up the hem of the underdress. "You see how deep this is? I always construct my ready-mades with ample hems. If they need to be shortened the excess can always be used for a hair ornament." Her eyes flickered to Honoria's hair, which was still uncovered after she'd tried on the red hat. "You have exceptionally lovely hair. Perhaps a string of pearls woven through your coiled braid." She pursed her lips speculatively.

Honey fingered the golden material and tried to suppress the excitement she felt when she thought about wearing such a gown. It wasn't that she did not have some pretty dresses, but she had always purchased for functionality and rarely bought anything that was the kick of fashion. She caressed the intricate lace. "How would you make this longer?"

Mrs. Fenton took her hands and pulled her to her feet. "You let me worry about such mundane matters. Come, let's slip you into this."

***

Peel was waiting for Simon when they returned to the hotel several hours later.

Simon had left Honoria in their shared sitting room, her eyes glistening at the mountain of boxes that awaited her at the hotel after their orgy of shopping.

"Ah, Peel, you are a sight for sore eyes."

The older, phlegmatic man looked pained, his gaze fastened to Simon's neck. "I wish I could say the same, my lord."

"Yes, I know my cravat is a bloody embarrassment and these clothes fit like grain sacks. And my footwear." He glanced down at his Hessians, which he'd allowed the inn boots in Grunstead to polish. "You may need to throw them out."

Peel sniffed and helped him out of his coat.

He grinned at his servant. "I think you missed me."

"Yes, my lord, there is nothing quite so disagreeable as having a holiday. And it was terribly flat having only myself to wash, groom, feed, and clothe for over a week."

Simon laughed at his chilling sarcasm. "There, that's more the thing, Peel. Now, did you collect the new toggery I ordered in London?"

"I did, my lord."

His servant's stiff, brief response told Simon his feelings were hurt. "Well, don't get all bent up, man. I'm sorry I had the audacity to choose garments without your approval. You can go out and break the bank while we're here if you don't care for my selections."

"If I may, sir, how long shall we be in Brighton?" Peel finished with his coats and Simon sat so he could pull off his boots.

"Until the end of the month—and then we'll be returning to Everley. I shall probably send you on ahead."

Simon scratched at a ridge of scar tissue beneath his hair. It hadn't been just his ear that had been damaged. Smooth, hairless slashes of raised skin snaked all over his head. He was fortunate he'd always had thick, curly hair which now helped to hide many of the ugly wounds. He'd not had a haircut in some time; not since deciding to allow his hair to grow a bit longer, to conceal the ugly stump of an ear. For a long time, he'd felt almost belligerent about exhibiting his mutilations. But Honey shouldn't have to look at such a thing all day. It was already bad enough she had to look at his face.

Peel set his second boot aside with a thump that brought him back. "You were saying, my lord?"

"I was saying I might send you back to Everley before us. The place should be ready for our arrival, but it can't hurt if you are there to supervise her ladyship's unpacking."

"You will not be returning to Whitcomb?"

"No. And that is another thing you can handle, moving my possessions from my chambers there to Everley."

The valet nodded, assembling Simon's shaving gear. Simon pulled off his shirt and tossed it onto the floor, wincing as he lowered his arm.

Peel bent to snatch up his shirt. "You have not been applying the salve Doctor Cruikshank gave you, my lord?"

Simon snorted and ignored his servant's pained sigh. Instead, he rolled his shoulder, the joint clicking softly with each rotation. Something was still in there; something the doctors in Belgium had not managed to extract. It did not hurt often, usually only if he slept on it, but he was always aware of it.

He dropped his arm and went to sit in front of the mirror.

Peel wrapped a steaming towel around his face and he let out a contented sigh. "I'm always too much in a hurry to do this part, Peel."

Peel mumbled something that sounded like, "Or too bloody lazy, more like."

"What's that?" he said, smiling.

"I can see the skin on your side is cracking—there is a little blood."

"Drop it already," he said, no longer amused. "You can slather me in pig fat after my bath." His eyes located Peel's in the mirror. "You *did* order me a bath, didn't you?"

Peel's expression told him what he thought of such a question.

Simon grunted. "Good." He'd been washing himself in a damned basin since he was too much of a bloody scatterbrain to remember to send for a bath most of the time.

Peel removed the towel and began to lather his face. Simon closed his eyes and relaxed.

***

Simon was half asleep as his valet rubbed the not unpleasant smelling substance into the slick, shiny skin that ran along his left side.

He'd not applied any of the unguent since Whitcomb and his scarred skin had begun to tug and shrink and pain him. Specks and streaks of blood showed up on his shirts with increasing regularity.

There was a soft knock on the connecting door.

"Come," he called, lazily turning his head.

His wife stood in the open doorway, her expression like the one she'd worn this morning, when she'd caught him tugging on his prick.

"Oh!" she began to take a step back.

"Don't leave," he ordered, and she froze. "We are finished here. Leave us, Peel."

His valet left swiftly and quietly through the entrance that led to his small room.

Simon rolled onto his side, the towel Peel used to protect his modesty sliding and drawing her eyes to his hips.

"What can I do for you, my lady?" he asked when he thought she might run.

She hesitated, holding out a rectangle of paper.

"What is that you have?" he asked.

"A letter from the duke."

"Oh? Why was it delivered to you?"

"I don't know, but I thought you should have it. Er, quickly. So that's why I'm here."

Simon bit back a grin at her uncharacteristic babbling. So, he made her nervous, did he? He knew his behavior was uncouth; the average aristocratic wife would be shocked at seeing her husband without a cravat.

But he didn't want to behave like average aristocrats.

He sat up, watching her watch him as he wrapped the towel snuggly around his hips, tucked in one corner and stood. She eyed him as if he were a demon sprung from the hideously patterned carpet.

"You look very beautiful," he said, his eyes hovering on the exceptionally—for her—low neckline of her bodice. "That is one of the new gowns?"

She blinked, thrown off balance by either the change of topic, the compliment, or both.

She'd been correct in the carriage; Simon enjoyed keeping people off balance, but her especially.

He could see it was a struggle to wrench her eyes from his towel and the erection that was growing beneath it. It was bad of him to keep her with him when he was all but naked, but he did not want to hide himself from her. And he had no intention of allowing her to hide from him.

She smoothed her gown with one hand. "Mrs. Fenton worked very quickly on it but the others are not ready, of course."

Simon wagered they'd be ready before the week was done. A sharper businesswoman he'd yet to meet.

"Turn around."

She cocked her head.

He twirled a finger in the air. "Turn around, I want to see you."

Her blushes were an aphrodisiac to him, he'd realized that early on.

She turned rather awkwardly, the diaphanous silk rippling like water against her long, subtle curves. When she came to a halt Simon was full hard. Her eyes dropped to his towel and it was all he could do not to tear it off, rip that pretty new dress from her body, and bend her over the back of the nearby chair.

It was a struggle, but he suppressed his savage urges. This was civilization; such behavior would be viewed harshly.

Besides, she was a maiden; he wanted to take her slowly and make her first time a pleasure for her.

Thinking about being the first man to enter her body made him almost woozy with desire. He'd never been interested in virgins, but something about being her first made him burn to possess her.

She was clenching the letter so tightly it was almost bent in half. "Are you not yet healed?"

He lifted his eyebrows. "Hmm?"

She gestured to his shoulder, to the raw scar from the poacher's bullet. "Was your valet applying medication?"

"That ointment wasn't for this scratch. It's a salve to keep the burnt skin supple. The scarring has left me without the essentials that keep skin pliable and oiled. I will have to apply it for the rest of my life." Simon felt his resolve not to touch her slipping, like shards of rock shearing off the face of a cliff. He took a step toward her and she tensed. "It is difficult for me to reach some of the scar tissue, so Peel applies it for me." Not to mention the fact that Simon was lazy and too impatient to massage his battered body.

Her eyes flickered over him as she digested this information.

"How is the other injury?" her lips twisted mockingly. "The one you just called a *scratch*."

"It is a scratch," he said, shrugging. "The bullet did little damage. Poor Raymond came out of that far worse." With barely a pause, he asked, "Do you find my scars repellent."

Her eyes flickered over him again lingering on his hips. "No." The word was barely a croak.

He took the letter from her unresisting fingers and tossed it onto a nearby table.

"Don't you want to read it?"

"No." He had absolutely no interest in anything Wyndham had to say. No doubt it contained orders cloaked as suggestions. "I want to talk about you."

"M-Me?"

He nodded slowly. "Last night I bit you and handled you quite roughly." He reached out and pushed back the neck of her gown, exposing one of the marks he'd likely left.

She trembled under his hand and her jaw dropped in a comical expression of shock.

"Did I hurt you?"

She hesitated, and then said, "No."

The soft word sent blood thundering through his veins. "Did you like it?" he asked, his eyes raking over her like red hot nails pulled from a forge. "Did you?" he repeated when she only gaped up at him.

She gave a jerky nod.

More telling than her nod was the way her pupils flared.

"You know that I've been away from polite society for a decade and a half. I lived among my men, many of whom were from the lower orders. What that means is that I am blunt and vulgar and less than gentlemanly in some ways." He snorted. "Likely in many ways." He flexed his jaws as he took in her flushed cheeks. "I daresay I'm especially raw when it comes to sexual matters." She jolted at the word *sexual.* "You must tell me to stop if I ever do something you do not like. Do you understand?"

The pulse at the base of her throat was fluttering madly by the end of his ungentlemanly speech. She gave an infinitesimal nod.

"No, this is too important, Honoria. Please answer me."

She cleared her throat. "I understand."

"Good." He took her hand and placed it over the obscene bulge beneath his towel. "Do you find this repellent?" he asked, his second question an echo of the first.

Her eyelids lowered and she swayed slightly. But she did not pull away. "No."

"I am pleased and relieved to hear that." Simon leaned forward and kissed the fine down of her jaw. "I want to put it inside your body." She shuddered, but still did not move away. "I want to make love to you, Honoria," he said, using a French phrase he'd heard for coitus—one he'd thought pretty for such an earthy act.

"Ma-make love?"

"Mmm-hmm." He kissed her neck beneath her ear, grazing the madly pounding vein in her throat, his hands moving to the back of her dress where he encountered—thank God—only a short row of buttons.

Her palm rested limply over his cock.

"Stroke me," he ordered.

Finesse, you dog. Show some damned finesse. This woman is an innocent— or near enough.

I won't hide my true self from her.

Even if he could pretend to be somebody different—a cool, bloodless, elegant dandy, for instance—he wouldn't do it, especially not with somebody important to him.

Simon wanted to know this fascinating woman—the real Honoria Keyes—and he wanted her to know the real him, warts and all.

The sexual part of marriage was important to him and he refused to go to her under the cloak of darkness and hide their actions beneath blankets.

Just when he started to believe that his raw command might have repulsed or frightened her, her fingers traced jerkily up his shaft.

Simon grunted with pleased surprise. "That feels good," he said roughly, his clumsy fingers coming to the last button of her gown. He leaned back so he could see her. "Open your eyes, Honoria." He wanted her to know who it was she was giving herself to—every step of the way.

Her pupils were huge and her breaths were uneven and shallow, but her hand continued to move.

"Yes, like that, but harder."

They stood that way for a moment: Simon struggling to seize control of his desire and her driving him to the brink of madness.

"Remove your hand. I want to take off your pretty dress," he said through clenched jaws when he could bear her stroking no longer.

When she jerked away, as if he'd rejected her, he realized that he needed to do better—to explain what was happening.

"Look at me, love."

He'd guessed correctly: she had taken his rough words as a rejection of her touch.

"I cannot recall ever wanting a woman as badly as I want you, Honoria. It is difficult for me to go slowly—to stop myself from rushing."

Her lips parted in surprise.

"I want to make your first time as pleasurable for you as I can." He gazed down at her darkly flushing face. "It will be a first for me, too."

"You cannot mean—"

Simon smiled. "No, love, I don't mean that I am a virgin. But I have never been with a virgin." His expression became serious. "Are you anxious?"

She stared up at him. "I am anxious," she admitted.

And then she surprised him, "But not enough to want to stop, Simon."

Chapter Twenty-Seven

Honoria felt like an epic heroine who had journeyed half a lifetime to reach this moment.

She had known since last night that she would have to continue this process of discovery. There was no other decision. And if it only lasted for a brief time—

She crushed the painful thought and ground it under foot; there was the rest of her life to think of such things.

Honey lifted her arms and Simon slowly raised her gauzy gown over her head, and then stood frozen, clutching the dress in his big hands, his eyes riveted to her body.

His chest expanded as he inhaled forever, and his lips barely moved. "Beautiful."

She fought the urge to cross her arms over her body. She *did* look pretty; she'd known that in the shop when the older woman had frowned at her serviceable, plain stays and chemise and had shaken her head.

"Your husband looks like the kind of man who might appreciate something like this," she had said, holding up the crème silk stays, embroidered with white butterflies. Before Honoria could ask her how she knew what Lord Saybrook would want the other woman added some garters that matched.

The woman had been right. Simon had actually taken a step back to look at her. He looked positively poleaxed.

Never had anyone looked at her with such raw want; even her toenails must be blushing.

Her dress fluttered from his hand and he shook his head. "It will almost be a shame to take that off you," he said in a rough voice. He looked up and met her gaze, his own black with lust. The unscarred corner of his mouth curved slowly upwards. "But I will do it anyway."

He held out a hand and she took it, letting him lead her toward his bed. It was dark outside but the room blazed with the light of at least two dozen candles.

Honey glanced at the candelabrum nearest the bed. "Could you—"

"I need to see you. And I want you to see me."

She saw the grim line of his mouth and understood. For all his bravado about not caring about his appearance he obviously felt it keenly. Honey was glad—not that he worried about his scars, but that the lights would remain. Her modesty would not have permitted her to admit that she wanted to see what he looked like, especially that part of him she had watched with such yearning this morning.

He reached behind her, his fingers going to her laces. "I think this must be Mrs. Fenton's work?" he asked, his hands working more skillfully than a French maid's to unlace her.

It pained her to know that he could only have gained such experience in practice. All those years that she had been yearning for him, he had been undressing countless women.

Honey turned away from the unpleasant thought, watching as her beautiful new garment slid down and over her narrow hips, landing on the floor.

He stood back again, holding out a hand to steady her while she stepped out of the fallen corset. The new chemise she wore was cobweb-thin muslin and she knew from looking at his face that it did nothing to hide her body.

He grunted and again shook his head, as if he were engaged in some fierce inner argument.

Yearning and desire burned in his eyes as he lifted her chemise over her head.

"Good God." He looked like a man standing before an altar and his hands shook as he dropped her chemise and closed the distance between them.

Honey wrenched her eyes from his adoring face and shook her head, stopping him in his tracks. "No."

His mouth fell open and she almost laughed at his expression of shock. "You have undressed me. I wish to—" she stumbled over her bold intentions.

But she didn't need to finish.

He stepped back, his eyes kindling so brightly she was surprised she didn't burst into flames. "By all means, strip me."

Her hand shook as she reached for the towel slung low on his hips. There was not an ounce of fat on him and his navel was a taut oval stretched over muscles that were one of God's masterpieces.

She'd seen many naked bodies—male and female—as her father had made sure she had all the models she needed to master her art. But never had she seen one as chiseled and battered and glorious as her husband's.

And never had she seen one so aroused.

The tips of her finger slid over the satiny skin beneath his navel and he sucked in a sharp breath, the bulge under the towel straining against the thick fabric like some kind of wild beast.

Honey slid her fingers back and forth over the soft golden hairs that dusted the fascinating ridges that tapered into a V somewhere beneath the towel. His abdomen tightened and became even more defined as she stroked.

"You are a cruel woman," he hissed between clenched teeth when she slid a single finger between flesh and fabric and then halted.

Her mouth curved into a smile that she couldn't recall ever wearing before.

He chuckled. "And so pleased with yourself." He swooped in and nipped her ear, making her jump. "Let me out, Honoria. Free me." His voice was hoarse and throbbed with need.

She gave the towel a tug.

He was on her in an instant, pressing a length of unimaginably hard, hot skin against her belly, kissing and biting her throat in that way he had, as if she were something to be consumed, something delicious, something—

He stepped back suddenly and she rocked unsteadily on her feet and took a step toward him. He shook his head and she stopped, confused.

"What—?"

"You still have one more garment to shed." He took a step back and dropped onto the bed, lounging on his elbows, his feet planted on the floor, his membrum virile red, hard, and jutting almost straight up.

He smiled, his eyes going from his erect manhood to her. "If you come closer, I will take them off for you. Or you could drive me mad," he snorted, "*madder* by stripping for my pleasure."

The mocking challenge in his voice—the absolute *certainty*—that she would not dare do such a thing gave her strength.

Honey dropped her hand to the tape that held up her fancy silk drawers and his gaze tracked her fingers like a falcon following prey. She hesitated, but his eyes never wavered. Honey bit back a smile.

His eyes rose to hers. "It's entertaining to torment me, isn't it?"

Honey smiled; it was.

She plucked the tape and the drawers slipped down. He watched and waited. She let them fall a little but still held the tie.

His expression was the very definition of avid. She could not believe that it was staid, scrawny, towering Honoria Keyes who held this handsome, powerful man in the palm of her hand.

Apparently, she didn't. He growled and launched himself at her, scooping her into his arms while a startled laugh broke from her.

"That's *enough*," he said, right before his mouth crushed hers, his tongue a hot, slick sword stabbing into her.

And then she found herself floating through the air before bouncing on the mattress. He was beside her, his long body pressing against hers. His hand stroking her the way it had last night, but he was facing her, his mouth trailing kisses down her chin, neck, chest—

She gave a choked cry as his tongue flicked over a hard nipple.

"God, I've been wanting to do this," he muttered, tormenting one nipple while his palm swirled lightly over the other. "Lie back," he ordered, nudging her breastbone with his forehead.

She toppled onto her back and he crawled over her, his knees between her thighs, shoving them wide, his hands planted by her shoulders.

This was it. He was going to put himself inside her and it would hurt. She knew that. It would—

His teeth grazed her nipple and her back arched.

"Mmmm, yes," he whispered against her skin, nudging her thighs wider, leaving her unspeakably exposed.

His hand slid down her belly, through her damp curls, and between her swollen lips.

"Oh, Honey." He thrust a finger into her, his wicked thumb insistent and caressing. Her back arched, her hips thrusting for his touch. Honey writhed as he worked her toward her climax with the same erotic, ruthless efficiency that he'd employed last night.

Hot breath fanned against her skin and she dazedly realized his mouth had moved from her breast to her stomach to—

"Simon!"

He chuckled against the divinely sensitive place he'd already mastered with his fingers.

And then he began to master her with his mouth.

***

Simon braced his hands on her velvety thighs and opened her wide as he impaled her with his tongue, ignoring the source of her pleasure while she recovered from the climax that had just wracked her, leaving the room echoing with his name.

While he explored her folds with his mouth, lips, and tongue he imagined another part of himself stroking into her and plunging deeply into her tight heat. She rode his thrusting tongue, bucking and grinding and using him for her pleasure.

Her fingers tangled in his hair, pulling, kneading, and causing him sweet pain as her nails raked his battered scalp.

Simon reluctantly abandoned her tight, clenching passage to stroke her tiny jewel. He cradled her bud with his tongue, laving and sucking until she shouted out his name and yanked hair out by the roots.

She was still shuddering when he rose to his knees, placed his fat crown at her entrance, and thrust into her, not stopping until he was hilted.

Her eyes flew open and he saw shock, pain, awareness, curiosity, relief, and—finally—submission, as her pliant body accommodated his thick shaft as nature intended.

Her tight sheath pulsed around him, but she remained still, her eyes wide and trusting.

Simon swallowed hard as his body quivered with need. "Good?" he asked gruffly, the single word all he could manage.

She nodded slowly. And then her hips moved a little, the change in angle bringing him even deeper.

A deep groan of pleasure burst from between his tightly clenched jaws. "That felt exquisite," he gritted out, holding her gaze as he withdrew almost all the way before entering her with another long, firm thrust. She shivered and squirmed but he saw no pain in her eyes as he kept her impaled.

Once again, she opened herself to him, tilting even more this time, taking him deeper, until she was utterly filled and stretched and dominated.

My wife.

The thought acted as an aphrodisiac on his already aroused body, sending a rush of blood and a throb of desire to his already engorged shaft; Honey gave a soft grunt of pleasure when he flexed inside her.

Simon could restrain himself no longer. He began to move, stroking into her with slow, deep thrusts that gave her his entire length, but without too much force.

He shook with the effort of restraining himself.

He'd been too close to the edge by the time he entered her and not even a miracle could hold back his orgasm.

Soon his eyelids began to droop and his control started to slip. His hips drummed into her, his thrusts savage and deep.

Pulling himself from her wet heat before he exploded wasn't the hardest thing he'd ever done, but it was agonizing. He was so primed that he needed no help from his hand to spend, covering her quivering belly in ribbons of hot spend.

Even in his lust-drunk state, Simon knew that he had left it close. Too close. He would have to take more care—next time.

Chapter Twenty-Eight

When Honey woke, the room was full dark and only shards of light penetrating the heavy window coverings.

She tried to turn but something warm and heavy held her pinned. Two somethings, actually: one across her breasts and one over her hip; a man's arm and leg.

Simon.

An uncharacteristic wave of giddiness rolled over her. Of course, it was Simon. They were married. Truly married, now, for better or for worse.

Well, this seemed good—very good—and she should seize it with both hands.

What did it matter if he were not the boy he'd once been? She was not that girl, either. She no longer expected fairy tale endings.

Besides, while he was no longer sweet and innocent—and although he was often distant and unknowable and cold—he had been gentle and kind with her.

It was not by his design that they were in this marriage, but he had accepted his part in the scandal and hadn't behaved as if he were throwing himself on his sword to marry her.

He stirred behind her and she tensed.

"I know you're awake." His voice was rough with sleep, and then he pulled her tighter and kissed the back of her neck, his scratchy night beard making her shiver. "Mmm." He held her closer. "I can almost *hear* your mind churning away," he whispered, his lips soft and warm against the sensitive skin.

That part of him was pressed tightly between them and seemed a good twenty degrees hotter than the rest of him.

He turned her onto her back. "What are you thinking about, Lady Saybrook?"

The name made her smile.

"Ah," he said, his finger tracing the curve of her mouth.

She blinked up at him, barely able to see an outline in the gloom. "You must have eyes like an owl."

"I do have very good night vision, although you are barely a shadow right now." He stroked her lower lip. "But you were going to tell me what you were thinking."

"I was?"

"Mmm-hmmm." Back and forth he swept.

"You never tell me what you are thinking."

"Men are easy to read." His finger moved again, stopping in the middle of her lower lip. "Our needs are basic, our thoughts disappointingly simple." He pressed lightly and her lips parted. "Food, shelter, rest, a good horse—" His finger pushed and she opened, her tongue acting without instruction from her brain and stroking the rough pad. He pulled out and then pushed back in, the motion just like—

Honey gasped and grabbed his hand, stilling it. "You are *wicked*."

He laughed and took her chin, tilting her toward him for a kiss that was disappointingly brief. "I don't know what you mean, my lady."

She was too embarrassed to speak. Did he really want to do that? To put himself inside her—

"Now that you know what I am thinking—when I'm thinking at all—it is your turn. What were you thinking about, lying awake in the dark?"

"I was thinking about your niece's portrait."

"*Liar*," he whispered in her ear.

"Fine. What do you think I was thinking about?"

"Me. Us. This."

"Are you always so arrogant, my lord?"

"Most of the time."

She laughed.

"There, that's better." He propped himself up on his elbow. "What do you want to do tomorrow? More shopping?" He caressed her throat in the darkness, his big, powerful hand making her feel delicate ... vulnerable ... *aroused*.

"Only if it is for you. I picked out too much today."

"I did my shopping in London. Peel brought it with him. You will no longer have to tolerate a shabby husband."

"That is a relief."

He chuckled. "What a sharp-tongued viper you are."

"Tell me about Everley."

His hand stopped, and she could tell that, for once, she had surprised him.

"Did you ever ride over and see it while you were staying at Whitcomb?"

"Raymond took me over once but I could only see part of it and didn't feel comfortable riding up their drive."

He resumed his stroking. "He should have brought you to meet them; the Amberlies are nice people."

"Amberlies—why do I know that name?"

"They were at your going away dinner."

"Ah."

"They have rented Everley since I was young, raised their family there. Their children were between Wyndam and me in age and we used to run wild together."

"How old is the duke?"

"He just turned nine-and-thirty."

Honey had thought he was older.

"Amberlie is an admiral and would be gone for long stretches, even before the War. Their two sons are both naval men themselves, and their daughter, far younger than the rest of us, recently married."

"So, too young for you to run wild with."

He traced the inside of her ear and she shivered. "Why? Would that have made you jealous?"

She snorted.

"You are right, she was too young for me and Raymond to run with." He hesitated, and Honey felt a strange tension in his body. "But their neighbors to the west had five daughters."

"Who are they? Did I meet them at the party?"

His hand dropped. "No. The local people are not invited to Whitcomb very often. The duke is not fond of country gentry or commoners. He liked the Amberlies because they were friends of our father." His voice had become cold, hollow, distant—the way it always did when he spoke of his brother.

"You have married a commoner."

"Ah, but your grandfather was Baron Yancy—bosom beau to my mother. In fact, it is quite possible she might have married the baron had her father not decided a duke was a better catch."

Honey had sensed the same thing in her few conversations with the duchess.

Simon resumed his soothing petting. "Everley is far, far less grand than Whitcomb, of course. It has been the abode of younger sons for generations. The only reason it stood vacant in my father's time is because he was an only child. Well, the only one who survived to adulthood—he actually had five brothers and sisters."

Honey shivered at the thought of so much death.

"You are right to shiver. Childbirth is a cruel process. My grandmother died in the childbed, as did my grandfather's second wife. He did not take a third."

Honey wanted to ask if that was part of his refusal to have children, but she didn't want to raise such a topic when he seemed so willing to confide.

"Like Whitcomb, the house is Tudor. But unlike Whitcomb it was not added to endlessly. You might find it small and dark or you might find it snug and cozy—people either love it or hate it."

"I have always enjoyed Tudor architecture."

"I hope you continue to feel that way." There was a warmth in his voice that made her wish she could see his face. "The house is in excellent condition but the stables are barely adequate and that will be my first project."

She turned onto her side, to face him, even though she could not see him. "Do you have plans drawn up?"

"I have had plans for at least fifteen years. I will take Wilkins with me."

"Your brother's stable master?"

"Not for much longer. We've been plotting and planning this for ages. He grew up in one of the cottages on the estate and was as horse-mad as I was." The enthusiasm in his voice warmed her.

"Will you breed horses like Loki?"

Once the floodgates opened, she no longer needed to pry each answer from him. He spoke about the studs and mares he either possessed or would soon purchase. He explained the stable improvements and the general structure of a breeding operation.

The more he talked, the more he sounded like himself—like the Simon of old. Honey's heart felt lighter. Perhaps—just perhaps—some distance from the duke's manipulations and machinations would do both Simon and their marriage some good.

"Listen to me! Boring on about horses when I have a lovely, naked woman beside me."

"I like listening to you, and you weren't boring on."

He kissed her squarely on the mouth, proving his boast about excellent vision. "What a perfect wife you are turning out to be. Listening to my yammering and then flattering me." Before she could protest, he went on. "There is a room at Everley that would be perfect for painting. In fact, I can't help but think it was used for such a purpose in the past—some long dead ancestor who dabbled." His hand slid from her throat to one of her breasts. "Is there something in particular one looks for in a studio?"

"Good lighting, a fair amount of space, a—" his finger settled on an already taut nipple and gave it a gentle tweak. "Urgh."

"What was that last thing, Honoria? I'm afraid I missed it."

"I said—"

He pinched her again and she sucked in a noisy breath and clamped her teeth shut, determined not to whimper this time.

"Am I distracting you?" His voice was rough, and his hand moved to her other nipple, stroking, pulling, and pinching her, the combination of pleasure and pain sending whorls of delight through her body, until the sensations all pooled low in her belly.

Suddenly he was straddling her, working her nipples with two hands instead of one. He pinched one nipple especially hard and she gasped.

"Does that hurt?" he asked, sounding amused rather than concerned.

It did hurt, but it also felt strangely delicious. She shook her head back and forth, vigorously, unable to speak.

He pinched the other, and she groaned. "Am I being too rough?"

Again she shook her head.

"What's that? I can't hear you?"

"No! Not ... too ... rough." The words came out in between rough tweaks.

He cupped her breasts, his big hands dwarfing them. "Mmm," he groaned, lowering his hot wet mouth over one tormented peak and sucked.

"Mmmm." He alternated breasts, the ache between her thighs intensifying with each kiss and caress.

"Or perhaps you like rough?" he whispered, giving her a sharp nip.

"Simon!" Honey bucked, her sex clenching around nothing, making her feel empty and needy.

Simon chuckled evilly, his mouth—one again gentle—kissing, laving, sucking, and then a nip.

She shook and whimpered like a wanton.

Shame hovered just beyond the exquisite pleasure.

What was wrong with her to like such treatment?

His hand slid between her thighs, wiping her worries from her mind, and she parted for him without being asked.

"Ah, such a good, obedient wife," he praised, the words causing a dizzying blend of mortification and lust to swirl in her belly. She was grateful it was dark—at least she could not see his face.

But then he chuckled, as if he *could* see her expression, his touch as light as a feather as he stroked her mound, his finger maddeningly avoiding the source of her pleasure.

Honey spread her legs a little and pushed her hips up, trying to unobtrusively lead him in the right direction.

He laughed—this time no mere chuckle, but a belly laugh. "Such a hungry little pussey."

Honey gasped—both at the finger that flicked her swollen bud and his shocking words. "*What* did you say?"

"*As fleet as my Feet,*
Could convey me I sped,
To Johnny who many Times Pussey has fed."

Honey could hear the grin in his voice.

"That's—that's—" she couldn't help laughing. "That's *dreadful*. Is that something you learned in the army?"

"No, I learned this when I was a boy—from a contraband copy of something by Thomas D'Urfey."

Honey had heard of the infamous wit, but never read any of his work. Now she knew why.

"It's actually a song." He stroked her again, grazing her bundle of nerves and drawing out another sharp gasp. "Shall I sing it for you, my love?" he offered.

"*No*," she said, choking on her laughter. "Please don't."

He made a purring sound. "Pussey needs feeding, and I have just the thing," he whispered. He parted her lips, sliding a finger inside her entrance.

Honey's hips rose to take him deeper.

"Mmm, so wet and eager—I like that very much," he praised, gently pumping. "But are you too sore to take me again, sweetheart? We can amuse ourselves in other ways if you are."

His voice was so tender and solicitous that Honey almost didn't recognize it. She *was* sore, but she was also wet, hot, and pulsing for him. She spread her legs wider in answer.

He laughed, the sound low and sinful. "I love that you are so eager to be filled, darling," he whispered in her ear, his knees pushing her thighs wider. "Take me in your hand, stroke me before you put me inside." He took her hand and guided it to his hot, heavy length.

"Oh," she said, stunned by how soft the skin was and how it seemed to slide over something as hard as bone.

"God that feels good, Honoria."

Honey thought his words were almost as exciting as the feel of him, and the way he groaned when she touched him.

And then his hips began to pump. "Like that. Hold me tight. *Yessss*. Just. Like. That." He punctuated each word with a sharp, controlled thrust.

And then she made a miraculous discovery: men could become wet, too.

He stopped abruptly, his breathing harsh in the darkness. "Put me inside you, lover."

Honey thrilled at the word, her thighs shaking with want as she guided him to her entrance. When he pushed inside her, it stung, but only for a moment, and then—unlike the first time—it was deliciousness without any discomfort.

He moved with the same deep, slow rhythm as before, and she could feel the restraint he was exercising and knew it was for her. She wished she knew what to do to let him know she was no porcelain doll that would break.

"Am I hurting you?" he asked, his voice harsh beside her ear.

"No." She hesitated, and then added, "I like it, Simon. You aren't hurting me."

Her words were like a match to a fuse and his next thrust went deeper, harder. "Like that?" he asked. "You like it hard? You want all of me?"

She shivered at his rough, crude demand.

"Yes," she whispered.

He pummeled her, driving them both up the bed with his savage thrusts. Honey wrapped her legs around him and tilted her pelvis to take him deeper.

He groaned, his hand finding its way between them, his fingers stroking her core while his hips drummed a brutal tattoo.

When she neared the precipice, it was as if Simon knew—as if he could read her body. "Come with me, Honoria."

And she hurled herself over the edge with him.

***

They stayed in Brighton for almost three weeks.

They made love every night—several times—and most days; her husband was not a man who paid any lip service to modesty.

He had no qualms about displaying any part of his body or inspecting every part of hers. He also approached what they did with an earthy enthusiasm that was nothing like what Freddie had warned her about.

"I want to do everything with you, Honey," he'd whispered one night, after he'd finished loving her a second time.

"There are other things?" she'd gasped, her body soaked with sweat from the vigor of their actions.

That had made him laugh. "So many other things. But we will take it slowly. Perhaps one new *thing* a week. What do you say to that?"

She could only laugh foolishly.

"I shall take that for a yes," he'd murmured, his mouth already moving toward her sex even though they had hardly finished their last bout. "I love to give you orgasms; it is an excellent pastime for a country gentleman."

That was another thing she adored about him: their love-making was not only passionate, it was filled with silliness, smiles, and so much laughter.

He had taught her more new words in the past three weeks than she'd learned in years. And the words were all forbidden and fascinating and private: words they used only with each other.

Simon rode every morning, renting a hack from the hotel stable. He'd wanted Honey to join him, and she'd gone once or twice, but she knew she held him back, even though he denied it.

She could spend time in the saddle when they moved to Everley. It would be easier to become more comfortable without the confusion of the city to distract her.

During the days they roamed the city. Twice Simon paid a man for the use of his sailboat and took Honey out on beautiful, sunny days.

After their first visit to the local assembly room, they did not return.

"I shall go if you like it, Honey. But not to please anyone else," he'd told her.

It was when he said words like that Honey knew she was in danger of falling back into love with her husband. He was not the man of his youth, he was something far more interesting, subtle, and complex than the fairy tale prince she'd loved as a girl.

Honey believed that the aloofness she often sensed in him was yet another scar from the war. His reserve was a constant in the background, waiting to drop like a barrier between them, but she learned to avoid the two topics that brought down the iron curtain: the war and his brother.

She was not offended; everyone had subjects they held close to their breast. Perhaps one day he might open to her, but if he did not? Well, the close, sensual friendship they shared, which strengthened with each day, was more than she'd ever hoped for.

During the day he was an entertaining, curious, and thoughtful companion.

And at night …

Her cheeks burned when she thought of what they did in the bed they shared all night, every night.

Simon not only made love with her, he slept with her, holding and stroking and cuddling her, as if he could not get enough of being near her.

He was earthy, open, and joyous. He saw no shame in the pleasure they gave and took—no matter how shocking society would have found the things they did—and would have been happy to remain naked with her all day and night.

Honey knew that he'd not been a monk. She'd heard the rumors at Whitcomb, seen the way the female servants eyed him. He was scarred and battered, but his wounds—some of them quite severe— seemed to add to his allure.

Women liked to nurse and heal the sick and wounded. Not that Simon presented himself as either. Certainly not when they were in bed. But there was something deep inside him that was broken, and she had to warn herself against the compulsion to fix him. He had not asked for fixing and it was nobody's place—not even a wife's—to impose such help.

The Duke of Plimpton sent messages at least twice a week.

And, at least twice a week, Simon tossed them into the fire.

"I don't wish to think about my brother," he told her when she protested that perhaps something bad had happened. "And I particularly do not wish to know if there has been some disaster that I most likely could do nothing to fix. No doubt he's missing me, with only poor, downtrodden Raymond there to do his bidding." His eyes had hardened then, and she had quickly backed away from the encroaching bleakness, too much of a coward to press the matter.

And so the days had passed in a happy, sensual blur.

Until it was their last day, which they decided to spend dining in their room.

The meal was delicious and they talked and laughed and bickered as they always did, now. But even so she sensed an extra layer of reserve settling upon him.

"Are you excited to be going home?" she asked as they finished a delicious berry trifle and lazed at the table with glasses of wine.

He shrugged, his smile fading a little. "This has been a pleasant idyll, but our real lives beckon, do they not? You must be eager to paint—have you been away from your work this long in the past?"

"Not for years," she admitted. "But I have my sketchpad, which fills a void."

He raised his eyebrows. "Is tonight the night you allow me to see it?"

It was a game between them: she sketched, he begged to see them, she deprived him. She didn't know why, maybe it was just that she enjoyed his teasing attention. But part of her wanted to keep something that was just her own. After all, he had hardly opened himself to her, yet she was already so vulnerable to him.

"Not yet," she said, swirling her glass and gazing at the ruby liquid.

"Not even if I show you something new and astonishing tonight?"

She blushed even as she laughed. "I do not believe there is anything left."

He shook his head, taking her glass and setting it on the table before leading her into the bedroom. "The fact that you would doubt me breaks my heart."

"Well, you will just have to convince me, my lord."

Which is exactly what he set about doing.

Chapter Twenty-Nine

The journey to Shropshire took several days longer than her first visit to Whitcomb.

Honey had assumed the task of massaging salve into Simon every evening and learned that his thin, damaged skin caused him more pain than he ever let on. Riding in a carriage—even the luxurious coach he had engaged—was never enjoyable for days on end.

They read to each other, played a game of chess on a traveling board, looked out the windows, and talked. But on the last day of their journey Simon became more morose with every mile.

Peel had left several days before them so, they traveled with only the services of Simon's groom, John, a man who'd accompanied Peel from Whitcomb and was riding back with them.

"We are almost there."

Honoria looked up from the book she'd been trying to read to see a long, tree-lined drive flickering past the windows.

Simon swung onto the seat beside her and pointed out the window, "This is Everley at its best. Watch for it—now!" His excitement was contagious and Honey gasped when the peaked roof of the big structure grew and grew until there was the entire building.

She squeezed his arm. "It is lovely, Simon."

He grinned and kissed her soundly, his excitement almost manic.

By the time the carriage rumbled to a stop in front of the entrance there were perhaps a dozen servants lined up and waiting.

"We'll need to hire more," he said, his eyes flickering rapidly over the house, the servants, everything. "The ones here are a few old retainers and those the Amberlies did not take with them. Some families have worked here for generations." He shot her a smile. "They'll be glad to have Fairchilds back in residence."

He was out of the carriage and handing her down almost before it rolled to a stop. Never had she seen him so excited.

"Hume, you look no older than you did when I was a boy." Simon grabbed the older man's—butler?—hand, his warm greeting clearly startling the stiff, proper servant

"It is a great pleasure to have you back, my lord."

"It is wonderful to *be* back, Hume. This is my wife, Lady Saybrook."

Hume bowed low. "Welcome to Everley, my lady." He turned back to Simon. "Mr. Peel arrived two days ago and has been unpacking your trunks from Whitcomb. We have recently received a shipment from your house in London," he said to Honey, "but have not begun to unpack until you were here to direct the staff as to where you wished to place your painting things. We have prepared the master and mistress's—"

"Yes, yes. Very good Hume, let us go in." Simon took Honoria's arm and led her through the gauntlet, pausing just long enough to let her nod but not exchange a word, with all the gawking servants.

"You are in a tearing hurry," she muttered as he all but dragged her up the steps.

He nodded, his eyes on the open doors ahead of them. "I've not been here for fourteen years."

"What?" She stopped and stared, but he pulled her on. "I thought you were great friends with the Amberlies?"

"When I was a boy. Not ... after."

"After what?"

Either he didn't hear the question or decided to ignore it.

They entered the foyer and he released her, turning to look at the rough-timbered entry hall like a man in a trance. "Not a thing has changed," he murmured, turning in a circle, either unaware or uncaring that several servants were staring.

He strode down the long gallery that went off to the left.

Honoria smiled at the waiting footman and let him take her cloak before hurrying after her husband, tugging off her gloves while she gazed at the pictures on the wall—all of them portraits. They were nowhere near as grand as those at Whitcomb, but there were dozens of very good pieces.

"Honoria!" Simon's head popped around a corner. "Why are you slow-poking? Hurry up." His head disappeared and she laughed. He was like a boy—a young, carefree boy.

The corner he'd disappeared behind led to another long hall and she recollected that he'd said the house was built like an 'E.'

Double doors made of stained glass illuminated the hall with fantastical colors and shapes. Simon was nowhere to be seen.

"Simon?" she called, her voice echoing eerily over the hard plaster and warped and cupped ancient wood floors.

"In here." His voice floated out of a room down near the end, to the inside of the "E."

The door was open and she paused upon entering, entranced.

There were floor-to-ceiling windows on two sides and late afternoon sunshine streamed through the beveled glass, refracting the light to make the room feel like it blazed with a hundred candles.

"Oh, Simon, it's lovely."

He grinned as he came toward her. "A perfect studio, isn't it?"

She nodded, turning in a circle, enchanted. "It is."

"And look," he said, leading her over to the south-facing bank of windows. "There are the stables. We shall be able to wave to one another while we sweat and slave over our respective labors."

In an act of unprecedented joy, he grabbed her by the waist and spun her around, and around, and around. Until she was dizzy from the motions as well as joy.

"I want to take you right now—right here," he whispered, his scandalous words and passionate urgency making her heart pound. "I will claim you in every room in our house. Would you like that, my beautiful lover?"

Honey shivered at his words and the erotic images they evoked.

"Would you?" he growled, lowering his mouth over her neck and making her squeal.

"Yes! Yes, I would," she laughed.

When he stopped, he was panting, his eyes so full of warmth she could only stare. All this happiness for them? For their life? For *her?*

"We will be happy here, won't we, Honey?" he asked, the question strangely somber, his gaze intense.

Honey nodded, swallowing convulsively but unable to banish the lump in her throat.

In that moment, she knew that he would come to love her—she could see it in the hope fairly beaming out of his remarkable blue eyes

She already loved him, and she would see her love returned. She knew it.

He lowered his mouth hungrily, kissing her the way he did when they were on the verge of ecstasy.

The sound of a clearing throat made them both jump, and Simon stepped in front of her, as if to protect her.

She was not surprised to see the Duke of Plimpton standing in the open doorway.

***

It was all Simon could do not to slam the door in his brother's face. But he could tell by Wyndham's cool, resolute stare that he would stay there until Simon listened to him.

"Hello Simon, Honoria." The duke strode forward. "How was your journey?"

Honoria dropped a curtsey. "It was pleasant, Your Grace."

Simon smiled at the ice in his wife's voice. Good, she would not be intimidated by his brother.

"My wife would like to go to her room and freshen up after the long journey, Wyndham. I will meet you in the library."

His brother hesitated, irritation flaring briefly at being dismissed, but he nodded and left the room without another word.

Simon turned to Honey. "I wanted to show you your chambers, myself," he said, forcing an air of lightness into his voice he was far from feeling. He took her hand and led her back to the family wing.

He leaned in close as he opened the door to her suite of rooms. "I plan to spend a lot of time with you in here," he murmured, enjoying her shiver.

She *oohed* and *ahhed* her way through the tour, but Simon could see her heart wasn't in it. Everything had changed the moment Wyndham had appeared. His brother would not have hastened over here to impart good news.

Simon turned to her after showing her the large copper tub and water heating tank, setting his hands on her shoulders. "I want you to take a long, hot bath and pay attention to all the details so you can tell me about it later." She blushed, which he loved, and he kissed her hard. "I shall see you at dinner. Just the two of us," he promised when he saw the question in her eyes.

Yes, just the two of them, he thought as he went storming down the stairs.

Wyndham was looking out the picture window, his hands clasped behind his back, which was ramrod straight, just like Simon's own—thanks to their father.

His brother would have made a good soldier, far better than Simon, who'd never really relished the discipline.

No, you only enjoyed the mayhem, killing, and carnage.

He ignored the cold, critical voice; dealing with Wyndham would be enough without dealing with his interfering conscience.

His brother, not surprisingly, exuded discipline; discipline and duty were what composed the ichor in his ice-cold veins.

He turned when Simon slammed the door. "I'd ask you if you wanted a drink, but I know you won't be staying long."

Wyndham ignored his rudeness. "I am pleased to see you getting on so well with your new wife."

"I'll wager you are." Simon snorted, heading for the brandy decanter and pouring one for himself, perfectly aware of how boorish his actions were. "Well," he said, turning with the tumbler of whiskey in his hand. "I wouldn't go congratulating her, if I were you. She hates you." *A lot,* he could have added, but he thought his brother got the picture.

"That is unfortunate," Wyndham said coolly, turning his dead stare from the glass in Simon's hands to Simon.

An emotion Simon couldn't recognize flickered through his brother's eyes, leaving him feeling uneasy. *Any* emotion on Wyndham's face was worth noticing and generally cause for concern.

"I must admit I am both grateful and relieved to see you have given yourself over to your new life with such enthusiasm."

Simon wished his brother would shut up but he knew telling him that would only prolong their encounter.

Instead, he gave him a stiff smile. "Thank you, brother. But you mustn't speak of it as if I've made a big sacrifice. She is a beautiful, talented, intelligent, *sensual* woman." He paused to enjoy the unusual sight of the duke's razor-sharp cheekbones flushing. Poor Wyndham. His brother probably hadn't been with a woman since his wife booted him from her bed. Too proud and rigid to bend his principles even though he would die without ever having another lover. A fool and a prude, in other words.

"How nice of you to come see that we are settling in," Simon cocked his head. "Or have you come to supervise the consummation of our union?"

Wyndham's cheeks went even darker at Simon's vulgar words.

He smiled and tossed back half his glass. "I daresay my wife will not allow such a thing, no matter how much you might enjoy it."

His brother's jaws were so tight he could see the muscles flexing beneath the skin.

"So, with that out of the way. Was there anything else you wanted?" Simon poured the rest of the drink down his throat. When he looked up, he saw the duke giving him an odd stare.

"Did you read my letters—you never answered, but then I did not expect any response."

"I'm glad to hear it. And yes, I received your letters, two per week." He turned his glass in his hands, "And I threw each of them in the fire, not wishing to contaminate my bridal holiday with missives from you."

The duke's normally impassive face seemed to close in on itself, and Simon felt a twinge of remorse.

He'd told himself that he was going to move on from annoying his brother, that he was enjoying the marriage he'd been forced into—a great deal, in fact. That he would begin trying to forgive Wyndham and leave his corrosive rage behind.

What Wyndham had done to him and Bella had happened a long, long time ago. Yes, his brother had also manipulated and controlled Simon since he'd returned from the war, but his rage over that had already begun to drain away; after all, it was because of Wyndham's manipulation that Simon was married to a woman he already cared a great deal for. Who knew, maybe love would come someday, or at least happiness and contentment, since he no longer believed in the calf love that had once sustained him.

Fortified by that thought, Simon set down his glass, took a step toward his only brother, and smiled, "Look here, Wyndham, I don't want to keep—"

"Arabella MacLeish has returned to live at her father's house."

Nobody had said her name for so long that it took Simon a moment to absorb his brother's words. And then there was the issue of the name—MacLeish. He had continued to think of her—on those occasions she stole into his well-guarded mind—as Bella Frampton.

Simon took his glass back to the console and sloshed more alcohol into it, so distracted was he that it almost overflowed. When he tried to pick it up, amber liquid sloshed over the rim onto his hand.

He put the glass down but did not turn. "She has come for a visit with her family?"

"She has come back here to live; she is a widow, Simon."

Simon laughed—a frightening sound that should not have originated in his body. He was still laughing when he felt a hand on his shoulder.

"How long?" Simon asked, not needing to explain what he meant.

"You are married now, Simon," his brother said in an uncharacteristically gentle voice. "*Happily* married and—"

Simon violently shrugged away the duke's hand and spun. "How. Long."

Wyndham's jaw worked, but he didn't speak.

Simon could only gape in horrified wonder. "You knew she was widowed and kept it from me." He grabbed his brother's coat lapels and rammed him back into the wall, knocking against the console and sending glasses and decanters crashing to the floor.

"Goddammit, Wyndham! How bloody long have you known?"

"Six months."

Another bark of half-mad laughter broke from him before he could catch it. "You could have told me this months ago?"

"You might have learned of it yourself if you'd actually behaved like a man instead of an angry child. You've been back almost two years and have refused to socialize with our neighbors and friends. And for twelve years before that you never paid us *one* visit." Wyndham shoved his face close to Simon's. "All those years you stayed away. You didn't just punish me—you punished our mother.

And then, after you finally *do* return, you go straight from the sickbed to The George and proceeded to drink yourself blind."

"You could have told me this six months ago."

"Good God! She is no good, Simon." It was the closest the Duke of Plimpton had ever come to yelling.

Simon watched in morbid fascination as the muscles of his brother's face rippled with the force of his emotions.

He stared at Simon with an openly beseeching look. "You need to believe that much: Arabella bloody Frampton was never any good."

This time, when Simon swung his fist, the duke caught his wrist, holding Simon's arm in a granite-hard grasp. "No. I will not take any more abuse from you." Wyndham's hair was mussed, but his voice and face were utterly bland, as if the emotional episode of a few seconds earlier had never happened.

Simon wrenched his arm from his grasp. "Get the hell out of my house." He stalked to the door and flung it open. "Get out and never, ever come here again. Do you hear me? I've tolerated you as long as I had to, and now I don't ever want to see you again."

The duke did not move.

"Fine," Simon shouted, "I'll leave. But you'd better be bloody gone when I come down for dinner or I'll kick you down the goddamned steps, myself."

Chapter Thirty

Honey ate her first dinner at Everley in the big dining room, alone.

She'd taken her time bathing and dressing and had waited for Simon. And then waited. And waited.

It had been full dark when she'd finally given up and come downstairs. Only to learn that her husband had sent word he was indisposed and not to be disturbed, and that Honey should dine alone.

She'd wanted nothing more than to go to his chamber and demand an explanation, but the silent, judging eyes of a half-dozen servants had forced her to take her seat and behave as if she'd already known of his indisposition.

She made her way through three courses with a dozen dishes each, every mouthful tasting like sawdust.

Finally, when the dessert tray came in, she waved it aside. "Please give my compliments to the cook, but I have had a long day and wish to retire."

The footman nodded, but Honey saw something that looked like pity in his eyes.

When she reached her chambers, she went to the connecting door. The handle was locked. She knocked and it immediately opened. Peel stood in the doorway.

"Good evening my lady."

"I wish to speak to my husband."

Peel's narrow, pale face flushed. "He is in bed, my lady." He hesitated. "I'm afraid his lordship is suffering one of his migraines."

Honey had heard of such things but had never experienced one herself.

"Is there something I might do?"

He gave her a look of profound regret—and again, a flash of something that looked like pity. "I'm afraid only sleep and quiet, my lady."

She felt her face heat under his kind, reserved scrutiny. "Please let me know if there is any assistance that I can offer."

He nodded and pushed the door shut.

Honey stood staring at the smooth mahogany, her mind a complete and utter blank.

***

Simon heard Peel and Honoria talking in hushed voices and knew he should invite her in, reassure her that everything would be fine, but it felt as though somebody was using the flat part of an ax on his scull again and again and again. Just opening his eyes a crack, in the dark, was causing his stomach to heave; he'd thrown up twice already.

He needed to be alone, where he could indulge in his pain without disgracing himself. He especially did not want to disgrace himself in front of a wife he'd begun to like and respect.

These blasted headaches were a dehumanizing orgy of torment that left him weak and feeling like a worm—even without an audience. He had no desire for her to see what she had married. Too much familiarity led to contempt—this would lead to worse: pity and disgust.

It had been over a year since his last headache—or migraine, as the doctors in Spain had called them. This was the first one he'd had since returning to England. For some reason, he had hoped it was a pain that would disappear along with the nightmares and night sweats—a suffering associated with the Continent and his life there. But here it was again.

They'd begun nine years ago, after his first serious injury. He'd been in the van of an assault and a company of French had appeared out of thin air. He'd been lucky enough to avoid sabers, but his horse had stumbled and must have broken its leg because both he and the animal went down hard. His had struck a rock or another horse clipped his skull, either way, he lost consciousness. When he came to, hours later, he had a ringing in his ears that persisted for weeks, until the giant goose egg went down. And then the migraine came.

He would have shot himself in the head if the doctors hadn't taken away his pistols. For the second time in his life, he'd found himself lashed to a bed. This time they force fed him laudanum, which only made him vomit, which only made the pain worse.

Finally, a hand had shoved a pea-sized piece of something in his mouth and bliss had descended: Opium.

Although laudanum was an opium derivative, there was something about pure opium that didn't make him sick and took away his pain. The doctor who gave it to him warned him about its power—its lure.

"Use only as much as you need. And use it only when you are afraid you might do yourself harm."

Simon hadn't told the man that he'd already had experience with the milk of the poppy—he'd been too concerned the physician wouldn't have given it to him.

Besides, he knew what he faced and could control his actions because he was older and wiser.

At first, Simon had only taken a pea-sized piece when one of his headaches struck.

But the road to hell was paved with intentions every bit as good and better than his had been.

Three years after the head injury he was hospitalized for a bayonet wound through his thigh. It was then that his other problem was discovered.

They would have sent him home for good at that point, if he hadn't threatened the doctor who was treating him.

"Send me back, and my death will be on your hands."

The man had been horrified. "But I cannot treat here. You need some place safe, with the right care, and—"

"Do it here; break the chains of this thing."

"You don't understand," the doctor kept saying. But Simon was accustomed to dealing with the Duke of Plimpton, everyone else in the world was mere clay in his hands after Wyndham.

Breaking his reliance on opium a second time made his migraines seem like a Wednesday at Almacks. If Simon had known how agonizing it would be, he never would have agreed to such torment.

The doctor had told him the next time he capitulated to opium, it would kill him, and Simon had believed it.

So here he was again, in the dark, with only a cool cloth on his forehead to soothe his pain, wanting to blow his brains out.

He knew Peel's inner workings; on the off chance that Simon could actually get out of bed, he would never find his guns.

His mind careened from frustrated thoughts of guns to the information his brother had shared.

So, Bella was a widow and free to marry. He shook his head and then gasped as a wave of nausea rolled through him.

Blast!

Simon weathered the violent churning and pounding for a few moments before the pain stabilized into a steady, brutal throbbing.

He hated that the duke would think it was the news of Bella's return that had launched this bout of sickness. The truth was, Simon had lost many of his memories of Bella along with all the others. The holes, gaps, and pure absences of days, weeks, and even months extended to her—the erstwhile love of his life.

No, what had upset him was his brother's behavior .

If Wyndham believed that Simon still loved the woman, why would he do such a thing? Did his brother really hate him so much? Was Wyndham's desire to manipulate and control him more important than Simon's well-being?

Anger at his brother's actions caused his temperature to rise and made every muscle in his body clench; his fury only made his head worse.

Simon inhaled and exhaled deeply but slowly several times.

Once he'd taken control of his anger, he let his mind drift back to the source of this mess: Bella's return.

Honestly, his visceral reaction had largely been habit. Not only did he have few actual memories of Bella, but he was a married man. And while he and Honoria had discussed lovers, that had been before their time together in Brighton. He liked the way their marriage was developing and believed she did, too.

Simon didn't want any other lover.

There was no doubt in his mind that what he had with his new wife was a very good thing indeed. She was clever, sensual, and fascinating; they spent their time together loving, laughing, and discovering each other.

As for Bella? Well, there would always be some nostalgia about what they'd once shared. Simon suspected the nostalgia was even more powerful because his recollections were so foggy. No doubt his imagination had done its job filling in the blanks.

But now he and Bella were neighbors and Simon would see her whether he wanted to, or not. He would tackle the task of normalizing his relations with Bella and her family when he wasn't writhing in agony.

Simon knew better than anyone that ghosts might appear insubstantial, but they could still exert a powerful influence.

The sooner he banished any remaining specters from his past, the better it would be for everyone.

***

Simon did not come out of his room for three days.

After the second day passed with no sign of her new husband Honey began to doubt that migraines were the real cause of his current seclusion.

Did such headaches really come on so suddenly? Could they be so severe as to keep him bed bound for three days? He had not suffered anything like it during their time together—why now? Why only when he reached home and spoke with his brother? Was it something else keeping him locked in his room? Was he a dipsomaniac? She had seen him in his cups more than a few times. Was that the sort of man she'd married—a drunkard?

Not knowing what was wrong with him was agonizing.

It was her new mother-in-law, the dowager, who finally put paid to her miserable wondering.

The older woman waited three days after they'd arrived at Everley to pay a visit.

"I'd planned to give you at least a week to settle in—I know how bothersome it is to have callers before one has unpacked—but then I heard Simon was suffering one of his notorious headaches and decided you must be feeling very neglected indeed."

Honey liked her new mother-in-law—very much—and knew the kindly, somewhat vague older woman liked her, too.

The duchess's ready confirmation of Simon's migraines had relieved her—at first.

But then the dowager had related the object of the duke's visit.

"Wyndham wanted to deliver the news in person."

"News?" Honey repeated, pouring two cups of tea.

"Yes, about the return of Countess MacLeish." She must have noticed Honey's questioning look. Her pale cheeks flushed, and she said, "The countess was called Arabella Frampton before she married."

Arabella? Bella? *That* Bella?

Honey had still been working through the confusing information when the older woman resumed her story.

"Bella and Simon were inseparable as youngsters." The dowager cleared her throat. "At one time there was an understanding between them."

So, the beautiful Bella, who'd so scattered Simon's wits on that long ago day, was back in the neighborhood. But why should that be enough to drive Simon into his chambers for three days?

"Lady MacLeish is recently widowed," the dowager added, plunging the knife a little deeper and twisting it.

Honey could not stop herself from asking the question, "How recently?"

"Six months."

Six months?

Honey's mind reeled; had there been some understanding between her and Simon? Had they been waiting for her mourning to be over to marry? Had the debacle in the library and Simon and Honey's subsequent marriage wrecked their plans and—

Stop it, a cool voice in her head commanded. *You are letting your imagination run wild. Why would news of Bella MacLeish drive your husband into a stupor? It's not as if she was widowed three weeks ago, Simon would have known about her status. Whatever the duke told him—if anything—it wasn't about this woman.*

Honey sighed. Those were all excellent points.

She finished preparing the dowager's tea and handed it to her.

"Thank you, my dear." She took a sip and continued. "We were all surprised when she suddenly married MacLeish." She flushed slightly and said, "I know it is unchristian of me, but I never did like Arabella Frampton, even when she was just a girl." She clucked her tongue. "She was simply too beautiful for people to behave with any sense around her."

Honey still recalled that sick churning in her belly on that long ago day outside Gunters, when Simon had introduced her to Bella, his face transformed by love.

Not for the first time did she burn with curiosity to know why the two had never married.

The duchess continued, looking blissfully unaware of the heartburn she'd unleashed in Honey, "She was the apple of her parents' eye and it was plain they had great plans for her. I don't hold that against her, of course."

She paused, her vague stare sharpening when Honey gestured to a tray arrayed with a selection of cakes and biscuits.

"Oh, I shouldn't, my dear." But her eyes gleamed speculatively as they landed on a light and puffy pastry horn that oozed lemon curd and cream. Her small, plump hand pointed. "Well, perhaps just one."

Honey smiled and scissored the delicacy onto a lace-edged plate using two forks, handing the dowager an ancient linen napkin along with it.

The older woman studied the linen. "These were mine."

"They are lovely," Honey said. The edges were trimmed in lace, tiny, perfect vines wending their way around the entire square.

"I made them for my wedding trunk." The dowager looked up with a mischievous smile that made her appear younger. "Back in my day that was something a good girl did no matter whether she married a butcher or a duke"

Honey chuckled. "I'm afraid my needlework efforts would not be fit to grace anyone's tea tray."

The duchess lowered the napkin. "You bring something so much more wonderful to your marriage."

Honey's brow wrinkled.

"Your paintings, my dear," the duchess said. "Wyndham says there will be a delay with them given your wedding. But Rebecca and I are simply longing to see them. She would have accompanied me today to see you—was in fact bouncing up and down to do so—but her governess had scheduled fittings for her and my son does not believe in discommoding others on a whim."

Honey barely restrained a snort at the thought of the duke even recognizing anyone else was a genuine leaving, breathing, feeling human being. Honey briefly wondered if he expected to have her labor without pay—as they were now *family*. She realized her mother-in-law was waiting for a response of some kind.

"Please tell her she may ride over any time and be welcome. I started Rebecca's portrait in London, before the wedding. It was delivered before we arrived at Everley and I've been working on it these past few days."

The older woman nodded and sipped her tea, but Honey could see her mind was elsewhere; she wasn't surprised when the duchess returned to the subject of Bella.

"I mentioned that it astonished me that Arabella met and wed the Earl MacLeish the way she did." Her face puckered and she fiddled with the handle of her cup before she looked up. "It is an ugly thought I've had in my head for over a decade and will sound even uglier out loud. She married the earl only a few days before my grandson Edward's death—it was a rushed affair in London, I believe. I think she did so because she'd decided that Simon would not inherit the title."

The duchess's pale, papery cheeks reddened and Honey suspected the other woman wished she could pull the words back.

Could what the duchess said really be true? It was beyond comprehension to her how any woman could trade Simon for a title or money or anything.

Her grace continued, "Edward had survived those first dangerous months of infancy and seemed to be a healthy baby—if not particularly strong. Simon had always been a sunny child, but he became even more light-hearted after Edward's birth. He was so thrilled to have an heir between himself and the dukedom. And he was so eager to marry and settle into the life he'd always dreamed about."

That was Simon that Honey had met all those years ago: lighthearted and sunny.

"Wyndham was—" the duchess looked at Honey through glassy eyes and then bit her lip, her gaze imploring. "Wyndham was almost afraid to be happy. You see, the two children between Rebecca and Edward had not survived an hour and my son took their deaths very hard. I know the duke must seem cold to you, but he shoulders many burdens and has weathered great pain and disappointment. He continues to do so in many ways."

Honey could only assume she meant the duke's strange, distant marriage.

The duchess's smile was tremulous. "But he was deeply pleased to hear that you and Simon married. Deeply pleased."

It took a great deal of self-restraint to smile back at the fragile old lady. She was a mother who loved her son—both of her sons—and had suffered a lifetime of not being able to help them. If Simon's father had been anything like the current duke, then the dowager—sweet, gentle, and retiring—would have been trapped between three strong, willful men.

Her grace cleared her throat, setting her tea aside, her impeccably straight spine seeming to straighten even more. "I don't know why I even raised such an ancient topic," she said, turning brisk. "You and my son are married and we must have a celebration."

Honoria opened her mouth to protest.

But the duchess was not finished. "Not now, of course. We will give Simon time to get through this dreadful headache." She shook her head. "They last for days, I understand."

"Oh, he has not had one at Whitcomb?"

"Not since before Belgium—or so his valet told us. Peel has been with him since he was a young man—well before the War. He is a great comfort to Simon."

So, her husband had been without a migraine until his brother closeted him in his office on their return. The connection seemed too direct to ignore; whatever the duke told Simon on his arrival sent him from relative contentment to bedridden.

The older woman's face puckered with concern. "I do hope I haven't said anything upsetting or—"

Honey smiled. "You have not upset me, ma'am. Indeed, I am grateful to know about any potential for, er, awkwardness."

The duchess was visibly relieved.

Honey knew her mother-in-law had meant to warn—not hurt—her by disgorging the information that Simon's former betrothed had returned to the area.

Although Honey didn't want Simon to suffer pain—especially not the debilitating sort he was apparently enduring—neither did she like to think that his current condition was somehow linked to Bella MacLeish. She really wished she knew what his brother had said.

"Well, it is time for me to be getting home." The dowager rose.

Honey escorted her to her waiting carriage, promising to consider a possible date for a dinner party. She watched the ducal coach, complete with four outriders, trundle down the drive, staring even after it had disappeared.

She returned to her sitting room; her mind oddly blank. She was still staring at nothing a short time later when a gentle knock made her look up.

Hume stood in the doorway. "I'm sorry to interrupt you, my lady, but there is a gentleman here who has asked to see you."

"Who is it, Hume?"

"A Mister Heyworth, he was scheduled to meet with the marquess about a steward position. He has come all the way from Leeds to meet with his lordship, but …"

Honey understood: But Simon was indisposed.

"I shall meet with him. Show him in."

Hume left and Honey gratefully turned her mind to a situation less fraught than that of her marriage. If the man had come all the way from Leeds to speak to Simon, then they must put him up, at least for the night, and hope that Simon could meet with him tomorrow or later today.

Again, the door opened and Hume ushered a tall, dark-haired man into the room.

"Good afternoon, my lady, I am Benjamin Heyworth."

"Please, have a seat." Honey gestured to one of the chairs across from her. "I understand you had a meeting with my husband. I'm afraid he is indisposed."

"I am very sorry to hear that, my lady. I hope it is nothing serious." It wasn't a question, but she felt she owed him at least a little information.

"Lord Saybrook was injured in Belgium and is still recovering from some of his injuries." That should be vague enough—not exposing Simon's condition yet still communicating its seriousness.

Heyworth's forehead creased with concern that appeared genuine. His green-brown eyes were clear and intelligent beneath expressive brows. "I know of his lordship's service; it is most impressive. I would not have disturbed you, but I'm afraid I only have a certain amount of time set aside for this visit." He flashed her a rueful smile. "I seem to have found myself with two possible positions at the same moment."

"Ah, an embarrassment of riches."

"Normally I would agree with you, but, you see, I am scheduled to meet my other prospective employer in four days. I informed his lordship of this in my letter," he added hastily. He lifted his broad shoulders and let them drop. "So, you see my predicament."

"I shall see what I can do this afternoon, although I can promise you nothing. You must stay for dinner and be our guest for the evening." Honey stood and he rose with her.

"I will have Hume show you to a room and send up some tea to tide you over."

"You are most kind." He hesitated and Honey raised her eyebrows. "I hope you won't think me impertinent, but I was wondering—as long as I am here—if there is anyone who could show me around the estate?"

As a woman who'd always worked for her living Honey did not think this was impertinent at all. But she did not know who could accompany him on such a journey. "I'd offer my own services, but I'm afraid I only arrived here a few days ago, myself. But I will see what I can arrange."

The door opened and it was Hume who answered the bell so she turned Heyworth over to her butler and went to look for some answers.

Chapter Thirty-One

Simon felt as weak as a baby bird, but at least the incessant drumming had gone away. It had stopped sometime in the middle of last night, but he'd still managed to lose his breakfast of weak tea and toast half an hour after eating it. So, he'd stayed in bed until noon, when he could stand the boredom no longer.

"I will have a bath, Peel," he'd said over his servant's mild demur. "The pain has gone. For now. And I have abandoned my bride for days. It is time I was up."

That had proved more arduous than it sounded. It had taken a good two hours before he was ready to leave his chambers and he was just donning his coat when there was a light knock on the door.

"Come," he called, waving away Peel when he would have buttoned Simon's coat, as if he were a boy of five.

His wife peeked through the small gap and Simon smiled. "Come in, Honoria. Why did you not use our connecting door?"

She stepped inside, her face taut and stiff, the way it had been before they'd become lovers.

Simon took her hand and kissed her palm. "You are a sight for sore eyes, my dear."

She blushed but remained stiff. "Are you well?"

"Yes, the pain has passed." He tucked a stray stand of hair back behind her ear. "I'm sorry to have abandoned you. You'll be thinking me a poor, sickly thing."

"Of course I don't. I'm glad you are feeling better."

"And *I'm* glad you came to me."

She dropped her eyes, suddenly shy, as if the weeks in Brighton had not happened.

Well, Simon would soon take care of that.

"There is a Mr. Heyworth here to see you."

Simon frowned, taking his watch and fob from Peel. "I don't recognize the name. Who is he?"

"He said he was here about the steward position."

Simon fiddled with his watch, playing for time as he struggled to recall the name. He could not.

Peel, who had been watching him like a hen with one chick, stepped forward to pluck a non-existent piece of lint from his sleeve.

"That would be the gentleman from Leeds, would it not, my lord?"

Simon still had no recollection of such a meeting, but it was easy enough to play along until he did. "Ah, yes." He looked at Honoria. "You have spoken to him?"

"I have invited him to dine with us and stay the night."

"Excellent." She still looked hesitant. "Is aught amiss?"

"He asked if there was anyone to show him around the property."

"That sounds like a fine idea." He nodded to Peel, "Let Mr. Heyworth know I will meet him in the stables in three-quarters of an hour."

Peel opened his mouth but then closed it again when he met Simon's glare.

Once he'd gone, Simon turned to Honoria, put his hands on her shoulders, and gave her a rueful smile. "Do you forgive me for abandoning you on your first few days in our new home?"

"It was hardly your fault," she said. "Are you sure it is a good idea to go riding so soon after—"

"I am feeling very well—just restless from a lack of exercise." He leaned down and kissed her, letting his mouth linger on her plush, warm lips. "Mmm," he murmured, pulling away with regret and looking deep into her cool gray eyes. "I will need *lots* of exercise."

She flushed wildly, but at least she was smiling, now.

"Why don't you join us?"

"You mean on your ride?"

"Why not? You haven't seen the place yet."

"Very well, I shall."

"Good. I'll need to change; shall we say an hour?"

She cocked her head. "I thought you said three-quarters of an hour?"

"That was before a woman was involved," he teased, giving her a kiss on the cheek and a gentle push toward their connecting doors, which he fully intended to use tonight.

***

It was all Honey could do not to skip and sing; Simon was the same man who'd come here with her a few days ago. He wasn't some love-struck swain grieving for another woman, after all. It was just as he'd claimed: a terrible headache.

Honey changed into the new habit Simon had picked out for her during their orgy of shopping in Brighton.

"You must have this habit," he'd said, pointing at a fashion plate. "But it should be in crimson, to match that dashing hat."

When she'd demurred about the color being too bright, he had surprised her.

"Don't shy away from the colors that suit you merely because you are a tall woman, Honoria. That shade of red could have been invented just for you."

Honey had almost collapsed sobbing at his feet. He was right, and she knew it. After all, she was an artist—she knew about colors. Oh, the gowns she wore were in colors that flattered her, but they were in the calmer, more unobtrusive part of the palette.

For years she had yearned to wear deep jewel tones.

Now that she'd begun wearing such colors, she was ashamed it had taken her so long.

She was ready and down in the stables a full quarter of an hour early. So was Mr. Heyworth, but her husband was not yet there.

Mr. Heyworth's eyes widened flatteringly when he saw her.

"I am going to join you, Mr. Heyworth, as I have not yet seen much of the estate." She had to tip her head back to meet his eyes; he was even taller than Simon.

"I learned that you and his lordship are only recently married?"

Ah, so somebody had been talking. It wasn't really a surprise; nor was it some kind of secret. "Yes, it is less than a month."

"I see I'm late."

They both turned at the sound of Simon's voice.

He gave Honey an apologetic smile. "And here I was teasing you about tardiness." He turned to Heyworth.

"It is good to meet you, Mr. Heyworth. I was very impressed with your work experience."

"Thank you, my lord. I am eager to see your estate. I believe you have plans to breed horses?"

"I do, after my stables have been overhauled and expanded." He gestured the other man ahead into the courtyard before leaning close and whispering into Honey's ear, "You look smashing."

Her face heated with pleasure.

Several servants were bustling around three horses, Simon led Honey to a very pretty dark bay roan—whose coloring just so happened to compliment her habit. She cut him a sideways glance and he winked, letting her know he was responsible. The tiny act of sweet, playfulness made her chest expand with love and she looked away, afraid of what her eyes might expose to him.

"Are you ready?" he asked her.

She nodded and he waved away the groom who'd pushed over the mounting block. Instead, he lifted her into the saddle himself.

He ignored her look of concern at such exertion and gave her booted ankle a quick squeeze before turning to the steward, who was already on a handsome gelding named Saturn. Simon himself rode Loki. She couldn't help wishing he had a less volatile mount, but it was hardly her place to say such a thing.

Honey rode between the two men, Simon including her in their discussion of land, tenant farms, and other estate matters. She enjoyed the desultory pace and sunshine and thought the two men seemed to get on quite well; it was easy to like the tall, earnest steward.

They were cresting a gentle rise when a voice called out. Honey saw there was a little gazebo that overlooked a bend in the stream.

She knew who it would be before the person stepped out of the shadows. Not that she recognized the woman's voice after all these years, but it just seemed like no part of arriving at her new home could proceed without something coming along to ruin it. First it had been the duke, and now it was Arabella MacLeish.

The other woman floated toward them with a sinuous grace, her smile blinding. "Simon! I just knew it was you."

Sometimes in life, one exaggerated the grandeur or beauty of a person or event, only to later see said object and discover that one's imagination had built it up.

This was not one of those occasions.

Countess MacLeish was even more beautiful than Honey remembered.

Simon's face was so blank that she wondered if he didn't recognize his former love. But Loki shifted beneath him with a nervousness that came from the man on his back.

"Bella," he said.

It was not the same joyous exclamation of that long-ago day in London, outside Gunters, but the word still throbbed with some emotion, not that Honey could identify it.

She could not look at either of them, which left Heyworth.

When she turned to the steward, he was looking directly at her, and Honey would have sworn she recognized the same expression she'd been seeing on Simon's servants: pity.

Chapter Thirty-Two

Simon hadn't drunk this much since that night at Grunstead. Indeed, he'd not had any spirits at all since that evening—a conscious decision.

But tonight, the alcohol kept sliding down his throat, as if somebody else's hand were pouring it.

Earlier today, when Honey had come to his room, he'd been annoyed that Heyworth would be at dinner with them—he'd wanted his wife all to himself.

But then they had run into Bella.

Simon snorted and his hand lifted the glass to his mouth without any encouragement from his brain.

She was as beautiful as ever. Not as slender, but lush—the body of a mature woman.

He had no idea why she was back here—he'd never given Wyndham a chance to tell him—but assumed her husband had left her destitute. Had she failed to bear him an heir? Or was it some other catastrophe that had brought her back to her childhood home?

She certainly hadn't looked like a mother—at least not like any mother that Simon had ever seen. She had looked like a green-eyed siren and he'd gawked at her like a stunned, smitten boy—right there in front of his new wife and a complete stranger.

His wife.

"Hell," he muttered, topping up his glass from the almost empty bottle, filling it all the way to the rim.

As addled as Bella had made him, it had taken him almost until the end of their brief visit to shake himself from his fugue and see that she was bent on mischief. She'd all but ignored Honoria, fawning over Simon and Heyworth, remind him suddenly of how she'd always behaved when other women were around: dismissively.

He recalled that she'd claimed to be a victim of feminine jealousy. As beautiful as she was, he suspected there was a grain of truth to her assertion. But he thought she worsened the situation by always seeking to be the center of attention.

By the time Simon had gathered his wits and disengaged his party from her, Honey had become as cool and aloof as she'd been before Brighton, which told him that somebody had informed her about Bella and her place in his past.

Simon suspected his mother. Wyndham would not want Bella's name mentioned or her existence acknowledged—and Honey wouldn't speak to him, anyway.

He closed his eyes and thought about his encounter with Bella today. He would need to speak to her again—alone, this time. She could not continue to ambush him—or, God forbid, Honey—the way she'd done today.

While it was true that he'd been stunned to see her after all these years, that had only been his initial reaction. What had truly rattled him was the tangled barrage of memories her face had unleashed. It had been too much, too fast.

He suspected that he'd appeared tongue-tied and besotted, when, in reality, he'd simply been overwhelmed.

She had walked out of his life fourteen years earlier without a word to him. Only that letter, a letter that—remarkably—he'd somehow managed to hold on to all these years, although it had been ages since he'd taken out the short missive and re-read it.

He glanced at it now, where it lay open on his desk. Unlike in the past, reading it no longer incited his anger.

He felt … nothing.

Simon let his drink-addled mind wander, unsurprised when it led him hip-deep into a flood of memories.

Chief among them was an image of Bella at seventeen, rising from his tattered, turbulent memory like Venus emerging from the waves. Only more beautiful.

He'd been eighteen and it was to be a summer of freedom before he went to Oxford. Simon didn't want to go—he was an indifferent student at best—but Wyndham had insisted he give it at least two years before he would consider Simon's plans for Everley.

At first, he'd been disgruntled, but then he realized he would enjoy the freedom of university, which he planned to fill with entertainment rather than studies.

He'd come home to find his cousin, Raymond, dogging his every step. Although Raymond was a year older than Simon, he had always behaved like a far younger man.

Raymond had finished school and returned to Whitcomb the year before. Wyndham took his responsibilities as the head of the family seriously and he'd personally set about teaching Raymond estate management. Simon knew that the duke had always given Raymond and Simon the same allowance but wanted Raymond to have a skill that would keep him from being dependent.

Whereas Simon would inherit his own estate and money when he came of age, there was nothing like that waiting for Raymond, who'd been left destitute by his feckless gambler of a father.

While Simon was anticipating university, Raymond had taken up a position as Wyndham's steward and spent his time traveling between the duke's six estates.

Simon hadn't believed Raymond had the brains for such work, but he could see that Wyndham's faith in his skills made his cousin happy. Because they were so close in age, they had always spent their school breaks riding, carousing, and wenching together.

But, for some reason, Raymond had gotten on his nerves that summer and Simon found himself constantly escaping the other man's cloying attention.

He'd been out riding the estate when he'd come upon Bella. It had been years since he'd last seen her, not since before he went to Eton, which would have made him eight or nine.

She'd been reading in the small gazebo that overlooked the stream. His brother had built it and allowed everyone in the area to use it.

She'd looked up, surprise in her wide green eyes, her impossibly red lips curving. He still recalled how her beauty had robbed him of his wits and words.

"Simon, I'd heard you were back."

Even back then he'd wondered if that was why she'd chosen such an improbable place to read—because she knew he rode that way.

But the cynical thought had evaporated, burnt away by her beauty after he'd dismounted and they had chatted.

That was the first of many chats they had that summer. She should have had a Season but her elder sisters had both been out for several years and had not yet formed suitable attachments.

"I will never get my turn," she'd told him more than once, heaving a sigh that made her plump bosom swell to twice its size.

Simon had fervently hoped that she did not. He'd already decided that he had to have her—but she was a lady, not like the serving wenches and two widows who'd been his sporting partners up until that point. No, he wanted her as his wife.

But Wyndham had remained adamant: Simon had to spend two years—until he was twenty—at university. Once he'd done that, his brother said he could marry Bella and settle down to horse breeding if that was still on his mind.

As if Simon would ever want to do anything else.

So, he'd waited two long years.

He would miss Bella, of course, but they were in love and it would one day all be worth the wait.

In the middle of his first year at Oxford—which he'd found astoundingly enjoyable, to his surprise—the duchess gave birth to another stillborn son. The house had been a grim place of mourning when he'd gone home that summer.

He and Bella had needed to snatch bits of time here and there. On her eighteenth birthday he'd given her a diamond bracelet. He'd saved half of each of his quarterly allowances to afford it, and she had loved it. Of course she could not wear it in public—not without raising questions—but it had been a tangible token of Simon's love.

Throughout the next year they had sent letters to each other, using devious means, becoming closer than ever.

And then, miracles of miracles, Cecily had become pregnant again.

This time, the child—a boy—appeared healthy.

But while the baby had survived, his sister-in-law had suffered some sort of injury during the birth and her already fragile health had become even worse. There would be no more children.

Simon went to Wyndham not long after his son was born.

While not elated by his decision to marry Bella, his brother had acquiesced to his plans. He'd only asked that Simon wait until Cecily was well enough to entertain before they made the official announcement.

It wouldn't be long, he'd promised, just after Simon sat for his portrait.

Simon's last leave-taking from Bella was burnt into his brain.

"He really said *yes*?" Bella asked, more than once.

Simon had laughed at her amazement. "You must have begun to wonder if I'd ever come to the sticking point. It's just—"

Bella had nodded. "I know, Simon, your family—especially your brother—have had their share of problems."

Simon recalled thinking that it was Cecily who'd suffered the most, but that had been an afternoon to celebrate—not to discuss his family.

But then Edward had died and Bella had married and Simon had gone to war.

Simon opened his eyes and gazed at the coffered ceiling above his head, those long-ago memories dissipating like mist.

It felt like a story he'd read—something that happened to other people. Seeing Bella had jarred everything loose—things he'd not considered in years. And, for the first time, he felt nothing when he thought of Bella and what they had once shared.

Nothing at all.

It was a different woman who took up all the space in his addled mind; a woman with cool gray eyes and a self-contained dignity that incited him. He loved his tightly-laced wife—and he loved being the only man to see her break free of those restraints.

He was, he realized, happy. Happier than he could recall being in a long, long time.

Smiling at the thought, he sighed and pulled his gaze from the ceiling. When he looked down, he saw the empty glass and bottle on his desk.

Damn and blast! How had that happened?

The clock chimed and Simon looked up, stunned: it was half-past midnight. He'd had a drink with Heyworth after dinner and had come to the library, promising to join his wife and new employee in the drawing room after a bit.

That had been almost three hours ago.

Holy Hell. Where had the time gone? He'd forgotten all about returning to the drawing room.

***

Honey heard the connecting door open but did not move. She was facing away from the door but recognized the shadow he cast across the plush carpet beside the bed. Besides, who else would be opening the door between their rooms close to one o'clock in the morning?

For a moment she thought he could come inside—perhaps come into her bed. But the door closed with a soft click.

She rolled onto her back and stared up at the blackness above her head.

Fury and shame fought for dominance in her mind and had been doing so ever since he failed to show up in the drawing room after dinner.

It would have been bad enough if he had simply abandoned her. But Mr. Heyworth had been there as well. The conversation had become more and more awkward as the other man realized Simon was not going to appear. Honoria had refused to tuck her tail between her legs and flee to her chambers. Instead, she had ordered tea when the time came and they had pretended that everything was normal.

Well, maybe this *was* normal. Maybe three weeks of married bliss was all she would have. But then why had he come up now—after all these hours?

She thought about today—about the woman who just *happened* to appear during their ride. It was foolishly suspicious to believe she could have been waiting for them—after all, what would she do, wait there all day, every day? She might have waited a year in that little gazebo by the stream without encountering anyone at all.

But there had been something in her eyes, some sly light that had said she knew exactly where to find Simon.

They'd only lingered a quarter of an hour, but it had felt like a century.

The surge of jealousy she'd experienced had infuriated her. Of all the base human emotions she *despised* jealousy the most. Not since she'd been a girl had she been plagued by it.

Simon had been correct when he'd said that she was the reason her father never remarried.

He'd also been right when he'd said that her father should have insisted that she go to school.

If she had gone away and had friends then she wouldn't have relied on her father for everything. The lovers he'd taken had not all been unpleasant to her—several had been quite lovely. But, to Honey, those women had been a threat to the only life she knew.

She had never wanted to share him because he was all she had.

Was that what she was feeling right now?

Or was it just that she was upset to be caught in the middle of something she didn't understand?

Honey sighed; she refused to let jealousy rule her—especially when she didn't yet know if she had anything to be jealous *about*.

If Simon was in love with Bella—and judging from his stunned expression he certainly felt something for her—and she was a widow, then why hadn't they married?

Simon had not acted like a broken-hearted lover when he'd asked her to marry him. She'd only been his wife for a month but she already knew that he was not the sort of man to hide his emotions. He was not stealthy or manipulative: what he felt he showed and then acted upon.

If he loved Bella, he would have married her.

So what was going on?

He hadn't been acting strangely before their ride, or during their ride—at least not until the lovely Countess MacLeish had materialized like a fairy from a Shakespeare play.

The conversation had been amiable, vague, and that of old neighbors seeing one another after an absence of many years. But the currents beneath the words had been vicious undertows of emotion and burning, unasked questions.

Honey might not understand it, but she'd felt it.

She turned onto her side, hugging a pillow to her chest, the pain of missing him physical. They had only been together for a few weeks, how had her attachment to him grown so strong, so quickly?

She squeezed the pillow so hard it was a wonder that stuffing did not pop out of it.

What was she supposed to do? Sit here and wait for her husband to pursue his old love—who was clearly interested in pursuing him?

Honey heaved a sigh. Why couldn't anything in life be the way one hoped and expected?

She immediately felt petty and childish for even thinking such a stupid thing. The truth was that Simon had promised her a marriage of convenience, nothing more. No matter what she might be feeling, she needed to recall *that*.

How could a marriage founded on the mutual agreement never to have children ever be anything other than a business arrangement?

Chapter Thirty-Three

Honey did not join Simon for breakfast, which was a first—at least when they'd been in Brighton. But he'd been ill every morning at Everley, so perhaps she didn't come down to eat?

Heyworth was there, however, and they settled matters between them quickly.

"How soon can you begin?" Simon asked the younger man as he made his way through a heaping plate of food.

"I can return in a week."

"Excellent. I will want to begin breaking ground for the new stable block. I'll show you my plans before you set off." *Which I should have done last night, if I hadn't been so jug-bitten ...*

Simon's face heated at the thought, but he pushed past it and talked of local builders and how much could be done before winter.

Heyworth accompanied him to his study after they'd finished breakfast. While the other man looked at the plans for the expansion, Simon brooded. He couldn't deny he was on edge. He'd behaved badly last night and now would have to apologize. It wasn't the act of apologizing he minded—he was willing to accept his blame—it was the subject and reason for his behavior. He'd never believed he was a drunkard, but last night he had begun drinking at dinner and then he drank and drank and drank and forgot everything else. It was mortifying.

A knock made him look up.

Honoria was in the open doorway. "I'm sorry to disturb you, my lord, but your mother has come to see you. I've put her in the smaller sitting room."

"Of course, thank you." Simon stood. "You're welcome to stay as long as you like, Heyworth."

Heyworth looked up from the plans, and a small leather-bound book in which he had made some notations. "Thank you, my lord, but I had better be on my way."

Simon went toward Honoria, who did not meet his eyes. Instead, she took a step toward the other man, turning her back to Simon. "I will show you out, Mr. Heyworth."

He felt a spark of anger at the obvious cut, but Simon knew it was what he had earned with his behavior. The sooner he apologized, the better.

His mother smiled nervously at him when he entered the sitting room and kissed her cheek.

"I think I did something unwise," she blurted.

"Oh?" he said, sinking into the chair across from her.

Her pale cheeks flushed. "I'm so sorry, Simon, but I'm afraid I may have mentioned your, er, past attachment to Arabella MacLeish."

Well, he supposed that might account for part of her frosty behavior.

He smiled. "It's fine, Mother. My past with Bella is no secret— it's also very much in my past."

"Oh, thank goodness," she murmured, her cheeks flushing even darker when she saw him staring at her. "I didn't mean it the way you think, Simon. I just … well, she is a siren."

His lips twitched at her dramatic language. "She can be somebody else's siren," he said drily. "We saw her yesterday, by the way."

Her pale gray eyes, so much like Wyndham's, widened. "We?"

"I was out riding with Honoria and Heyworth—my new steward."

"Oh," she said, and then asked, "And?"

"Something she said gave me the impression that Wyndham has been hard on her family."

His mother grimaced. "Well, you know how he can be."

"I *do* know. But I shan't give them all the cut, Mama."

"No, no, I didn't think you would," she said faintly, her expression saying that she'd still hoped.

"If I behave stiffly and fuel the already existing mystery around her it will only make our past a bigger subject for gossip. If I treat her like anyone else, the dust will quickly settle."

"Yes, I suppose that makes sense."

He chuckled at her dubious frown. "Tell Wyndham what I said, Mother. Let's put all this behind us."

"Perhaps you might tell him?"

"I will say something when I see him again," he promised, not bothering to mention that he had no plans to see his brother any time soon.

What he *did* need to do soon was go see Bella and make sure that days like yesterday didn't happen again.

Chapter Thirty-Four

At dinner that night it was just the two of them.

Honey had spent the day with her housekeeper, Mrs. Lowell, taking pains to avoid her husband.

Avoiding Simon wasn't difficult as he'd saddled up Loki and disappeared almost immediately after speaking to his mother.

By the time she went upstairs to bathe and dress for dinner and he still hadn't returned, Honey's nerves were stretched taut. Would he come to dine? Or would he drink himself into a stupor again, letting a half hour of port stretch to four hours?

But, no, there he was—freshly groomed and looking sinful in his blacks—when she entered the dining room at eight o'clock. His blue eyes widened as he took in her gown—the golden lace confection he'd bought for her in Brighton.

He came toward her, his expression … adoring.

Honey's pulse thudded deafeningly at the way he consumed her with his eyes.

"You look divine, Honoria." He took both her hands and held them out, his hot gaze roaming lazily over her body, sending the predictable spirals of lust to her belly and causing a distracting aching between her thighs.

It infuriated her how was he able to disarm her with so little effort.

You love it.

Yes, she did. But that didn't mean it didn't infuriate her, too.

Once Hume and the footman left to fetch the first course Simon took her hand.

Honey swallowed as she stared down at his long fingers; they were work-roughened but still elegant, and easily twice as thick as hers.

He reached for her chin with his other hand and tilted her face up, until she couldn't avoid his consuming stare. "Are you still angry with me? You have every right to be," he said before she could answer, his smile wry.

Honey hesitated. She considered just accepting his apology and moving on.

That is a bad habit, Honey. Begin as you would go on.

"What happened last night?"

He released her chin but not her hand. "Heyworth asked several sticky questions about the improvements during dinner and I got caught up in those." He shrugged. "I'm afraid I'm a bit, er, well, obsessed with the project and I simply lost track of time."

Honey nodded slowly; she swore he was not telling her the truth. At least not all of it.

She certainly believed the part about being obsessed, but she wasn't convinced it was the stables that had kept him occupied last night.

He squeezed her hand. "I will guard against it happening again—whether we have guests, or not." He hesitated, and then said, "I would be obliged if you came to me if it were ever to occur again. I dislike blaming my injuries, but the truth is that I'm not always aware of the passage of time. And I do tend to forget what I'm supposed to be doing."

That, at least, sounded honest. "I can do that," she said.

Before he could reply the door opened and the first course arrived.

***

Simon was grateful that his new wife was not churlish or tending toward grudges—not that he deserved easy forgiveness.

Still, it was fortunate she was understanding because he *did* have a tendency to focus on one matter to the exclusion of all others.

And if he'd fibbed a little by neglecting to mention the other issue that had consumed his thoughts last night? Well, he believed that it had been better to pass along a small falsehood than to hurt her.

Wasn't it?

Besides, his conversation with Bella today had put to rest any concerns he might have had about lingering feelings for her.

Other than a certain nostalgic fondness and admiration for a beautiful woman, he'd felt nothing for her when he'd sat in the shabby sitting room at Frampton Park.

Not only was his own mind settled, but, after today's conversation, Bella now knew that Simon was very married.

He knew that Bella didn't love or yearn for him; he'd recognized the familiar glint in her eyes: she'd been hoping for a bit of sport—a diversion from what likely a very mundane existence.

The only sport he'd offered her was the use of one of the new hunters he'd bought, a fine mare he intended to breed as soon as his new stud was delivered.

Bella was one of the most skilled equestriennes he'd ever seen. Hell, she was a better rider than most men.

Simon had planned to pay a rough rider this hunting season as he had several hunters he wished to sell. This way he could pay Bella, even though money had never been mentioned.

She'd told him that her husband had been hunting mad and she'd gone with him every year, so he knew she'd kept up with the sport.

Apparently, MacLeish had been deeply dipped and when he'd died the ancestral home had gone to a cousin, since Bella and her husband had only had one daughter.

She'd been forced to move back in with her parents because all MacLeish's personal property had gone for debts.

Since Bella was too bloody poor to even own a riding hack, he'd opened his stables to her, as well. Not only was it a small kindness that he could well afford, but he wanted her in top fettle if she was going to be hunting one of his horses this year.

Like most females who hunted seriously, Bella rode astride. His niece Rebecca did, as well, at Wyndham's insistence. Simon was proud that his stiff brother valued his daughter's health over a bit of scandalous clothing. It was just too damned dangerous to hunt on a woman's pleasure saddle, in Simon's opinion.

There would be plenty of riders with the local hunt who would recall Bella from years ago. He couldn't help smiling at the thought of how she would shake up many of the parochial men—and then ride them into the dirt.

Simon saw that Honey was looking at him and realized he'd been woolgathering rather than entertaining his wife.

"Wine?" he asked, picking up the bottle that had been decanting.

"Yes, please."

He was eager to talk of something other than himself, Everley, his stables project, or his family. "How was your day? You've been working on Becca's portrait."

She took a sip, looking pleased by the vintage. "I worked on her portrait and began stretching a canvas for the duchess's."

"You don't mind working on two at once?"

"Not at all. Preparing a canvas is easy work that needs to be done. It is perfect for those times you cannot bring yourself to focus."

Simon didn't have to ask what had been disturbing her focus. "I see there were a great pile of letters for you this morning. I'm assuming one or two are from Lady Sedgwick and Ingram. Are the others also from your teacher friends?"

The countess and Miles Ingram had despised him—he'd seen that straight away. Of course, Ingram had good reason to dislike him. He wondered if Honey's other friends would loathe him, as well. It surprised him to realize that he'd much rather her friends *liked* him. Or at least didn't take him in active dislike.

She swallowed her oyster and dabbed her plump lower lip with her napkin, the action making him harden. Of course, that wasn't anything unusual; the juxtaposition between his wife's cool outward appearance and the firebrand she was in private kept him in a state of arousal whenever he was around her.

"Indeed," she said. "It was an unprecedented *nine* letters."

Simon chuckled. "Lord, I scarcely have nine acquaintances. All from teachers?"

"One from each of my friends—those who couldn't attend our wedding sending their felicitations—and also two possible commissions."

Simon paused, his oyster halfway to his mouth. "Commissions?" As soon as he spoke, he felt like a fool. Of course, she would continue painting—no matter where she lived.

"Yes, Freddie forwarded them."

He swallowed his food before asking, "Who from?"

"One from a client of Freddie's—a man named Thurston Lloyd—and one from Baron Stoke."

"Yes, the shipping magnate," he said, familiar with Lloyd's name from the newspapers.

"The very same. It appears that he wants a portrait of his son and Baron Stoke wants one of himself."

Simon ate another oyster, considering his reaction to the news that his wife would have two male subjects, men she would spend hours alone with.

Something dark and ugly churned in his belly.

Ah, jealousy. Yet another attractive emotion to add to your already impressive collection.

Simon scowled at the voice in his head. What kind of man wanted his wife to spend hours with other men? He knew Stoke—the man looked like a cross between a toad and a tree stump; so, no problem, there.

But Lloyd's son? What if he were young and handsome and unscarred? What if—

"*Simon?*"

His head whipped up. Judging by his wife's tone and concerned expression, this wasn't the first time she'd spoken his name.

"I'm sorry, Honoria, what was that?"

"I said I would like to schedule both sittings back-to-back, which would mean a longer visit to London, but I think that is better than two separate trips. I daresay I wouldn't need longer than three weeks."

"When did you want to go? Perhaps I could go with you."

"I thought I'd go at the end of the month."

Simon frowned. "You wish to go during hunting season," he asked, more than a little surprised.

"That's probably just as well. I don't care for hunting," she said.

Simon gasped and clutched at his chest. "Lord save me. I've married a woman who doesn't like hunting." When her face tightened, he reached for her hand. "I'm teasing you, love. Of course, you needn't hunt if you don't wish to. My mother never cared for it, nor does Cecily. Becca is mad for it, so she can come along and make sure her doddering old uncle doesn't fall off his hunter."

She gave him an uncertain smile, making him realize how raw her emotions must be—thanks to his recent idiocy.

"The end of the month is probably a good time to go," he said, releasing her hand and turning back to his meal. "Between the hunting and the construction, I'll not be especially entertaining." He lowered his eyelids. "I'd better make up for that starting tonight." He was pleased when she blushed.

"So, tell me about these other friends of yours," he said.

"Well, you've met Freddie and Miles, but there is also Portia—"

"She's the one who married Broughton?"

"Yes, not long ago."

"It seems like I heard something unusual about him?" Simon frowned as he tried to recall.

"The Earl of Broughton has albinism. Also, he only recently inherited the title."

"Ah," Simon nodded.

"There is Annis, who is currently living with her grandmother." Honey chuckled fondly. "Annis is ... well, she is one of a kind."

"Oh, how is that?"

"She is almost otherworldly—not only does she look like a fairy—dainty, delicate, with enormous blue eyes and hair the color of cornsilk—but she never seems to be entirely in the present. She was the language teacher and taught French, Italian, and German. I have no idea how many other languages she speaks. She is also rather astounding when it comes to knowing word and idiom origins." She gave him a wry look. "Having a conversation with her is like chasing kittens."

"You sound like you miss her," he said.

"I do. I miss all of them. Working at the Stefani Academy was one of the best times of my life. It was too bad that Ivo Stefani was so profligate."

"I heard him play once—in Portugal, years ago. He was ... well, I'm no expert, but he was astounding."

"I never heard him. By the time he opened the school with Portia he'd injured one of his hands. But Portia is an amazing musician in her own right."

"Who is next?" Simon asked, loving seeing her so animated.

"Serena Lombard taught sculpting and botany."

"She is the Duke of Remington's daughter-in-law—French, isn't she?"

"Half-French and half-English. Yes, she was married to the youngest son, who died in the war." She cocked her head. "Did you know him?"

"I never had the pleasure," he admitted.

"Serena is currently working at Gareth Lockheart's estate—she is in charge of landscaping his entire park, as well as doing several sculptures."

"That is impressive," Simon said, not exaggerating. "I've heard that Lockheart is a genius, but that he's also a bit … odd."

"I know nothing about that. Serena said that he is delightful to work for and that money is no object."

Simon laughed. "That *would* be delightful." He lifted his hand and ticked off his fingers, "So, that's Freddie, Miles, Portia, Annis, Serena—am I missing anybody?"

"Last but not least, there is Lorelei Fontenot."

"Now *there's* a name. Let me guess—was she a mistress of theatrical arts?"

"Shame on you! Young ladies do *not* get instruction in treading the boards. No, Lorelei taught English composition, as well as the classics. She is a rather vehement proponent of Mary Wollstonecraft."

Simon groaned—only partly in jest. "A bluestocking, eh?"

"She would chide you for employing such a term." She pursed her lips, as if suppressing something especially amusing. "I daresay you and Lorelei would lock horns instantly."

"Whatever do you mean? Am I not an open, modern-minded male?"

She made an adorable snorting sound. "You epitomize masculinity."

Simon grinned. "That doesn't sound bad at all."

"Well, it does to Lorelei. I doubt she'll ever get married, but, if she did, it would be to a supportive proponent of Wollstonecraftian ideals who would be her equal in all ways."

Simon could only stare.

"I can see by your expression that you find the notion of such equality unpalatable."

"No," he drawled, trying to formulate an answer that wouldn't end with a locked door between their rooms. "I suppose I believe men and women possess different strengths and weaknesses—not that the sexes are the same."

"She's not arguing that. Rather, she believes that women deserve the same rights over our persons and our money as men possess."

Simon nodded. "I'm in agreement with her, there." Her eyes widened in surprised. "I cannot believe you look so stunned by my admission. Have I really behaved like such an ogre? You just informed me that you were going to London to pursue your business—a business which involves you spending time alone with strange men, I might add—and I made nary an objection."

"That is true," she admitted, her color high, for some reason.

"As to women having rights over their own person, I couldn't agree more. Lots of men are cruel brutes who use their superior strength against women—and children. And once they are married, they may do so with impunity." His lips curled in distaste. "There should be protections in place."

The smile she gave him was almost blinding.

"What?" he asked.

"It's just—well, you are so enlightened."

Simon sputtered.

"I don't mean I thought you were brutish, I just thought you would support the status quo."

"Not when the status quo is unjust."

"I am very pleased to hear that, Simon."

The look she gave him arrowed straight to his cock and the sound of his name on her lips fed intensely masculine thoughts that she probably would not be so approving of.

Simon couldn't wait until dinner was over.

Chapter Thirty-Five

Honey had just dismissed Nora, her maid, and finished brushing her hair when there was a brief knock and then Simon entered.

It had only been five nights since she'd last seen him in his robe, but it felt like a year. As ever, he wore nothing beneath it, the satin brocade obscenely tented by his erection.

Without a word, he strode toward her and caught her up in his arms, his mouth crushing hers.

A loud groan filled her ears and she realized that it had come from her.

He kissed her with lips, tongue, and teeth, grazing and nipping and sucking. "God, I missed you so much, Honey," he muttered gruffly as he lightly bit her earlobe and then kissed it. "Did you miss me?"

She wanted to say something sophisticated and clever, but her wits were already scrambled. "You know I did," she whispered as he nudged her head back and then trailed cruel nips and soothing kisses down her exposed throat.

"I think it's time we resume our evening lessons, don't you?" he said against the sensitive skin at the base of her throat—right before he sucked in a mouthful of tender flesh and worried it with his lips and teeth.

Honey squirmed at the insistent throbbing deep in her sex. What was wrong with her that she liked his rough touches so?

"You marked me," she said in a dreamy voice.

It wasn't a question, but he chuckled and nodded. "Guilty." A big warm hand slid down her belly, toward her damp curls, making her aware that he'd unbuttoned the front of her nightgown without Honey even noticing.

He parted her lower lips, the pad of his finger calloused but gentle.

"Ah, Honey—how I love the feel of these prim little lips of yours."

Her face heated, more at his lewd, suggestive words than the pleasurable stroking.

His other hand slid down her neck, not stopping until he held one of her breasts. He groaned. "What a delicious little bud." He pinched her nipple hard enough to make her bite her lip and whimper. "Don't hold anything in, love," he chided with a growl. "I want all your noises. His finger stroked between her swollen folds. "So wet," he praised in a breathy, harsh voice, caressing from her entrance to the tight bundle of nerves but never actually touching her needy core.

Honey tilted her hips to lure him closer.

He laughed, the sensual sound sending a shiver down her spine. "Such a greedy cunt," he whispered.

She gasped, her body stiffening in shock. That was a word she'd only read one time—in a book she'd sneaked out of her father's *private* library.

"Does that word shock you? *Cunt*," he murmured.

Another wicked chuckle rumbled through his chest as he continued kissing and licking until he reached a nipple. He sucked her hard, taking in as much of her small breast as possible. The sounds he made were crude and animalistic, his finger teasing and teasing and teasing.

Honey made a noise of frustration, shoving her sex against his hand.

He moved so quickly that she found herself bouncing on her mattress before she even realized that he'd picked her up.

He grinned down at her, breathing raggedly. He tugged at the sash and then carelessly shrugged out of his robe, his fist closing around his thrusting organ.

Honey couldn't help staring. She'd seen him naked and erect dozens of times, but his appeal never diminished.

He clenched his big hand tightly enough to make the veins on the back of his hand stand out, the ropey muscles in his forearm flexing beneath his sun-browned skin.

"I was hard all the way through dinner," he said, his conversational tone at odds with his shockingly erotic actions and words. "Peel was most displeased when he undressed me for bed as there was a big wet spot on my pantaloons. I told him it was your fault."

She gasped. "You didn't!"

He grinned. "Did."

His eyes dropped to where he was pumping into his fist and Honey's eyes could only follow. "See how slick you make me?"

Honey made a mortifying gulping sound as she took in the most erotic sight she'd ever seen. Even his big hand could not dwarf his thick, ruddy shaft. The crown was a darker shade of red, the tiny slit glinting with moisture.

"Taste it."

Honey blinked, as if that would improve her hearing. When she looked up, he reached for the bed, snatched up a pillow, and tossed it onto the floor between his spread feet. "Kneel and taste me."

Her jaw dropped and whatever he saw on her face made him release himself.

He took a step toward her, his expression shifting in an instant from cruelly sensual to lovingly concerned. "I'm sorry, love." He grimaced. "I've shocked you. You needn't—"

"I want to." It was the truth, she did—more than she could recall wanting anything in her life.

In fact, she wanted to please him so badly she frightened herself. "I'm not angry—or frightened. I was just, er, surprised."

He studied her for a long moment before nodding, as if to himself. He leaned down, kissing her tenderly on the lips. "I'm a bad man for asking these things of you, Honey—it's not the sort of thing a gentleman requests from his wife."

"I want to," she repeated. She shoved from her mind the images of all the women that he'd asked such things of in the past, unable to bear the thought of him sharing intimacies with anyone but her.

She placed her hand flat on his chest and gave him a shove.

He staggered back a step, grinning. "That's my brave girl," he praised. And then his lips curled into a savage smile and his nostrils flared. "Strip for me, first."

***

Simon's cock throbbed when she instantly complied, the pulse beneath the brutal love bite he'd given her racing.

He was a bastard. He was treating a young—near-virginal—woman like an experienced harlot. But he felt the yearning in her every time he pinched or bit or used her roughly: she was aroused by such play.

So was he.

She tossed the nightgown to the floor, her trusting, aroused eyes staring up at him. Simon wrenched his gaze away from her hard nipples and perfect little breasts and pointed again to the floor. "Kneel."

She sank to her knees, her lips slightly parted, her gray eyes dark.

"Bloody hell," he whispered, cupping the sweet curve of her jaw with his free hand, pausing his rough pumping. "Kiss it," he ordered gruffly, squeezing his shaft until liquid beaded on the tip of his crown. "Taste me."

She didn't hesitate and Simon felt shallow, rapid puffs of air on his prick as she leaned closer, her lips parted to take him. The urge to seize her hair and give free reign to his savage passions was strong. Only by leashing his lust was he able to keep himself under control.

And it was all worth it when her delicate pink tongue flicked his weeping slit.

"Oh God, Honoria," he whispered, his body shaking.

When she pulled back, a strand of clear liquid connected her tongue to his crown.

Simon groaned as his head fell back; he was so boneless with lust that merely standing was a challenge.

Slender warm fingers closed around his hand and lifted it off his cock.

"Like this?" she asked.

He swore his head weighed a thousand pounds as he lifted it to gaze down at her.

She'd made a fist around him and was stroking; it was a beautiful bloody sight.

"Yes, just so—a bit harder," he encouraged, sucking in a breath when she flexed her strong fingers. "Just below the crown is the most sensitive part. Urgh, yes, very good," he praised, letting her get the feel of him for a moment.

And then he said, "Put me in your mouth while your hand works my shaft."

Her already parted lips opened wider in shock, her hand freezing in mid-stroke.

Simon chuckled, running a finger across her full lower lip. "I want to see you take me."

She shuddered, her eyelids fluttering but not closing.

"Open," he urged, "and lick your lips. Yes, just like that." He smiled as she swallowed several times and then leaned toward him, her wet lips stretching to surround his swollen crown, her eyes never leaving his.

If Simon had seen anything more beautiful in his life than her pouty lips wrapped around him, he couldn't recall it.

"Ah, *Christ*," he swore, his body shuddering as he forced his hips to remain still, gritting his teeth as she explored him rather enthusiastically. Her hand had stilled, but he didn't give a damn. Watching his thick shaft fill her mouth was better than a gamahuching from the most skilled courtesan in the world.

Her tongue caressed from root to tip, flicking the sensitive underside and he knew he wouldn't be able to maintain control.

Simon groaned. "That feels too good, love." He withdrew and grabbed her beneath her arms, lifting her onto the bed. The action painfully stretched the scars on his left side but he didn't give a damn.

"Hands and knees, darling," he ordered, reaching for her slim hips and effortlessly flipping her onto her front. He hooked his hands beneath her and pulled her hips up, laying his hand between her shoulders and pressing her until her head rested on the bed.

When he had her positioned how he wanted he leaned back to admire her. "Bloody hell you're gorgeous." He slid a hand over her long, lean flank, tracing the generous curve of her arse, his fingers dipping into her cleft.

She jolted when he grazed her tight little pucker and he smiled. There would be plenty of time for that some other night.

He parted her delicate folds and lightly circled her bud. "You're wet, Honey. I think you enjoyed putting your mouth on me."

She squirmed beneath his erotic petting, pushing against his hand.

On his next stroke, he slid a finger inside her. *Good God she felt like heaven.*

He kept that blasphemous thought to himself but continued his thorough exploration.

"Answer me, Honey—did you like pleasuring me with your mouth and tongue?"

She growled, sounding a bit like an angry badger. "Yes, I liked it," she said in a mulish voice that made him grin.

"You liked what?"

"Doing *that*."

"Doing what?"

"You won't quit asking until I say it will you?" Her voice was muffled by the bedding, but he could hear her desire clearly beneath her frustration.

"That's right, darling, I want to hear you say it."

"I liked—" she stopped, making the most adorable huffing sound.

"Hmm?" He stroked her a few more times before positioning his crown at her entrance. "I can't hear you, love."

"I liked licking your—"

Simon slammed into her, fingers digging into her hips as he buried himself as deeply as he could.

"Simon!" she cried, loudly enough to rattle the windows.

"*Honoria*," he whispered in response, his pulse pounding in his ears as he kept himself sheathed. "Did I hurt you, love?"

She whimpered, shaking her head back and forth, her hands clutching the bedding.

When she clenched around him and pushed back, Simon did a little whimpering of his own.

And then he proceeded to make his wife scream.

Chapter Thirty-Six

Simon? *Simon?*"

"Hmm?" he removed the spectacles he needed in order to read most writing and looked up, his lips curving into a smile when he saw his wife.

But they turned down when he saw she wasn't smiling back at him.

"What is it, love?"

"Lady MacLeish and Lady Frampton are here."

Simon frowned; was there some reason he should know this? Something he'd forgotten?

"Yes?" he asked when it was clear she had nothing else to add.

"Lady MacLeish said that you called on her and told her to visit."

"Yes, that is true, I called on her last week—the day after we encountered her on our ride with Heyworth."

She stared at him, her posture rigid.

Simon suppressed a sigh. Had he done wrong? Lord.

He took a step toward her; she didn't retreat from him, but her body language did not beckon him closer, either. "My mother said she'd told you about my past with Bella."

Honey nodded.

"My mother isn't the only person who will recall that Bella and I were once very close." He shoved a hand through his hair. "My brother took her family in dislike years ago, and because his behavior sets the social standard, it has been difficult for the Framptons. Rather than cause any gossip to fade, I believe Wyndham's unkind treatment of them has kept old rumors fed and healthy. I decided to take the bull by the horns, so to speak. The sooner people see that Bella means no more to me than any other acquaintance, the better."

"And that is why you called on her in secret? To tell her such things?" she asked.

He restrained his annoyance at her sarcasm. After all, he could understand her reaction because he wouldn't like having an ex-lover of Honey's living a mere mile away. And he would be furious if she went to call on such an imaginary person without telling him.

He held her gaze. "Yes, that was one of the matters I wished to discuss with her," he admitted. "I see that perhaps I didn't handle it as wisely as—"

John Murphy, the foreman of the stables project, appeared in the doorway of Simon's makeshift office. "Oh, I beg your pardon, my lord—"

"It's quite all right, Mr. Murphy," Simon said.

A construction site was not the place for the discussion he and Honey were conducting.

He nodded at the other man. "I've looked at the plans and agree with your assessment. Go ahead and double the number of beams."

"Aye, my lord." Murphy disappeared back into the corridor.

"Lady MacLeish expressed a desire to speak to you," his wife said in clipped accents, and then spun on her heel.

Simon bit back a curse. Bloody Bella. What the devil could she want from him? "Hold a moment, Honoria, I'll come with you."

She paused and gave a jerky nod.

"I'm not exactly fit for the drawing room," he said as they walked toward the house. "Should I go change?" he asked, hoping her answer would be *no*.

"I told them you were busy working," she said, tightly.

Simon took her arm and stopped her. "You are angry. No," he said when she opened her mouth to demur. "I might be insensitive and oblivious a good deal of the time, but I can see that you are unhappy with me. Is it because—"

"Lady MacLeish brought her daughter along with her."

Simon frowned, confused. "And that upsets you? Er, is the chit ill-behaved?"

"No." Her pinched expression was singular and Simon could not decipher what it meant. "Honey, what is it?"

She pulled away, heading toward the front door, which Hume was holding open

Simon followed his wife, a heavy feeling in his chest.

***

As she strode toward the sitting room Honey knew she was behaving badly, but never in her life had she been so furious: first at Lady MacLeish's gall, second at herself for being consumed by anger and jealousy, and third—and not least—at Simon.

Why hadn't he *told* her that he'd paid a call on the woman? She'd looked like a fool showing her surprise.

Probably because he knew you'd react like you're reacting.

She gritted her teeth against the annoying, yet accurate, thought.

"Honey." Simon's hand landed on her arm.

She whirled around and glared up at him. "What?"

"What the hell is the matter?" he demanded.

Honey snorted and reached for the door to the sitting room before he could open it and hissed, *"This,* my lord."

She didn't take her eyes off him as he looked over the denizens of the room. A dozen emotions flickered across his face when his gaze landed on Lady MacLeish's daughter.

"Thank you for allowing us to interrupt you, Simon," Bella MacLeish said, her mesmerizing green eyes on Honey, rather than Simon as she spoke.

But Simon's attention was all for the girl standing beside her.

"You remember my mother, of course," the countess said. "And this is my daughter, Enola."

Lady Frampton's face was a mask of mortification.

Enola looked uncertainly from her mother to Simon—who still hadn't spoken or moved—her unusual hydrangea-colored eyes wide as she dropped a coltish curtsey. "My lord."

As if waking from a dream, Simon strode across the room, stopped in front of the girl and took her chin in fingers, raising her face to his. While the exotic tilt of Enola's eyes was just like her mother's, her patrician profile, complete with strong, aquiline nose, was a duplicate of Simon's.

"Enola," he said in a low, wondering voice, breaking the brittle silence that filled the room. "What a pretty name." He dropped his hand and turned to Bella.

The sultry beauty gave him an innocent smile that didn't fool Honey for a minute: she had purposely engineered this scene.

Honey realized she was a spectator in her own drawing room and moved toward the untouched tea tray.

For the next quarter of an hour, she smiled and made tea and distributed biscuits, nodding when appropriate and even answering the few questions directed her way.

When the women rose to leave, it was Simon who walked them out to their carriage.

Honey slumped back in her chair, staring at the remains of the tray.

Part of her wanted Simon to just return to the stables and they could pretend this hadn't happened.

Part of her wanted to shout and throw things at him, and demand why he had not warned her.

And part of her wanted to pack her valise and get on a mail coach and go home.

They'd talked about separate lives before they'd married. Perhaps it was now—

She heard Simon's distinctive, uneven tread before the door opened.

Honey could not make herself look at him.

"You are angry with me," he said, taking the seat he'd just vacated.

Her head whipped up at his weary words. "Why didn't you tell me?"

"I just wanted to speak to her alone—to make sure she knew that I wouldn't tolerate her games. Bella has always been a bit, er, mischievous. In any case, the visit was harmless and I didn't mean for my actions to appear secretive."

"I'm not talking about your visit to Lady MacLeish," she spat—although that *did* rankle. "I'm talking about the girl."

"What about the girl?" he asked, but she could see that he was not as sanguine as he was attempting to sound.

"Don't," she said with a withering look.

"Fine. So, the child looks like a Fairchild—is that what you mean?"

"She could be your female double, Simon."

His distinctive blue eyes widened. "Are you accusing me of fathering Bella's child?"

Honey snorted and threw up her hands, as if to say, *how could I not.*

His frown deepened and the chill in his blue eyes was enough to make her shiver. "The child is not mine, Honey."

"Are you *sure?* Perhaps it is one of the many things you claim not to remember?" she snapped, and then bit her lower lip, wishing she could take the words back.

He stood and came toward her. Honey shot to her feet, refusing to have to look up at him.

"How dare you?" he said, his voice menacingly soft.

"What am I supposed to think?"

"Good God! You could think dozens of other things—none of them as insulting to me as what you just said. Can you really believe I'd parade Bella and her daughter in front of you if the girl were *mine?*"

Honey sucked in a breath but caught an ill-advised retort before it slipped from her mouth.

He nodded, even though she'd not spoken. "I see you believe me capable of such cruelty—not only to you, but to the girl, if she really was my daughter." He took a step closer, until she felt the heat from his body. "As bad as my memory might be, I know that I have *never* put my cock in Bella MacLeish."

She gasped at his crude words.

Simon's lips curled into an unpleasant smile, the likes of which she'd not seen since her first week at Whitcomb. "And believe me, my dear, I doubt that any man would ever forget fucking a woman like that—no matter how badly his brain had been damaged."

He turned and strode from the room, slamming the door hard enough to rattle the tea tray.

Even after he'd gone his vicious taunt echoed in the empty room, pitting her soul the way the hot shrapnel had once pierced his skin.

***

Not surprisingly, dinner was a frosty and brief affair.

Simon knew he should apologize for his vulgar words and cruel baiting, but he couldn't believe she thought him capable of treating her so shabbily. Shouldn't *she* be the one to apologize.

Very mature thinking, Simon. It's too bad you're not nine years of age and this isn't a schoolyard.

He growled as Peel shaved him, glaring at his own foolish face in the glass.

Fine. He would apologize when he went to her chambers.

He'd considered not going to her bed at all, but to hell with that. The last thing he wanted was for their marriage to settle into cold, prolonged hostilities. He'd been at war too goddamned long to want to wage another one under his own roof.

No, he would go to her and they would spend a pleasurable night together.

Somehow, I don't think it will be so simple …

He would *make* it that simple.

Once Peel finished, Simon went to the connecting door, half expecting to find it locked. But the handle turned and he entered her room.

She was in bed, reading. Her cool look told him that she'd not expected him to come to her.

"I don't wish for there to be strife between us," he said, as she grudgingly put a marker in her book, set it on the nightstand, and crossed her arms.

"You are correct that the girl's eye color is similar to mine. It is a trait in my father's side of the family. My grandfather had the same eyes as does one of my aunts. There are portraits in the galleries of other Fairchilds with the same eyes." He sighed. "There is also a portrait at Frampton Park of some ancestor of mine—I daresay my mother or Wyndham would recall which one—who married an ancestor of Bella's. It's several generations back, but you will recognize the distinctive eye color." He hesitated. "I'll admit I was … surprised by the family resemblance today, but the child is not mine, Honoria. That would be impossible." He paused to make sure his words sank in. "I'm sorry for what I said earlier," he continued. "It was inexcusable."

Simon waited—both for her to accept his apology and make one of her own.

He was beginning to think he'd grossly miscalculated when she sighed.

"I apologize for accusing you of something you didn't do." The words were an apology, but they were grudgingly spoken.

Simon decided that he didn't care.

"Thank you," he said.

He pulled the sash on his robe, shrugged out if it, and tossed it over the foot of the bed.

Her gaze dropped to his erection, bounced back up, and she swallowed.

Simon adored the hunger in her angry gray eyes. She was still mad at him, but she wanted him, all the same. Good.

"Did it make you jealous to think of me putting a baby inside her, Honey? Did you think of me doing the things to her body that I now do to yours?"

Her eyes grew so round he was honestly surprised they didn't roll out of her head. Despite her shock—and wrath—her pupils flared, until only a thin silver ring surrounded the black.

It didn't matter how she answered his questions, her eyes gave her away.

Ah, I've got you, my love.

You're a bad man, Simon.

Yes, he was.

She shook her head, sputtering. "You—You arrogant *bastard*."

Simon laughed and took his engorged cock in his hand, giving himself a few pumps, amused and aroused by the way her eyes could not look away.

"Why is that arrogant, darling? I would be foaming at the mouth if I thought some other man had put a child in your belly." He narrowed his eyes, nostrils flaring, a dangerous yet erotic cocktail swirling in his stomach at the infuriating thought. "It incenses me to think of another man even touching you. I'd want to hunt down such a man and rip out his heart."

Her jaw dropped.

"But strangely," he said musingly, still stroking his slickening shaft, "It also makes me ferociously hard."

A sound of strangled disbelief slipped from her lips.

Simon smiled and then thrust hard into his fist, displaying his full length and girth for her like an animal in rut. "It seems that jealousy is an ugly emotion with some surprisingly beneficial side-effects." He jerked his chin at her. "How about you? Are you wet, Honey? I'll bet you were swollen and soaking for me before I even entered your room."

She drew herself up like a queen. "How *dare* you—"

"Show me."

"I most certainly will n—"

"Do you wish me to leave?" he asked. "You need only say the word. I will never touch you without your permission."

Her eyes blazed as a titanic battle raged inside her.

"Tell me that you want me or I'm walking out that door."

"Don't go." The words were explosive and harsh—almost feral, as if somebody had tortured them out of her lungs.

Simon strode to the bed, grabbed the blankets, and jerked them off her body.

She gasped, trying to scoot backward, but there was nowhere to go; she was already up against the headboard.

He eyed her prim nightgown with dislike; it was old and ugly and prudish. He took the hem with both hands and yanked.

The *riiiiiip* that cut through the silence enflamed him and made her yelp.

"You *tore* it," she accused in a breathy voice as Simon took the two halves, which were open over her belly, and gave another vicious yank that went all the way up to the high neck.

"I bought you pretty nightgowns and I expect you to wear them for me," he said in a lust-roughened voice. "Or better yet, wear nothing at all." He grabbed her hips and pulled her down the bed before kneeling between her thighs and shoving her legs wide.

Simon thrust two fingers into her tight passage and she cried out, her hips bucking.

He grunted like the animal he was; her wet heat made his head spin.

"I make you this way," he accused, lifting his glistening fingers, holding them up for her stunned gaze, and then putting them in his mouth, licking them clean.

She clutched at her throat with a shaking hand, her mouth gaping with shock.

Simon smirked, dropped his damp fingers, and slowly lowered his body between her thighs. "Watch me while I make you come."

Honey's gaze followed him, the look in her eyes making him ache painfully

"I think of you all day long," he said harshly. "You interrupt my thoughts—smashing and scattering them, until I am nothing but a moony-eyed fool for you. You keep me hard and wanting and I can scarcely think of anything but being deep inside your delicious body."

Honey bit her lower lip, the corners of her mouth curling ever so slightly.

"Ah, you *like* what you do to me."

She didn't demur.

"You witch," he hissed, parting her folds and thrusting his tongue into her.

Their groans blended into a primitive rumble of need.

Simon laved from her core to her pearl, her eyelids fluttering as she struggled to keep her eyes open.

"Who do you belong to?" he demanded when she began grinding and bucking against his face.

Her eyes were lust-drunk and she was panting, her pale torso passion-splotched.

"Who?" he snarled.

"You, Simon. I belong to you."

"Mine," he growled, lowering his mouth and showing her that she was, in every way, his to command.

***

When Honey woke, Simon was already gone. That wasn't unusual as he preferred to ride at the break of dawn. She'd gone with him once or twice, but he was like a demon in the saddle and she'd only held him back.

He'd been like a demon in bed last night, as well.

Honey's face heated at the memory of what he'd done—what *they'd* done. He'd taken her four times, seemingly insatiable.

You were more than a bit insatiable yourself.

Honey could not deny that. The last time they'd joined, just before dawn, it had been Honey who'd reached between his thighs and woken him.

She covered her hot face with her hands, shocked by her behavior in the bright light of day.

He has you so tied in knots that you'd do anything—believe anything.

She dropped her hands and stared at nothing as the words sank in. It was true what he'd said last night—about the jealousy—

shameful, but true. Thinking about Simon with that woman had given her upsetting, but erotic feelings. She'd also felt violent toward him.

Her emotional response was more than a little irrational; after all, if he'd fathered a child more than a decade before they were married, why should it affect her so?

The question had an equally irrational answer: it bothered her because he was *hers*. He belonged to her.

Honey sighed. As he'd said, jealousy made no sense.

She rose from the tangled sheets, grimacing at the aches and stiffness. You'd think after so many nights with him that her body would no longer be sore, but Simon seemed to find new ways to stretch and bend her.

Smiling to herself, she slipped into her robe and then pulled back the drapes. It was a perfect fall day, the cerulean sky a gorgeous backdrop for the changing foliage. She would take her sketchpad and—

Something moved down by the edge of the park; it was a rider—no, two.

As they drew closer, she recognized Simon, but not the other man. He was small; perhaps it was Wilkins. The two men were as thick as—

The smaller person suddenly removed their hat, shaking out long dark hair.

So, not Wilkins, after all ....

Honey's jaw sagged. "What in the name of—"

It was Bella MacLeish.

Chapter Thirty-Seven

Simon was pleased to find Honey in the breakfast room when he came in from his ride.

"Good morning," he said, unable to look at her without thinking about last night.

She must have guessed what he was thinking because her face flushed a fiery red.

He chuckled and leaned over to kiss her, aiming for her mouth but getting her cheek when she moved away—no doubt horrified by all his dirt.

"I'm sorry," he said. "I must smell like horse. Shall I go change?"

"It doesn't matter. I'm nearly done." Her smile was cool and polite.

Simon glanced down at her plate; it was three-quarters full.

"You've hardly eaten. Do you not feel well?"

"I am fine," she said, so frosty he was surprised there were not icicles on her tongue.

Simon dropped into the chair beside her. When she began to rise, he grabbed her arm and pulled her down.

She turned on him. "Don't think you can just manhandle me whenever you like." Her eyes glittered coldly.

Simon tightened his grip when she tried to yank away. "You will sit here and tell me what is amiss," he said, more than a bit irked. "I thought we'd settled our misunderstanding last night. What have I done to displease you?" The *now* at the end of his sentence was unspoken, but hung in the air between them, all the same.

She jerked hard and he released her arm before she hurt herself.

"I woke up this morning to the sight of you riding with Lady MacLeish."

He blinked. "So?"

She sneered. "Last night you claimed to have no interest in her— yet now you are riding with her? So that all and sundry might see the two of you together?"

Simon gave a perplexed laugh. "But we are neighbors—we shall have to socialize with Bella and her family for the rest of our lives. I would far rather be on easy terms with them." He paused and frowned. "Especially as Wyndham has treated them all so shabbily."

"So that means riding with her? Even when I am not welcome to come?"

She bit her lip and Simon saw regret and mortification flood her lovely face.

"That is hardly fair, Honey. I've asked you repeatedly to join me on my morning rides but you never wish to come."

Her jaw moved from side to side, but she didn't speak.

"As for riding with Bella, you were there in the sitting room yesterday—didn't you hear what we talked about? Our arrangement?"

"What arrangement?"

"That Bella would ride some of my hunters."

The way her eyes widened told him that she had not been listening.

"She's a bruising rider and her father, Sir Charles, has no money to keep hunters for her," he explained.

"So *you're* going to furnish her with horses?" she asked in disbelief.

He took a deep breath and told himself to be patient. "Have you ever heard of rough riders?"

She crossed her arms. "No."

"They are skilled equestrians who will ride other people's horses for pay—usually in hunts or races. It is an excellent way to exhibit one's horseflesh."

"But I thought you would do that?"

"And I will. So will Becca. But I'm keeping several hunters at Whitcomb that I'd very much like to sell so that I might afford more bloodstock. I'm inviting some men with deep pockets to join our hunts this season." He could see she was trying to wrap her mind around all of it. As a stranger to fox hunting, he supposed it was bewildering to her.

"So, she'll ride your horses," she said, clearly skeptical.

"Yes. I'm also giving her access to the stables as those at Frampton are a disgrace."

"She will be here often?" she asked flatly.

"As often as she wishes to ride—daily, I hope, as it's been some time since her husband died so she'll need to get back in form."

Simon could see the idea didn't sit well with her. But if he could become accustomed to the thought of her spending days on end with strange men then surely she could accept him associating with a woman that he'd already said he had no interest in?

He was trying to be patient, but his patience only stretched so far.

As sexually stimulating as a bit of jealousy was, he didn't want to make his wife unhappy or give her the wrong idea.

Then tell her so, you dolt, the voice in his head ordered. *You owe her that much.*

For once, the voice was right. "You are my wife, Honey—the only woman I want or need."

Her eyes went wide and he knew it had been right to speak plainly. Strangely, he hadn't realized exactly how he felt until he'd spoken the words. She *was* the only woman he wanted or needed.

Simon squeezed her hand. "Bella is nothing more than a neighbor. She might not be your favorite person, but she can do my nascent enterprise a great deal of good by riding my hunters. It will also be a kindness to her family if they are seen to be welcomed by me—by *us*. The squire and his wife are lovely people, Honey. They don't deserve to suffer. Nor does Bella, whose only crime is that she was once betrothed to me and Wyndham dislikes her for it." He hesitated and then asked. "Do you understand why I'm doing this?"

She swallowed once, and then again. And then she sighed, the anger seeming to drain out of her. "I understand, Simon."

His relief was so strong it floored him. While he did not wish to hurt her, he also did not want to live under the cat's paw. It would be a relief if they could resolve issues without unnecessary dramatics.

He pulled her close and kissed her, fiercely claiming her with tongue and teeth, rather than a mere peck. When he finally let her go, her mouth was bruised and wet, her skin flushed.

He ached to bury himself inside her. "I should drag you upstairs, strip you naked, and ride you until you are lathered."

Her face went scarlet. "*Simon*." She glanced around, as if somebody might have heard.

He chuckled. "Don't worry, I've got the roofer arriving in less than an hour, so you're safe from my demands. Until tonight." He gave her a second, only slightly less incendiary, kiss. "So," he said after he'd pulled away. "Are we good, darling? Can you bear being civil—kind, even—to Bella and her family?"

"Yes, I can. You are right, Simon. It is the best way to dispel gossip."

He grinned and kissed her one last time. "Of course, I'm right. I'm your lord and master. I am always right."

When she laughed, he knew that all between them was on the mend.

***

In the days that followed that conversation, Honey had to remind herself often of his words: *You are my wife, Honey—the only woman I want or need. Bella is nothing more than a neighbor.*

It seemed like every time she turned around Bella MacLeish was with her husband. She came to the stables every day, but never up to the house. Honey couldn't decide if she was relieved or slighted.

Not only did Bella linger around the stables, but Simon spent his days outside, as well, so Honey often saw the two of them together.

He now made a point of inviting her to ride every morning, but she had no desire to expose her lack of skill to Bella, who was achingly graceful in the saddle.

In the evenings they were no longer alone at dinner as Heyworth had settled into his new position, so *that* intimacy was gone, as well.

But you still have him all to yourself at night.

Honey blushed even though there was nobody to see her; yes, she had him all to herself all night, every night.

He was insatiable for her and she for him. Just when she thought he couldn't be more shocking—he showed her some new manner of wickedness.

And she adored him for it.

No, you love him.

Fine, that was true. But there was no reason for him to know that. Although he was clearly infatuated by the things they did in bed, he did not love her. Perhaps he never would. Sometimes she thought there was a barrier in his blue eyes—a line that he couldn't or wouldn't cross.

So, the nights were theirs, but their days were spent apart.

Was she happy that Bella was always there—and always dressed in her scandalously snug leather breeches?

No.

But she had to admit there appeared to be nothing untoward going on. While it was unusual for women to ride astride, many who hunted—Becca, for instance—wore breeches on hunt days.

Of course, Bella wore them *every* day.

It was unfortunate that Honey's studio window faced the stables. At first, she had loved being able to watch Simon come and go. Now it was like salt on a wound. Not only did she have to watch Bella, but she had to watch every male in her vicinity drop what they were doing to gawk at the other woman.

That's not fair, Honey. Simon doesn't gawk.

She sighed, cleaning her brush and putting it aside before she destroyed the duchess's portrait. It was never good to paint when she was in this sort of mood.

As for Bella's behavior? Well, she flirted with Simon, but she also flirted with Heyworth, Hume, and every other male servant or worker on the property. Or perhaps she wasn't flirting. Perhaps that was just Honey's gut-wrenching jealousy at work.

She loosely covered the painting and stepped closer to the window as Raymond Fairchild rode up.

Simon's cousin had brought a second horse behind him, probably the mare the duke wanted bred. She was lovely—as black as coal, just like Loki, but daintier.

Simon emerged from the stables, Bella—naturally—two steps behind him.

That's unfair, Honey. There is Becca, too.

All right, all right—that is true.

Becca rode over most days and Honey often watched the three of them—Simon and the two women—tearing across the countryside in a neck-or-nothing way that left her breathless.

Honey couldn't help smiling as she read Becca's posture just now; the younger woman did not like Bella. In fact, Honey had overheard Becca complaining to Simon, just a few days ago, that *she* could ride Epiphany—the huge hunter that Simon was hoping to sell as quickly as possible—in this year's first hunt.

"You aren't ready for him yet, Beccs," Simon had chided. "Your father would skin me alive if I mounted you on that beast."

"What? You think *Bella* is a better rider than I am?"

Simon's eyes had narrowed at that. "Oi!" He'd snapped out crudely, no longer playful. "She's your elder—Lady MacLeish, to you. Show some respect. And yes, by the way, I *know* she is a better rider. That's not surprising since she was hunting before you were born." He'd softened when he'd seen Becca's crushed expression. "Come on, love," he'd cajoled, "you're not too big yet for me to do this." He'd picked her up under her arms and spun her in a circle until she'd squealed.

"Stop it, Uncle Simon!" she'd breathlessly demanded, but Honey could see that she loved it. Becca was teetering on the verge of womanhood and these last glimpses of childhood had inspired Honey to make a few subtle changes to her portrait.

For all her uncle's chiding, Honey could tell that Becca had not resigned herself to Bella's presence.

Neither, it seemed, had Raymond, who was regarding the siren with a derisive smirk as she proceeded to inspect the horse he'd brought.

Honey was about to turn away when Raymond looked up. His smile spread when he saw her, a markedly more pleased expression than only a moment before, and he waved—drawing everyone else's attention to her, as well.

"Wonderful. Thank you, Raymond," she muttered through clenched teeth, waving back.

When he strode toward the house, Honey sighed and prepared to meet him. She removed her painting smock and then smoothed her hair before going to the smaller, and cozier, sitting room that she favored.

It wasn't that she didn't like Raymond—she did. But he was strangely … cloying.

When she'd told Simon that, he'd chuckled. "That he is—and always has been. I think it's a result of being orphaned at such a young age. He has never spoken about what his life was like when Wyndham went to collect him and bring him back to Whitcomb, but I know he lived in squalor. He can be annoying at times, but, overall, he's a good egg," he'd added, "And he adores you, Honey."

Unfortunately, Raymond made that all too plain. Indeed, sometimes his affection was a little overwhelming.

But he was family—something she had always dreamed of having—and so Honey pasted on a smile.

***

Honey stood back from the Duchess of Plimpton's portrait and smiled.

Although the woman was bland, self-centered, and aloof, there'd been something beneath her beautiful features that Honey hadn't even realized existed until she saw it on the canvas.

Cecily Fairchild was a strong woman, for all that she languished on her chaise longue as the world went on around her.

Oh, Honey didn't believe that the woman's physical delicacy was contrived, but it was clear that the duchess wielded her invalid status like a weapon—a very powerful, effective weapon.

Honey was proud that she'd managed to capture the woman's subtle strength—it was the sort of detail that separated a workmanlike painting from a great one. Honey believed this portrait came close to that second category.

She was pleased that she'd managed to finish the portrait before she left for London two days hence. When she returned from her commissions in the city there would be a grand ceremony to unveil both canvases.

"It will be a ball," the dowager had told her with a sparkle in her eyes. "Wyndham wants this to be a combination celebration of your marriage as well as an unveiling of the portraits. You must invite all your friends, Honoria. If you don't have room at Everley we can accommodate them at Whitcomb."

Honey had to admit the prospect of a grand event intrigued her.

And so she'd written to her friends, not having much hope as most of them worked for their crust. Still, it would be lovely to get everyone together again.

She untied her smock and went to hang it up when activity from the stables drew her attention; it was Simon and Bella, mounted and headed out.

Honey looked at the clock; it was after five. Tonight, was the night they'd have his family over to dine for the first time—Simon had relented toward the duke, and Honey had agreed. Where could he be going so late? With Bella.

Honey grimaced at the unwanted pang of jealousy—at least the pangs were getting milder rather than worse—and left the studio.

She encountered Mr. Heyworth on the stairs.

"I was just looking for you, my lady. His lordship wanted you to know he'd be back in time for dinner. He had to run out to the Turnbull farm to inspect some work." He grimaced. "I'm afraid the man who was in charge of the job isn't reliable enough to trust and the new tenants will be arriving sometime tomorrow."

"Ah, I recall him mentioning that at breakfast," Honey said, although she wished he'd not left it so late. She smiled at the steward, "I shall see you at dinner, Mr. Heyworth."

As she made her way up the stairs, she tried to understand why she was so nervous about tonight. She'd acted as her father's hostess on hundreds of occasions. She could only assume it was the duke's presence that made her so anxious. She'd not seen him since the day they'd arrived at Everley, almost a month ago.

"I told Wyndham never to step foot in my house without my express invitation," Simon had said when she'd asked if the duke would be coming to see the portraits.

To tell the truth, Honey could hardly be angry at Plimpton for being the force behind her marriage, as much as she might resent the high-handed behavior he'd employed to achieve his ends. Being married to Simon might be turbulent, but she had never been happier.

She was glad her husband was mending fences with his only sibling, but that didn't mean that hosting Plimpton for dinner was without its worries. The man *was* a duke, after all, and she would be conscious of that fact as she entertained him tonight.

As her maid undressed her, Honey couldn't help thinking about the nights of passion since what she thought of as the *Bella Incident.*

Simon's open, honest approach to a potential misunderstanding had been the right one to take. There was no reason to try and hide a past that everyone knew about.

Honey stepped out of her petticoat, her skin heating at his outrageous claims about jealousy.

Well, it seemed his claims were not so outrageous as they'd proven correct. In small doses, jealousy *did* enhance what they did in the bedroom.

Honey had tormented herself more than once with thoughts of all the lovers he'd had. And there must have been many given his extraordinary skills.

"My lady?"

She reluctantly pulled her mind from her erotic musings. "Yes, Nora?"

The younger woman was blushing, too—almost like she'd seen the scandalous contents of Honey's head.

"It's about your courses, my lady?"

"Goodness, is it time?"

"It's past time, my lady—two weeks past."

"Are you sure?"

"If what you said when you engaged me is correct, then I'm sure."

Honey blinked at this news. "A baby?" she asked stupidly.

"Aye, milady, if what you said about bein' regular-like was the case."

Honey stared at her reflection as her hands dropped to her flat midriff, a foolish grin blooming on her face. She might be preg—

Simon's face rose up in her mind's eye, his words from six weeks ago replaying in her ears: *I mean, no children. Ever.*

"Oh no," she whispered.

Nora frowned. "I'm sorry, milady? I didn't quite catch that."

Honey met the woman's rather curious gaze and forced a smile. "Please keep this just between us for the time being."

Nora bristled. "Why of course, my lady. I'd never speak of such a thing."

"Of course, you wouldn't," Honey soothed, swallowing down her incipient hysteria. "Now, I believe I'll wear the turquoise gown this evening."

***

The last time Honey had felt so humiliated had been in the Duke of Plimpton's library the night of her imbroglio with Simon.

She supposed it was only fitting that this occasion centered around her husband, as well.

"Thank you for a lovely evening, Honoria," the duchess said, offering up her powdered cheek for a kiss.

"Thank you for coming, Mama." The word did not yet feel comfortable on her tongue, but she could see it pleased the older woman.

Raymond was next, and he caught her in a one-armed embrace that startled her. "I had a smashing time. Tell Simon that you were more than enough—we didn't even miss him." He released her and held her at arm's length for a long moment, his gaze far too probing—and knowing.

"Thank you for inviting me, Honey," Becca said, giving her a quick peck on the cheek and a hug. "I'm sure Uncle Simon is fine," she whispered in Honey's ear, so that when Honey turned, finally, to Plimpton, her face was likely flaming.

His stern mouth twitched into a faint smile, "Dinner was delightful," the duke said in the cool monotone that suited his bland features so well.

Honey had been shocked by his appearance when he'd arrived for dinner. He looked a decade older than he had a month ago. His pale skin was even paler and the skin beneath his eyes was bruised almost purple.

She'd had no idea that he'd been so sick. Doubtless it was the duke's persistent illness that was behind Simon's recent desire for rapprochement with his brother.

"Thank you also for allowing me to peek at the portraits," the duke said. "I'd promised myself that I could wait until the unveiling, but it was simply too tempting."

Honey felt a rush of warmth at his confession. It flattered her that such an aloof, powerful man would be so excited to see her work.

"They are spectacular," he added, bowing over her hand.

Before she could think up a suitable response, he'd gone, handing his mother into the ducal coach that was waiting.

Honey waved and watched until the carriage disappeared.

She smiled at her butler as he shut the door, forcing herself to ignore the questioning look in his eyes. "Good night, Hume."

"Good night, my lady."

"Excuse me, my lady."

Honey turned to find Heyworth descending the stairs; he'd changed into his riding leathers.

"I'm going out to the Turnbull farm." His handsome face darkened and he dropped his gaze, staring at his gloves as he pulled them on. "I worry that perhaps his horse pulled up lame and he is stranded. It is a very long walk on foot. I'll bring a mount with me, so that—"

The door swung open and Honey and Mr. Heyworth turned at the sound.

Simon stood in the doorway, dusty and disheveled. He smiled at Honey, his expression wry. "I supposed I missed dinner?"

Chapter Thirty-Eight

Simon could see that his wife was very unhappy and worried; he could not blame her.

He was enraged, even though he'd had three hours to do nothing but sort out his anger.

But right now, he was starving and his blisters had blisters. He turned to Hume, who was hovering. "Could you please have a tray sent up to my chambers? Something cold is fine."

"Very good, my lord."

Simon turned to Heyworth once the butler had left. "You'll need to send a wagon to fetch Saturn."

Honey raised her hand to her mouth and Heyworth stared.

Simon gestured to the leg of his breeches.

Because he wore leathers that had been died dark brown, the blood stains had not immediately been apparent; Honey saw them now.

"My God, Simon—is that *blood?*" She grabbed his coat and pulled him closer to a nearby candelabrum.

Simon's lips twitched; as angry as he was, he couldn't help being amused by the sight of his steward blushing as the lady of the house bent low to stare at her husband's groin.

"It is not mine, love," he said.

His voice brought her back to herself, and she straightened up, blushing as furiously as his steward. "What happened?"

"Somebody shot in my direction—by mistake, I expect. No doubt whoever it was didn't expect anyone to be out on that remote path so late. Probably a poacher." Simon grimaced, sickened as he recalled the equine scream of pain just before Saturn staggered and fell.

"Thankfully, the horse didn't suffer, but I couldn't get my foot out quickly enough, so it's a bit sore." He lifted his injured leg—his left, of course—and winced.

"Come," she said, shaking off her shock. "Let's get you upstairs." She turned to the footman who'd just appeared. "Have a bath brought up to his lordship's room immediately."

"Very good, my lady."

"Here," she said, thrusting her delicate shoulder beneath his arm. "You can lean on me."

Simon could walk well enough—he'd done so for hours—but he found that he liked being coddled by his wife.

"I'll be off if you don't need anything?" Heyworth said.

"Just collect Saturn—don't go looking for anything," Simon warned as he limped toward the stairs. "We'll comb the area tomorrow and speak to the sheriff."

Heyworth nodded and left them alone.

"I'm sorry I missed dinner, love," he said as they made slow progress up the stairs; Simon might have held her tighter than strictly necessary.

"You were missed," she said, and then asked, "Why didn't you send Lady MacLeish for help?"

Simon frowned. "Bella wasn't with me," he said. And then it hit him. "Oh, you saw us leave together. She only rode as far as the turnoff to Frampton Park and then headed home. I told her she could stable Bacchus at her father's." Simon actually felt the tension drain from her long, slender body. So, she still worried about Bella.

Honey took control of matters when they reached his chambers. She ordered Peel to strip him, inspect him for injuries, and then put him in his bath.

"Your meal will be waiting for you in a quarter of an hour," she told Simon, before bustling from the room.

A throat cleared beside him and Simon realized that he'd been staring after his wife, likely with a foolish, adoring grin on his face.

One look at his valet's faintly amused, superior expression told him he was right.

Simon was notorious for loathing coddling of any sort.

Until now.

He smirked down at his valet and then dropped into his chair, lifting up one dusty, battered boot. "We'd best do as my lady says and get me into that tub, Peel."

***

Honey was seated across from Simon at a small table that a footman must have had brought up.

Her husband was wearing only his robe and his gold curls were damp from his bath. His poor feet were bare rather than in slippers due to the bloody blisters he had from toe-to-heel on both feet.

"This cannot be normal," she said, absently watching as Simon took a second piece of ham from the platter of cold meats Cook had sent up.

"Hmm?" he said.

"That's *twice* you've been shot in less than three months, Simon."

He nodded, finishing chewing before taking a drink of wine to wash the food down.

"It's outrageous," he agreed. "But last year's brutal winter and this year's lingering chill have been damnably hard on people. Both Wyndham and I have opened up more land to hunting—but not near where Saturn was shot. It's bloody irresponsible to hunt so close to a road, no matter how lightly trafficked it is."

"What are you going to do?"

"What *can* I do? When people learn that one of my horses was killed nobody in their right mind will come forward to take responsibility. I can only hope it will be enough to stop such dangerous behavior in the future." He cut her an intense look. "That bullet came closer to me than any during the war, Honey."

There was a sort of wondrous horror in his voice.

Honey just felt sick.

"Can you imagine that?" he asked, visibly stunned. "To spend over a decade at war and then die from a stray bullet on my own land?"

Honey grabbed his wrist and squeezed hard. "Don't."

His eyes met hers and he seemed to come back to himself. He laid a hand over hers. "Why, I believe you'd miss me, Lady Saybrook."

"That isn't funny," she said, her voice a hoarse whisper.

His expression shifted from teasing to concerned and he leaned toward her, caressing her cheek. "What's this?" he asked, holding up a damp finger.

She sniffed and pulled away. "Nothing."

But he wouldn't release her. "Don't cry, Honey." He stood and pulled her up and into his arms. "I didn't mean to worry you—the bullet didn't hit me. I'm fine. I've always been fortunate when it comes to bullets—it's cannons and cannon balls I have to worry about, and there aren't many of them in East Shropshire."

Her tears were running freely now, and she pushed her face into his neck. "*This* bullet didn't hit you, but the last one did, Simon."

She felt him chuckle. "So, it did. I'm guessing I've now had my full complement of stray bullets, love. Please don't cry, Honey." He held her at arm's length, tipping her face toward his. "It was an accident, sweetheart. And I am as fit as a fiddle—except for a few blisters." He smiled and brushed a tear from her cheek.

"You should finish your supper," she said, mortified by her emotional display. Only Simon could make her come apart this way.

He shook his head and then winced.

"What is it?" she demanded. "Are you hurt?"

He grimaced. "A bit of chaffing on my left side from all that walking," he admitted.

"Lie down on the bed and I shall put on your salve."

His beautiful lips curled up at the edges, his sinful smile causing the predictable reactions in her body. "Take off your clothes," he ordered.

Honey froze like a startled hare, her heart pounding at the hungry glint in his eyes.

Simon stepped away from her and pulled the sash that held his robe closed, shrugging the heavy brocade garment to the floor.

Honey wasn't surprised to see that he was erect—she rarely saw him any other way.

"Turn around," he said, "I'll be your maid."

"Simon, you need to—"

"Hush and turn."

Honey complied.

He nibbled at the back of her neck while his fingers worked on her gown. "You smell so good," he murmured, thrusting his hard shaft against her lower back, the heat of him scorching even through several layers of dress. "What is it?"

"It's lemon verbena soap," she said, her voice quivering.

"Mmm," he nuzzled, his hips lazily thrusting.

"You need your salve first." She'd meant the words to sound like an order, but they came out more like a plea.

He chuckled and pushed her dress to the floor. A moment later he had her out of petticoat, stays, and chemise, down to only her stockings and shoes.

He dropped to his haunches and Honey stared down at his broad, muscular back as he removed her slippers and rolled down her stockings, his motions gentle and almost worshipful.

His body was every bit as much of a canvas as those she stretched and prepared. He was raw, masculine beauty, the scars and burns only adding to his appeal. Her heart ached for the painful story his battered skin told—as clearly as any painting—and she loved him with a fierce, almost primal desire.

He stood, his eyes black with need. "I want—"

Honey shook her head. "Salve, first. Go lie on the bed."

His expression went from lusty to shocked to delighted. "Yes, ma'am."

He pulled back the bedding and sprawled out like a starfish, his erection jutting proudly.

Honey rolled her eyes at his shameless behavior.

"I can't believe you are so cruel," he murmured, his big hand curling around the base of his endlessly fascinating organ. "Can't you see my need?"

She snorted. "I think your need is probably visible from several miles away."

He gave a roar of laughter. "I'll take that as a compliment."

Honey yanked her gaze away from evidence of his *need*, fetching the salve from his dressing table before returning to the bed.

He was stroking himself, beads of moisture leaking from the tiny slit.

A mortifying grunt of desire slipped from between her lips before she could catch it. "Stop that," she ordered shakily.

"I don't know if I can."

"Simon."

His eyebrows shot up. "Oooh, I like that stern voice, Mistress Fairchild."

Her cheeks heated at the sensual taunt. "Stop it," she repeated.

He dropped his hand. "I'll behave. Come up here." He patted the bed.

Honey cautiously approached him and set the glass container of salve on the bed. His hand shot out so fast it was a blur. He caught her wrist and pulled her on top of him.

"Simon—you need—"

His mouth crushed hers, his arms closing around her like iron bands.

Honey managed to resist for perhaps a second before giving in to her own *need*.

His lips were hot—almost desperate—his stubble rough and scratchy against her skin. He nibbled, sucked, and left marks all up and down her throat.

"God," he breathed against her, his chest heaving beneath her, "I am desperate for you, Honey."

She shivered at the savage desire in his voice.

He flipped her onto her back, his mouth ravaging her throat and chest before landing on a nipple, sucking her so hard she cried out.

"Poor baby," he breathed against her tortured, pebbled nipple, kissing it tenderly before moving to her other breast and assaulting it with a sharp nip.

He slipped a hand between her thighs, stroking and penetrating and driving her quickly toward the summit of her pleasure.

"I need to be in you," he rasped, his hips pushing her legs wide, his actions almost frantic.

He entered her with a violent, claiming thrust. "Oh God, yes."

Honey didn't know where her moans ended and his began.

He stroked into her with brutal intensity, as if he were chasing something that was just out of reach.

"So good," he gasped, plunging hard enough to drive her up the bed. "Can't get enough—need you so much."

His hips drummed and he ground himself against her, angling his body in a way that shattered her into a thousand pieces.

"Honey!" he yelled as she convulsed around him, his big body shuddering.

He thrust into her twice more before freezing, his shaft jerking and flexing in her sensitive sheath, warmth flooding deep inside her body.

"I love you, Honey," he whispered.

***

As Simon came to, he realized three things at the exact same moment: first, he'd told his wife that he loved her; second, he'd meant what he said; and third, he'd spent inside her.

He pushed up onto his elbows and looked down, afraid of what he'd see.

Honey looked up at him, her gray eyes wide, her lips parted with what looked to be shock.

He grimaced; this did not look promising. "Er, I'm sorry. I'm afraid I lost control and—"

"Did you mean that?" she asked, her voice so low it took his brain a moment to decipher what she'd said.

Simon sighed. "I'm sorry."

Impossibly, her eyes opened even wider. "What?"

"I promised you a marriage of convenience and it seems I've—"

—fallen deeply, madly, hopelessly in love with you. If you try to take a lover it will be pistols at dawn for him, even though I told you—no, I promised you—before we were married that you could do what you pleased and—

"Oh, hell." Simon rolled onto his back, wincing as he pulled his sensitive shaft from her body, which reminded him—

"I spent in you," he said, glaring at the canopy—as if it were to blame for his weak will. "Yet another promise I broke."

She remained motionless beside him. Had she fallen asleep?

That might be just as well, Simon.

"Simon?"

He jolted at the sound of her voice. "Yes?"

"I'm pregnant."

His head whipped around so fast he cricked his neck.

Her eyes were still wide, but now worried rather than stunned.

"I'm sorry, I know you didn't—"

"Are you?" he blurted. When she gave him a confused look he explained, "Are you sorry that you're pregnant?"

She opened her mouth, but then closed it. Finally, she bit her lip and shook her head. "No. I'm glad."

Simon let out a half-moan, half-sigh. "Thank God."

"But—I don't understand," she said. "I thought *you'd* be angry? You said—"

Simon shuddered. "Don't remind me of what I said, Honey. I was such a fool to say something so stupid." He slid a hand over her flat belly, a grin pulling at his lips. "Really?" he asked, sounding like an idiot as he looked up at her, no doubt looking like an idiot, too.

"I think so." She bit her lip again, as if she were trying to hold back a smile.

Simon gave a joyous hoot of laughter and grabbed her. He rolled her on top of him, shifting her body until she was straddling his hips.

"Simon—" She began to cross her arms over her breasts and he caught her wrists, pulling her hands down.

"No covering yourself," he said sternly, only partly mocking.

She flushed charmingly.

"Ever," he added, his eyes greedily consuming her delicious body, a body that now had their child growing inside it.

The wave of possessive pride that rolled over him was almost crushing. He'd never even thought about having a child before, and here he was, all but *exploding* with joy. He met her gaze, unable to read her inscrutable expression. "Are you truly pleased, Honey?"

"I am, but—"

"But?" he prodded.

"I am even more pleased that *you* seem pleased. I never expected—"

"Shh," he said. "I've been an idiot." He pulled her down, claiming her mouth in a deep, dizzying kiss.

Far too quickly she pulled away, breathing heavily. "Did you mean it?"

Simon considered teasing her and asking her what she meant, but the look in her eyes—vulnerable and uncertain—told him now would be a bad time. "I love you, Honoria Elizabeth Fairchild. You are mine and there is no escaping," he added.

Her eyes glazed and a tear slid down one cheek.

Simon groaned. "Oh, no—"

"Hush!" she chided, smiling through her tears. "I love you, too."

"You don't have to say that because—"

"You dunce—I've loved you for almost fourteen years."

Simon blinked. "You—"

She nodded violently, the tears flowing faster than ever. "Yes. I loved you then—how could I not?"

"I could understand then," he admitted without shame, "But *now*, when I look like this and am—" his lips twisted, "well, I'm not only battered and damaged externally, but less than a bargain when it comes to my broken brain and savage personality."

She laughed and it was the sweetest sound he'd ever heard. "I love you even more now."

He raised an eyebrow, hoping to hide the riot of emotions currently threatening to make him sob like a two-year-old. "Hmm, sounds like maybe all isn't normal in your brain box, either."

She just laughed and cried harder, wrapping her arms around his body and squeezing him until he couldn't breathe. "I love you so much."

"I love you too, darling—more than I've ever loved anyone in my life."

Simon squeezed his eyes shut, but not quickly enough to stop a tear or two from leaking out.

Chapter Thirty-Nine

Honey opened her eyes and stretched.

"Good morning, slug-a-bed."

She yelped and pushed herself up.

Simon was sitting in front of her fireplace, looking relaxed in one of her armchairs, a book in his lap.

"You didn't go for a morning ride?" she asked, glancing at the clock; it was not quite seven.

He closed his book, smiling. "I wanted to wait for you."

Was it possible to die from too much happiness?

He cocked his head when she merely gazed at him. "You don't have to go, darling. If you'd rather sleep, I'll just—"

"No, I want to," she said, shoving back the blankets, trying not to break into song as she recalled last night. And now this morning.

"Ah, that's good," he said, sounding pleased. "I took the liberty of ordering up a pot of chocolate. If you'd not woken soon, I was going to waft it beneath your nose until you—" he broke off at a light knock on the door.

Nora entered, bearing a tray. "Good morning, my lady." She blushed, making Honey recall her state of dishabille

"I'll serve her ladyship," Simon said. He frowned and picked something off the tray. "What is this?"

"Oh, that's a letter that Mr. Hume sent up, sir. He said it was on the salver this morning."

"Thank you," he said, absently, relieving her of the tray.

Honey hopped out of bed and quickly wrapped her robe around herself while Simon turned the letter in his hands.

"What is it?" she asked.

"I don't know—there's no direction on it and no sender name." He slid his finger beneath the fold and pulled it open.

Honey poured herself a cup of chocolate, watching her husband's face as he read.

His expression went from confused to shocked to even more shocked to enraged. And then, surprisingly, to pained.

"Simon?"

He tore his gaze from the page and handed it to her, without speaking.

"What is it?" she asked, afraid to look at what he'd given her.

Simon only shook his head.

She turned to the letter. Letter wasn't really the right word, there was only one sentence:

"Bella MacLeish's child is also the duke's."

Honey had to read the sentence multiple times, and still her mind couldn't seem to absorb the meaning. When she finally looked up, Simon was staring at her with an expression she'd not seen since her first week at Whitcomb: deadness.

"I can't believe this is true," she said. "Who would send something like this? And why? It's just—"

"I'm going to talk to Wyndham." He turned on his heel and strode toward the door.

"Simon!"

He stopped, his hand on the doorknob, shoulders so rigid they looked like they would shatter if she touched him.

But she had to touch him.

She laid a hand on his back and he shuddered. "Wait a bit, Simon. If you go now—"

He turned on her. "You think I will forgive him an hour from now?" he demanded.

She flinched back from his rage, but he just took a step toward her, gripping both her upper arms, hurting her. "I want you to know this is not about *Bella*," he spat the word.

"I know that, Simon." Honey had no siblings, but she had an imagination and what she was imagining right now was pain and betrayal.

"How could he do this to me?" Simon asked. "Not just then—but all these years making me believe—" he broke off, his gaze dropping to his hands. He immediately released her. "Oh hell, Honey! I hurt you—"

"Shhh." She wrapped her arms around his body and laid her head over his heart; it was pounding almost out of his chest.

He stood as still and rigid as a statue. For a moment she thought he would push her away, but then his arms slid around her, crushing her.

"God, Honey," he whispered into her hair. "I used to love and admire Wyndham so bloody much. This is just—"

"I know." She felt the tautness—the need for action—and released him. "I know," she said again. "Just—well, just be careful, Simon. Don't let your anger guide your tongue."

He hesitated a moment and she thought her words might overcome his need for haste. But then his eyes shuttered and he nodded. He kissed her on the forehead and was gone.

***

Honey's brush hovered over the painting of Simon.

She'd been standing in front of the canvas for a good ten minutes, and still she hadn't painted so much as a stroke.

She lowered the brush. Today wasn't a good day to paint; it was a good day to work on canvasses and frames. She would—

Angry voices came from out in the corridor and the door swung open hard enough to slam against the wall.

It was Bella, with Hume close on her heels.

"I'm terribly sorry, my lady," Hume said before Honey could speak. Her butler shot the breeches-wearing beauty a cold look. "I told Lady MacLeish that you were not to be disturbed when you—"

"Has something happened to Simon?" Honey looked from her butler to Bella's wide-eyed and frightened face.

"Where is Simon?" Bella asked at almost the same moment, her magnificent eyes flickering around the room, as if Honey's husband might be hiding somewhere among the painting paraphernalia.

Honey went limp with relief; if Bella was looking for Simon, that meant he wasn't lying hurt or dead somewhere.

Her relief quickly turned to anger. "What can I do for you, Lady MacLeish?" Honey demanded.

"Where is Simon?" Bella repeated, louder this time.

"He has gone to speak to the duke," Honey said coolly. "If you must know," she added, "he has gone on a matter not so tangentially concerning *you*."

"What do you mean?"

Honey looked pointedly at Hume, her meaning clear: if Bella wanted to demand answers in such a rude, public fashion, Honey would gladly share the truth in front of her servant.

But the other woman either didn't catch her meaning or didn't care. "I saw Raymond's groom—Taft—last night and he was heading toward the Turnbull farm. I saw him not long after I left Simon."

Honey shook her head, confused. "Why are you telling me this?"

"Because I just *now* heard about Simon's accident from one of your stable lads."

Honey frowned, still unable to see her point. "And?"

"I don't think Simon's *horse* was the bullet's target, my lady," she bit out.

Hume's jaw sagged.

So did Honey's. "Please excuse us, Hume."

She could see the man didn't want to leave, but thirty-odd years of service made him nod and retreat.

The instant the door was closed she turned to Bella. "Explain," she ordered.

Bella was clutching her riding gauntlets, which she was wringing like laundry. "It's Raymond—" she stopped, the muscles in her jaw flexing, her expression agonized. "I hope to God I am wrong, but I think Raymond is trying to h-hurt—*no*—kill Simon."

"*What?*" Honey shrieked. "But why?"

"For the dukedom," she said, as though Honey were thick. "He wants the title—he always has. We don't speak at all, now—he hates me—but years ago, we were—" Bella bit her lip and stared at Honey.

"Yes?" she prodded.

"He used to be *obsessed* with the title. He might not speak to me anymore, but I can still see it in his eyes—the way he sometimes looks at Simon. I've not seen him with the duke, of course, but I'm guessing it is the same as it was before."

Honey's brain couldn't find purchase in the other woman's words. "But—the duke—" she stopped, the dowager's words from last week ringing in her ears:

Poor Wyndham has been so ill—this dreadful stomach problem just seems to go on and on. I don't know what to do if the doctor cannot discover what is wrong—

"Good God," Honey blurted.

She met Bella's startled, questioning gaze and explained, "The duke—he's been ill for months with some sort of stomach illness."

Bella nodded. "Everyone knows that he's been sick, but nobody knows what is wrong."

"If Raymond is trying to kill Simon, then he must also be—"

"He's poisoning the duke," Bella said.

They stared at each other in stunned silence, awed and horrified.

"I feel like a fool. I'm so sorry," Bella said, tears sliding down her cheeks. "I should have said something sooner. I'd heard of the duke's illness and it reminded me of the baby's, but of course I never had any proof—"

"Baby?" Honey repeated, her hands unconsciously going to her midriff. "*What baby?*"

Bella's beautiful face was pale. "Edward."

"Are you saying—"

Bella nodded.

Honey's mind shrieked out against the other woman's accusation: *No! That couldn't be true. Who would poison an infant?*

She raised a hand to her mouth, her stomach pitching and roiling at the sickening thought.

Honey barely made it to the basin where she usually washed her hands before she voided the contents of her stomach.

Good God. Had Raymond really poisoned Wyndham's son?

A small hand rubbed her back. "Are you ill, my lady?" Bella asked, and then gasped, "Lord, has Raymond been here? Do you think you've been—"

Honey dragged the back of her hand across her mouth, shaking her head. She didn't want to tell the other woman that she was pregnant.

"No, I was just sickened by such a thought," she said. "I don't see how Raymond could have done anything to us. He was at dinner last night but—"

The mysterious letter that was found in the salver. Simon rushing off to confront Wyndham—

Honey groaned. "God, what an idiot I am—it must have been Raymond who left the letter."

"What letter?" Bella asked.

"Simon received an anonymous letter saying your daughter was the duke's."

"That had to be Raymond's doing," Bella said.

Honey headed for the door. "I need to talk to Simon."

"Where is he?" Bella asked, right behind her.

"He went to confront the duke—

Honey stopped and spun around, comprehension dawning. "Wait—how foolish I've been. Your child is Raymond's—not the duke's."

Bella nodded. "If Raymond left a letter for Simon, it has to be some kind of trap. I daresay he's hoping Simon will harm the duke. Even in the village people know of the enmity between the two brothers."

"Good God! You think he hopes for one of them to kill the other?"

"Yes," Bella said grimly. "And then whoever remains will hang for murder and Raymond inherits."

"We need to get to Whitcomb." Honey turned and ran, almost colliding with Heyworth and Rebecca, who were coming from the direction of the foyer.

"Oh, you are here, Rebecca," she said, sounding foolish to her own ears.

"Why are you running? What is wrong with everyone this morning?" Rebecca demanded before Honey could speak. "I passed Uncle Simon on the way here and he was behaving so strangely I was frightened."

"He just wants to talk to your father," Honey said, striving for a normal tone. "I'm going over to Whitcomb right now to join them," she added, trying to smile and failing if Becca's expression was anything to go by.

"But Papa isn't at home. He's went to Lindthorpe today."

"Did you tell your uncle that?" Honey shot back.

Rebecca recoiled at her harsh tone. "Of course, I didn't want—"

Honey turned to Bella. "Take Simon's fastest horse and ride for the sheriff. Bring him to Lindthorpe."

Bella didn't argue or hesitate—she nodded and ran for the door.

"And Bella?" Honey called out just as Bella opened the door.

The other woman glanced over her shoulder.

"Bring a doctor, too."

Once again Bella nodded, and then she was gone.

Heyworth stepped toward her. "Lady Saybrook, what is—"

"Meet me in five minutes in the stables." Honey strode toward her chambers. "Fetch two pistols and saddle whatever horses Bella doesn't take. Rebecca, you stay put—go to the library," she called over her shoulder.

"But—"

"Don't argue!"

"You want *pistols* my lady—?" the steward gasped.

"Just do it, Mr. Heyworth—there is no time to explain right now, my husband's life might be in danger."

Chapter Forty

After half an hour of riding hell-bent-for-leather, Simon's temper had begun to abate and he slowed Bacchus to a canter. What in the name of the hell was he doing rushing off half-cocked like this?

You're thinking with your fists, Simon, just as you always do.

He grimaced at the all-too-apt description.

It's time to leave the past in the past. Whatever Wyndham did with Bella, it no longer matters. You are married and in love with a wonderful woman. You are going to be a father.

His face creased into a smile at the thought, the joy in his chest so intense that he felt like he would burst at the seams.

But then Wyndham's face thrust itself into his mind's eye and he recalled how his brother had looked Simon in the face all these years, lying and manipulating the entire time.

It was true that what Wyndham and Bella had done with each other no longer mattered. But what his brother had done to *him* was something they needed to discuss—if not resolve—the sooner the better.

Besides, he thought as he glanced at a passing road marker; he was almost to Lindthorpe and there was no point in turning back now.

It would probably always bother Simon that his brother had betrayed him, but it was a long time ago and Wyndham's life had been a such a misery at the time. Lord knew that Bella had been enough to tempt any man.

Whatever Wyndham had done, his brother was essentially an honorable man—Simon believed that with every fiber of his being. Wyndham would have suffered mightily for his sins all these years.

As for Bella? Well, she'd certainly been punished more than she deserved for her part in the indiscretion.

The more time Simon spent with her, the more he learned that her marriage to MacLeish had not held much pleasure.

Bella's letter from all those years ago had mentioned a hefty dowery—which he now knew to be the courtesy of Wyndham's guilty conscience.

Based on what Bella had said about her dead husband, Simon suspected the money might have been even more of a lure for the penniless Scotsman than a beautiful young wife, especially one who'd been pregnant with another man's child.

It was all sordid and sad and desperate.

And it had nothing to do with his current life.

Simon sighed as a weight seemed to lift from his heart; he would confront Wyndham with the truth and he then would forgive him.

He looked up from his thoughts to see that the turnoff to Lindthorpe was just ahead; he'd certainly made excellent time.

The driveway to duke's newest house was shaped like a horseshoe, with huge old oaks marching down both sides of the narrow drive. There were various hedges surrounding the house and grounds, giving one the feeling of entering a cave.

The Palladian-style house was of recent vintage—built sometime early in the last century—and a great deal smaller than Everley.

As he rode up to the entrance, Simon was surprised to see no sign of workmen or activity—not even a gardener.

He dismounted and tied off Bacchus before heading toward the entrance. Not until he was almost to the big, metal-strapped door did he notice that it was open a crack.

"Wyndham?" he called out.

He paused, but there was no answer.

As he reached for the doorhandle his gaze flickered to the light-colored flagstone at his feet. The hairs on the back of Simon's neck stood on end and some primitive part of his brain identified what he was looking at before Simon even recognized the red smear as blood.

His body reacted without prodding from his mind and he shoved the door while flinging himself through the opening.

He landed with a bone-jarring thud just as a pistol shot rang out. Bits of plaster rained down on him and his body again acted on instinct, rolling to the side, out of the doorway opening

"Simon!" It was Wyndham's voice and it came from the bowels of the house.

Simon scrambled clumsily for purchase on the bloodied, polished wooden floor, getting to his feet just as the sidelight next to the door shattered, sending splinters of glass glittering in the air around him.

He ran without a backward glance.

"Wyndham," he shouted breathlessly, heading deeper into the house.

"Back here," Wyndham yelled.

Simon followed the sound of his voice, turning down what he knew was a very short hall with only four or five rooms off it.

Long smears of blood on the wood floor led into the second room on the right.

Simon skidded to a halt in the open doorway.

His brother was opposite the door, lying on the floor next to the room's only window.

"Watch out for the wind—"

Something flickered past the window just before chips of wooden doorframe exploded beside Simon's head.

For the second time in less than a minute he dove, landing with a muffled grunt of pain

He crawled the rest of the way toward his brother, keeping clear of the window.

Only when he was beside Wyndham did he notice the state of his brother's clothing. "Good God! You're hit," he said stupidly.

Wyndham smiled, but it was weak. His left hand was pressed over his right side and blood was oozing from between his spread fingers.

Simon shrugged off his overcoat, coat, and waistcoat before pulling off his cravat.

He worked quickly to fashion a compression dressing for the wound. "Tell me what happened," he ordered, folding his waistcoat into a small square.

"Raymond was headed off on his quarterly rounds on estate business this morning, but he'd forgotten that he'd arranged to meet the builder here. I told him that I'd take care of it. When I got here, *he* was waiting for me." Wyndham pointed to the far corner of the room.

Simon turned to look. "Bloody hell," he said, noticing the unmoving body for the first time. "Is that—"

"It's Taft, Raymond's groom." Wyndham grimaced as Simon pressed the folded waistcoat onto his wound. "I unlocked the door and was about to come inside, when something just—" he shrugged and then moaned at the pain the action caused.

"Don't shrug, Wynd," Simon said, earning a glare for his unnecessary advice.

"For some reason, I hesitated at the doorway," Wyndham said, a hint of wonder in his voice.

"Survival instinct," Simon said. "It's a good thing you listened to it. Those instincts have saved my life times beyond counting. So, Taft shot you? Then what happened?"

"I played dead and the silly bugger came to riffle my pockets and I got him in the throat with *that*."

Simon glanced over at Taft's body and squinted. "Good Lord! Is that—"

"It's the handle of my quizzing glass."

Simon barked a laugh. "Death by quizzing glass. Where the hell was Raymond while all this was happening?"

"He got here not long after. I'd just started crawling toward the front door, toward my horse, when I heard him riding down the driveway. So, then I crawled right back here."

"Why hasn't he come in?"

"He thinks I have Taft's gun. But he knows I'm wounded. Right before you arrived, Raymond told me that he'd given you a message ensuring that you would come." Wyndham snorted, his expression one of disgust. "The bastard confessed that he's been poisoning me for months. He knows that I'm as weak as a bloody kitten."

"Good God, this is like the plot from a bad gothic novel," Simon said, shaking his head. "He expects to kill us both and step into your shoes, I take it? I expect he will set it up so it looks like we killed each other?"

"That is the plan. He's tried to shoot you twice—or had Taft do it for him."

"Ah, so that's our poacher, is it—Taft? Bastard must have learned how to shoot from Raymond," Simon muttered.

Wyndham chuckled and then groaned. "Lord, don't make me laugh."

"What do you suppose he's doing out there?" Simon asked.

"Figuring out the best way to kill us both." Wyndham squinted at Simon. "How did he get you here, by the way?"

It was Simon's turn to laugh. "Because I'm a bloody fool." He looked at his pale, bleeding brother. "But I can't say that I'm sorry for my impulsive foolishness. He would have finished you for sure if I'd not shown up."

"Now he might finish us *both*," Wyndham pointed out.

"I'll be damned if I survived the war only to die at the hands of a bloody land steward," Simon said tartly, earning another gasping laugh. "He sent a letter telling me that Bella's daughter was yours."

"Bastard," Wyndham hissed, his eyes closed.

"She's Raymond's, isn't she? And you got her sent away because you knew."

Wyndham nodded, but his eyes stayed closed. "I knew it would break your heart," he finally said. "And then there was Raymond. What would I do with him if you knew? You would have killed him." He snorted weakly. "Now that seems like a capital idea."

Simon laughed, but his humor quickly changed to disgust. "What a bloody muddle. If he wanted the title so bad why do you reckon he didn't kill us both years ago?"

"Lord only knows," Wyndham admitted. "I suppose he hasn't needed to, until now. His situation has become rather desperate recently. Gambling debts," he added at Simon's questioning look.

"I can't say I'm surprised; he's a wretched card player."

"I told him the last time—almost a year ago, which coincides with my mysterious *illness*—that I wouldn't pay them off a fourth time." He opened his eyes and gave Simon a wry smile. "I gave him a choice: I would give him enough money to set himself up, but he needed to leave England. If he stayed here, he would be on his own. I gave him until the year's end to decide."

"Christ, Wyndham—you signed your own death warrant."

"Let's hope not, Simon." His brother's cool gray eyes flared with determination. "That bastard can't inherit; he'll gamble every cent away. He'll—"

"Good God!" Fear stabbed Simon in the chest, almost doubling him over.

"What? What is it, Simon?" Wyndham demanded.

"Honey is pregnant."

Wyndham's eyes widened.

"We can't let him get away from here alive. Even if I have to—"

"I know you're in there, Simon!"

Both he and Wyndham jolted; Raymond's voice was so close it sounded like he was in the bloody room. It sounded like he was right outside the window.

"I know you can hear me, you'd better answer me, Simon!"

"He sounds scared," Wyndham whispered.

Simon agreed. And there was nothing more dangerous than a frightened, cornered animal.

"What do you want, Raymond?" he shouted.

"You know there's no way out, Simon. I can't let either of you live. But I can give you a less unpleasant death."

"Tell him I will still give him money to go to America," Wyndham whispered weakly.

Simon stared at his brother, but Wyndham mouthed, *tell him*.

"Wyndham doesn't want word of our murderous cousin to be the *on dit* of next Season, Raymond," Simon yelled. "You let us out right now and he'll give you enough money to live well for the rest of your life—in America."

His cousin's laughter was immediate. "You two must think I'm an idiot to believe such an offer. Besides, why would I take exile in bloody America when I'm going to be the Duke of Plimpton? There is no way out for you. I'll give you *five* minutes!" Raymond shrieked, his voice breaking. "And then I'm going to set fire to the house and burn you both alive."

"You will hang for this, Raymond," Simon said.

"No, I won't—because I'm miles away, on my quarterly journey to visit the duke's estates—just ask *his grace*. Dozens of people saw me leave today. And I have a witness who will swear I was nowhere near this place."

Simon met Wyndham's gaze.

"His valet," the duke said.

Simon had seen the man, of course—an almost hilariously villainous looking character.

"Everyone will know you came charging here in a rage," Raymond shouted. "You were infuriated that your brother impregnated the love of your life." Another peel of near-hysterical laughter drifted through the shattered glass. "I must admit that you've helped out immeasurably by tearing about the countryside with dear Bella. Ah, poor foolish Simon. How we laughed at you—Bella and I. You were such an honorable, noble sprig. And thanks to your nobility Bella gave *me* her maidenhead. And more. Maybe I'll kill her, too—after I'm done with both of you."

Simon ground his teeth but held back his retort. He looked at his brother, but Wyndham's eyes had drifted shut.

Simon's heart leapt into his throat. "Wyndham are you—"

The duke's heavy lids lifted half-way; his gray eyes clouded with pain. "I have an idea," he whispered.

"Yes?"

"If we both rush him—"

"You can't even *walk*," Simon hissed. His eyes darted around the empty room, looking for something to use as a weapon. There was *nothing*—not so much as a stick of furniture.

His gaze settled on the new section of wooden doorcase somebody must have just installed.

The door was visible from the window, so it would be a risk. But what other hope did he have?

"Wyndham—can you press on this?"

His brother's shaky hand rose and closed around the bloody neckcloth.

"Good, keep it there."

Wyndham blinked his hazy eyes. "What—"

"Shhh, you'll see." Simon crawled across the floor, biting his lip bloody at the pain in his knees. Once he reached the door, he dug his fingers beneath the door frame.

"You have *three* minutes!" Raymond shouted

Simon got a good grip and then yelled while he pulled, hoping to muffle any noise.

"Why don't you come in here and we can discuss the matter like gentlemen?" Simon shouted, wrenching with all his strength. The frame didn't even budge.

"Goddammit," he hissed.

"Why would I risk my neck? You must think I'm a fool," Raymond called back.

"Kick it," Wyndham wheezed.

Simon nodded and stood.

"At least come to the window and quit hiding like a coward," he yelled, kicking at the same time.

The wood splintered with a loud *crack* and pulled away from the wall.

"Two minutes!" Raymond sounded almost hysterical and Simon saw something burning outside the window.

"That wasn't a minute, Raymond. Do you need to borrow my watch?" Again he kicked and this time a two-foot piece broke away.

"This is the last time you'll mock me, Simon!" Raymond yelled in an ominous tone, black smoke billowing past the shattered glass.

Simon grabbed the wood and yanked it off the wall.

"Take my boot—throw it first to distract him," Wyndham gasped.

Simon saw that his brother had toed off his boot while he'd been kicking the doorframe.

He grabbed the boot and took one last look at his brother.

Wyndham was breathing in rough gasps through his mouth and his face was taut with pain. "Go."

Simon nodded, grabbed the boot, and threw it at the window with all his might.

Chapter Forty-One

How far past the mile marker did the farmer say it was?" Honey asked.

Mr. Heyworth squinted at the road ahead. "He said it was just past a big chestn—oh—" he pointed, "I think that must be it, on the right."

The unmistakable sound of gunfire came from the direction where Heyworth had just pointed.

Honey urged her horse into a gallop.

"My lady! Wait, you don't know what you're riding into. You could get shot—you might get your husband shot—"

His last words made her abruptly rein in and slow to a canter.

When Mr. Heyworth rode up beside her, she turned to him. "My husband might be the one getting shot right now," she said through gritted teeth.

"Let's get off the driveway and go in through there." He pointed toward the thicket that ran beside the driveway. "It will give us a bit of cover."

Honey nodded and headed in that direction. Once she was concealed from the drive, she swung off her horse without waiting for help.

"I'm going on foot," she said in a low voice, quickly fastening the skirt of her habit, which made it far easier to walk. She held out a hand. "Give me a gun."

He hesitated. "But—"

Another shot rang out and he swiftly handed her a pistol, butt first. "Let's stay in the trees and—"

But Honey was already moving. She kept walking until she could see the roof of the house ahead.

"The pistol is loaded and ready to fire," he whispered as they both made their way toward the left, to get around the hedge that cut off most of their view of the house.

Honey nodded; she knew the rest: aim and pull the trigger.

A third shot came from the direction of the house, which they could now see.

It was a moderately sized three-story structure. More trees and shrubs grew along the front and the side that faced them. It looked like a park bordered the back of the building.

Heyworth grabbed her arm and pulled her down into a crouch just as a man emerged from behind a tree near the house: it was Raymond.

His back was to where they were hiding and he was staring at something that was blocked from their view by a tree.

Whatever Raymond was looking at, it was agitating him and he paced back and forth, clutching something in his hands. He was gesticulating, as if he were talking to himself.

"If we could get to that tree, we could get a better look," Heyworth whispered, pointing to a big oak about twenty feet beyond the hedge. "But we'd need to expose ourselves to get there. We can't squeeze through this hedge because it's just too thick. That means going out in the open."

Honey was only listening with part of her brain. The other part was watching Raymond and trying to see how much time she might have to reach the tree that Heyworth had just pointed out.

"I'm going to follow the hedge in the other direction for a bit and see if there is a spot we might push through. You should wait here."

"We've got two guns and there is only one of him," she said. "Couldn't we rush him and—"

"Lady MacLeish said she saw his man Taft last night, didn't she? What if he's over there somewhere, too?"

Honey grimaced; he was right.

"Just give me a moment to go see." He cut her a pleading look. "If I can't find a way, we'll try our luck getting to that tree."

Honey nodded and Heyworth trotted off to the right.

The moment he was out of sight, Honey crept to the left, away from the protection of the hedge.

Right now, Raymond's side was to her; if he turned, he would see her.

He dropped into a crouch, doing something she couldn't see. In that position, his back was mostly facing her. If she made a run for the house she'd only be out in the open for a few seconds before she reached—

"I know you can hear me, you'd better answer me, Simon!"

Honey jumped at the sound of Raymond's voice.

Simon was inside that building!

Honey swallowed, forcing herself to remain still and listen.

After a long moment, a voice came from inside; it was Simon's voice but she wasn't close enough to understand the words."

Her husband was alive. "Thank God," she murmured.

But her relief was short-lived.

"You know there's no way out!" Raymond leapt to his feet. "I can't let you live. But I can give you both a much less unpleasant death."

Honey gasped at his words. Even though she'd mobilized Bella and Heyworth and had ridden like mad to get to Lindthorpe, she'd not really believed that Raymond was behind all these seeming accidents.

For the whole ride there, she'd worried that she was making a dreadful mistake and that the duke would be furious when he learned that she'd sent Bella to tell strangers that his cousin—his land steward—was a murderer.

And yet it was the bloody truth: Raymond was trying to kill Simon. And Raymond had said that he would kill <u>both</u> of them; so, the duke was in there with Simon.

It was like something out of a fantastical nightmare.

Raymond was now kneeling in front of whatever he had on the ground.

It's now or never, Honey.

With the gun in one hand and her skirts clutched in the other, she ran.

A voice came from inside the house when she was halfway there.

Raymond pushed to his feet. This time, instead of pacing, he marched toward the house, laughing.

Honey made it to the tree just as his voice rang out.

"Good God but you two must think I'm an idiot," Raymond yelled. He'd stopped a few feet from the house.

From where Honey now stood, she could see that he was facing a window.

"Why would I take exile in bloody America when I'm going to be the Duke of Plimpton? I'll give you *five* minutes to say your goodbyes," he shouted.

From where Honey was standing, she could see that Raymond was shaking with anger.

She could also see what he held in his hands: a lantern, of sorts, with a white cloth hanging from it. The cloth was burning and a thin whisp of black smoke was spiraling upward.

A muffled shout came from inside the house.

Raymond snorted. "I'm going to burn you both alive. *That's* what I'm going to do, dear cousin."

Honey bit down on her lip to stifle a gasp.

Simon called out something.

"No, I won't," Raymond yelled back, his tone one of excitement and triumph, "because I'm miles away, on my quarterly journey to visit the duke's estates. And I have a witness who will swear to it. Everyone will know that you came charging here in a rage—infuriated that your brother had impregnated the love of your life." He laughed, the sound chilling. "You've helped out immeasurably by tearing about the countryside with dear Bella, behaving like her devoted swain. Ah, poor foolish Simon. How we laughed at you—Bella and I—"

Honey blocked out his voice and looked down at the gun as she considered her few options.

Raymond was just too far away; there was no way she could hit him from this distance, especially when he kept jumping about.

She needed to get closer.

When she looked up, she saw that he was holding the flaming lantern—or whatever it was—in his left hand and a gun in his right.

"You have *three* minutes!" he screamed, his words jolting her out of her contemplation.

And then he dropped into a crouch and began stealthily moving toward the window.

There was one last tree between her and Raymond; it was another ten or fifteen feet from her. If she could make it to the tree, that would cut her distance in half. It would still be a difficult shot, but it was the best chance she had before he threw that lantern, which was clearly—

Quit dithering and do it now!

The voice in her head was like the report of a pistol and Honey ran.

It was no more than twenty feet, but it felt like miles.

She expected him to turn any moment and shoot her.

"Two minutes," he yelled, just as she reached the safety of the tree.

Raymond was crouched beside the window and was fiddling with the lantern; the white cloth began to flame.

"That wasn't a minute, Raymond. Do you want to borrow my watch," Simon shouted.

Honey slapped a hand over her mouth, smothering a half-laugh, half-sob; Simon was well enough to taunt.

"This is the last time you will mock me, Simon!" Raymond hollered.

The black smoke began to billow more thickly and Honey saw flames shooting from the lantern itself.

Raymond raised his arm just as a blood-curdling scream came from the direction that Heyworth had run.

Raymond spun around and Honey barely managed to duck out of sight.

He was still clutching the now-flaming lantern, his head jerking back and forth as he searched for the source of the scream. But all was silent.

Honey feared it had to be Heyworth. The other man— Raymond's groom—must have found him.

She was on her own.

Do it now.

Honey raised the gun with shaking hands and moved toward Raymond, who'd set down the lantern and was smacking his burning cuff against his thigh.

A boot came flying out of the window and Raymond spun around at the noise, kicking the lantern in the process.

Simon hurtled out of the jagged opening, screaming like a creature out of a nightmare. He held a stick in one hand and launched it like a javelin. He hit the ground running but lost his balance and the stick flew wide of its target.

"He's got a gun!" Honey screamed as Raymond raised the pistol.

Raymond turned at the sound of her voice and Honey squeezed the trigger.

The gun jumped in her palm and Raymond staggered back, stepping onto the still burning lantern. He raised his gun, his arm unsteady, and pulled the trigger just as Simon leaped onto his back, knocking him to the ground.

Honey heard a bang and felt a searing pain in her arm as she ran toward where Simon was sprawled facedown across Raymond's motionless body.

"Simon?" Honey dropped to her knees beside him.

When he looked up, she saw blood gushing from the side of his neck.

"You're bleeding!"

He smiled weakly and began to push up to his feet.

Honey stood and offered him a hand. He took it and rose with a groan, his weight almost pulling her to the ground.

Once he was standing, Honey peeled back the bloody collar of his shirt, wincing at the wound on his neck. "Simon—we need—"

"Shhhh," he murmured, taking her hand and squeezing it gently. Doesn't hurt." His eyes flickered to her shoulder. "Lord, Honey, you've been shot, too."

Honey turned and saw the shoulder of her coat was torn and bloody. "Oh, goodness," she said, a wave of nausea rolling through her.

"Here, let me have a look." He carefully parted the ragged wool. "It's a flesh wound—like mine—but it will soon begin to smart like the dickens."

"It already smarts."

He turned his brilliant blue gaze on her and grabbed her face with both hands, crushing her mouth with a passionate but far too brief, kiss. "We'll talk later about how you jumped in front of a man with a gun, love. Right now, I've got to get Wyndham to a doctor."

"What about him?" Honey pointed to Raymond. "Shouldn't we do something?"

Simon glanced down at his cousin, who'd rolled onto his back and was gazing wide-eyed at them.

Raymond was bleeding profusely from where Honey's bullet had entered his chest. He was gasping for breath and red froth was coming from his mouth.

A sneer contorted Simon's handsome features. "I think he's getting exactly what he deserved."

Some hours later …

Simon closed the door to the room where Wyndham was resting and made his way down the corridor.

For a moment he was tempted to go to the library, where he knew there was a cabinet with brandy or whiskey.

But then he recalled Raymond's last words and decided that he'd better not drink anything other than water that was pulled straight from the well.

When Simon opened the door to the room he was sharing with Honey, she looked up from a book she'd found in the pillaged library.

"How is he?"

"He's still sleeping. Doctor Powell says the wound looks good and the bullet did not hit any organs. He's got a fever, but Powell says it isn't becoming worse." Simon sank into the nearest chair, closed his eyes, and rubbed his temples with brutal fingers.

Hands landed on his shoulders, massaging hard on his right side, but caressing more gently on the damaged skin on his left.

Simon remembered that his brother wasn't the only one who'd been shot.

"What a horrid husband I am," he said, twisting around to smile up at her. "How is your arm?'

"It hurts, but—to be honest—the time I slammed my little finger in the front door of our London house was far worse."

Simon knew from personal experience that even a mild gunshot wound hurt a great deal. His wife was made of stern stuff.

"You had Powell look at it?" he asked, ashamed that he'd been so consumed with Wyndham that he'd not paid attention to Honey over the last eight hours.

"The doctor said the wound was shallow and clean. He gave me some laudanum, but it always makes me ill. What about you, Simon? You're rubbing your head. Are you getting a migraine?"

"No, just feeling like an arse."

Her hands froze and she came out from behind him. She sat on the arm of his chair and draped an arm around him. "Why?"

Simon sighed, looking up at her. "I can't believe I thought Wyndham was capable of fathering a child on Bella—or on any woman other than his wife. He's the most honorable man I know." He exhaled shakily. "I'm a hot-headed fool. He almost died today—and he's still not out of the woods. If he had died, the last memories I'd have of him were of back-biting and fighting."

Her arm tightened around him. "Don't punish yourself over this, Simon. It doesn't do anyone any good." She hesitated, and then said, "The duke is one of the most formidable men I've ever met. It will take more than a single bullet to stop him."

Simon gave her a weary smile. "You're right, love. He's tough. I just wish I'd said I was sorry for misjudging him when I had the chance this morning."

"You had a few other things to worry about," she said drily. "Like saving both your lives."

"No," he said firmly, "it wasn't me who saved us, it was you. Raymond would have shot me if not for you." He lifted her hand to his lips and kissed her palm. "You didn't just save me and Wyndham—you saved yourself and our unborn child. If Raymond had gotten away with this—" he shivered, sickened at the thought of what might have happened.

She stroked his cheek. "He didn't get away with it, and Wyndham will pull through."

"Once again thanks to my clever wife, who thought ahead enough to send for a doctor as well as a sheriff."

"I'll only take part of the thanks; the majority of it goes to Bella."

"She must have ridden like the wind to get them here so quickly. Loki earned a double serving of oats for the rest of his life."

And the doctor had arrived not a moment too soon, either.

Simon had been at wit's end when the three had thundered up.

Wyndham had lost consciousness and his heartbeat was so faint that Simon could barely feel his pulse.

The doctor hadn't bothered to move the duke to a bed before he began working on him.

While Simon had been with Wyndham, Honey had stayed with Raymond, who'd died in the arms of the woman he very likely would have killed.

Simon knew he should feel something at the other man's passing, but all he could muster was relief. At least Raymond had done one good thing before dying; he'd confessed to putting the poison in the duke's liquor decanters—within the sheriff's hearing.

Raymond's confession had gone a long way to helping Simon explain the two dead bodies and various gunshot wounds to the sheriff.

The man had agreed to wait until the duke could give testimony to announce an official cause of death for either Raymond or his groom.

Simon had also told the sheriff about Raymond's valet, but he suspected they would never catch the man.

It had slipped Honey's mind to tell anyone about Heyworth, and so the steward had surprised everyone when he'd come limping out of the woods about an hour after Bella and the two men arrived.

It seemed the steward had been caught in a snare—so there was a poacher, after all. The accident hadn't just mangled Heyworth's foot, his pride was considerably damaged from leaving his mistress to fend for herself.

Simon wasn't sure he could ever forgive the man for bringing Honey and their unborn child into such danger.

Unfortunately, his wife had read his expression correctly and had already threatened him with dire deeds if Simon sacked Heyworth.

Honey stood up from the arm of his chair and held out her hand. "Come to bed—you need sleep. You can trust your brother to Doctor Powell and the dowager."

Simon had sent for their mother, knowing she would want to be by Wyndham's bedside. She was a capable nurse and had cared for their father in his last years.

Honey was right; Wyndham was getting the best care possible.

He stood, but instead of following her to bed, he wrapped his arms around her, gazing down into her lovely gray eyes. "How did I ever get so lucky," he murmured, kissing the tip of her nose.

She blushed and squirmed, shy at his praise.

"There is a tradition among soldiers; if you save somebody's life, it then belongs to you."

She cocked her head, the slightest of smiles on her lips. "Are you saying that you now belong to me?"

"Utterly and completely."

"Hmmm. How interesting. What do you think I should do with you?"

Simon kissed her until they were both breathless. And then he said, "You're my clever wife, I'm sure you'll think of something fitting."

Epilogue

Several Months Later ...

Oh!" Honey said, pressing a hand against her stomach. "I think the baby just kicked me."

Simon looked up from the letter in his hand. He was sitting across the breakfast table from her, his blue eyes twinkling behind the spectacles he used for reading. "I don't believe it. No son of ours would be so rude."

"No, but our daughter might be."

They both smirked at their silly, private joke.

Honey had asked him once, early in her pregnancy, if he would be disappointed if their first child was not a son.

He'd given her the most serious look she'd ever seen on his handsome face. "All I want is for both of you to be healthy."

She'd heard the anxiety beneath his words and had seen it in his intense gaze; he was worried for her.

Not that there seemed to be any reason to worry. Thus far Honey had enjoyed a very easy pregnancy. She'd not been ill or off her feed—as the dowager had apparently been with her children—and she'd only recently begun to get tired and require a short nap in the afternoons.

The only unhappy side effect of her pregnancy was her reaction to the smell of paints: the oily scent nauseated her.

The doctor had assured her it was temporary and that women often developed strong dislikes for tastes or smells. It had upset her, at first, but she'd decided to look at the months that remained as an enforced holiday from work.

Of course, she was still sketching—more than ever—but she'd also taken up tatting, which her mother-in-law had been overjoyed to teach her. She had never been accomplished at any needlecraft and could hardly wait to show Freddie—who'd mastered all such feminine arts—the first length of lace that she'd made.

Simon grunted and tossed his letter aside "So, Morrison has finally come up to snuff on Epiphany."

Honey smiled. "I'm surprised you can part with him," she teased. She'd half-believed that her husband wouldn't be able to sell the magnificent hunter.

Simon muttered something beneath his breath and she saw a slight pinkness on his cheeks.

Honey knew he was embarrassed by his attachment to his animals.

He was only willing to sell them to people he liked and trusted. Honey thought his impulse spoke well of his character but knew that he lamented his sentimental approach to what was supposed to be a business.

She turned to her own letters, opening the one from Annis.

It was only a single page and was sparsely written—very unusual for her word-loving friend.

For a woman whose entire life revolved around languages, Annis's penmanship had always been dreadful, but this letter was almost illegible.

Honey squinted down at the page, re-reading the third sentence once, twice, and then again. "Oh, goodness," she said.

"Is your rude daughter kicking you again?" Simon asked with a snicker, frowning at something he was reading in the newspaper.

"No, it's a letter from my friend Annis."

Simon looked up. "The one who lives with her grandmother and could not come to the wedding?"

Simon meant Serena's wedding, which had been some months back.

"Yes, Annis could not come because she was in Scotland at the time."

"That's probably just as well. After meeting Lorelei, I think it might be better if you introduced your friends to me one at a time."

Honey laughed. "Don't worry, Annis is nothing like Lorelei.

Simon muttered something that sounded suspiciously like, "Thank God for small favors."

Honey smiled. "I wouldn't have believed you were such a staunch defender of the aristocracy until I heard you brangling with Lorelei."

"Ha! Your friend doesn't want to just eliminate the peerage, she'd like to eliminate all *peers*. At least all male ones."

"Poor Simon," she teased. "Did Lorelei pin your ears back?" Honey *knew* her friend had talked Simon into a corner because she'd heard at least two of the arguments the pair had engaged in over the week they'd spend in Kent.

"More like tried to cut my bollocks off," he groused in an under voice.

"*Simon!*"

"Well, it's true. Having a conversation with her was akin to shoving a weasel down my breeches."

Honey couldn't help laughing. "I'm not going to ask how you would know such a thing."

She'd have to pass that description of Lorelei's debating skills along to her friend in her next letter; Lorie would love it.

"So, what does your friend Annis have to say?" Simon asked, clearly eager to leave the subject of Lorie and weasels behind.

"She is getting married and you'll never believe to whom."

"Lord, Honey—how would I know such a thing?"

"You'll know because his name has been noised about in every paper for the last two months."

Simon's eyebrows shot up. "Good God—she's marrying Whosy-Whatsit? Er, the one they've taken to calling the mysterious Earl of Rotherhithe?"

"Apparently so." Honey was stunned. "My retiring, shy friend has somehow managed to land the catch of the decade."

Simon sputtered. "But, darling—you told me that *I* was the catch of the decade."

Honey looked up from the shocking letter and met the love of her life's twinkling hydrangea gaze. "No, Simon—you're the catch of a lifetime."

His pupils flared and his cheeks—tanned by all the time he spent out of doors—flushed darkly. "Did I tell you today how much I love you?" he asked, his voice husky.

Honey adored the fact that it took only a few words or a well-placed look to have her intensely masculine husband eating out of the palm of her hand.

"Actually, I think you overlooked that this morning."

That was a lie; Simon told her—and showed her—his love every single day.

But that didn't mean Honey wouldn't appreciate hearing it yet again.

He reached across the table and took her hand. "I love you, Lady Saybrook."

"I love you, too, my lord."

"A good way to show your love would be to paint my portrait—after you've delivered our son, of course."

Honey laughed; there were already two of portraits of her husband hanging in their house: the one she'd painted all those years ago and the one she'd finished only a few months ago.

Honey had given him the older portrait as a wedding gift. Her masculine, rugged husband had been so touched when he'd seen the painting that she'd thought there might have been a tear or two welling in his glorious eyes.

"I think my next portrait should be of me astride Loki," he mused, a smile pulling at his lips.

She shook her head. "I'm sorry, my dear, I'd love to paint you, *yet again,* but I'm afraid I'm engaged for the coming year."

"Ah, yes. Alvanley's spaniel, is it?"

Honey grinned.

"Wretch," he accused, kissing her hand before releasing her.

The door opened and Rebecca entered, trailed by Enola MacLeish. Even though Becca was a few years older than the other girl, the two had grown to enjoy each other's company a great deal. They were both single, lonely children who yearned for companionship.

"Good morning, girls," Simon said. "Come to eat us out of house and home again?"

Enola, who was shy to the point of paralysis, blushed, while Rebecca rolled her eyes.

"Ignore him, girls. Have some breakfast," Honey said.

She watched with tolerant amusement as the two attacked the sideboard.

Unlike her mother, Enola wasn't much of a horsewoman. She hadn't hunted with Bella, Becca, and Simon this past season. However, it turned out the girl had quite a talent for sketching and painting.

Honey knew that after Raymond's death Wyndham and Simon had discussed their dead cousin's child. She had been pleased to learn that Wyndham had already set up a trust for the girl and Enola would come into a tidy competence when she reached twenty-one.

When Simon had come to Honey with a suggestion to do more—pay for her schooling—Honey had been thrilled to offer such assistance. Enola was showing considerable artistic talent and Honey looked forward to helping her develop her skills.

Rebecca rode with Bella and Simon most days, and Enola came for a few hours of instruction in sketching and watercolors. While not Honey's favorite medium, Enola had expressed an interest in watercolors and Honey could work with the paints without becoming ill.

A few weeks after Raymond's death, Honey and Bella had had a private conversation about Enola's father.

After giving it some thought, they'd both agreed to keep Raymond's part in his nephew's death between themselves.

They had no real evidence and could never be sure that Raymond had committed such a monstrous crime.

Besides, passing along their suspicions to the duke would do no good for the baby—who could not be brought back—and might destroy Plimpton, who would likely blame himself for bringing a murderer to live beneath his roof.

No, neither of the brothers needed to know the full truth about the viper they'd nursed in the bosom of their family.

Honey never asked, but Bella had volunteered information about her history with Raymond.

"It was my fault, as much as Raymond's. I was young and foolish and impulsive. I'd not seen Simon for months and Raymond was always hovering around me. He told me that Plimpton would never allow Simon to marry me. Even though I knew that Raymond was using that information to manipulate me, I was lonely and eventually capitulated."

Bella had given Honey a wry, slightly embarrassed, look. "I'm not proud to admit that I wanted Simon because I thought he would inherit the title and money. My family has always been poor and I wanted a way out of that hand-to-mouth existence.

"Of course, after I learned that I was pregnant I knew I had no future with him. So, I went to Plimpton—not the other way around." Bella had laughed at whatever she'd seen on Honey's face—likely disgust. "I told you—I'm not blameless. I lied and schemed and was unfaithful to Simon. The duke knew the truth would devastate Simon. Indeed, Simon would have likely called out Raymond and killed him. Plimpton also knew that my interest in marrying Simon had diminished with the birth of his son. And I certainly had no interest in marrying Raymond."

Bella had shrugged, her expression world-weary. "And so Plimpton introduced me to MacLeish while Simon was still in London getting his portrait painted. I was pleased that I would become a countess—no matter that it was a Scottish title. The duke was pleased to solve a sticky problem so easily and cheaply, and MacLeish was pleased to get the money and also because I was pregnant and he was incapable of fathering children." Bella pulled a face. "The only one *not* pleased was Raymond."

"And Simon," Honey reminded her quietly.

Bella gave her a wry look. "Ah, but you and I know it was a fortunate escape for him, don't we, my lady?" Before Honey could answer, Bella continued. "Raymond was incensed when I told him I was to marry MacLeish. We had a tremendous row and he threatened all sorts of things—not so subtly hinting that I could face dire consequences if I refused to marry him. That was when he'd let slip what he knew about poisons and how to use them." Bella's humor had disappeared, replaced by revulsion—and even a tinge of fear. "Later, after I heard that the baby had died so unexpectedly, I simply could not believe that he would do such a thing." Bella had looked genuinely haunted, then. "I will hope, until the end of my life, that my suspicions about him were wrong."

Honey thought back to that conversation now, her gaze lingering on Bella and Raymond's daughter.

Honey felt drawn to the quiet girl, who reminded her a great deal of herself when she'd been younger, but without the benefit of a loving, doting parent.

Oh, she knew that Bella loved Enola in her own way—which was to say carelessly. From the few things the girl had said to Honey about her father, Enola had never received much affection from the Earl of MacLeish, either.

Enola might always be shy, but with a bit of affection and friendship, she was slowly coming out of her shell.

As Honey looked across the breakfast table at her own child's father, she felt a rush of almost suffocating love.

Right now, Simon was bickering good-naturedly with both girls, making them laugh and protest his outrageous behavior, teasing them as relentlessly as he'd likely done when he'd been their age. She could envision him doing the same with their own children in the years to come.

Honey's heart swelled as she watched the three of them, and it struck her that they were the boisterous, loving family she had always yearned for and was, in her own way, beginning to assemble around herself.

As she watched them together, she suddenly knew what her first painting would be when she went back to work. She would paint her family—not just the three people before her, but the rest of her new family, too: the dowager, the duke, and even her aloof sister-in-law, who perhaps she might one day know better.

Yes, she would paint a family portrait—the first one that she would paint that included herself.

Honey smiled at the image already forming in her mind's eye; she would need a large canvas for such a portrait of love.

THANKS SO MUCH FOR READING!

I hope you enjoyed Honoria and Simon's story.

THE ACADEMY OF LOVE is a 7-book series. In this book you briefly meet some of the other teachers from the Stefani Academy for Young Ladies: Frederika, Lady Sedgewick—or Freddie, as she is better known, Miles Ingram, and Serena Lombard.

Serena's book, A FIGURE OF LOVE, is already available and takes place at roughly the same time as this book.

Book 4 in the series is THE LANGUAGE OF LOVE, which features Annis Redmond, the languages teacher.

Book 5, DANCING WITH LOVE, features Miles Ingram, the newly anointed Earl of Avingdon.

Book 6, A STORY OF LOVE, features Lorelei Fontenot, the classics teacher.

Book 7, not only features Freddie, but you'll also get to see Wyndham Fairchild, the Duke of Plimpton again ….

If you liked my story and would like to read more, please leave me a review on your website of choice. Drop me a line at minervaspencerauthor@gmail.com if you would like to see a specific character get their story. Or tell me the sort of story that YOU'D like to read. I am always open to good ideas!

Please read on for a peek at THE FOOTMAN, Book 1 in THE MASQUERADERS series, a Regency Romance trilogy about heroes and heroines who are not always what they appear …

Chapter One

Iain Vale was examining a marble statue of some poor armless bloke
when the door beside it flew open and a whirlwind in skirts burst into
the hall.

"I *will not!*" the whirlwind yelled before slamming the door,
spinning around, and careening into Iain. "Ooof." She bounced off
him and stumbled backward, catching her foot in the hem of her dress
in the process.

Iain sprang forward, reached out one long arm, and caught her
slim waist, halting her fall. He looked down at his armful of warm
female and found surprised gray eyes glaring back at him. Her mouth,
which had been open in shock, snapped shut. Iain hastily righted his
bundle and took a step back.

"Who the devil are *you*?" the girl demanded, brushing at her dress
as though his gloved hands might have soiled it.

"I'm the new footman, Miss."

The gray eyes turned steely. "Are you stupid?" She didn't wait for an answer. "I'm not a *Miss*. I am Lady Elinor, your employer's *daughter*."

Iain's face heated under her contemptuous eyes. He'd been spoken down to many times, but never quite so . . . effectively.

"You are welcome, *Lady Elinor*."

"What?" she demanded. "*What* did you say?" Her eyes were so wide they looked to be in danger of popping out of their sockets.

"*I said,* 'you are welcome, my lady.'"

She planted her fists on her slim hips. "I'm welcome for what?"

"For saving you from a very nasty fall," he retorted, unable to keep his tongue behind his teeth even though he was breaking every rule in the footman's handbook. If such a thing existed.

The unladylike noise that slipped from her mouth told Iain she was thinking the same thing. "You are an intolerably insolent *boy*. Not to mention the most ignorant footman I've ever known."

Iain couldn't argue with her on that second point.

"Besides," she added, looking him up and down, "I wouldn't have needed your clumsy rescuing if you'd not been listening at keyholes."

Listening at keyholes? *Why the obnoxious little—*

Iain had just opened his mouth to say something foolish and most likely job-ending when the door Lady Elinor had exited so violently opened and Lady Yarmouth stood on the threshold. Her gray eyes, much like her daughter's, moved from Lady Elinor to her newest footman and back again.

"What is going out here, Elinor?"

The girl scowled. "I have just asked our new footman to run away with me, Mama."

Iain's jaw dropped.

Lady Yarmouth's lips thinned until they were pale pink lines. She raked the younger woman with a look designed to leave her quaking in her slippers. Her daughter glared back, un-quaked.

"Come back inside this instant, Elinor." The older woman turned and retreated into the room without waiting to see if her daughter obeyed.

The Footman

Lady Elinor gave an exaggerated sigh and rolled her eyes at her mother's back before limping toward the open doorway. She stopped and turned back to Iain before entering the room.

"You'll catch flies if you don't close your mouth." She slammed the door in his face.

Bloody hell.

***

Iain yawned. It was almost three in the morning and the festivities showed no sign of abating. Other than his encounter with Lady Elinor earlier, the evening had been quiet. Disappointingly quiet not only for his first ball, but also his first day as footman.

The only other entertainment had been watching an overdressed dandy cast up his accounts on his dancing slippers while trying, and failing, to make it to the men's necessary.

Iain adjusted the lacy cuffs of his fancy new shirt and examined the stranger who looked back at him in the ornate mirror. The black livery made him appear taller than his six feet and the well-tailored coat spanned his shoulders in a way that made him look lean and dangerous rather than scrawny and puppyish. His wiry red hair had been cropped to barely a stubble and was now concealed by a white powdered wig that gave him dignity. Of course his freckles were still there, but there was nothing he could do to hide them—unlike his age.

"You don't look five-and-ten, Iain," his Uncle Lonnie had said upon seeing Iain in his new clothes earlier today. He'd then grinned and squeezed Iain's shoulder. "Go ahead and give us yer story one last time, lad."

The story was one his uncle had concocted when Iain first came to work in Viscount Yarmouth's household three months ago: Iain was nineteen and had spent six years in Mr. Ewan Kennedy's household, two as a scrub boy, two as a boot boy, and two as a footman, even though he was unusually young for that last position. Uncle Lonnie also told Lord Yarmouth that Iain had come to London seeking employment after Mr. Kennedy died and there weren't any other suitable positions in the tiny town of Dannen, Scotland.

That last part was the only *true* part of the whole story. Dannen was more a collection of shacks than a real village and there'd never been any Mr. Kennedy, nor any work as scrub boy or footman. Iain had written the letter from "Mr. Kennedy" himself, under his uncle's direction.

"Admiring your pretty face?"

Iain yelped and jumped a good six inches. Female laughter echoed down the mahogany-paneled corridor. He turned to find Lady Elinor behind him, her small, almost boyish, frame propped against the wall in a very unladylike manner. Her white gown looked limp and tired, as if it were ready to go to bed. Her hair, a nondescript brown, had come loose from its moorings and fine tendrils wafted about her thin, pale face. Only her large gray eyes held any animation.

Iain drew himself up to his full height and glared over her shoulder at nothing. "How may I be of service, my lady?"

"Oh, stuff! You're angry with me, aren't you?" She didn't wait for an answer. "I'm sorry for being beastly earlier. I was wrong. Pax?" She held out her hand and limped forward. Iain stared, not because of her limp—he already knew she was lame—but because of the gesture. Surely a footman wasn't permitted to shake a lady's hand?

Besides, he hadn't forgiven her. His mother and uncle both accused him of being too grudging and slow to forgive. He looked down at her little hand and chewed his lip. Maybe they were right; perhaps it might be advisable to *appear* to forgive her. He'd just decided to say 'pax' when Lady Elinor grabbed his hand.

"Don't be angry with me. I apologized."

"I'm not angry," he lied, tugging not so subtly on his hand to free it from her grasp. He suspected it would not do to get caught holding the hand of the daughter of the house at three in the morning, or at any other time of the day or night, for that matter.

"Why aren't you in there," he gestured with his chin toward the ballroom, "dancing? Er, my lady," he added a trifle belatedly.

She snorted and hiked up her dress, exhibiting a shocking amount of leg. "With this?"

Iain gawked. He'd seen girl's legs, of course, but never a *lady's* leg. Her stockings were embroidered with flowers—daisies, perhaps.

330

The Footman

His groin gave an appreciative thump as he studied the gentle swell of her calf. She had shapely legs for such a tiny thing.

She dropped her skirts. "Are you ogling my limb?"

"What do you expect if you go around hiking up your skirt like that?" The words were out of his mouth before he could stop them. Iain squeezed his eyes shut and waited for her to start screeching. But the sound of giggling made him open them again.

She eyed him skeptically. "You're not like the other footmen."

What was Iain supposed to say to that?

"You look *very* young. How long have you been a footman?"

"Today is my first day."

"You shan't keep your job very long if you argue with any other members of my family. Or ogle their limbs."

His face heated and he pursed his lips.

She looked delighted by whatever she saw on his face. "How old are you?"

"Nineteen, my lady."

"What a bouncer!"

"How old are *you?*" Iain bit out, and then wanted to howl. At this rate, he would be jobless before breakfast.

"Sixteen." She stopped smiling and her eyes went dull, like a vivid sunset losing its color. "But I might as well be forty. I shan't even have a Season."

"I thought all young ladies had at least one Season." What drivel. What the devil did *he* know about aristocrats, Seasons, or any of it? It was as if some evil imp had taken over his body: some pixie or spirit determined to get him sacked. Or jailed. He clamped his mouth shut, vowing not to open it again until it was time to put food in it.

Luckily his employer's daughter was too distracted to find his behavior odd.

"Tonight was my betrothal ball." Her shapely, shell-pink lips turned down at the corners. "Why should my father go to the expense of a Season when he can dispose of me so cheaply without one?"

It seemed like an odd way to talk about a betrothal but Iain kept that observation behind his teeth.

"The Earl of Trentham is my betrothed," she added, not in need of any responses from him to hold a conversation. "He is madly in love."

The silence became uncomfortable. Iain cleared his throat. "You must be very happy, then," he said when he could bear it no longer.

Her eyes, which had been vague and distant, sharpened and narrowed. "He's not in love with *me*, you dunce. He is in love with a property that is part of my dowry. Some piece of land that is critical to a business venture he and my father have planned."

Iain's flare of anger at being called *dunce* quickly died when he saw the misery and self-loathing on her face.

"Lord Trentham will have his land, my father will get to take part in the earl's investment, and I? Well, I will have—" She stopped, as if suddenly aware of what she was saying and to whom she was saying it. She glared up at him, her gray eyes suddenly molten silver. "Why am I telling *you* any of this? How could you ever know what it is like to be an ugly *cripple*? You will never be forced to marry someone who is twice your age. A man who views you with less pleasure than he does a piece of dirt." Her mouth twisted. "I am no more than a broodmare to him."

Her expression shifted from agonized into a sneering mask. Iain hadn't thought her ugly before—plain, perhaps—but, at that moment, she became ugly. Fury boiled off her person like steam from a kettle and Iain recoiled, not wanting to get burned.

She noticed his reaction and laughed, the sound as nasty as the gleam in her eyes. "What? Do I scare you, *boy*?"

Iain felt as if she'd prodded him with a red-hot iron and he took two strides and closed the distance between them, seething at the undeserved insults and bile. He stared down at her, no idea as to what he planned to do. Not that it mattered. The second he came within reach, her hands slid up the lapels of his jacket like two pale snakes. He froze at her touch but she pushed closer. Small, firm mounds pressed hard against his chest.

Breasts! Breasts! a distant, but euphoric, part of his mind shrieked.

His breeding organ had already figured that out.

Iain looked down into eyes that had become soft and imploring.

The Footman

"What is your name?" she asked, her voice husky.

"I—" He coughed and cleared his throat. "Iain, my lady."

"Would you like to kiss me, Iain?" It was barely a whisper and Iain wondered if he'd heard her correctly. He cocked his head and was about to ask her to repeat herself, when she stood on tiptoes and pressed her lips against his.

Iain had kissed girls before. Just last week he'd done a whole lot more than kiss with one of the housemaids in the stables. But this kiss was different. It was a gentle, tentative offering, rather than a taking. To refuse it was somehow unthinkable. He leaned lower and slid his hands around her waist, pulling her closer. She was so slim his hands almost spanned her body. She made a small noise in her throat and touched the side of his face with caressing fingers, her pliant body melting against his.

"You bloody *bastard!*"

The girl jumped back and screamed just as Iain's head exploded. He staggered, his vision clouding with multi-colored spangles and roaring agony. When he reached out to steady himself on the wall, he encountered air. A foot kicked his legs out from under him and he slammed onto his back, his skull cracking against the wood floor.

"Lord Trentham, *no!*" Lady Elinor's voice was barely audible above the agonizing pounding filling Iain's head.

A body—Lord Trentham's?—dropped onto Iain's chest with crushing force. Soft but powerful hands circled his neck and squeezed.

"You rutting pig, how dare you touch *my* betrothed?" The choking eased on his throat just before a fist buffeted the right side of his head. "How *dare* you put your filthy hands on your betters?" Another blow slammed into his left temple.

"*Stop it! Stop this instant, he did nothing wrong. It was me!*"

"I'll deal with you next, you little whore," the earl said, his tone even harsher than his words as his fists cracked against Iain's head over and over again. Iain's mouth filled with blood and he struggled to spit it out before he choked on it. And then a knee jammed between his thighs and he screamed, the world going black.

"*You're going to kill him!*"

333

Iain retched and Trentham scrambled off him, clearly wishing to avoid becoming drenched in blood and vomit. Iain rolled to his side and cupped his hands protectively over his aching groin, his stomach convulsing until there was nothing left to expel.

He wanted to die.

"What the devil is going on here?"

Iain distantly recognized Lord Yarmouth's voice.

"Make him stop, Papa, he will kill him!"

"I will certainly make him *wish* he were dead," Trentham snarled just before a foot made contact with Iain's side.

"*Ooof!*" Iain groaned and rolled away, unwilling to take his hands from his groin and risk more gut-churning abuse.

"Trentham, what is going on?" Yarmouth asked again.

"This lout was in the process of mounting your bloody daughter when I caught them."

"That's not—" Lady Elinor began.

"Silence!" her father roared.

"Is this the kind of household you run, Yarmouth? Has this happened before? Is she even *intact*?"

"I assure you, Trentham, this is the first time such a thing has happened. Look at her. Do you think she poses much of a temptation to any man?" The viscount continued without waiting for an answer. "Besides, this is a mere boy. I told Lady Yarmouth he was too young to be fit for the position. We shall discharge him immediately and forget this ever happened."

"I won't forget it, Yarmouth. And I won't marry this lout's castoffs—not unless my doctor examines her and swears she is intact. And I want *him*— "a kick glanced off Iain's shoulder—"put where he belongs."

"We did nothing wrong, Papa. It was just—"

"Another word from you, Elinor, and you will regret it most severely." The viscount's normally soft voice was thick with disgust and rage. A pregnant pause followed his words before he spoke again. "Very well, Trentham."

"*Papa, no.* It was only a kiss. He didn't even want to, I begged him—"

The Footman

"*Enough!*" The word was followed by a loud crack and a muffled cry.

"I want him taken in for attempted rape," Trentham said, his voice suddenly cool and collected.

"Very well," the viscount said. "Thomas, Gerald, take him. You can put him down in the cellar while one of you fetches the constable."

Four hands closed around Iain's arms and began to lift. He struggled weakly against their efforts, squirming and thrashing his way across the plush carpet.

"You incompetent fools." The Earl of Trentham's voice came from behind. "Let me ensure this piece of rubbish gives you no trouble." Something hard slammed into Iain's head and the world faded to black.

CPSIA information can be obtained
at www.ICGtesting.com
Printed in the USA
LVHW092146040221
678432LV00034B/468

9 781951 662431